CW00820745

The Collected Supernatural and Weird Fiction of A. C. Benson

The Collected Supernatural and Weird Fiction of A. C. Benson

One Novel 'The Child of the Dawn,' One Novelette 'The Uttermost Farthing' and Eight Short Stories of the Strange and Unusual

A. C. Benson

LEONAUR

The Collected
Supernatural and Weird
Fiction of
A. C. Benson
One Novel 'The Child of the Dawn,' One Novelette 'The Uttermost Farthing' and
Eight Short Stories of the Strange and Unusual
by A. C. Benson

FIRST EDITION

Leonaur is an imprint of Oakpast Ltd

Copyright in this form © 2019 Oakpast Ltd

ISBN: 978-1-78282-794-8 (hardcover)
ISBN: 978-1-78282-795-5 (softcover)

http://www.leonaur.com

Publisher's Notes

The views expressed in this book are not necessarily
those of the publisher.

Contents

The Child of the Dawn

I think that a book like the following, which deals with a subject so great and so mysterious as our hope of immortality, by means of an allegory or fantasy, needs a few words of preface, in order to clear away at the outset any misunderstandings which may possibly arise in a reader's mind. Nothing is further from my wish than to attempt any philosophical or ontological exposition of what is hidden behind the veil of death. But one may be permitted to deal with the subject imaginatively or poetically, to translate hopes into visions, as I have tried to do.

The fact that underlies the book is this: that in the course of a very sad and strange experience—an illness which lasted for some two years, involving me in a dark cloud of dejection—I came to believe practically, instead of merely theoretically, in the personal immortality of the human soul, I was conscious, during the whole time, that though the physical machinery of the nerves was out of gear, the soul and the mind remained, not only intact, but practically unaffected by the disease, imprisoned, like a bird in a cage, but perfectly free in themselves, and uninjured by the bodily weakness which enveloped them. This was not all. I was led to perceive that I had been living life with an entirely distorted standard of values; I had been ambitious, covetous, eager for comfort and respect, absorbed in trivial dreams and childish fancies. I saw, in the course of my illness, that what really mattered to the soul was the relation in which it stood to other souls; that affection was the native air of the spirit; and that anything which distracted the heart from the duty of love was a kind of bodily delusion, and simply hindered the spirit in its pilgrimage.

It is easy to learn this, to attain to a sense of certainty about it, and yet to be unable to put it into practice as simply and frankly as one desires to do! The body grows strong again and reasserts itself; but the blessed consciousness of a great possibility apprehended and grasped remains.

There came to me, too, a sense that one of the saddest effects of what is practically a widespread disbelief in immortality, which affects many people who would nominally disclaim it, is that we think of the soul after death as a thing so altered as to be practically unrecognisable—as a meek and pious emanation, without qualities or aims or passions or traits—as a sort of amiable and weak-kneed sacristan in the temple of God; and this is the unhappy result of our so often making religion a pursuit apart from life—an occupation, not an atmosphere; so that it seems impious to think of the departed spirit as interested in anything but a vague species of liturgical exercise.

I read the other day the account of the death-bed of a great statesman, which was written from what I may call a somewhat clerical point of view. It was recorded with much gusto that the dying politician took no interest in his schemes of government and cares of State, but found perpetual solace in the repetition of childish hymns. This fact had, or might have had, a certain beauty of its own, if it had been expressly stated that it was a proof that the tired and broken mind fell back upon old, simple, and dear recollections of bygone love. But there was manifest in the record a kind of sanctimonious triumph in the extinction of all the great man's insight and wisdom. It seemed to me that the right treatment of the episode was rather to insist that those great qualities, won by brave experience and unselfish effort, were only temporarily obscured, and belonged actually and essentially to the spirit of the man; and that if heaven is indeed, as we may thankfully believe, a place of work and progress, those qualities would be actively and energetically employed as soon as the soul was freed from the trammels of the failing body.

Another point may also be mentioned. The idea of transmigration and reincarnation is here used as a possible solution for the extreme difficulties which beset the question of the apparently fortuitous brevity of some human lives. I do not, of course, propound it as literally and precisely as it is here set down—it is not a forecast of the future, so much as a symbolising of the forces of life—but *the renewal of conscious experience*, in some form or other, seems to be the only way out of the difficulty, and it is that which is here indicated. If life is a probation for those who have to face experience and temptation, how can it be a probation for infants and children, who die before the faculty of moral choice is developed? Again, I find it very hard to believe in any multiplication of human souls. It is even more difficult for me to believe in the creation of new souls than in the creation of new matter. Science has shown ns that there is no actual addition made to the sum of matter, and that the apparent creation of new forms of plants or animals is nothing more than a rearrangement of existing particles—that if a new form appears in one place, it merely means that so much matter is transferred thither from another place. I find it, I say, hard to believe that the sum total of life is actually increased.

To put it very simply for the sake of clearness, and accepting the assumption that human life had some time a beginning on this planet, it seems impossible to think that when, let us say, the two first progenitors of the race died, there were but two souls in heaven; that when the next generation died there were, let us say, ten souls in heaven; and that this number has been added to by thousands and millions, until the unseen world is peopled, as it must be now, if no reincarnation is possible, by myriads of human identities, who, after a single brief taste of incarnate life, join some vast community of spirits in which they eternally reside. I do not say that this latter belief may not be true; I only say that in default of evidence, it seems to me a difficult faith to hold; while a reincarnation of spirits, if one could believe it, would seem to me both to equalise the inequalities of human experience, and give one a lively belief in the virtue and worth of human endeavour. But all this is set down, as I say, in a tentative and not in a philosophical form.

And I have also in these pages kept advisedly clear of Christian doctrines and beliefs; not because I do not believe wholeheartedly in the divine origin and unexhausted vitality of the Christian revelation, but because I do not intend to lay rash and profane hands upon the highest and holiest of mysteries.

I will add one word about the genesis of the book. Some time ago I wrote a number of short tales of an allegorical type. It was a curious experience. I seemed to have come upon them in my mind, as one comes upon a covey of birds in a field. One by one they took wings and flew; and when I had finished, though I was anxious to write more tales, I could not discover any more, though I beat the covert patiently to dislodge them.

This particular tale rose unbidden in my mind. I was never conscious of creating any of its incidents. It seemed to be all there from the beginning; and I felt throughout like a man making his way along a road, and describing what he sees as he goes. The road stretched ahead of me; I could not see beyond the next turn at any moment; it just unrolled itself inevitably and, I will add, very swiftly to my view, and was thus a strange and momentous experience.

I will only add that the book is all based upon an intense belief in God, and a no less intense conviction of personal immortality and personal responsibility. It aims at bringing out the fact that our life is a very real pilgrimage to high and far-off things from mean and sordid beginnings, and that the key of the mystery lies in the frank facing of experience, as a blessed process by which the secret purpose of God is made known to us; and, even more, in a passionate belief in Love, the love of friend and neighbour, and the love of God; and in the absolute faith that we are all of us, from the lowest ani most degraded human soul to the loftiest and wisest, knit together with chains of infinite nearness and dearness, under God, and in Him, and through Him, now and hereafter and for evermore.

A. C. B.

The Old Lodge, Magdalene College,
Cambridge, January, 1912.

1

Certainly, the last few moments of my former material, worn-out life, as I most still call it, were made horrible enough for me. I came to, after the operation, in a deadly sickness and ghastly confusion of thought I was just dimly conscious of the trim, bare room, the white bed, a figure or two, but everything else was swallowed up in the pain, which filled all my senses at once. Yet surely, I thought, it is all something outside me? . . . my brain began to wander, and the pain became a thing. It was a tower of stone, high and blank, with a little sinister window high up, from which something was every now and then waved above the house-roofs. . . . The tower was gone in a moment, and there was a heap piled up on the floor of a great room with open beams—a granary, perhaps. The heap was of curved sharp steel things like sickles: something moved and muttered underneath it, and blood ran out on the floor.

Then I was instantly myself, and the pain was with me again; and then there fell on me a sense of faintness, so that the cold sweat-drops ran suddenly out on my brow. There came a smell of drugs, sharp and pungent, on the air. I heard a door open softly, and a voice said, "He is sinking fast—they must be sent for at once."

Then there were more people in the room, people whom I thought I had known once, long ago; but I was buried and crushed under the pain, like the thing beneath the heap of sickles. There swept over me a dreadful fear; and I could see that the fear was reflected in the faces above me; but now they were strangely distorted and elongated, so that I could have laughed, if only I had had the time; but I had to move the weight off me, which was crushing me. Then a roaring sound began to come and go upon the air, louder and louder, faster and faster; the strange pungent scent came again; and then I was thrust down under the weight, monstrous, insupportable; further and further down; and there came a sharp bright streak, like a blade severing the strands of a rope drawn taut and tense; another and another; one was left, and the blade drew near. . . .

I fell suddenly out of the sound and scent and pain into the most incredible and blessed peace and silence. It would have been like a sleep, but I was still perfectly conscious, with a sense of unutterable and blissful fatigue; a picture passed before me, of a calm sea, of vast depth and clearness. There were cliffs at a little distance, great headlands and rocky spires. I seemed to myself to have left them, to have come down through them, to have embarked. There was a pale light everywhere, flushed with rose-colour, like the light of a summer dawn; and I felt as I had once felt as a child, awakened early in the little old house among the orchards, on a spring morning; I had risen from my bed, and leaning out of my window, filled with a delightful wonder, I had seen the cool morning quicken into light among the dewy apple-blossoms. That was what I felt like, as I lay upon the moving tide, glad to rest, not wondering or hoping, not fearing or expecting anything—just there, and at peace.

There seemed to be no time in that other blessed morning, no need to do anything. The cliffs, I did not know how, faded from me, and the boundless sea was about me on every side; but I cannot describe the timelessness of it. There are no human words for it all, yet I must speak of it in terms of time and space, because both time and space were there, though I was not bound by them.

And here first I will say a few words about the manner of speech I shall use. It is very hard to make clear, but I think I can explain it in an image. I once walked alone, on a perfect summer day, on the South Downs. The great smooth shoulders of the hills lay left and right, and, in front of me, the rich tufted grass ran suddenly down to the plain, which stretched out before me like a map. I saw the fields and woods, the minute tiled hamlet-roofs, the white roads, on which crawled tiny carts. A shepherd, far below, drove his flock along a little deep-cut lane among high hedges. The sounds of earth came faintly and sweetly up, obscure sounds of which I could not tell the origin; but the tinkling of sheep-bells was the clearest, and the barking of the shepherd-dog. My own dog sat beside me, watching my face, impatient to be gone. But at the barking he pricked up his ears, put his head on one side, and wondered, I saw, where that companionable sound came from. What he made of the scene I do not know; the sight of the fruitful earth, the homes of men, the fields and waters, filled me with an inexpressible emotion, a wide- flung hope, a sense of the immensity and intricacy of life. But to my dog it meant nothing at all, though he saw just what I did. To him it was nothing but a great excavation in the earth, patched and streaked with green. It was not then the scene itself that I loved; that was only a symbol of emotions and ideas within me. It touched the spring of a host of beautiful thoughts; but the beauty and the sweetness were the contribution of my own heart and mind.

Now in the new world in which I found myself, I approached the thoughts of beauty and loveliness direct, without any intervening symbols at all. The emotions which beautiful things had aroused in me upon earth were all there, in the new life, but not confused or blurred, as they had been in the old life, by the intruding symbols of ugly, painful, evil things. That was all gone like a mist. I could not think an evil or an ugly thought.

For a period, it was so with me. For a long time—I will use the words of earth henceforth without any explanation—I abode in the same calm, untroubled peace, partly in memory of the old days, partly in the new visions. My senses seemed all blended in one sense; it was not sight or hearing or touch—it was but an instant apprehension of the essence of things. All that time I was absolutely alone, though I had a sense of being watched and tended in a sort of helpless and happy infancy. It was always the quiet sea, and the dawning light. I lived over the scenes of the old life in a vague, blissful memory. For the joy of the new life was that all that had befallen me had a strange and perfect significance. I had lived like other men. I had rejoiced, toiled, schemed, suffered, sinned.

But it was all one now. I saw that each influence had somehow been shaping and moulding me. The evil I had done, was it indeed evil? It had been the flowering of a root of bitterness, the impact of material forces and influences. Had I ever desired it? Not in my spirit,

I now felt Sin had brought me shame and sorrow, and they had done their work. Repentance, contrition—ugly words! I laughed softly at the thought of how different it all was from what I had dreamed. I was as the lost sheep found, as the wayward son taken home; and should I spoil my joy with recalling what was past and done with for ever? Forgiveness was not a process, then, a thing to be sued for and to be withheld; it was all involved in the glad return to the breast of God.

What was the mystery, then? The things that I had wrought, ignoble, cruel, base, mean, selfish—had I ever willed to do them? It seemed impossible, incredible. Were those grievous things still growing, seeding, flowering in other lives left behind? Had they invaded, corrupted, hurt other poor wills and lives? I could think of them no longer, any more than I could think of the wrongs done to myself. Those had not hurt me either. Perhaps I had still to suffer, but I could not think of that. I was too much overwhelmed with joy. The whole thing seemed so infinitely little and far away. So, for a time I floated on the moving crystal of the translucent sea, over the glimmering deeps, the dawn above me, the scenes of the old life growing and shaping themselves and fading without any will of my own, nothing within or without me but ineffable peace and perfect joy.

2

I knew quite well what had happened to me; that I had passed through what mortals call Death: and two thoughts came to me; one was this. There had been times on earth when one had felt sure with a sort of deep instinct that one could not really ever die; yet there had been hours of weariness and despair when one had wondered whether death would not mean a silent blankness. That thought had troubled me most, when I had followed to the grave some friend or some beloved. The mouldering form, shut into the narrow box, was thrust with a sense of shame and disgrace into the clay, and no word or sign returned to show that the spirit lived on, or that one would ever find that dear proximity again. How foolish it seemed now ever to have doubted, ever to have been troubled!

Of course, it was all eternal and everlasting. And then, too, came a second thought. One had learned in life, alas, so often to separate what was holy and sacred from daily life; there were prayers, liturgies, religious exercises, solemnities. Sabbaths—an oppressive strain, too often, and a banishing of active life. Brought up as one had been, there had been a mournful overshadowing of thought, that after death, and with

13

God, it would be all grave and constrained and serious, a perpetual liturgy, an unending Sabbath. But now all was deliciously merged together. All of beautiful and gracious that there had been in religion, all of joyful and animated and eager that there had been in secular life, everything that amused, interested, excited, all fine pictures, great poems, lovely scenes, intrepid thoughts, exercise, work, jests, laughter, perceptions, fancies— they were all one now; only sorrow and weariness and dullness and ugliness and greediness were gone.

The thought was fresh, pure, delicate, full of a great and mirthful content.

There were no divisions of time in my great peace; past, present, and future were alike all merged. How can I explain that? It seems so impossible, having once seen it, that it should be otherwise. The day did not broaden to the noon, nor fade to evening. There was no night there. More than that. In the other life, the dark low-hung days, one seemed to have lived so little, and always to have been making arrangements to live; so much time spent in plans and schemes, in alterations and regrets. There was this to be done and that to be completed; one thing to be begun, another to be cleared away; always in search of the peace which one never found; and if one did achieve it, then it was surrounded, like some cast carrion, by a cloud of poisonous thoughts, like buzzing blueflies. Now at last one lived indeed; but there grew up in the soul, very gradually and sweetly, the sense that one was resting, growing accustomed to something, learning the ways of the new place.

I became more and more aware that I was not alone; it was not that I met, or encountered, or was definitely conscious of any thought that was not my own; but there were motions as of great winds in the untroubled calm in which I lay, of vast deeps drawing past me. There were hoverings and poisings of unseen creatures, which gave me neither awe nor surprise, because they were not in the range of my thought as yet; but it was enough to show me that I was not alone, that there was life about me, purposes going forward, high activities.

The first time I experienced anything more definite was when suddenly I became aware of a great crystalline globe that rose like a bubble out of the sea. It was of an incredible vastness; but I was conscious that I did not perceive it as I had perceived things upon the earth, but that I apprehended it all together, within and without. It rose softly and swiftly out of the expanse. The surface of it was all alive. It had sea, and continents, hills and valleys, woods and fields, like our own earth. There were cities and houses thronged with living beings; it was a world like our own, and yet there was hardly a form upon it that resembled any earthly form, though all were articulate and definite, ranging from growths which I knew to be vegetable, with a dumb and sightless life of their own, up to beings of intelligence and purpose.

It was a world, in fact, on which a history like that of our own world was working itself out; but the whole was of a crystalline texture, if texture it can be called; there was no colour or solidity, nothing but form and silence, and I realised that I saw, if not materially yet in thought, and recognised then, that all the qualities of matter, the sounds, the colours, the scents—all that depends upon material vibration—were abstracted from it; while form, of which the idea exists in the mind apart from all concrete manifestations, was still present.

For some time after that, a series of these crystalline globes passed through the atmosphere where I dwelt, some near, some far; and I saw in an instant, in each case, the life and history of each. Some were still all aflame, mere currents of molten heat and flying vapour. Some had the first signs of rudimentary life—some, again, had a full and organised life, such as ours on earth, with a clash of nations, a stream of commerce, a perfecting of knowledge. Others were growing cold, and the life upon them was artificial and strange, only achieved by a highly intellectual and noble race, with an extraordinary command of natural forces, fighting in wonderfully constructed and guarded dwellings against the growing deathliness of a frozen world, and with a tortured despair in their minds at the extinction which threatened them.

There were others, again, which were frozen and dead, where the drifting snow piled itself up over the gigantic and pathetic contrivances of a race living underground, with huge vents and chimneys, burrowing further into the earth in search of shelter, and nurturing life by amazing processes which I cannot here describe. They were marvellously wise, those pale and shadowy creatures, with a vitality infinitely ahead of our own, a vitality out of which all weakly or diseased elements had long been eliminated. And again, there were globes upon which all seemed dead and frozen to the core, slipping onwards in some infinite progress. But though I saw life under a myriad of new conditions, and with an endless variety of forms, the nature of it was the same as ours. There was the same ignorance of the future, the same doubts and uncertainties, the same pathetic leaning of heart to heart, the same wistful desire after permanence and happiness, which could not be there or so attained.

Then, too, I saw wild eddies of matter taking shape, of a subtlety that is as far beyond any known earthly conditions of matter as steam is above frozen stone. Great tornadoes whirled and poised; globes of spinning fire flew off on distant errands of their own, as when the heavens were made; and I saw, too, the crash of world with world, when satellites that had lost their impetus drooped inwards upon some central sun, and merged themselves at last with a titanic leap. All this enacted itself before me, while life itself flew like a pulse from system to system, never diminished, never increased, withdrawn from one to settle on another. All this I saw and knew.

3

I thought I could never be satiated by this infinite procession of wonders. But at last there rose in my mind, like a rising star, the need to 'be alone no longer. I was passing through a kind of heavenly infancy; and just as a day comes when a child puts out a hand with a conscious intention, not merely a blind groping, but with a need to clasp and caress, or answers a smile by a smile, a word by a purposeful cry, so in a moment I was aware of someone with me and near me, with a heart and a nature that leaned to mine and had need of me, as I of him. I knew him to be one who had lived as I had lived, on the earth that was ours—lived many lives, indeed; and it was then first that I became aware that I had myself lived many lives too.

My human life, which I had last left, was the fullest and clearest of all my existences; but they had been many and various, though always progressive. I must not now tell of the strange life histories that had enfolded me—they had risen in dignity and worth from a life far back, unimaginably elementary and instinctive; but I felt in a moment that my new friend's life had been far richer and more perfect than my own, though I saw that there were still experiences ahead of both of us; but not yet. I may describe his presence in human similitudes, a presence perfectly defined, though apprehended with no human sight. He bore a name which described something clear, strong, full of force, and yet gentle of access, like water.

It was just that; a thing perfectly pure and pervading, which could be stained and troubled, and yet could retain no defilement or agitation; which a child could scatter and divide, and yet was absolutely powerful and insuperable. I will call him Amroth. Him, I say, because though there was no thought of sex left in my consciousness, his was

16

a courageous, inventive, masterful spirit, which gave rather than received, and was withal of a perfect kindness and directness, love undefiled and strong. The moment I became aware of his presence, I felt him to be like one of those wonderful, pure youths of an Italian picture, whose whole mind is set on manful things, untroubled by the love of woman, and yet finding all the world intensely gracious and beautiful, full of eager frankness, even impatience, with long, slim, straight limbs and close-curled hair. I knew him to be the sort of being that painters and poets had been feeling after when they represented or spoke of angels.

And I could not help laughing outright at the thought of the meek, mild, statuesque draped figures, with absurd wings and depressing smiles, that encumbered pictures and churches, with whom no human communication would be possible, and whose grave and discomfiting glance would be fatal to all ease or merriment. I recognised in Amroth a mirthful soul, full of humour and laughter, who could not be shocked by any truth, or hold anything uncomfortably sacred—though indeed he held all things sacred with a kind of eagerness that charmed me. Instead of meeting him in dolorous pietistic mood, I met him, I remember, as at school or college one suddenly met a frank, smiling, high-spirited youth or boy, who was ready at once to take comradeship for granted, and walked away with one from a gathering, with an outrush of talk and plans for further meetings. It was all so utterly unlike the subdued and cautious and sensitive atmosphere of devotion that it stirred us both, I was aware, to a delicious kind of laughter. And then came a swift interchange of thought, which I must try to represent by speech, though speech was none.

"I am glad to find you, Amroth," I said. "I was just beginning to wonder if I was not going to be lonely."

"Ah," he said, "one has what one desires here; you had too much to see and learn at first to want my company. And yet I have been with you, pointing out a thousand things, ever since you came here."

"Was it you" I said, "that have been showing me all this? I thought I was alone."

At which Amroth laughed again, a laugh full of content. "Yes," he said, "the crags and the sunset—do you not remember? I came down with you, carrying you like a child in my arms, while you slept; and then I saw you awake. You had to rest a long time at first; you had had much to bear—uncertainty—that is what tires one, even more than pain. And I have been telling you things ever since, when you could

17

listen."

"Oh," I said, "I have a hundred things to ask you; how strange it is to see so much and understand so little!"

"Ask away," said Amroth, putting an arm through mine.

"I was afraid," I said, "that it would all be so different—like a catechism 'Dost thou believe—is this thy desire?' But instead it seems so entirely natural and simple!"

"Ah," he said, "that is how we bewilder ourselves on earth. Why, it is hard to say! But all the real things remain. It is all just as surprising and interesting and amusing and curious as it ever was: the only things that are gone—for a time, that is—are the things that are ugly and sad. But they are useful too in their way, though you have no need to think of them now. Those are just the discipline, the training."

"But," I said, "what makes people so different from each other down there—so many people who are sordid, grubby, quarrelsome, cruel, selfish, spiteful? Only a few who are bold and kind—like you, for instance?"

"No," he said, answering the thought that rose in my mind, "of course I don't mind—I like compliments as well as ever, if they come naturally! But don't you see that all the little poky, sensual, mean, disgusting lives are simply those of spirits struggling to be free; we begin by being enchained by matter at firsts and then the stream runs clearer. The divine things are imagination and sympathy. That is the secret."

4

Once I said:

"Which kind of people do you find it hardest to help along?"

"The young people," said Amroth, with a smile.

"Youth!" I said. "Why, down below, we think of youth as being so generous and ardent and imitative! We speak of youth as the time to learn, and form fine habits; if a man is wilful and selfish in after-life, we say that it was because he was too much indulged in childhood—and we attach great importance to the impressions of youth."

"That is quite right," said Amroth, "because the impressions of youth are swift and keen; but of course, here, age is not a question of years or failing powers. The old, here, are the wise and gracious and patient and gentle; the youth of the spirit is stupidity and unimaginativeness. On the one hand are the stolid and placid, and on the other are the brutal and cruel and selfish and unrestrained."

"You confuse me greatly," I said; "surely you do not mean that spiritual life and progress are a matter of intellectual energy?"

"No, not at all," said he; "the so-called intellectual people are often the most stupid and youngest of all. The intellect counts for nothing: that is only a kind of dexterity, a pretty game. The imagination is what matters."

"Worse and worse!" I said. "Does salvation belong to poets and novelists?"

"No, no," said Amroth, "that is a game too! The imagination I speak of is the power of entering into other people's minds and hearts, of putting yourself in their place—of loving them, in fact. The more you know of people, the better chance there is of loving them; and you can only find your way into their minds by imaginative sympathy. I will tell you a story which will show you what I mean. There was once a famous writer on earth, of whose wisdom people spoke with bated breath. Men went to see him with fear and reverence, and came away, saying, 'How wonderful!'

"And this man, in his age, was waited upon by a little maid, an ugly, tired, tiny creature. People used to say that they wondered he had not a better servant. But she knew all that he liked and wanted, where his books and papers were, what was good for him to do. She did not understand a word of what he said, but she knew both when he had talked too much, and when he had not talked enough, so that his mind was pent up in itself, and he became cross and fractious. Now, in reality, the little maid was one of the oldest and most beautiful of spirits. She had lived many lives, each apparently humbler than the last. She never grumbled about her work, or wanted to amuse herself. She loved the silly flies that darted about her kitchen, or brushed their black heads on the ceiling; she loved the ivy tendrils that tapped on her window in the breeze.

"She did not go to church, she had no time for that; or if she had gone, she would not have understood what was said, though she would have loved all the people there, and noticed how they looked and sang. But the wise man himself was one of the youngest and stupidest of spirits, so young and stupid that he had to have a very old and wise spirit to look after him. He was eaten up with ideas and vanity, so that he had no time to look at any one or think of anybody, unless they praised him. He has a very long pilgrimage before him, though he wrote pretty songs enough, and his mortal body, or one of them, lies in the Poets' Corner of the Abbey, and people come and put wreaths there with tears in their eyes."

"It is very bewildering," I said, "but I see a little more than I did. It is all a matter of feeling, then? But it seems hard on people that they should be so dull and stupid about it all—that the truth should lie so close to their hand and yet be so carefully concealed."

"Oh, they grow out of dullness!" he said, with a movement of his hand; "that is what experience does for us—it is always going on; we get widened and deepened. Why," he added, "I have seen a great man, as they called him, clever and alert, who held a high position in the State. He was laid aside by a long and painful illness, so that all his work was put away. He was brave about it, too, I remember; but he used to think to himself how sad and wasteful it was, that when he was most energetic and capable he should be put on the shelf—all the fine work he might have done interrupted; all the great speeches he would have made unuttered.

"But as a matter of fact, he was then for the first time growing fast, because he had to look into the minds and hearts of all sorrowful and disappointed people, and to learn that what we do matters so little, and that what we are matters so much. When he did at last get back to the world, people said, 'What a sad pity to see so fine a career spoilt!' But out of all the years of all his lives, those years had been his very best and richest, when he sat half the day feeble in the sun, and could not even look at the papers which lay beside him, or when he woke in the grey mornings, with the thought of another miserable day of idleness and pain before him."

I said, "Then is it a bad thing to be busy in the world, because it takes off your mind from the things which matter?"

"No," said Amroth, "not a bad thing at all: because two things are going on. Partly the framework of society and life is being made, so that men are not ground down into that sordid struggle, when little experience is possible because of the drudgery which clouds all the mind. Though even that has its opportunities! And all depends, for the individual, upon how he is doing his work. If he has other people in mind all the time, and does his work for them, and not to be praised for it, then all is well. But if he is thinking of his credit and his position, then he does not grow at all; that is pomposity—a very youthful thing indeed; but the worst case of all is if a man sees that the world must be helped and made, and that one can win credit thus, and so engages in work of that kind, and deals in all the jargon of it, about using influence and living for others, when he is really thinking of himself all the time, and trying to keep the eyes of the world upon him. But it is all growth really, though sometimes, as on the beach when the tide is coming in, the waves seem to draw backward from the land, and poise themselves in a crest of troubled water."

"But is a great position in the world," I said, "whether inherited or attained, a dangerous thing?"

"Nothing is *dangerous*, child," he said. "You must put all that out of your mind. But men in high posts and stations are often not progressing evenly, only in great jogs and starts. They learn very often, with a sudden surprise, which is not always painful, and sometimes is very beautiful and sweet, that all the ceremony and pomp, the great house, the bows and the smiles, mean nothing at all—absolutely nothing, except the chance, the opportunity of not being taken in by them. That is the use of all pleasures and all satisfactions—the frame of mind which made the old king say, 'Is not this great Babylon, which I have builded?'—they are nothing but the work of another class in the great school of life. A great many people are put to school with self-satisfaction, that they may know the fine joy of humiliation, the delight of learning that it is not effectiveness and applause that matters, but love and peacefulness.

"And the great thing is that we should feel that we are growing, not in hardness or indifference, nor necessarily even in courage or patience, but in our power to feel and our power to suffer. As love multiplies, suffering must multiply too. The very Heart of God is full of infinite, joyful, hopeful suffering; the whole thing is so vast, so slow, so quiet, that the end of suffering is yet far off. But when we suffer, we climb fast; the spirit grows old and wise in faith and love; and suffering is the one thing we cannot dispense with, because it is the condition of our fullest and purest life."

5

I said suddenly, "The joy of this place is not the security of it, but the fact that one has not to think about security. I am not afraid of anything that may happen, and there is no weariness of thought. One does not think till one is tired, but till one has finished thinking."

"Yes," said Amroth, "that was the misery of the poor body!"

"And yet I used to think," I said, "in the old days that I was grateful to the body for many pleasant things it gave me—breathing the air, feeling the sun, eating and drinking, games and exercise, and the strange thing one called love."

"Yes," said Amroth, "all those things have to be made pleasant, or to appear so; otherwise no one could submit to the discipline at all; but of course, the pleasure only got in the way of the thought and of the happiness; it was not what one saw, tasted, smelt, felt, that one desired, but the real thing behind it; even the purest thing of all, the sight and contact of one whom one loved, let us say, with no sensual passion at all, but with a perfectly pure love; what a torment that was—desiring something which one could not get, the real fusion of feeling and thought! But the poor body was always in the way then, saying, 'Here am I—please me, amuse me.'"

"But then," I said, "what is the use of all that? Why should the pure, clear, joyful, sleepless life I now feel be tainted and hampered and drugged by the body? I don't feel that I am losing anything by losing the body."

"No, not losing," said Amroth, "but, happy though you are, you are not gaining things as fast now—it is your time of rest and refresh-ment—but we shall go back, both of us, to the other life again, when the time comes: and the point is this, that we have got to win the best things through trouble and struggle."

"But even so," I said, "there are many things I do not understand—the child that opens its eyes upon the world and closes them again; the young child that suffers and dies, just when it is the darling of the home; and at the other end of the scale, the helpless, fractious invalid, or the old man who lives in weariness, wakeful and tortured, and who is glad just to sit in the sun, indifferent to everyone and everything, past feeling and hoping and thinking— or, worst of all, the people with diseased minds, whose pain makes them suspicious and malig-nant. What is the meaning of all this pain, which seems to do people nothing but harm, and makes them a burden to themselves and others too?"

"Oh," said he, "it is difficult enough; but you must remember that we are all bound up with the hearts and lives of others; the child that dies in its helplessness has a meaning for its parents; the child that lives long enough to be the light of its home, that has a significance deep enough; and all those who have to tend and care for the sicky to lighten the burden and the sorrow for them, that has a meaning surely for all concerned? The reason why we feel as we do about broken lives, why they seem so utterly purposeless, is because we have the proportion so wrong. We do not really, in fact, believe in immortality, when we are bound in the body—some few of us do, and many of us say that we do. But we do not realise that the little life is but one in a great chain of lives, that each spirit lives many times, over and over. There is no such thing as waste or sacrifice of life.

"The life is meant to do just what it does, no more and no less; bound in the body, it all seems so long or so short, so complete or so incomplete; but now and here we can see that the whole thing is so endless, so immense, that we think no more of entering life, say, for a few days, or entering it for ninety years, than we should think of counting one or ninety water-drops in the river that pours in a cataract over the lip of the rocks. Where we do lose, in life, is in not taking the particular experience, be it small or great, to heart. We try to forget things, to put them out of our minds, to banish them. Of course, it is very hard to do otherwise, in a body so finite, tossed and whirled in a stream so infinite; and thus, we are happiest if we can live very simply and quietly, not straining to multiply our uneasy activities, but just getting the most and the best out of the elements of life as they come to us. As we get older in spirit, we do that naturally; the things that men call ambitions and schemes are the signs of immaturity; and when we grow older, those slip off us and concern us no more; while the real vitality of feeling and emotion runs ever more clear and strong."

"But," I said, "can one revive the old lives at will? Can one look back into the long range of previous lives? Is that permitted?"

"Yes, of course it is permitted," said Amroth, smiling; "there are no rules here; but one does not care to do it overmuch. One is just glad it is all done, and that one has learnt the lesson. Look back if you like—there are all the lives behind you."

I had a curious sensation—I saw myself suddenly a stalwart savage, strangely attired for war, near a hut in a forest clearing. I was going away somewhere; there were other huts at hand; there was a fire, in the side of a mound, where some women seemed to be cooking something and wrangling over it; the smoke went up into the still air. A child came out of the hut, and ran to me. I bent down and kissed it, and it clung to me. I was sorry, in a dim way, to be going out—for I saw other figures armed too, standing about the clearing. There was to be fighting that day, and though I wished to fight, I thought I might not return. But the mind of myself, as I discerned it, was full of hurtful, cruel, rapacious thoughts, and I was sad to think that this could ever have been I.

"It is not very nice," said Amroth with a smile; "one does not care to revive that! You were young then, and had much before you."

Another picture flashed into the mind. Was it true? I was a woman, it seemed, looking out of a window on the street in a town with high, dark houses, strongly built of stone: there was a towered gate at a little distance, with some figures drawing up sacks with a pulley to a door in the gate. A man came up behind me, pulled me roughly back, and spoke angrily; I answered him fiercely and shrilly. The room I was in seemed to be a shop or store; there were barrels of wine, and bags of corn. I felt that I was busy and anxious—it was not a pleasant retrospect.

"Yet you were better then," said Amroth; "you thought little of your drudgery, and much of your children."

Yes, I had had children, I saw. Their names and appearance floated before me. I had loved them tenderly. Had they passed out of my life? I felt bewildered.

Amroth laid a hand on my arm and smiled again. "No, you came near to some of them again. Do you not remember another life in which you loved a friend with a strange love, that surprised you by its nearness? He had been your child long before; and one never quite loses that."

I saw in a flash the other life he spoke of. I was a student, it seemed, at some university, where there was a boy of my own age, a curious, wilful, perverse, tactless creature, always saying and doing the wrong thing, for whom I had felt a curious and unreasonable responsibility. I had always tried to explain him to other people, to justify him; and he had turned to me for help and companionship in a singular way. I saw myself walking with him in the country, expostulating, gesticulating; and I saw him angry and perplexed. . . . The vision vanished.

"But what becomes of all those whom we have loved?" I said; "it cannot be as if we had never loved them."

"No, indeed," said Amroth, "they are all there or hare; but there lies one of the great mysteries which we cannot yet attain to. We shall be all brought together some time, closely and perfectly; but even now, in the world of matter, the spirit half remembers; and when one is strangely and lovingly drawn to another soul, when that love is not of the body, and has nothing of passion in it, then it is some close ancient tie reasserting itself. Do you not know how old and remote some of our friendships seemed—so much older and larger than could be accounted for by the brief, days of companionship? That strange hunger for the past of one we love is nothing but the faint memory of what has been. Indeed, when you have rested happily a little longer, you will move farther afield, and you will come near to spirits you have loved.

You cannot bear it yet, though they are all about you; but one regains the spiritual sense slowly after a life like yours."

"Can I revisit," I said, "the scene of my last life—see and know what those I loved are doing and feeling?"

"Not yet," said Amroth; "that would not profit either you or them. The sorrow of earth would not be sorrow, it would have no cleansing power, if the parted spirit could return at once. You do not guess, either, how much of time has passed already since you came here—it seems to you like yesterday, no doubt, since you last suffered death. To meet loss and sorrow upon earth, without either comfort or hope, is one of the finest of lessons. When we are there, we must live blindly, and if we here could make our presence known at once to the friends we leave behind, it would be all too easy. It is in the silence of death that its virtue lies."

"Yes," I said, "I do not desire to return. This is all too wonderful. It is the freshness and sweetness of it all that comes home to me. I do not desire to think of the body, and, strange to say, if I do think of it, the times that I remember gratefully are those when the body was faint and weary. The old joys and triumphs, when one laughed and loved and exulted, seem to me to have something ugly about them, because one was content, and wished things to remain for ever as they were. It was the longing for something different that helped me; the acquiescence was the shame."

6

One day I said to Amroth, "What a comfort it is to find that there is no religion here!"

"I know what you mean," he said. "I think it is one of the things that one wonders at most, to remember into how very small and narrow a thing religion was made, and how much that was religious was never supposed to be so."

"Yes," I said, "as I think of it now, it seems to have been a game played by a few players, a game with a great many rules."

"Yes," he said, "it was a game often enough; but of course, the mischief of it was, that when it was most a game it most pretended to be something else—to contain the secret of life and all knowledge."

"I used to think," I said, "that religion was like a noble and generous boy with the lyrical heart of a poet, made by some sad chance into a king, surrounded by obsequious respect and pomp and etiquette, bound by a hundred ceremonious rules, forbidden to do this and that,

25

taught to think that his one duty was to be magnificently attired, to acquire graceful arts of posture and courtesy, subtly and gently prevented from obeying natural and simple impulses, made powerless—a crowned slave; so that, instead of being the freest and sincerest thing in the world, it became the prisoner of respectability and convention, just a part of the social machine."

"That was only one side of it," said Amroth. "It was often where it was least supposed to be."

"Yes," I said, "as far as I resent anything now, I resent the conversion of so much religion from an inspiring force into a repressive force. One learnt as a child to think of it, not as a great moving flood of energy and joy, but as an awful power apart from life, rejoicing in petty restrictions, and mainly concerned with creating an unreal atmosphere of narrow piety, hostile to natural talk and laughter and freedom. God's aid was invoked, in childhood, mostly when one was naughty and disobedient, so that one grew to think of Him as grim, severe, irritable, anxious to interfere.

"What wonder that one lost all wish to meet God and all natural desire to know Him! One thought of Him as impossible to please except by behaving in a way in which it was not natural to behave; and one thought of religion as a stern and dreadful process going on somewhere, like a law-court or a prison, which one had to keep clear of if one could. Yet I hardly see how, in the interests of discipline, it could have been avoided. If only one could have begun at the other end!"

"Yes," said Amroth, "but that is because religion has fallen so much into the hands of the wrong people, and is grievously misrepresented. It has too often come to be identified, as you say, with human law, as a power which leaves one severely alone, if one behaves oneself, and which punishes harshly and mechanically if one outsteps the limit. It comes into the world as a great joyful motive; and then it becomes identified with respectability, and it is sad to think that it is simply from the fact that it has won the confidence of the world that it gains its awful power of silencing and oppressing. It becomes hostile to frankness and independence, and puts a premium on caution and submissiveness; but that is the misuse of it and the degradation of it; and religion is still the most pure and beautiful thing in the world for all that; the doctrine itself is fine and true in a way, if one can view it without impatience; it upholds the right things; it all makes for peace and order, and even for humility and just kindliness; it insists, or tries

26

to insist, on the fact that property and position and material things do not matter, and that quality and method do matter.

"Of course, it is terribly distorted, and gets into the hands of the wrong people—the people who want to keep things as they are. Now the Gospel, as it first came, was a perfectly beautiful thing—the idea that one must act by tender impulse, that one must always forgive, and forget, and love; that one must take a natural joy in the simplest things, find everyone and everything interesting and delightful . . . the perfectly natural, just, good-humoured, uncalculating life—that was the idea of it; and that one was not to be superior to the hard facts of the world, not to try to put sorrow or pain out of sight, but to live eagerly and hopefully in them and through them; not to try to school oneself into hardness or indifference, but to love lovable things, and not to condemn or despise the unlovable. That was indeed a message out of the very heart of God.

"But of course, all the acrid divisions and subdivisions of it come, not from itself, but from the material part of the world, that determines to traffic with the beautiful secret, and make it serve its turn. But there are plenty of true souls within it all, true teachers, faithful learners—and the world cannot do without it yet, though it is strangely fettered and bound. Indeed, men can never do without it, because the spiritual force is there; it is full of poetry and mystery, that ageless brotherhood of saints and true-hearted disciples; but one has to learn that many that claim its powers have them not, while many who are outside all organisations have the secret."

"Yes," I said, "all that is true and good; it is the exclusive claim and not the inclusive which one regrets. It is the voice which says, 'Accept my exact faith, or you have no part in the inheritance,' which is wrong. The real voice of religion is that which says, 'You are my brother and my sister, though you know it not.' And if one says, 'We are all at fault, we are all far from the truth, but we live as best we can, looking for the larger hope and for the dawn of love,' that is the secret. The sacrament of God is offered and eaten at many a social meal, and the Spirit of Love finds utterance in quiet words from smiling lips. One cannot teach by harsh precept, only by desirable example; and the worst of the correct profession of religion is that it is often little more than taking out a licence to disapprove."

"Yes," said Amroth, "you are very near a great truth. The mistake we make is like the mistake so often made on earth in matters of human government—the opposing of the individual to the State, as if the State were something above and different to the individual—like the old thought of the Spirit moving on the face of the waters. The individual is the State; and it is the game with the soul and God. God is not above the soul, seeing and judging, apart in isolation. The Spirit of God is the spirit of humanity, the spirit of admiration, the spirit of love. It matters little what the soul admires and loves, whether it be a flower or a mountain, a face or a cause, a gem or a doctrine.

"It is that wonderful power that the current of the soul has of setting towards something that is beautiful: the need to admire, to worship, to love. A regiment of soldiers in the street, a procession of priests to a sanctuary, a march of disordered women clamouring for their rights—if the idea thrills you, if it uplifts you, it matters nothing whether other people dislike or despise or deride it—it is the voice of God for you. We must advance from what is merely brilliant to what is true; and though in the single life many a man seems to halt at a certain point, to have tied up his little packet of admirations once and for all, there are other lives where he will pass on to further loves, his passion growing more intense and pure.

"We are not limited by our circle, by our generation, by our age; and the things which youthful spirits are divining and proclaiming as great and wonderful discoveries, are often being practised and done by silent and humble souls. It is not the concise or impressive statement of a truth that matters, it is the intensity of the inner impulse towards what is high and true which differentiates. The more we live by that, the less are we inclined to argue and dispute about it. The base, the impure desire is only the imperfect desire; if it is gratified, it reveals its imperfections, and the soul knows that not there can it stay; but it must have faced and tested everything. If the soul, out of timidity and conventionality, says 'No' to its eager impulses, it halts upon its pilgrimage. Some of the most grievous and shameful lives on earth have been fruitful enough in reality.

"The reason why we mourn and despond over them is, again, that we limit our hope to the single life. There is time for everything; we must not be impatient. We must despair of nothing and of no one; the true life consists not in what a man's reason approves or disapproves, not in what he does or says, but in what he sees. It is useless to explain things to souls; they must experience them to apprehend them. The one treachery is to speak of mistakes as irreparable, and of sins as unforgivable. The sin against the Spirit is to doubt the Spirit, and the sin against life is not to use it generously and freely; we are happiest if we love others well enough to give our life to them; but it is better to use life for ourselves than not to use it at all."

7

One day I said to Amroth, "Are there no rules of life here? It seems almost too good to be true, not to be found fault with and censured and advised and blamed."

"Oh," said Amroth, laughing, "there are plenty of *rules*, as you call them; but one feels them, one is not told them; it is like breathing and seeing."

"Yes," I replied, "yet it was like that, too, in the old days; the misery was when one suddenly discovered that when one was acting in what seemed the most natural way possible, it gave pain and concern to someone whom one respected and even loved. One knew that one's action was not wrong, and yet one desired to please and satisfy one's friends; and so, one fell back into conventional ways, not because one liked them but because other people did, and it was not worth while making a fuss—it was a sort of cowardice, I suppose?"

"Not quite," said Amroth; "you were more on the right lines than the people who interfered with you, no doubt; but of course, the truth is that our principles ought to be used, like a stick, to support ourselves, not like a rod to beat other people with. The most difficult people to teach, as you will see hereafter, are the self-righteous people, whose lives are really pure and good, but who allow their preferences about amusements, occupations, ways of life, to become matters of principle. The worst temptation in the world is the habit of influence and authority, the desire to direct other lives and to conform them to one's own standard. The only way in which we can help other people is by loving them; by frightening another out of something which he is apt to do and of which one does not approve, one effects absolutely nothing: sin cannot be scared away; the spirit must learn to desire to cast it away, because it sees that goodness is beautiful and fine; and this can only be done by example, never by precept."

"But it is the entire absence of both that puzzles me here," I said, "Nothing to do and a friend to talk to; it's a lazy business, I think."

Amroth looked at me with amusement. "It's a sign," he said, "if you feel that, that you are getting rested, and ready to move on; but you will be very much surprised when you know a little more about the life here. You are like a baby in a cradle at present; when you come to enter one of our communities here, you will find it as complicated a business as you could wish. Part of the difficulty is that there are no rules, to use your own phrase. It is real democracy, but it is not complicated by any questions of property, which is the thing that clogs all political progress in the world below. There is nothing to scheme for, no ambitions to gratify, nothing to gain at the expense of others; the only thing that matters is one's personal relation to others; and this is what makes it at once so simple and so complex. But I do not think it is of any use to tell you all this; you will see it in a flash, when the time comes. But it may be as well for you to remember that there will be no one to command you or compel you or advise you. Your own heart and spirit will be your only guides. There is no such thing as compulsion or force in heaven. Nothing can be done to you that you do not choose or allow to be done."

"Yes," I said, "it is the blessed and beautiful sense of freedom from all ties and influences and fears that is so utterly blissful."

"But this is not all," said Amroth, shaking his head with a smile. "This is a time of rest for you, but things are very different elsewhere. When you come to enter heaven itself, you will be constantly surprised. There are labour and fear and sorrow to be faced; and you must not think it is a place for drifting pleasantly along. The moral struggle is the same—indeed it is fiercer and stronger than ever, because there is no bodily languor or fatigue to distract. There are choices to be made, duties to perform, evil to be faced. The bodily temptations are absent, but there is still that which lay behind the bodily frailties—curiosity, love of sensation, excitement, desire; the strong duality of nature—the knowledge of duty on the one hand and the indolent shrinking from performance—that is all there; there is the same sense of isolation, and the same need for patient endeavour as upon earth.

"All that one gets is a certain freedom of movement; one is not bound to places and employments by the material ties of earth; but you must not think that it is all to be easy and straightforward. We can each of us by using our wills shorten our probation, by not resisting influences, by putting our hearts and minds in unison with the will of God for us; and that is easier in heaven than upon earth, because there is less to distract us. But on the other hand, there is more temptation to drift, because there are no material consequences to stimulate us. There are many people on earth who exercise a sort of practical virtue simply to avoid material inconveniences, while there is no such motive in heaven; I say all this not to disturb your present tranquillity, which it is your duty now to enjoy, but just to prepare you. You must be prepared for effort and for endeavour, and even for strife. You must use right judgment, and, above all, common sense; one does not get out of the reach of that in heaven!"

8

These are only some of the many talks I had with Amroth. They ranged over a great many subjects and thoughts. What I cannot indicate, however, is the lightness and freshness of them; and above all, their entire frankness and amusingness. There were times when we talked like two children, revived old simple adventures of life—he had lived far more largely and fully than I had done—and I never tired of hearing the tales of his old lives, so much more varied and wonderful than my own. Sometimes we merely told each other stories out of our imaginations and hearts. We even played games, which I cannot describe, but they were like the games of earth. We seemed at times to walk and wander together; but I had a sense all this time that I was, so to speak, in hospital, being tended and cared for, and not allowed to do anything wearisome or demanding effort.

But I became more and more aware of other spirits about me, like birds that chirp and twitter in the ivy of a tower, or in the thick bushes of a shrubbery. Amroth told me one day that I must prepare for a great change soon, and I found myself wondering what it would be like, half excited about it, and half afraid, unwilling as I was to lose the sweet rest, and the dear companionship of a friend who seemed like the crown and sum of all hopes of friendship. Amroth became utterly dear to me, and it was a joy beyond all joys to feel his happy and smiling nature bent upon me, hour by hour, in sympathy and understanding and love. He said to me laughingly once that I had much of earth about me yet, and that I must soon learn not to bend my thoughts so exclusively one way and on one friend.

"Yes," I said, "I am not fit for heaven yet! I believe I am jealous; I cannot bear to think that you will leave me, or that any other soul deserves your attention."

"Oh," he said lightly, "this is my business and delight now—but you will soon have to do for others what I am doing for you. You like this easy life at present, but you can hardly imagine how interesting it is to have someone given you for your own, as you were given to me. It is the delight of motherhood and fatherhood in one; and when I was allowed to take you away out of the room where you lay—I admit it was not a pleasant scene—I felt just like a child who is given a kitten

31

for its very own."

"Well," I said, "I have been a very satisfactory pet—I have done little else but purr." I felt his eyes upon me in a wonderful nearness of love; and then I looked up and I saw that we were not alone.

It was then that I first perceived that there could be grief in heaven. I say "first perceived," but I had known it all along. But by Amroth's gentle power that had been for a time kept away from me, that I might rest and rejoice.

The form before me was that of a very young and beautiful woman—so beautiful that for a moment all my thought seemed to be concentrated upon her. But I saw, too, that all was not well with her. She was not at peace with herself, or her surroundings. In her great wide eyes there was a look of pain, and of rebellious pain. She was attired in a robe that was a blaze of colour; and when I wondered at this, for it was unlike the clear hues, pearly grey and gold, and soft roseate light that had hitherto encompassed me, the voice of Amroth answered my unuttered question, and said, "It is the image of her thought. Her slim white hands moved aimlessly over the robe, and seemed to finger the jewels which adorned it. Her lips were parted, and anything more beautiful than the pure curves of her chin and neck I had seldom seen, though she seemed never to be still, as Amroth was still, but to move restlessly and wearily about. I knew by a sort of intuition that she was unaware of Amroth and only aware of myself. She seemed startled and surprised at the sight of me, and I wondered in what form I appeared to her; in a moment she spoke, and her voice was low and thrilling.

"I am so glad," she said in a half-courteous, half-distracted way, "to find someone in the place to whom I can speak. I seem to be always moving in a crowd, and yet to see no one—they are afraid of me, I think; and it is not what I expected, not what I am used to. I am in need of help, I feel, and yet I do not know what sort of help it is that I want. May I stay with you a little?"

"Why, yes," I said; "there is no question of 'may' here."

She came up to me with a sort of proud confidence, and looked at me fixedly. "Yes," she said, "I see that I can trust you; and I am tired of being deceived!" Then she added with a sort of pettishness, "I have nowhere to go, nothing to do—it is all dull and cold. On earth it was just the opposite. I had only too much attention and love. . . . Oh, yes," she added with a strange glance, "it was what you would probably call sinful. The only man I ever loved did not care for me, and I was loved by many for whom I did not care. Well, I had my pleasures, and I suppose I must pay for them. I do not complain of that. But I am determined not to give way: it is unjust and cruel. I never had a chance. I was always brought up to be admired from the first.

"We were rich at my home, and in society—you understand? I made what was called a good match, and I never cared for my husband, but amused myself with other people; and it was splendid while it lasted: then all kinds of horrible things happened—scenes, explanations, a lawsuit—it makes me shudder to remember it all; and then I was ill, I suppose, and suddenly it was all over, and I was alone, with a feeling that I must try to take up with all kinds of tiresome things—all the things that bored me most. But now it may be going to be better; you can tell me where I can find people, perhaps? I am not quite unpresentable, even here? No, I can see that in your face. Well, take me somewhere, show me something, find something for me to do in this deadly place. I seem to have got into a perpetual sunset, and I am so sick of it all."

I felt very helpless before this beautiful creature who seemed so troubled and discontented. "No," said the voice of Amroth beside me, "it is of no use to talk; let her talk to you; let her make friends with you if she can."

"That's better," she said, looking at me. "I was afraid you were going to be grave and serious. I felt for a minute as if I was going to be confirmed."

"No," I said, "you need not be disturbed; nothing will be done to you against your wish. One has but to wish here, or to be willing, and the right thing happens."

She came close to me as I said this, and said, "Well, I think I shall like you, if only you can promise not to be serious." Then she turned, and stood for a moment disconsolate, looking away from me.

All this while the atmosphere around me had been becoming lighter and clearer, as though a mist were rising. Suddenly Amroth said, "You will have to go with her for a time, and do what you can. I must leave you for a little, but I shall not be far off; and if you need me, I shall be at hand. But do not call for me unless you are quite sure you need me." He gave me a hand-clasp and a smile, and was gone.

Then, looking about me, I saw at last that I was in a place. Lonely and bare though it was, it seemed to me very beautiful. It was like a grassy upland, with rocky heights to left and right. They were most delicate in outline, those crags, like the crags in an old picture, with sharp, smooth curves, like a fractured crystal. They seemed to be of a creamy stone, and shadows fell blue and distinct. Down below was a great plain full of trees and waters, all very dim, A path, worn lightly in the grass, lay at my feet, and I knew that we must descend it. The girl with me—I will call hep Cynthia—was gazing at it with delight.

"Ah," she said, "I can see clearly now. This is something like a real place, instead of mist and light. We can find people down here, no doubt; it looks inhabited out there." She pointed with her hand, and it seemed to me that I could see spires and towers and roofs, of a fine and airy architecture, at the end of a long horn of water which lay very blue among the woods of the plain. It puzzled me, because I had the sense that it was all unreal, and, indeed, I soon perceived that it was the girl's own thought that in some way affected mine. "Quick, let us go," she said; "what are we waiting for?"

The descent was easy and gradual. We came down, following the path, over the hill-shoulders. A stream of clear water dripped among stones; it all brought back to me with an intense delight the recollection of long days spent among such hills in holiday times on earth, but all without regret; I only wished that an old and dear friend of mine, with whom I had often gone, might be with me. He had quitted life before me, and I knew somehow or hoped that I should before long see him; but I did not wish things to be otherwise; and, indeed, I had a strange interest in the fretful, silly, lovely girl with me, and in what lay before us. She prattled on, and seemed to be recovering her spirits and her confidence at the sights around us. If I could but find anything that would draw her out of her restless mood into the peace of the morning!

She had a charm for me, though her impatience and desire for amusement seemed uninteresting enough; and I found myself talking to her as an elder brother might, with terms of familiar endearment, which she seemed to be grateful for. It was strange in a way, and yet it all appeared natural. The more we drew away from the hills, the happier she became. "Ah," she said once, "we have got out of that hateful place, and now perhaps we may be more comfortable,"—and when we came down beside the stream to a grove of trees, and saw something which seemed like a road beneath us, she was delighted. "That's more like it," she said, "and now we may find some real people perhaps,"—she turned to me with a smile—"though you are real enough too, and very kind to me; but I still have an idea that you are a clergyman, and are only waiting your time to draw a moral."

9

Now before I go on to tell the tale of what happened to us in the valley there were two very curious things that I observed or began to observe.

The first was that I could not really see into the girl's thought. I became aware that though I could see into the thought of Amroth as easily and directly as one can look into a clear sea-pool, with all its rounded pebbles and its swaying fringes of seaweed, there was in the girl's mind a centre of thought to which I was not admitted, a fortress of personality into which I could not force my way. More than that. When she mistrusted or suspected me, there came a kind of cloud out from the central thought, as if a turbid stream were poured into the sea-pool, which obscured her thoughts from me, though when she came to know me and to trust me, as she did later, the cloud was gradually withdrawn; and I perceived that there must be a perfect sacrifice of will, an intention that the mind should lie open and unashamed before the thought of one's friend and companion, before the vision can be complete.

With Amroth I desired to conceal nothing, and he had no concealment from me. But with the girl it was different. There was something in her heart that she hid from me, and by no effort could I penetrate it; and I saw then that there is something at the centre of the soul which is our very own, and into which God Himself cannot even look, unless we desire that He should look; and even if we desire that He should look into our souls, if there is any timidity or shame or shrinking about us, we cannot open our souls to Him. I must speak about this later, when the great and wonderful day came to me, when I beheld God and was beheld by Him. But now, though when the girl trusted me I could see much of her thought, the inmost cell of it was still hidden from me.

And then, too, I perceived another strange thing; that the landscape in which we walked was very plain to me, but that she did not see the same things that I saw. With me, the landscape was such as I had loved most in my last experience of life; it was a land to me like the English hill-country which I loved the best; little fields of pasture mostly, with hedgerow ashes and sycamores, and here and there a clear stream of water running by the wood-ends. There were buildings, too, low white-walled farms, roughly slated, much-weathered, with evidences of homely life, byre and barn and granary, all about them. These sloping fields ran up into high moorlands and little grey crags, with the trees and thickets growing in the rock fronts. I could not think that people lived in these houses and practised agriculture, though I saw with surprise and pleasure that there were animals about, horses and sheep grazing, and dogs that frisked in and out. I had always believed and hoped that animals had their share in the inheritance of light, and now I thought that this was a proof that it was indeed so, though I could not be sure of it, because I realised that it might be but the thoughts of my mind taking shape, for, as I say, I was gradually aware that the girl did not see what I saw.

To her it was a different scene, of some southern country, because she seemed to see vineyards, and high-walled lanes, hill-crests crowded with houses and crowned with churches, such as one sees at a distance in the Campagna, where the plain breaks into chestnut-clad hills. But this difference of sight did not make me feel that the scene was in any degree unreal; it was the idea of the landscape which we loved, its pretty associations and familiar features, and the mind did the rest, translating it all into a vision of scenes which had given us joy on earth, just as we do in dreams when we are in the body, when the sleeping mind creates sights which give us pleasure, and yet we have no knowledge that we are ourselves creating them. So, we walked together, until I perceived that we were drawing near to the town which we had discerned.

And now we became aware of people going to and fro. Sometimes they stopped and looked upon us with smiles, and even greetings; and sometimes they went past absorbed in thought

Houses appeared, both small wayside abodes and larger mansions with sheltered gardens. What it all meant I hardly knew; but just as we have perfectly decided tastes on earth as to what sort of a house we like and why we like it, whether we prefer high, bright rooms, or rooms low and with subdued light, so in that other country the mind creates what it desires.

Presently the houses grew thicker, and soon we were in a street— the town to my eyes was like the little towns one sees in the Cotswold country, of a beautiful golden stone, with deep plinths and cornices, with older and simpler buildings interspersed. My companion became strangely excited, glancing this way and that. And presently, as if we were certainly expected, there came up to us a kindly and grave person, who welcomed us formally to the place, and said a few courteous words about his pleasure that we should have chosen to visit it.

I do not know how it was, but I did not wholly trust our host. His mind was hidden from me; and indeed, I began to have a sense, not of evil, indeed, or of oppression, but a feeling that it was not the place appointed for me, but only where my business was to lie for a season. A group of people came up to us and welcomed my companion with great cheerfulness, and she was soon absorbed in talk.

10

Now before I come to tell this next part of my story, there are several things which seem in want of explanation. I speak of people as looking old and young, and of there being relations between them such as fatherly and motherly, sonlike and loverlike. It bewildered me at first, but I came to guess at the truth. It would seem that in the further world spirits do preserve for a long time the characteristics of the age at which they last left the earth; but I saw no very young children anywhere at first, though I came afterwards to know what befell them. It seemed to me that, in the first place I visited, the only spirits I saw were of those who had been able to make a deliberate choice of how they would live in the world and which kind of desires they would serve; it is very hard to say when this choice takes place in the world below, but I came to believe that, early or late, there does come a time when there is an opening out of two paths before each human soul, and when it realises that a choice must be made.

Sometimes this is made early in life; but sometimes a soul drifts on, guileless in a sense, though its life may be evil and purposeless, not looking backwards or forwards, but simply acting as its nature bids it act. What it is that decides the awakening of the will I hardly know; it is all a secret growth, I think; but the older that the spirit is, in the sense of spiritual experience, the earlier in mortal life that choice is made; and this is only another proof of one of the things which Amroth showed me, that it is, after all, imagination which really makes the difference between souls, and not intellect or shrewdness or energy; all the real things of life—sympathy, the power of entering into fine relations, however simple they may be, with others, loyalty, patience, devotion, goodness—seem to grow out of this power of imagination; and the reason why the souls of whom I am going to speak were so content to dwell where they were, was simply that they had no imagination beyond, but dwelt happily among the delights which upon earth are represented by sound and colour and scent and comeliness and comfort.

This was a perpetual surprise to me, because I saw in these fine creatures such a faculty of delicate perception, that I could not help believing again and again that their emotions were as deep and varied too; but I found little by little, that they were all bent, not on loving, and therefore on giving themselves away to what they loved, but in gathering in perceptions and sensations, and finding their delight in them; and I realised that what lies at the root of the artistic nature is its deep and vital indifference to anything except what can directly give it delight, and that these souls, for all their amazing subtlety and discrimination, had very little hold on life at all, except on its outer details and superficial harmonies; and that they were all very young in experience, and like shallow waters, easily troubled and easily appeased; and that therefore they were being dealt with like children, and allowed full scope for all their little sensitive fancies, until the time should come for them to go further yet.

Of course, they were one degree older than the people who in the world had been really immersed in what may be called solid interests and serious pursuits—science, politics, organisation, warfare, commerce—all these spirits were very youthful indeed, and they were, I suppose, in some very childish nursery of God. But what first bewildered me was the finding of the earthly proportions of things so strangely reversed, the serious matters of life so utterly set aside, and so much made of the things which many people take no sort of trouble about, as companionships and affections, which are so often turned into a matter of mere propinquity and circumstance. But of this I shall have to speak later in its place.

Now it is difficult to describe the time I spent in the land of delight, because it was all so unlike the life of the world, and yet was so strangely like it. There was work going on there, I found, but the nature of it I could not discern, because that was kept hidden from me. Men and women excused themselves from our company, saying they must return to their work; but most of the time was spent in leisurely converse about things which I confess from the first did not interest me. There was much wit and laughter, and there were constant games and assemblies and amusements. There were feasts of delicious things, music, dramas. There were books read and discussed; it was just like a very cultivated and civilised society. But what struck me about the people there was that it was all very restless and highly-strung, a perpetual tasting of pleasures, which somehow never pleased. There were two people there who interested me most. One was a very handsome and courteous man, who seemed to desire my company, and spoke more freely than the rest; the other a young man, who was very much occupied with the girl, my companion, and made a great friendship with her. The elder of the two, for I must give them names, shall be called Charmides, which seems to correspond with his stately charm, and the younger may be known as Lucius.

I sat one day with Charmides, listening to a great concert of stringed and wind instruments, in a portico which gave on a large sheltered garden. He was much absorbed in the music, which was now of a brisk and measured beauty, and now of a sweet seriousness which had a very luxurious effect upon my mind.

"It is wonderful to me," said Charmides, as the last movement drew to a close of liquid melody, "that these sounds should pass into the heart like wine, heightening and uplifting the thought—there is nothing so beautiful as the discrimination of mood with which it affects one, weighing one delicate phrase against another, and finding all so perfect."

"Yes," I said, "I can understand that; but I must confess that there seems to me something wanting in the melodies of this place. The music which I loved in the old days was the music which spoke to the soul of something further yet and unattainable; but here the music seems to have attained its end, and to have fulfilled its own desire."

"Yes," said Charmides, "I know that you feel that; your mind is very clear to me, up to a certain point; and I have sometimes wondered why you spend your time here, because you are not one of us, as your friend Cynthia is."

I glanced, as he spoke, to where Cynthia sat on a great carved settle among cushions, side by side with Lucius, whispering to him with a smile.

"No," I said, "I do not think I have found my place yet, but I am here, I think, for a purpose, and I do not know what that purpose is."

"Well," he said, "I have sometimes wondered myself. I feel that you may have something to tell me, some message for me. I thought that when I first saw you; but I cannot quite perceive what is in your mind, and I see that you do not wholly know what is in mine. I have been here for a long time, and I have a sense that I do not get on, do not move; and yet I have lived in extreme joy and contentment, except that I dread to return to life, as I know I must return. I have lived often, and always in joy—but in life there are constantly things to endure, little things which just ruffle the serenity of soul which I desire, and which I may fairly say I here enjoy. I have loved beauty, and not intemperately; and there have been other people—men and women—whom I have loved, in a sense; but the love of them has always seemed a sort of interruption to the life I desired, something disordered and strained, which hurt me, and kept me away from the peace I desired—from the fine weighing of sounds and colours, and the pleasure of beautiful forms and lines; and I dread to return to life, because one cannot avoid love and sorrow, and mean troubles, which waste the spirit in vain."

"Yes," I said, "I can understand what you feel very well, because I too have known what it is to desire to live in peace and beauty, not to be disturbed or fretted; but the reason, I think, why it is dangerous, is not because life becomes too easy. That is not the danger at all—life is never easy, whatever it is! But the danger is that it grows too solemn! One is apt to become like a priest, always celebrating holy mysteries, always in a vision, with no time for laughter, and disputing, and quarrelling, and being silly and playing. It is the poor body again that is amiss. It is like the camel, poor thing; it groans and weeps, but it goes on. One cannot live wholly in a vision; and life does not become more simple so, but more complicated, for one's time and energy are spent in avoiding the sordid and the tiresome things which one cannot and must not avoid. I remember, in an illness which I had, when I was depressed and fanciful, a homely old doctor said to me, 'Don't be too careful of yourself: don't think you can't bear this and that—go out to dinner—eat and drink rather too much!' It seemed to be coarse advice, but it was wise."

"Yes," said Charmides, "it was wise; but it is difficult to feel it so at the time. I wonder! I think perhaps I have made the mistake of being too fastidious. But it seemed so fine a goal that one had in sight, to chasten and temper all one's thoughts to what was beautiful—to judge and distinguish, to choose the right tones and harmonies, to be always rejecting and refining. It had its sorrows, of course. How often in the old days one came in contact with some gracious and beautiful personality, and flung oneself into close relations; and then one began to see this and that flaw. There were lapses in tact, petulances, littlenesses; one's friend did not rightly use his beautiful mind; he was jealous, suspicious, trivial, petty; it ended in disillusionment. Instead of taking him as a passenger on one's vessel, and determining to live at peace, to overlook, to accommodate, one began to watch for an opportunity of putting him down courteously at some stopping-place; and instead of being grateful for his friendship, one was vexed with him for disappointing one. We must speak more of these things. I seem to feel the want of something commoner and broader in my thoughts; but in this place it is hard to change."

"Will you forgive me then," I said, "if I ask you plainly what this place is? It seems very strange to me, and yet I think I have been here before."

Charmides looked at me with a smile. "It has been called," he said, "by many ugly names, and men have been unreasonably afraid of it. It is the place of satisfied desire, and, as you see, it is a comfortable place enough. The theologians in their coarse way call it Hell, though that is a word which is forbidden here; it is indeed a sort of treason to use the word, because of its unfortunate association—and you can see with your own eyes that I have done wrong even to speak of it."

I looked round, and saw indeed that a visible tremor had fallen on the groups about us; it was as though a cold cloud, full of hail and darkness, had floated over a sunny sky. People were hurrying out of the garden, and some were regarding us askance and with frowns of disapproval. In a moment or two we were left alone.

"I have been indiscreet," said Charmides, "but I feel somehow in a rebellious mood; and indeed, it has long seemed absurd to me that you should be unaware of the fact, and so obviously guileless! But I will speak no more of this today. People come and go here very strangely, and I have sometimes wondered if it would not soon be time for me to go; but it would be idle to pretend that I have not been happy here."

11

What Charmides had told me filled me with great astonishment; it seemed to me strange that I had not perceived the truth before. It made me feel that I had somehow been wasting time. I was tempted to call Amroth to my side, but I remembered what he had said, and I determined to resist the impulse. I half expected to find that our strange talk, and the very obvious disapproval of our words, had made some difference to me. But it was not the case. I found myself treated with the same smiling welcome as before, and indeed with an added kind of gentleness, such as older people give to a child who has been confronted with some hard fact of life, such as a sorrow or an illness. This in a way disconcerted me; for in the moment when I had perceived the truth, there had come over me the feeling that I ought in some way to bestir myself to preach, to warn, to advise.

But the idea of finding any sort of fault with these contented, leisurely, interested people, seemed to me absurd, and so I continued as
before, half enjoying the life about me, and half bored by it. It seemed
so ludicrous in any way to pity the inhabitants of the place, and yet I
dimly saw that none of them could possibly continue there. But I soon
saw that there was no question of advice, because I had nothing to
advise. To ask them to be discontented, to suffer, to inquire, seemed as
absurd as to ask a man riding comfortably in a carriage to get out and
walk; and yet I felt that it was just that which they needed.

But one effect the incident had; it somehow seemed to draw me
more to Cynthia. There followed a time of very close companionship
with her. She sought me out, she began to confide in me, chattering
about her happiness and her delight in her surroundings, as a child
might chatter, and half chiding me, in a tender and pretty way, for not
being more at ease in the place.

"You always seem to me," she said, "as if you were only staying
here, while I feel as if I could live here for ever. Of course, you are very
kind and patient about it all, but you are not at home—and I don't
care a bit about your disapproval now." She talked to me much about
Lucius, who seemed to have a great attraction for her. "He is all right,"
she said. "There is no nonsense about him—we understand each other; I don't get tired of him, and we like the same things. I seem to
know exactly what he feels about everything; and that is one of the
comforts of this place, that no one asks questions or makes mischief;
one can do just as one likes all the time. I did not think, when I was
alive, that there could be anything so delightful as all this ahead of me."

"Do you never think—?" I began, but she put her hand to my
lips, like a child, to stop me, and said, "No, I never think, and I never
mean to think, of all the old hateful things. I never wilfully did any
harm; I only liked the people who liked me, and gave them all they
asked—and now I know that I did right, though in old days serious
people used to try to frighten me. God is very good to me," she went
on, smiling, "to allow me to be happy in my own way."

While we talked thus, sitting on a seat that overlooked the great
city—I had never seen it look so stately and beautiful, so full of all that
the heart could desire—Lucius himself drew near to us, smiling, and
seated himself the other side of Cynthia. "Now is not this heavenly?"
she said; "to be with the two people I like best—for you are a faithful
old thing, you know—and not to be afraid of anything disagreeable or
tiresome happening—not to have to explain or make excuses, what

could be better?"

"Yes," said Lucius, "it is happy enough," and he smiled at me in a friendly way. "The pleasantest point is that one can *wait* in this charming place. In the old days, one was afraid of a hundred things—money, weather, illness, criticism. One had to make love in a hurry, because one missed the beautiful hour; and then there was the horror of growing old. But now if Cynthia chooses to amuse herself with other people, what do I care? She comes back as delightful as ever, and it is only so much more to be amused about. One is not even afraid of being lazy, and as for those ugly twinges of what one called conscience—which were only a sort of rheumatism after all—that is all gone too; and the delight of finding that one was right after all, and that there were really no such things as consequences!"

I became aware, as Lucius spoke thus, in all his careless beauty, of a vague trouble of soul. I seemed to foresee a kind of conflict between myself and him. He felt it too, I was aware; for he drew Cynthia to him, and said something to her; and presently they went off laughing, like a pair of children, waving a farewell to me. I experienced a sense of desolation, knowing in my mind that all was not well, and yet feeling so powerless to contend with happiness so strong and wide.

12

Presently I wandered off alone, and went out of the city with a sudden impulse. I thought I would go in the opposite direction to that by which I had entered it. I could see the great hills down which Cynthia and I had made our way in the dawn; but I had never gone in the further direction, where there stretched what seemed to be a great forest. The whole place lay bathed in a calm light, all unutterably beautiful. I wandered long by streams and wood-ends, every corner that I turned revealing new prospects of delight I came at last to the edge of the forest, the mouths of little open glades running up into it, with fern and thorn-thickets. There were deer here browsing about the dingles, which let me come close to them and touch them, raising their heads from the grass, and regarding me with gentle and fearless eyes. Birds sang softly among the boughs, and even fluttered to my shoulder, as if pleased to be noticed. So, this was what was called on earth the place of torment, a place into which it seemed as if nothing of sorrow or pain could ever intrude!

Just on the edge of the wood stood a little cottage, surrounded by a quiet garden, bees humming about the flowers, the scents of which came with a homely sweetness on the air. But here I saw something which I did not at first understand. This was a group of three people, a man and a woman and a boy of about seventeen, beside the cottage porch. They had a rustic air about them, and the same sort of leisurely look that all the people of the land wore. They were all three beautiful, with a simple and appropriate kind of beauty, such as comes of a contented sojourn in the open air. But I became in a moment aware that there was a disturbing element among them.

The two elders seemed to be trying to persuade the boy, who listened smilingly enough, but half turned away from them, as though he were going away on some errand of which they did not approve. They greeted me, as I drew near, with the same cordiality as one received everywhere, and the man said, "Perhaps you can help us, sir, for we are in a trouble?" The woman joined with a murmur in the request, and I said I would gladly do what I could; while I spoke, the boy watched me earnestly, and something drew me to him, because I saw a look that seemed to tell me that he was, like myself, a stranger in the place. Then the man said, "We have lived here together very happily a long time, we three—I do not know how we came together, but so it was; and we have been more at ease than words can tell, after hard lives in the other world; and now this lad here, who has been our delight, says that he must go elsewhere and cannot stay with us; and we would persuade him if we could; and perhaps you, sir, who no doubt know what lies beyond the fields and woods that we see, can satisfy him that it is better to remain."

While he spoke, the other two had drawn near to me, and the eyes of the woman dwelt upon the boy with a look of intent love, while the boy looked in my face anxiously and inquiringly. I could see, I found, very deep into his heart, and I saw in him a need for further experience, and a desire to go further on; and I knew at once that this could only be satisfied in one way, and that something would grow out of it both for himself and for his companions.

So, I said, as smilingly as I could, "I do not indeed know much of the ways of this place, but this I know, that we must go where we are sent, that no harm can befall us, and that we are never far away from those whom we love. I myself have lately been sent to visit this strange land; it seems only yesterday since I left the mountains yonder, and yet I have seen an abundance of strange and beautiful things; we must remember that here there is no sickness or misfortune or growing old; and there is no reason, as there often seemed to be on earth, why we should fight against separation and departure. No one can, I think, be hindered here from going where he is bound. So, I believe that you will let the boy go joyfully and willingly, for I am sure of this, that his journey holds not only great things for himself, but even greater things for both of you in the future. So be content and let him depart."

At this the woman said, "Yes, that is right, the stranger is right, and we must hinder the child no longer. No harm can come of it, but only good; perhaps he will return, or we may follow him, when the day comes for that."

I saw that the old man was not wholly satisfied with this. He shook his head and looked sadly on the boy; and then for a time we sat and talked of many things. One thing that the old man said surprised me very greatly. He seemed to have lived many lives, and always lives of labour; he had grown, I gathered from his simple talk, to have a great love of the earth, the lives of flocks and herds, and of all the plants that grew out of the earth or flourished in it. I had thought before, in a foolish way, that all this might be put away from the spirit, in the land where there was no need of such things; but I saw now that there was a claim for labour, and a love of common things, which did not belong only to the body, but was a real desire of the spirit. He spoke of the pleasures of tending cattle, of cutting fagots in the forest wood-land among the copses, of ploughing and sowing, with the breath of the earth about one; till I saw that the toil of the world, which I had dimly thought of as a thing which no one would do if they were not obliged, was a real instinct of the spirit, and had its counterpart beyond the body.

I had supposed indeed that in a region where all troublous accidents of matter were over and done with, and where there was no need of bodily sustenance, there could be nothing which resembled the old weary toil of the body; but now I saw gladly that this was not so, and that the primal needs of the spirit outlast the visible world. Though my own life had been spent mostly among books and things of the mind, I knew well the joys of the country-side, the blossoming of the orchard-close, the high-piled granary, the brightly-painted waggon loaded with hay, the creaking of the cider-press, the lowing of cattle in the stall, the stamping of horses in the stable, the mud-stained implements hanging in the high-roofed, cobwebbed barn.

I had never known why I loved these things so well, and had invented many fancies to explain it; but now I saw that it was the natural delight in work and increase; and that the love which surrounded all

45

these things was the sign that they were real indeed, and that in no part of life could they be put away.

And then there came on me a sort of gentle laughter at the thought of how much of the religion of the world spent itself on bidding the heart turn away from vanities, and lose itself in dreams of wonders and doctrines, and what were called higher and holier things than barns and byres and sheep-pens. Yet the truth had been staring me in the face all the time, if only I could have seen it; that the sense of constraint and unreality that fell upon one in religious matters, when some curious and intricate matter was confusedly expounded, was perfectly natural and wholesome; and that the real life of man lay in the things to which one returned, on work-a-day mornings, with such relief—the acts of life, the work of homestead, library, barrack, office, and class-room, the sight and sound of humanity, the smiles and glances and unconsidered words.

When we had sat together for a time, the boy made haste to depart. We three went with him to the edge of the wood, where a road passed up among the oaks. The three embraced and kissed and said many loving words; and then to ease the anxieties of the two, I said that I would myself set the boy forward on his way, and see him well bestowed. They thanked me, and we went together into the wood, the two lovingly waving and beckoning, and the boy stepping blithely by my side.

I asked him whether he was not sorry to go and leave the quiet place and the pair that loved him. He smiled and said that he knew he was not leaving them at all, and that he was sure that they would soon follow; and that for himself the time had come to know more of the place. I learned from him that his last life had been an unhappy one, in a crowded street and a slovenly home, with much evil of talk and act about him; he had hated it all, he said, but for a little sister that he had loved, who had kissed and clasped him, weeping, when he lay dying of a miserable disease. He said that he thought he should find her, which made part of his joy of going; that for a long while there had come to him a sense of her remembrance and love; and that he had once sent his thought back to earth to find her, and she was in much grief and care; and that then all these messages had at once ceased, and he knew that she had left the body.

He was a merry boy, full of delight and laughter, and we went very cheerfully together through the sunlit wood, with its green glades and open spaces, which seemed all full of life and happiness, creatures living together in goodwill and comfort. I saw in this journey that all things that ever lived a conscious life in one of the innumerable worlds had a place and life of their own, and a time of refreshment like myself. What I could not discern was whether there was any interchange of lives, whether the soul of the tree could become an animal, or the animal progress to be a man. It seemed to me that it was not so, but that each had a separate life of its own.

But I saw how foolish was the fancy that I had pursued in old days, that there was a central reservoir of life, into which at death all little lives were merged; I was yet to learn how strangely all life was knit together, but now I saw that individuality was a real and separate thing, which could not be broken or lost, and that all things that had ever enjoyed a consciousness of the privilege of separate life had a true dignity and worth of existence; and that it was only the body that had made hostility necessary; that though the body could prey upon the bodies of animal and plant, yet that no soul could devour or incorporate any other soul. But as yet the merging of soul in soul through love was unseen and indeed unsuspected by me.

Now as we went in the wood, the boy and I, it came into my mind in a flash that I had seen a great secret. I had seen, I knew, very little of the great land yet—and indeed I had been but in the lowest place of all: and I thought how base and dull our ideas had been upon earth of God and His care of men. We had thought of Him dimly as sweeping into His place of torment and despair all poisoned and diseased lives, all lives that had clung to the body and to the pleasures of the body, all who had sinned idly, or wilfully, or proudly; and I saw now that He used men far more wisely and lovingly than thus. Into this lowest place indeed passed all sad, and diseased, and unhappy spirits: and instead of being tormented or accursed, all was made delightful and beautiful for them there, because they needed not harsh and rough handling, but care and soft tendance.

They were not to be frightened hence, or to live in fear and anguish, but to live deliciously according to their wish, and to be drawn to perceive in some quiet manner that all was not well with them; they were to have their heart's desire, and learn that it could not satisfy them; but the only thing that could draw them thence was the love of some other soul whom they must pursue and find, if they could. It was all so high and reasonable and just that I could not admire it enough. I saw that the boy was drawn thence by the love of his little sister, who was elsewhere; and that the love and loss of the boy would presently draw the older pair to follow him and to leave the place of heart's delight. And then I began to see that Cynthia and Charmides and Lucius were being made ready, each at his own time, to leave their little pleasures and ordered lives of happiness, and to follow heavenwards in due course. Because it was made plain to me that it was the love and worship of some other soul that was the constraining force; but what the end would be I could not discern.

And now as we went through the wood, I began to feel a strange elation and joy of spirit, severe and bracing, very different from my languid and half-contented acquiescence in the place of beauty; and now the woods began to change their kind; there were fewer forest trees now, but bare heaths with patches of grey sand and scattered pines; and there began to drift across the light a grey vapour which hid the delicate hues and colours of the sunlight, and made everything appear pale and spare.

Very soon we came out on the brow of a low hill, and saw, all spread out before us, a place which, for all its dullness and darkness, had a solemn beauty of its own. There were great stone buildings very solidly made, with high chimneys which seemed to stream with smoke; we could see men, as small as ants, moving in and out of the buildings; it seemed like a place of manufacture, with a busy life of its own. But here I suddenly felt that I could go no further, but must return. I hoped that I should see the grim place again, and I desired with all my soul to go down into it, and see what eager life it was that was being lived there. And the boy, I saw, felt this too, and was impatient to proceed. So, we said farewell with much tenderness, and the boy went down swiftly across the moorland, till he met someone who was coming out of the city, and conferred a little with him; and then he turned and waved his hand to me, and I waved my hand from the brow of the hill, envying him in my heart, and went back in sorrow into the sunshine of the wood.

And as I did so I had a great joy, because I saw Amroth come suddenly running to me out of the wood, who put his arm through mine, and walked with me. Then I told him of all I had seen and thought, while he smiled and nodded and told me it was much as I imagined.

"Yes," he said, "it is even so. The souls you have seen in this fine country here are just as children who are given their fill of pleasant things. Many of them have come into the state in which you see them from no fault of their own, because their souls are young and ignorant. They have shrunk from all pain and effort and tedium, like a child that does not like his lessons. There is no thought of punishment, of course.

No one learns anything of punishment except a cowardly fear. We never advance until we have the will to advance, and there is nothing in mere suffering, unless we learn to bear it gently for the sake of love. On earth it is not God but man who is cruel.

"There is indeed a place of sorrow, which you will see when you can bear the sight, where the self-righteous and the harsh go for a time, and all those who have made others suffer because they believed in their own justice and insight. You will find there all tyrants and conquerors, and many rich men, who used their wealth heedlessly; and even so you will be surprised when you see it. But those spirits are the hardest of all to help, because they have loved nothing but their own virtue or their own ambition; yet you will see how they too are drawn thence; and now that you have had a sight of the better country, tell me how you liked it."

"Why," I said, "it is plain and austere enough; but I felt a great quickening of spirit, and a desire to join in the labours of the place."

Amroth smiled, and said, "You will have little share in that. You will find your task, no doubt, when you are strong enough; and now you must go back and make unwilling holiday with your pleasant friends. You have not much longer to stay there; and surely"—he laughed as he spoke—"you can endure a little more of those pretty concerts and charming talk of art and its values and pulsations!"

"I can endure it," I said, laughing, "for it does me good to see you and to hear you; but tell me, Amroth, what have you been about all this time? Have you had a thought of me?"

"Yes, indeed," said Amroth, laughing. "I don't forget you, and I love your company; but I am a busy man myself, and have something pleasanter to do than to attend these elegant receptions of yours—at which, indeed, I have sometimes thought you out of place."

As we thus talked we came to the forest lodge. The old pair came running out to greet me, and I told them that the boy was well bestowed. I could see in the woman's face that she would soon follow him, and even the old man had a look that I had not seen in him before; and here Amroth left me, and I returned to the city, where all was as peaceable as before.

13

But when I saw Cynthia, as I presently did, she too was in a different mood. She had positively missed me, and told me so with many endearments. I was not to remain away so long. I was useful to her.

Charmides had become tiresome and lost in thought, but Lucius was as sweet as ever. Some newcomers had arrived, all pleasant enough. She asked me where I had been, and I told her all the story. "Yes, that is beautiful enough," she said, "but I hate all this breaking up and going on. I am sure I do not wish for any change." She made a grimace of disgust at the idea of the ugly town I had seen, and then she said that she would go with me some time to look at it, because it would make her happier to return to her peace; and then she went off to tell Lucius.

I soon found Charmides, and I told him my adventures.

"That is a curious story," he said. "I like to think of people caring for each other so; that is picturesque! These simple emotions are interesting. And one likes to think that people who have none of the finer tastes should have something to fall back upon—something hot and strong, as we used to say."

"But," I said, "tell me this, Charmides, was there never any one in the old days whom you cared for like that?"

"I thought so often enough," said he, a little peevishly, "but you do not know how much a man like myself is at the mercy of little things! An ugly hand, a broken tooth, a fallen cheek . . . it seems little enough, but one has a sort of standard. I had a microscopic eye, you know, and a little blemish was a serious thing to ma I was always in search of something that I could not find; then there were awkward strains in the characters of people—they were mean or greedy or selfish, and all my pleasure was suddenly dashed. I am speaking," he went on, "with a strange candour! I don't defend it or excuse it, but there it was. I did once, as a child, I believe, care for one person—an old nurse of mine—in the right way. Dear, how good she was to me! I remember once how she came all the way, after she had left us, to see me on my way through town. She just met me at a railway station, and she had bought a little book which she thought might amuse me, and a bag of oranges—she remembered that I used to like oranges.

"I recollect at the time thinking it was all very touching and devoted; but I was with a friend of mine, and had not time to say much. I can see her old face, smiling, with tears in her eyes, as we went off. I gave the book and the oranges away, I remember, to a child at the next station. It is curious how it all comes back to me now; I never saw her again, and I wish I had behaved better. I should like to see her again, and to tell her that I really cared! I wonder if that is possible? But there is really so much to do here and to enjoy; and there is no one to tell me where to go, so that I am puzzled. What is one to do?"

"I think that if one desires a thing enough here, Charmides," I said, "one is in a fair way to obtain it. Never mind! a door will be opened. But one has got to care, I suppose; it is not enough to look upon it as a pretty effect, which one would just like to put in its place with other effects—'*Open, sesame*'—do you remember? There is a charm at which all doors fly open, even here!"

"I will talk to you more about this," said Charmides, "when I have had time to arrange my thoughts a little. Who would have supposed that an old recollection like that would have disturbed me so much? It would make a good subject for a picture or a song."

14

It was on one of these days that Amroth came suddenly upon me, with a very mirthful look on his face, his eyes sparkling like a man struggling with hidden laughter. "Come with me," he said; "you have been so dutiful lately that I am alarmed for your health." Then we went out of the garden where I was sitting, and we were suddenly in a street. I saw in a moment that it was a real street, in the suburb of an English town; there were electric trams running, and rows of small trees, and an open space planted with shrubs, with asphalt paths and ugly seats. On the other side of the road was a row of big villas, tasteless, dreary, comfortable houses, with meaningless turrets and balconies.

I could not help feeling that it was very dismal that men and women should live in such places, think them neat and well-appointed, and even grow to love them. We went into one of these houses; it was early in the morning, and a little drizzle was falling, which made the whole place seem very cheerless. In a room with a bow-window looking on the road there were three persons. An old man was reading a paper in an armchair by the fire, with his back to the light. He looked a nice old man, with his clear skin and white hair; opposite him was an old lady in another chair, reading a letter. With his back to the fire stood a man of about thirty-five, sturdy-looking, but pale, and with an appearance of being somewhat overworked. He had a good face, but seemed a little uninteresting, as if he did not feed his mind. The table had been spread for breakfast, and the meal was finished and partly cleared away. The room was ugly and the furniture was a little shabby; there was a glazed bookcase, full of dull-looking books, a sideboard, a table with writing materials in the window, and some engravings of royal groups and celebrated men.

The younger man, after a moment, said, "Well, I must be off." He nodded to his father, and bent down to kiss his mother, saying, "Take care of yourself—I shall be back in good time for tea." I had a sense that he was using these phrases in a mechanical way, and that they were customary with him. Then he went out, planting his feet solidly on the carpet, and presently the front door shut. I could not understand why we had come to this very unemphatic party, and examined the whole room carefully to see what was the object of our visit. A maid came in and removed the rest of the breakfast things, leaving the cloth still on the table, and some of the spoons and knives, with the salt-cellars, in their places.

When she had finished and gone out, there was a silence, only broken by the crackling of the paper as the old man folded it. Presently the old lady said: "I wish Charles could get his holiday a little sooner; he looks so tired, and he does not eat well. He does stick so hard to his business."

"Yes, dear, he does," said the old man," but it is just the busiest time, and he tells me that they have had some large orders lately. They are doing very well, I understand."

There was another silence, and then the old lady put down her letter, and looked for a moment at a picture, representing a boy, a large photograph a good deal faded, which hung close to her—underneath it was a small vase of flowers on a bracket. She gave a little sigh as she did this, and the old man looked at her over the top of his paper. "Just think, father," she said, "that Harry would have been thirty-eight this very week!"

The old man made a comforting sort of little noise, half sympathetic and half deprecatory. "Yes, I know," said the old lady, "but I can't help thinking about him a great deal at this time of the year. I don't understand why lie was taken away from us. He was always such a good boy—he would have been just like Charles, only handsomer—he was always handsomer and brighter; he had so much of your spirit! Not but what Charles has been the best of sons to us—I don't mean that—no one could be better or more easy to please! But Harry had a different way with him." Her eyes filled with tears, which she brushed away. "No," she added, "I won't fret about him. I daresay he is happier where he is—I am sure he is—and thinking of his mother too, my bonny boy, perhaps."

The old man got up, put his paper down, went across to the old lady, and gave her a kiss on the brow. "There, there," he said sooth-ingly, "we may be sure it's all for the best; "and he stood looking down fondly at her. Amroth crossed the room and stood beside the pair, with a hand on the shoulder of each. I saw in an instant that there was an unmistakable likeness between the three; but the contrast of the mar-vellous brilliance and beauty of Amroth with the old, world-wearied, simple-minded couple was the most extraordinary thing to behold.

"Yes, I feel better already," said the old lady, smiling; "it always does me good to say out what I am feeling, father; and then you are sure to understand."

The mist closed suddenly in upon the scene, and we were back in a moment in the garden with its porticoes, in the radiant, untroubled air. Amroth looked at me with a smile that was full, half of gaiety and half of tenderness. "There," he said, "what do you think of that? If all had gone well with me, as they say on earth, that is where I should be now, going down to the city with Charles. That is the prospect which to the dear old people seems so satisfactory compared with this! In that house I lay ill for some weeks, and from there my body was car-ried out. And they would have kept me there if they could—and I myself did not want to go. I was afraid. Oh, how I envied Charles go-ing down to the city and coming back for tea, to read the magazines aloud or play backgammon. I am afraid I was not as nice as I should have been about all that—the evenings were certainly dull!"

"But what do you feel about it now?" I said, "Don't you feel sorry for the muddle and ignorance and pathos of it all? Can't something be done to show everybody what a ghastly mistake it is, to get so tied down to the earth and the things of earth?"

"A mistake?" said Amroth. "There is no such thing as a mistake. One cannot sorrow for their grief, any more than one can sorrow for the child who cries out in the tunnel and clasps his mother's hand. Don't you see that their grief and loss is the one beautiful thing in those lives, and all that it is doing for them, drawing them hither? Why, that is where we grow and become strong, in the hopeless suffering of love. I am glad and content that my own stay was made so brief. I wish it could be shortened for the three—and yet I do not, because they will gain so wonderfully by it. They are mounting fast; it is their very ignorance that teaches them. Not to know, not to perceive, but to be forced to believe in love, that is the point."

"Yes," I said, "I see that; but what about the lives that are broken and poisoned by grief, in a stupor of pain—or the souls that do not feel it at all, except as a passing shadow—what about them?"

"Oh," said Amroth lightly, "the sadder the dream the more blessed the awakening; and as for those who cannot feel—well, it will all come to them, as they grow older."

"Yes," I said, "it has done me good to see all this—it makes many things plain; but can you bear to leave them thus?"

"Leave them!" said Amroth. "Who knows but that I shall be sent to help them away, and carry them, as I carried you, to the crystal sea of peace? The darling mother, I shall be there at her awakening. They are old spirits, those two, old and wise; and there is a high place prepared for them."

"But what about Charles?" I said.

Amroth smiled. "Old Charles?" he said. "I must admit that he is not a very stirring figure at present. He is much immersed in his game of finance, and talk a great deal in his lighter moments about the commercial prospects of the Empire and the need of retaliatory tariffs. But he will outgrow all that! He is a very loyal soul, but not very adventurous just now. He would be sadly discomposed by an affection which came in between him and his figures. He would think he wanted a change—and he will have a thorough one, the good old fellow, one of these days. But he has a long journey before him."

"Well," I said, "there are some surprises here! I am afraid I am very youthful yet."

"Yes, dear child, you are very ingenuous," said Amroth, "and that is a great part of your charm. But we will find something for you to do before long! But here comes Charmides, to talk about the need of exquisite pulsations, and their symbolism—though I see a change in him too. And now I must go back to business. Take care of yourself, and I will be back to tea." And Amroth flashed away in a very cheerful mood.

15

There were many things at that time that were full of mystery, things which I never came to understand. There was in particular a certain sort of people, whom one met occasionally, for whom I could never wholly account. They were unlike others in this fact, that they never appeared to belong to any particular place or community. They were both men and women, who seemed—I can express it in no other way—to be in the possession of a secret so great that it made everything else trivial and indifferent to them. Not that they were

54

impatient or contemptuous—it was quite the other way; but to use a similitude, they were like good-natured, active, kindly elders at a children's party. They did not shun conversation, but if one talked with them, they used a kind of tender and gentle irony, which had something admiring and complimentary about it, which took away any sense of vexation or of baffled curiosity. It was simply as though their concern lay elsewhere; they joined in anything with a frank delight, not with any touch of condescension. They were even more kindly and affectionate than others, because they did not seem to have any small problems of their own, and could give their whole attention and thought to the person they were with. These inscrutable people puzzled me very much. I asked Amroth about them once.

"Who are these people," I said, "whom one sometimes meets, who are so far removed from all of us? What are they doing here?"

Amroth smiled. "So, you have detected them!" he said. "You are quite right, and it does your observation credit. But you must find it out for yourself. I cannot explain, and if I could, you would not understand me yet."

"Then I am not mistaken," I said, "but I wish you would give me a hint—they seem to know something more worth knowing than all beside."

"Exactly," said Amroth. "You are very near the truth; it is staring you in the face; but it would spoil all if I told you. There is plenty about them in the old books you used to read—they have the secret of joy." And that is all that he would say.

It was on a solitary ramble one day, outside of the place of delight, that I came nearer to one of these people than I ever did at any other time. I had wandered off into a pleasant place of grassy glades with little thorn-thickets everywhere. I went up a small eminence, which commanded a view of the beautiful plain with its blue distance and the enamelled green foreground of close-grown coverts. There I sat for a long time lost in pleasant thought and wonder, when I saw a man drawing near, walking slowly and looking about him with a serene and delighted air. He passed not far from me, and observing me, waved a hand of welcome, came up the slope, and greeting me in a friendly and open manner, asked if he might sit with me for a little.

"This is a pleasant place," he said, "and you seem very agreeably occupied."

"Yes," I said, looking into his smiling face, "one has no engagements here, and no need of business to fill the time—but indeed I am not sure that I am busy enough." As I spoke I was regarding him with some curiosity. He was a man of mature age, with a strong, firm-featured face, healthy and sunburnt of aspect, and he was dressed, not as I was for ease and repose, but with the garments of a traveller. His hat, which was large and of some soft grey cloth, was pushed to his back, and hung there by a cord round his neck. His hair was a little grizzled, and lay close-curled to his head; in his strong and muscular hand he carried a stick. He smiled again at my words, and said:

"Oh, one need not trouble about being busy until the time comes; that is a feeling one inherits from the life of earth, and I am sure you have not left it long. You have a very fresh air about you, as if you had rested, and rested well."

"Yes, I have rested," I said; "but though I am content enough, there is something unquiet in me, I am afraid!"

"Ah!" he said, "there is that in all of us, and it would not be well with us if there were not. Will you tell me a little about yourself? That is one of the pleasures of this life here, that we have no need to be cautious, or to fear that we shall give ourselves away."

I told him my adventures, and he listened with serious attention.

"Ah, that is all very good," he said at last, "but you must not be in any hurry; it is a great thing that ideas should dawn upon us gradually—one gets the full truth of them so. It was the hurry of life which was so bewildering—the shocks, the surprises, the ugly reflections of one's conduct that one saw in other lives—the corners one had to turn. Things, indeed, come suddenly even here, but one is led up to them gently enough; allowed to enter the sea for oneself, not soused and ducked in it. You will need all the strength you can store up for what is before you, and I can see in your face that you are storing up strength—but the weariness is not quite gone out of your mind."

He was silent for a little, musing, till I said, "Will you not tell me some of your own adventures? I am sure from your look that you have them; and you are a pilgrim, it seems. Where are you bound?"

"Oh," he said lightly, "I am not one of the people who have adventures—just the journey and the talk beside the way."

"But," I said, "I have seen some others like you, and I am puzzled about it. You seem, if I may say so—I do not mean anything disrespectful or impertinent—to be like the gipsies whom one meets in quiet country places, with a secret knowledge of their own, a pride too great to be worth expressing, not anxious about life, not weary or dissatisfied, caring not for localities or possessions, but with a sort of eager pleasure in freedom and movement."

He laughed. "Yes," he said, "you are right! I am no doubt a sort of nomad, as you say, detached from life perhaps. I don't know that it is desirable; there is a great deal to be said for living in the same place and loving the same things. Most people are happier so, and learn what they have to learn in that manner."

"Yes," I said, "that is true and beautiful—the same old house, the same trees and pastures, the stream and the water-plants that hide it, the blue hills beyond the nearer wood—the dear familiar things; but even so the road which passes through the fields, over the bridge, up the covert-side . . . it leads somewhere, and the heart on sunny days leaps up to follow it! Talking with you here, I feel a hunger for something wider and more free; your voice has the sound of the wind, with the secret knowledge of strange hill-tops and solitary seas! Sometimes the heart settles down upon what it knows and loves, but sometimes it reaches out to all the love and beauty hidden in the world, and in the waters beyond the world, and would embrace it all if it could. The faces one sees as one passes through unfamiliar cities or villages, how one longs to talk, to question, to ask what gave them the look they wear. . . . And you, if I may say it, seem to have passed beyond the need of wanting or desiring anything . . . but I must not talk thus to a stranger; you must forgive me."

"Forgive you?" said the stranger; "that is only an earthly phrase—the old terror of indiscretion and caution. What are we here for but to get acquainted with one another—to let our inmost thoughts talk together? In the world we are bounded by time and space, and we have the terror of each other's glances and exteriors to contend with. We make friends on earth in spite of our limitations; but in heaven we get to know each other's hearts; and that blessing goes back with us to the dim fields and narrow houses of the earth. I see plainly enough that you are not perfectly happy; but one can only win content through discontent. Where you are now, you are not in accord with the souls about you. Never mind that! There are beautiful spirits within reach of your hand and heart; a little clouded by mistaking the quality of joy, no doubt, but great and everlasting for all that You must try to draw near to them, and find spirits to love.

"Do you not remember in the days of earth how one felt sometimes in an unfamiliar place—among a gathering of strangers—at church perhaps, or at some school which one visited, where one saw the young faces, which showed so clearly, before the world had stamped itself in frowns and heaviness upon them, the quality of the soul within? Don't you remember the feeling at such times of how many there were in the world whom one might love, if one had leisure and opportunity and energy? Well, there is no need to resist that, or to deplore it here; one may go where one's will inclines one, and speak as one's heart tells one to speak. I think you are perhaps too conscious of waiting for something. Your task lies ahead of you, but the work of love can begin at once and anywhere."

"Yes," I said, "I feel that now and here. Will you not tell me something of yourself in return? I cannot read your mind clearly—it is occupied with something I cannot grasp—what is your work in heaven?"

"Oh," he said lightly, "that is easy enough, and yet you would not understand it. I have been led through the shadow of fear, and I have passed out on the other side. And my duty is to release others from fear, as far as I can. It is the darkest shadow of all, because it dwells in the unknown. Pain, without it, is no suffering at all; indeed, pain is almost a pleasure, when one knows what it is doing for one.

But fear is the doubt whether pain or suffering are really helping us; and just as memory never has any touch of fear about it, so hope may likewise have done with fear."

"But how did you learn this?" I said.

"Only by fearing to the uttermost," he replied. "The power—it is not courage, because that only defies fear—cannot be given one; it must be painfully won. You remember the blessing of the pure in heart, that they shall see God? There would be little hope in that promise for the soul that knew itself to be impure, if it were not for the other side of it—that the vision of God, which is the most terrible of all things, can give purity to the most sin-stained soul. In that vision, all desire and all fear have an end, because there is nothing left either to desire or to dread. That vision we may delay or hasten. We may delay it, if we allow our prudence, or our shame, or our comfort, to get in the way: we may hasten it, if we cast ourselves at every moment of our pilgrimage upon the mercy and the love of God.

"His one desire is that we should be satisfied; and if He seems to put obstacles in our way, to keep us waiting, to permit us to be miserable, that is only that we may learn to cast ourselves into love and service—which is the one way to His heart. But now I must be going, for I have said all that you can bear. Will you remember this—not to reserve yourself, not to think others unworthy or hostile, but to cast your love and trust freely and lavishly, everywhere and anywhere? We must gather nothing, hold on to nothing, just give ourselves away at every moment, flowing like the stream into every channel that is open, withholding nothing, retaining nothing. I see," he added, "very great and beautiful things ahead of you, and very sad and painful things as well. But you are close to the light, and it is breaking all about you with a splendour which you cannot guess." He rose up, he took my hand in his own and laid the other on my brow, and I felt his heart go out to mine and gather me to him, as a child is gathered to a father's arms. And then he went silently and lightly upon his way.

16

The time moved on quietly enough in the land of delight I made acquaintance with quite a number of the soft-voiced contented folk. Sometimes it interested me to see the change coming upon one or another, a wonder or a desire that made them sit withdrawn and abstracted, and breaking with a sort of effort out of the dreamful mood. Then they would leave us, sometimes quite suddenly, sometimes with courteous adieus. Newcomers, too, kept arriving, to be made pleasantly at home. I found myself seeing more of Cynthia. She was much with Lucius, and they seemed as gay as ever, but I saw that she was sometimes puzzled. She said to me one day as we sat together, "I wish you would tell me what this is all about? I do not want to change it, and I am very happy, but isn't it all rather pointless? I believe you have some secret you are keeping from me." She was sitting close beside me, like a child, resting her head on my arm, and she took my hand in both of hers.

"No," I said, "I am keeping nothing from you, pretty child! I could not explain to you what is in my mind, and it would spoil your pleasure if I could. It is all right, and you will see in good time."

"I hate to be put off like that," she said. "You are not really interested in me; and you do not trust me; you do not care about the things I care about, and if you are so superior, you ought to explain to me why."

"Well," I said, "I will try to explain. Do you ever remember having been very happy in a place, and having been obliged to leave it, always hoping to return; and then when you did return, finding that, though nothing was changed, you were yourself changed, and could not, even if you would, have taken up the old life again?"

"Yes," said Cynthia, musing, "I remember that sort of thing hap-

59

pening once, about a house where I stayed as a child It seemed so stupid and dull when I went back that I wondered how I could ever have really liked it."

"Well," I said, "it is the same sort of thing here. I am only here for a time, and though I do not know where I am going or when, I think I shall not be here much longer."

At this Cynthia did what she had never done before—she kissed me. Then she said, "Don't speak of such disagreeable things. I could not get on without you. You are so convenient, like a comfortable old armchair."

"What a compliment!" I said. "But you see that you don't like my explanation. Why trouble about it? You have plenty of time. Is Lucius like an armchair, too?"

"No," she said, "he is exciting, like a new necklace—and Charmides, he is exciting too, in a way, but rather too fine for me, like a ball-dress!"

"Yes," I said, "I noticed that your own taste in dress is different of late. This is a much simpler thing than what you came in."

"Oh, yes," she said, "it doesn't seem worthwhile to dress up now. I have made my friends, and I suppose I am getting lazy."

We said little more, but she did not seem inclined to leave me, and was more with me for a time. I actually heard her tell Lucius once that she was tired, at which he laughed, not very pleasantly, and went away.

But my own summons came to me so unexpectedly that I had but little time to make my farewell.

I was sitting once in a garden-close watching a curious act proceeding, which I did not quite understand. It looked like a religious ceremony; a man in embroidered robes was being conducted by some boys in white dresses through the long cloister, carrying something carefully wrapped up in his arms, and I heard what sounded like an antique hymn of a fine stiff melody, rapidly sung.

There had been nothing quite like this before, and I suddenly became aware that Amroth was beside me, and that he had a look of anger in his face, "You had better not look at this," he said to me; "it might not be very helpful, as they say."

"Am I to come with you?" I said. "That is well—but I should like to say a word to one or two of my friends here."

"No, not a word!" said Amroth quickly. He looked at me with a curious look, in which he seemed to be measuring my strength and courage. "Yes, that will do!" he added. "Come at once—don't be surprised—it will be different from what you expect."

He took me by the arm, and we hurried from the place; one or two of the people who stood by looked at us in lazy wonder. We walked in silence down a long alley, to a great gate that I had often passed in my strolls. It was a barred iron gate, of a very stately air, with high stone gateposts, I had never been able to find my outward way to this, and there was a view from it of enchanting beauty, blue distant woods and rolling slopes. Amroth came quickly to the gate, seemed to unlock it, and held it open for me to pass. "One word," he said with his most beautiful smile, his eyes flashing and kindling with some secret emotion, "whatever happens, do not be *afraid!* There is nothing whatever to fear, only be prepared and wait." He motioned me through, and I heard him close the gate behind me.

17

I was alone in an instant, and in terrible pain—pain not in any part of me, but all around and within me. A cold wind of a piercing bitterness seemed to blow upon me; but with it came a sense of immense energy and strength, so that the pain became suddenly delightful, like the stretching of a stiffened limb. I cannot put the pain into exact words. It was not attended by any horror; it seemed a sense of infinite grief and loss and loneliness, a deep yearning to be delivered and made free. I felt suddenly as though everything I loved had gone from me, irretrievably gone and lost. I looked round me, and I could discern through a mist the bases of some black and sinister rocks, that towered up intolerably above me; in between them were channels full of stones and drifted snow.

Anything more stupendous than those black-ribbed crags, those toppling precipices, I had never seen. The wind howled among them, and sometimes there was a noise of rocks cast down. I knew in some obscure way that my path lay there, and my heart absolutely failed me. Instead of going straight to the rocks, I began to creep along the base to see whether I could find some easier track. Suddenly the voice of Amroth said, rather sharply, in my ear, "Don't be silly!" This homely direction, so peremptorily made, had an instantaneous effect. If he had said, "Be not faithless," or anything in the copybook manner, I should have sat down and resigned myself to solemn despair. But now I felt a fool and a coward as well.

So, I addressed myself, like a dog who hears the crack of a whip, to the rocks.

It would be tedious to relate how I clambered and stumbled and agonised. There did not seem to me the slightest use in making the attempt, or the smallest hope of reaching the top, or the least expectation of finding anything worth finding. I hated everything I had ever seen or known; recollections of old lives and of the quiet garden I had left came upon me with a sort of mental nausea. This was very different from the amiable and easy-going treatment I had expected. Yet I did struggle on, with a hideous faintness and weariness—but would it never stop? It seemed like years to me, my hands frozen and wetted by snow and dripping water, my feet bruised and wounded by sharp stones, my garments strangely torn and rent, with stains of blood showing through in places. Still the hideous business continued, but progress was never quite impossible. At one place I found the rocks wholly impassable, and choosing the broader of two ledges which ran left and right, I worked out along the cliff, only to find that the ledge ran into the precipices, and I had to retrace my steps, if the shuffling motions I made could be so called.

Then I took the harder of the two, which zigzagged backwards and forwards across the rocks. At one place I saw a thing which moved me very strangely. This was a heap of bones, green, slimy, and ill-smelling, with some tattered rags of cloth about them, which lay in a heap beneath a precipice. The thought that a man could fall and be killed in such a place moved me with a fresh misery. What that meant I could not tell. Were we not away from such things as mouldering flesh and broken bones? It seemed not; and I climbed madly away from them. Quite suddenly I came to the top, a bleak platform of rock, where I fell prostrate on my face and groaned.

"Yes, that was an ugly business," said the voice of Amroth beside me, "but you got through it fairly well. How do you feel?"

"I call it a perfect outrage," I said. "What is the meaning of this hateful business?"

"The meaning?" said Amroth; "never mind about the meaning. The point is that you are here!"

"Oh," I said, "I have had a horrible time. All my sense of security is gone from me. Is one indeed liable to this kind of interruption, Amroth?"

"Of course," said Amroth, "there must be some tests; but you will be better very soon. It is all over for the present, I may tell you, and you will soon be able to enjoy it. There is no terror in past suffering— it is the purest joy."

"Yes, I used to say so and think so," I said, closing my eyes. "But this was different—it was horrible! And the time it lasted, and the despair of it! It seems to have soaked into my whole life and poisoned it."

Amroth said nothing for a minute, but watched me closely.

Presently I went on. "And tell me one thing. There was a ghastly thing I saw, some mouldering bones on a ledge. Can people indeed fall and die there?"

"Perhaps it was only a phantom," said Amroth, "put there like the sights in the *Pilgrim's Progress*, the fire that was fed secretly with oil, and the robin with his mouth full of spiders, as an encouragement for wayfarers!"

"But that," I said, "would be too horrible for anything—to turn the terrors of death into a sort of conjuring trick—a dramatic entertainment, to make one's flesh creep! Why, that was the misery of some of the religion taught us in old days, that it seemed often only dramatic—a scene without cause or motive, just displayed to show us the anger or the mercy of God, so that one had the miserable sense that much of it was a spectacular affair, that He Himself did not really suffer or feel indignation, but thought it well to feign emotions, like a schoolmaster to impress his pupils—and that people too were not punished for their own sakes, to help them, but just to startle or convince others."

"Yes," said Amroth, "I was only jesting, and I see that my jests were out of place. Of course, what you saw was real—there are no pretences here. Men and women do indeed suffer a kind of death—the second death—in these places, and have to begin again; but that is only for a certain sort of self-confident and sin-soaked person, whose will needs to be roughly broken. There are certain perverse sins of the spirit which need a spiritual death, as the sins of the body need a bodily death. Only thus can one be born again."

"Well," I said, "I am amazed—but now what am I to do? I am fit for nothing, and I shall be fit for nothing hereafter."

"If you talk like this," said Amroth, "you will only drive me away. There are certain things that it is better not to confess to one's dearest friend, not even to God. One must just be silent about them, try to forget them, hope they can never happen again. I tell you, you will soon be all right; and if you are not you will have to see a physician. But you had better not do that unless you are obliged."

This made me feel ashamed of myself, and the shame took off my thoughts from what I had endured; but I could do nothing but lie aching and panting on the rocks for a long time, while Amroth sat beside me in silence.

"Are you vexed?" I said after a long pause.

"No, no, not vexed," said Amroth, "but I am not sure whether I have not made a mistake. It was I who urged that you might go forward, and I confess I am disappointed at the result. You are softer than I thought."

"Indeed, I am not," I said. "I will go down the rocks and come up again, if that will satisfy you."

"Come, that is a little better," said Amroth, "and I will tell you now that you did well—better indeed at the time than I expected. You did the thing in very good time, as we used to say."

By this time, I felt very drowsy, and suddenly dropped off into a sleep—such a deep and dreamless sleep, to descend into which was like flinging oneself into a river-pool by a bubbling weir on a hot and dusty day of summer,

I awoke suddenly with a pressure on my arm, and, waking up with a sense of renewed freshness, I saw Amroth looking at me anxiously. "Do not say anything," he said. "Can you manage to hobble a few steps? If you cannot, I will get some help, and we shall be all right—but there may be an unpleasant encounter, and it is best avoided." I scrambled to my feet, and Amroth helped me a little higher up the rocks, looking carefully into the mist as he did so. Close behind us was a steep rock with ledges. Amroth flung himself upon them, with an agile scramble or two. Then he held his hand down, lying on the top; I took it, and, stiffened as I was, I contrived to get up beside him. "That is right," he said in a whisper. "Now lie here quietly, don't speak a word, and just watch."

I lay, with a sense of something evil about. Presently I heard the sound of voices in the mist to the left of us; and in an instant there loomed out of the mist the form of a man, who was immediately followed by three others. They were different from all the other spirits I had yet seen—tall, lean, dark men, very spare and strong. They looked carefully about them, mostly glancing down the cliff, and sometimes conferred together. They were dressed in close-fitting dark clothes, which seemed as if made out of some kind of skin or untanned leather, and their whole air was sinister and terrifying. They passed quite close beneath us, so that I saw the bald head of one of them, who carried a sort of hook in his hands.

When they got to the place where my climb had ended, they

stopped and examined the stones carefully: one of them clambered a few feet down the cliff. Then he came back and seemed to make a brief report, after which they appeared undecided what to do; they even looked up at the rock where we lay; but while they did this, another man, very similar, came hurriedly out of the mist, said something to the group, and they all disappeared very quickly into the darkness the same way they had come. Then there was a silence. I should have spoken, but Amroth put a finger on his lips. Presently there came a sound of falling stones, and after that there broke out among the rocks below a horrible crying, as of a man in sore straits and instant fear. Amroth jumped quickly to his feet. "This will not do," he said. "Stay here for me." And then leaping down the rock, he disappeared, shouting words of help—"Hold on—I am coming."

He came back some little time afterwards, and I saw that he was not alone. He had with him an old stumbling man, evidently in the last extremity of terror and pain, with beads of sweat on his brow and blood running down from his hands. He seemed dazed and bewildered. And Amroth too looked ruffled and almost weary, as I had never seen him look. I came down the rock to meet them. But Amroth said, "Wait here for me; it has been a troublesome business, and I must go and bestow this poor creature in a place of safety—I will return." He led the old man away among the rocks, and I waited a long time, wondering very heavily what it was that I had seen.

When Amroth came back to the rock he was fresh and smiling again: he swung himself up, and sat by me, with his hands clasped round his knees. Then he looked at me, and said, "I daresay you are surprised? You did not expect to see such terrors and dangers here? And it is a great mystery."

"You must be kind," I said, "and explain to me what has happened."

"Well," said Amroth, "there is a large gang of men who infest this place, who have got up here by their agility, and can go no further, who make it their business to prevent all they can from coming up. I confess that it is the hardest thing of all to understand why it is allowed; but if you expect all to be plain sailing up here, you are mistaken. One needs to be wary and strong. They do much harm here, and will continue to do it."

"What would have happened if they had found us here?" I said.

"Nothing very much," said Amroth; "a good deal of talk no doubt, and some blows perhaps. But it was well I was with you, because I could have summoned help. They are not as strong as they look either—it is mostly fear that aids them."

"Well, but who are they?" I said,

"They are the most troublesome crew of all," said Amroth, "and come nearest to the old idea of fiends—they are indeed the origin of that notion. To speak plainly, they are men who have lived virtuous lives, and have done cruel things from good motives. There are some kings and statesmen among them, but they are mostly priests and schoolmasters, I imagine—people with high ideals, of course! But they are not replenished so fast as they used to be, I think. Their difficulty is that they can never see that they are wrong. Their notion is that this is a bad place to come to, and that people are better left in ignorance and bliss, obedient and submissive.

"A good many of them have given up the old rough methods, and hang about the base of the cliff, dissuading souls from climbing: they do the most harm of all, because if one does turn back here, it is long before one may make a new attempt. But enough of this," he added; "it makes me sick to think of them—the old fellow you saw with me had an awful fright—he was nearly done as it was! But I see you are feeling stronger, and I think we had better be going. One does not stay here by choice, though the place has a beauty of its own. And now you will have an easier time for a while."

We descended from our rock, and Amroth led the way, through a long cleft, with rocks, very rough and black, on either side, and fallen fragments under foot. It was steep at first; but soon the rocks grew lower; and we came out presently on to a great desolate plain, with stones lying thickly about, among a coarse kind of grass. At each step I seemed to grow stronger, and walked more lightly, and in the thin fine air my horrors left me, though I still had a dumb sense of suffering which, strange to say, I found it almost pleasant to resist. And so, we walked for a time in friendly silence, Amroth occasionally indicating the way. The hill began to slope downwards very slowly, and the wind to subside. The mist drew off little by little, till at last I saw ahead of us a great bare-looking fortress with high walls and little windows, and a great blank tower over all.

18

We were received at the guarded door of the fortress by a porter, who seemed to be well acquainted with Amroth, Within, it was a big, bare place, with stone-arched cloisters and corridors, more like a monastery than a castle. Amroth led me briskly along the passages, and took me into a large room very sparely furnished, where an elderly man sat writing at a table with his back to the light. He rose when we entered, and I had a sudden sense that I was coming to school again, as indeed I was. Amroth greeted him with a mixture of freedom and respect, as a well-loved pupil might treat an old schoolmaster. The man himself was tall and upright, and serious-looking, but for a twinkle of humour that lurked in his eye; yet I felt he was one who expected to be obeyed.

He took Amroth into the embrasure of a window, and talked with him in low tones. Then he came back to me and asked me a few questions of which I did not then understand the drift—but it seemed a kind of very informal examination. Then he made us a little bow of dismissal, and sat down at once to his writing without giving us another look. Amroth took me out, and led me up many stone stairs, along whitewashed passages, with narrow windows looking out on the plain, to a small cell or room near the top of the castle. It was very austerely furnished, but it had a little door which took us out on the leads, and I then saw what a very large place the fortress was, consisting of several courts with a great central tower.

"Where on earth have we got to now?" I said.

"Nowhere '*on earth*,'" said Amroth. "You are at school again, and you will find it very interesting, I hope and expect, but it will be hard work. I will tell you plainly that you are lucky to be here, because if you do well, you will have the best sort of work to do."

"But what am I to do, and where am I to go?" I said. "I feel like a new boy, with all sorts of dreadful rules in the background."

"That will all be explained to you," said Amroth. "And now good-bye for the present Let me hear a good report of you," he added, with a parental air, "when I come again. What would not we older fellows give to be back here!" he added with a half-mocking smile. "Let me tell you, my boy, you have got the happiest time of your life ahead of you. Well, be a credit to your friends!"

He gave me a nod and was gone. I stood for a little looking out rather desolately into the plain. There came a brisk tap at my door, and a man entered. He greeted me pleasantly, gave me a few directions, and I gathered that he was one of the instructors. "You will find it hard work," he said; "we do not waste time here. But I gather that you have had rather a troublesome ascent, so you can rest a little. When you are required, you will be summoned."

When he left me, I still felt very weary, and lay down on a little couch in the room, falling presently asleep. I was roused by the entry of a young man, who said he had been sent to fetch me: we went down along the passages, while he talked pleasantly in low tones about the arrangements of the place. As we went along the passages, the doors of the cells kept opening, and we were joined by young men and women, who spoke to me or to each other, but all in the same subdued voices, till at last we entered a big, bare, arched room, lit by high windows, with rows of seats, and a great desk or pulpit at the end. I looked round me in great curiosity. There must have been several hundred people present, sitting in rows. There was a murmur of talk over the hall, till a bell suddenly sounded somewhere in the castle, a door opened, a man stepped quickly into the pulpit, and began to speak in a very clear and distinct tone.

The discourse—and all the other discourses to which I listened in the place—was of a psychological kind, dealing entirely with the relations of human beings with each other, and the effect and interplay of emotions. It was extremely scientific, but couched in the simplest phraseology, and made many things clear to me which had formerly been obscure. There is nothing in the world so bewildering as the selective instinct of humanity, the reasons which draw people to each other, the attractive power of similarity and dissimilarity, the effects of class and caste, the abrupt approaches of passion, the influence of the body on the soul and of the soul on the body.

It came upon me with a shock of surprise that while these things are the most serious realities in the world, and undoubtedly more important than any other thing, little attempt is made by humanity to unravel or classify them. I cannot here enter into the details of these instructions, which indeed would be unintelligible, but they showed me at first what I had not at all apprehended, namely the proportionate importance and unimportance of all the passions and emotions which regulate our relations with other souls. These discourses were given at regular intervals, and much of our time was spent in discussing together or working out in solitude the details of psychological problems, which we did with the exactness of chemical analysis.

What I soon came to understand was that the whole of psychology is ruled by the most exact and immutable laws, in which there is nothing fortuitous or abnormal, and that the exact course of an emotion can be predicted with perfect certainty if only all the data are known.

One of the most striking parts of these discourses was the fact that they were accompanied by illustrations. I will describe the first of these which I saw. The lecturer stopped for an instant and held np his hand. In the middle of one of the sidewalls of the room was a great shallow arched recess. In this recess there suddenly appeared a scene, not as though it were cast by a lantern on the wall, but as if the wall were broken down, and showed a room beyond.

In the room, a comfortably furnished apartment, there sat two people, a husband and wife, middle-aged people, who were engaged in a miserable dispute about some very trivial matter. The wife was shrill and provocative, the husband curt and contemptuous. They were obviously not really concerned about the subject they were discussing—it only formed a ground for disagreeable personalities.

Presently the man went out, saying harshly that it was very pleasant to come back from his work, day after day, to these scenes; to which the woman fiercely retorted that it was all his own fault; and when he was gone, she sat for a time mechanically knitting, with the tears trickling down her cheeks, and every now and then glancing at the door. After which, with great secrecy, she helped herself to some spirits which she took from a cupboard.

The scene was one of the most vulgar and debasing that can be described or imagined; and it was curious to watch the expressions on the faces of my companions. They wore the air of trained doctors or nurses, watching some disagreeable symptoms, with a sort of trained and serene compassion, neither shocked nor grieved. Then the situation was discussed and analysed, and various suggestions were made which were dealt with by the lecturer, in a way which showed me that there was much for us to master and to understand.

There were many other such illustrations given. They were, I discovered, by no means imaginary cases, projected into our minds by a kind of mental suggestion, but actual things happening upon earth. We saw many strange scenes of tragedy, we had a glimpse of lunatic asylums and hospitals, of murder even, and of evil passions of anger and lust. We saw scenes of grief and terror; and, stranger still, we saw many things that were being enacted not on the earth, but upon other planets, where the forms and appearances of the creatures concerned were fantastic and strange enough, but where the motive and the emotion were all perfectly clear. At times, too, we saw scenes that were beautiful and touching, high and heroic beyond words. These seemed to come rather by contrast and for encouragement; for the work was distinctly pathological, and dealt with the disasters and complications of emotions, as a rule, rather than with their glories and radiances. But it was all incredibly absorbing and interesting, though what it was to lead up to I did not quite discern.

What struck me was the concentration of effort upon human emotion, and still more the fact that other hopes and passions, such as ambition and acquisitiveness, as well as all material and economic problems, were treated as infinitely insignificant, as just the framework of human life, only interesting in so far as the baser and meaner elements of circumstance can just influence, refining or coarsening, the highest traits of character and emotion.

We were given special cases, too, to study and consider, and here I had the first inkling of how far it is possible for disembodied spirits to be in touch with those who are still in the body.

As far as I can see, no direct intellectual contact is possible, except under certain circumstances. There is, of course, a great deal of thought-vibration taking place in the world, to which the best analogy is wireless telegraphy. There exists an all-pervading emotional medium, into which every thought that is tinged with emotion sends a ripple. Thoughts which are concerned with personal emotion send the firmest ripple into this medium, and all other thoughts and passions affect it, not in proportion to the intensity of the thought, but to the nature of the thought.

The scale is perfectly determined and quite unalterable; thus, a thought, however strong and intense, which is concerned with wealth or with personal ambition sends a very little ripple into the medium, while a thought of affection is very noticeable indeed, and more noticeable in proportion as it is purer and less concerned with any kind of bodily passion. Thus, strange to say, the thought of a father for a child is a stronger thought than that of a lover for his beloved. I do not know the exact scale of force, which is as exact as that of chemical values—and of course such emotions are apt to be complex and intricate; but the purer and simpler the thought is, the greater is its force.

Perhaps the prayers that one prays for those whom one loves send the strongest ripple of all. If it happens that two of these ripples of personal emotion are closely similar, a reflex action takes place; and thus, is explained the phenomenon which often takes place, the sudden sense of a friend's personality, if that friend, in absence, writes one a letter, or bends his mind intently upon one. It also explains the way in which some national or cosmic emotion suddenly gains simultaneous force, and vibrates in thousands of minds at the same time.

The body, by its joys and sufferings alike, offers a great obstruction to these emotional waves. In the land of spirits, as I have indicated, an intention of congenial wills gives an instantaneous perception; but this seems impossible between an embodied spirit and a disembodied spirit. The only communication which seems possible is that of a vague emotion; and it seems quite impossible for any sort of intellectual idea to be directly communicated by a disembodied spirit to an embodied spirit

On the other hand, the intellectual processes of an embodied spirit are to a certain extent perceptible by a disembodied spirit; but there is a condition to this, and that is that some emotional sympathy must have existed between the two on earth. If there is no such sympathy, then the body is an absolute bar.

I could look into the mind of Amroth and see his thought take shape, as I could look into a stream, and see a fish dart from a covert of weed. But with those still in the body it is different. And I will therefore proceed to describe a single experience which will illustrate my point.

I was ordered to study the case of a former friend of my own who was still living upon earth. Nothing was told me about him, but, sitting in my cell, I put myself into communication with him upon earth. He had been a contemporary of mine at the university, and we had many interests in common. He was a lawyer; we did not very often meet, but when we did meet it was always with great cordiality and sympathy. I now found him ill and suffering from overwork, in a very melancholy state. When I first visited him, he was sitting alone, in the garden of a little house in the country. I could see that he was ill and sad; he was making pretence to read, but the book was wholly disregarded.

When I attempted to put my mind into communication with his, it was very difficult to see the drift of his thoughts. I was like a man walking in a dense fog, who can just discern at intervals recognisable objects as they come within his view; but there was no general prospect and no distance. His mind seemed a confused current of distressing memories; but there came a time when his thought dwelt for a moment upon myself; he wished that I could be with him, that he might speak of some of his perplexities. In that instant, the whole grew clearer, and little by little I was enabled to trace the drift of his thoughts.

I became aware that though he was indeed suffering from overwork, yet that his enforced rest only removed the mental distraction

71

of his work, and left his mind free to revive a whole troop of painful thoughts. He had been a man of strong personal ambitions, and had for twenty years been endeavouring to realise them. Now a sense of the comparative worthlessness of his aims had come upon him. He had despised and slighted other emotions; and his mind had in consequence drifted away like a boat into a bitter and barren sea. He was a lonely man, and he was feeling that he had done ill in not multiplying human emotions and relations. He reflected much upon the way in which he had neglected and despised his home affections, while he had formed no ties of his own. Now, too, his career seemed to him at an end, and he had nothing to look forward to but a maimed and invalided life of solitude and failure.

Many of his thoughts I could not discern at all—the mist, so to speak, involved them—while many were obscure to me. When he thought about scenes and people whom I had never known, the thought loomed shapeless and dark; but when he thought, as he often did, about his school and university days, and about his home circle, all of which scenes were familiar to me, I could read his mind with perfect clearness. At the bottom of all lay a sense of deep disappointment and resentment. He doubted the justice of God, and blamed himself but little for his miseries. It was a sad experience at first, because he was falling day by day into more hopeless dejection; while he refused the pathetic overtures of sympathy which the relations in whose house he was—a married sister with her husband and children—offered him. He bore himself with courtesy and consideration, but he was so much worn with fatigue and despondency that he could not take any initiative.

But I became aware very gradually that he was learning the true worth and proportion of things—and the months which passed so heavily for him brought him perceptions of the value of which he was hardly aware. Let me say that it was now that the incredible swiftness of time in the spiritual region made itself felt for me. A month of his sufferings passed to me, contemplating them, like an hour.

I found to my surprise that his thoughts of myself were becoming more frequent; and one day when he was turning over some old letters and reading a number of mine, it seemed to me that his spirit almost recognised my presence in the words which came to his lips, "It seems like yesterday!" I then became blessedly aware that I was actually helping him, and that the very intentness of my own thought was quickening his own.

I discussed the whole case very closely and carefully with one of our instructors, who set me right on several points and made the whole state of things clear to me.

I said to him, "One thing bewilders me; it would almost seem that a man's work upon earth constituted an interruption and a distraction from spiritual influences. It cannot surely be that people in the body should avoid employment, and give themselves to secluded meditation? If the soul grows fast in sadness and despondency, it would seem that one should almost have courted sorrow on earth; and yet I cannot believe that to be the case."

"No," he said, "it is not the case; the body has here to be considered. No amount of active exertion clouds the eye of the soul, if only the motive of it is pure and lofty, and if the soul is only set patiently and faithfully upon the true end of life. The body indeed requires due labour and exercise, and the soul can gain health and clearness thereby. But what does cloud the spirit is if it gives itself wholly up to narrow personal aims and ambitions, and uses friendship and love as mere recreations and amusements. Sickness and sorrow are not, as we used to think, fortuitous things; they are given to those who need them, as high and rich opportunities; and they come as truly blessed gifts, when they break a man's thought off from material things, and make him fall back upon the loving affections and relations of life. When one re-enters the world, a woman's life is sometimes granted to a spirit, because a woman by circumstance and temperament is less tempted to decline upon meaner ambitions and interests than a man; but work and activity are no hindrances to spiritual growth, so long as the soul waits upon God, and desires to learn the lessons of life, rather than to enforce its own conclusions upon others."

"Yes," I said, "I see that. What, then, is the great hindrance in the life of men?"

"Authority," he said, "whether given or taken. That is by far the greatest difficulty that a soul has to contend with. The knowledge of the true conditions of life is so minute and yet so imperfect, when one is in the body, that the man or woman who thinks it a duty to disapprove, to correct, to censure, is in the gravest danger. In the first place it is so impossible to disentangle the true conditions of any human life; to know how far those failures which are lightly called sins are inherited instincts of the body, or the manifestation of immaturity of spirit. Complacency, hard righteousness, spiritual security, severe judgments, are the real foes of spiritual growth; and if a man is in a position

73

to enforce his influence and his will upon others, he can fall very low indeed, and suspend his own growth for a very long and sad period. It is not the criticism or the analysis of others which hurts the soul, so long as it remains modest and sincere and conscious of its own weaknesses. It is when we indulge in secure or compassionate comparisons of our own superior worth that we go backwards."

This was but one of the many cases which I had to investigate. I do not say that this is the work of all spirits in the other world—it is not so; there are many kinds of work and occupation. This was the one now allotted to me; but I did become aware of the intense and loving interest which is bent upon the souls of the living by those who are departed. There is not a soul alive who is not being thus watched and tended, and helped, as far as help is possible; for no one is ever forced or compelled or frightened into truth, only drawn and wooed by love and care.

I must say a word, too, of the great and noble friendships which I formed at this period of my existence. We were not free to make many of these at a time. Love seems to be the one thing that demands an entire concentration, and though in the world of spirits I became aware that one could be conscious of many of the thoughts of those about me simultaneously, yet the emotion of love, in the earlier stages, is single and exclusive.

I will speak of two only. There were a young man and a young woman who were much associated with me at that time, whom I will call Philip and Anna. Philip was one of the most beautiful of all the spirits I ever came near. His last life upon earth had been a long one, and he had been a teacher. I used to tell him that I wished I had been under him as a pupil, to which he replied, laughing, that I should have found him very uninteresting. He said to me once that the way in which he had always distinguished the two kinds of teachers on earth had been by whether they were always anxious to teach new books and new subjects, or went on contentedly with the old.

"The pleasure," he said, "was in the teaching, in making the thought clear, in tempting the boys to find out what they knew all the time; and the oftener I taught a subject the better I liked it; it was like a big cog-wheel, with a number of little cog-wheels turning with it. But the men who were always wanting to change their subjects were the men who thought of their own intellectual interest first, and very little of the small interests revolving upon it." The charm of Philip was the charm of extreme ingenuousness combined with daring insight. He never seemed to be shocked or distressed by anything.

He said one day, "It was not the sensual or the timid or the ill-tempered boys who used to make me anxious. Those were definite faults and brought definite punishment; it was the hard-hearted, virtuous, ambitious, sensible boys, who were good-humoured and respectable and selfish, who bothered me; one wanted to shake them as a terrier shakes a rat—but there was nothing to get hold of. They were a credit to themselves and to their parents and to the school; and yet they went downhill with every success."

Anna was a woman of singularly unselfish and courageous temperament. She had been, in the course of her last life upon earth, a hospital nurse; and she used to speak gratefully of the long periods when she was nursing some anxious case, when she had interchanged day and night, sleeping when the world was awake, and sitting with a book or needlework by the sick-bed, through the long darkness. "People used to say to me that it must be so depressing; but those were my happiest hours, as the dark brightened into dawn, when many of the strange mysteries of life and pain and death gave up their secrets to me. But of course," she added with a smile, "it was all very dim to me. I felt the truth rather than saw it; and it is a great joy to me to perceive now what was happening, and how the sad, bewildered hours of pain and misery leave their blessed marks upon the soul, like the tools of the graver on the gem. If only we could learn to plan a little less and to believe a little more, how much simpler it would all be!"

These two became very dear to me, and I learnt much heavenly wisdom from them in long, quiet conferences, where we spoke frankly of all we had felt and known.

19

It was at this time, I think, that a great change came over my thoughts, or rather that I realised that a great change had gradually taken place. Till now, I had been dominated and haunted by memories of my latest life upon earth; but at intervals there had visited me a sense of older and purer recollections. I cannot describe exactly how it came about—and, indeed, the memory of what my heavenly progress had hitherto been, as opposed to my earthly experience, was never very clear to me; but I became aware that my life in heaven—I will call it heaven for want of a better name—was my real continuous life, my home-life, so to speak, while my earthly lives had been, to pursue the metaphor, like terms which a boy spends at school, in which he is aware that he not only learns definite and tangible things, but that his character is hardened and consolidated by coming into contact with the rougher facts of life—duty, responsibility, friendships, angers, treacheries, temptations, routine.

The boy returns with gladness to the serener and sweeter atmosphere of home; and just in the same way I felt I had returned to the larger and purer life of heaven. But, as I say, the recollection of my earlier life in heaven, my occupations and experience, was never clear to me, but rather as a luminous and haunting mist. I questioned Amroth about this once, and he said that this was the universal experience, and that the earthly lives one lived were like deep trenches cut across a path, and seemed to interrupt the heavenly sequence; but that as the spirit grew more pure and wise, the consciousness of the heavenly life became more distinct and secure. But he added, what I did not quite understand, that there was little need of memory in the life of heaven, and that it was to a great extent the inheritance of the body. Memory, he said, was to a great extent an interruption to life; the thought of past failures and mistakes, and especially of unkindnesses and misunderstandings, tended to obscure and complicate one's relations with other souls; but that in heaven, where activity and energy were untiring and unceasing, one lived far more in the emotion and work of the moment, and less in retrospect and prospect.

What mattered was actual experience and the effect of experience; memory itself was but an artistic method of dealing with the past, and corresponded to fanciful and delightful anticipations of the future. "The truth is," he said, "that the indulgence of memory is to a great extent a mere sentimental weakness; to live much in recollection is a sign of exhausted and depleted vitality. The further you are removed from your last earthly life, the less tempted you will be to recall it. The highest spirits of all here," he said, "have no temptation ever to revert to retrospect, because the pure energies of the moment are all-sustaining and all-sufficing."

The only trace I ever noticed of any memory of my past life in heaven was that things sometimes seemed surprisingly familiar to me, and that I had the sense of a serene permanence, which possessed and encompassed me. Indeed, I came to believe that the strange feeling of permanence which haunts one upon earth, when one is happy and content, even though one knows that everything is changing and shifting around one, and that all is precarious and uncertain, is in itself a memory of the serene and untroubled continuance of heaven, and a desire to taste it and realise it.

Be this as it may, from the time of my finding my settled task and ordered place in the heavenly community the memories of my old life upon earth began to fade from my thoughts. I could, indeed, always recall them by an effort, but there seemed less and less inclination to do so the more I became absorbed in my heavenly activities.

One thing I noticed in these days; it surprised me very greatly, till I reflected that my surprise was but the consequence of the strange and mournful blindness with regard to spiritual things in which we live under the dark skies of earth. We have there a false idea that somehow or other death takes all the individuality out of a man, obliterating all the whims, prejudices, the thorny and unreasonable dislikes and fancies, oddities, tempers, roughnesses, and subtlenesses from a temperament. Of course, there are a good many of these things which disappear together with the body, such as the glooms, suspicions, and cloudy irritabilities, which are caused by fatigue and malaise, and by ill-health generally.

But a man's whims and fancies and dislikes do not by any means disappear on earth when he is in good health; on the contrary, they are often apt to be accentuated and emphasised when he is free from pain and care and anxiety, and riding blithely over the waves of life. Indeed, there are men whom I have known who are never kind or sympathetic till they are in some wearing trouble of their own; when they are prosperous and cheerful, they are frankly intolerable, because their mirth turns to derision and insolence.

But one of the reasons why the heavenly life is apt to appear in prospect so wearisome a thing is, because we are brought up to feel that the whole character is flattened out and charged with a serene kind of priggishness, which takes all the salt out of life. The word "saintly," so terribly misapplied on earth, grows to mean, to many of us, an irritating sort of kindness, which treats the interests and animated elements of life with a painful condescension, and a sympathy of which the basis is duty rather than love.

The true sanctification, which I came to perceive something of later, is the result of a process of endless patience and infinite delay, and the attainment of it implies a humility, seven times refined in the fires of self-contempt, in which there remains no smallest touch of superiority or aloofness. How utterly depressing is the feigned interest of the imperfect human saint in matters of mundane concern! How it takes at once both the joy out of holiness and the spirit out of human effort!

It is as dreary as the professional sympathy of the secluded student for the news of athletic contests, as the tolerance of the shrewd man of science for the feminine logic of religious sentiment!

But I found to my great content that whatever change had passed over the spirits of my companions, they had at least lost no fibre of their individuality. The change that had passed over them was like the change that passes over a young man, who has lived at the University among dilettante literary designs and mild sociological theorising, when he finds himself plunged into the urgent practical activities of the world. Our happiness was the happiness which comes of intense toil, with no fatigue to dog it, and from a consciousness of the vital issues which we were pursuing.

But my companions had still intellectual faults and preferences, self-confidence, critical intolerance, boisterousness, wilfulness. Stranger still, I found coldness, anger, jealousy, still at work. Of course, in the latter case reconciliation was easier, both in the light of common enthusiasm and, still more, because mental communication was so much swifter and easier than it had been on earth. There was no need of those protracted talks, those tiresome explanations which clever people, who really love and esteem each other, fall into on earth—the statements which affirm nothing, the explanations which elucidate nothing, because of the intricacies of human speech and the fact that people use the same words with such different implications and meanings.

All those became unnecessary, because one could pierce instantaneously into the very essence of the soul, and manifest, without the need of expression, the regard and affection which lay beneath the crosscurrents of emotion. But love and affection waxed and waned in heaven as on earth; it was weakened and it was transferred. Few souls are so serene on earth as to see with perfect equanimity a friend, whom one loves and trusts, becoming absorbed in some new and exciting emotion, which may not perhaps obliterate the original regard, but which must withdraw from it for a time the energy which fed the flame of the intermitted relation.

It was very strange to me to realise the fact that friendships and intimacies were formed as on earth, and that they lost their freshness, either from some lack of real congeniality or from some divergence of development. Sometimes, I may add, our teachers were consulted by the aggrieved, sometimes they even intervened unasked.

I will freely confess that this all immensely heightened the interests to me of our common life. One could see two spirits drawn together by some secret tie of emotion, and one could see some further influence strike across and suspend it. One case of this I will mention, which is typical of many. There came among us an extremely lively and rather whimsical spirit, more like a boy than a man. I wondered at first why he was chosen for this work, because he seemed both fitful and even capricious; but I gradually realised in him an extraordinary fineness of perception, and a swiftness of intuition almost unrivalled. He had a power of weighing almost by instinct the constituent elements of character, which seemed to me something like the power of tonality in a musician, the gift of recognising, by pure faculty, what any notes may be, however confusedly jangled on an instrument. It was wonderful to me how often his instantaneous judgments proved more sagacious than our carefully formed conclusions.

This boy became extraordinarily attractive to an older woman who was one of our number, who was solitary and abstracted, and of an intense seriousness of devotion to her work. It was evident both that she felt his charm intensely and that her disposition was wholly alien to the disposition of the boy himself. In fact, she simply bored him. He took all that he did lightly, and achieved by an intense momentary concentration what she could only achieve by slow reflection. This devotion had in it something that was strangely pathetic, because it took the form in her of making hep wish to conciliate the boy's admiration, by treating thoughts and ideas with a lightness and a humour to which she could by no means attain, and which made things worse rather than better, because she could read so easily, in the thoughts of others, the impression that she was attempting a handling of topics which she could not in the least accomplish.

But advice was useless. There it was, the old, fierce, constraining attraction of love, as it had been of old, making havoc of comfortable arrangements, attempting the impossible; and yet one knew that she would gain by the process, that she was opening a door in her heart that had hitherto been closed, and learning a largeness of view and sympathy in the process. Her fault had ever been, no doubt, to estimate slow and accurate methods too highly, and to believe that all was insecure and untrustworthy that was not painfully accumulated. Now she saw that genius could accomplish without effort or trouble what no amount of homely energy could effect, and a new horizon was unveiled to her. But on the boy, it did not seem to have the right result. He might have learned to extend his sympathy to a nature so dumb and plodding; and this coldness of his called down a rebuke of what seemed almost undue sternness from one of our teachers.

It was not given in my presence, but the boy, bewildered by the severity which he did not anticipate, coupled indeed with a hint that he must be prepared, if he could not exhibit a more elastic sympathy, to have his course suspended in favour of some more simple discipline, told me the whole matter. "What am I to do?" he said. "I cannot care for Barbara; her whole nature upsets me and revolts me. I know she is very good and all that, but I simply am not myself when she is by; it is like taking a run with a tortoise!"

"Well," I said, "no one expects you to give up all your time to taking tortoises for runs; but I suppose that tortoises have their rights, and must not be jerked along on their backs, like a sledge."

"Oh," said he, "you are all against me, I know; and I am not sure that this place is not rather too solemn for me. What is the good of being wiser than the aged, if one has more commandments to keep?"

Things, however, settled down in time. Barbara, I think, must have been taken to task as well, because she gave up her attempts at wit; and the end of it was that a quiet friendship sprang up between the incongruous pair, like that between a wayward young brother and a plain, kindly, and elderly sister, of a very fine and chivalrous kind.

It must not be thought that we spent our time wholly in these emotional relations. It was a place of hard and urgent work; but I came to realise that, just as on earth, institutions like schools and colleges, where a great variety of natures are gathered in close and daily contact, are shot through and through with strange currents of emotion, which some people pay no attention to, and others dismiss as mere sentimentality, so it was also bound to be beyond, with this difference, that whereas on earth we are shy and awkward with our friendships, and all sorts of physical complications intervene, in the other world they assume their frank importance. I saw that much of what is called the serious business of life is simply and solely necessitated by bodily needs, and is really entirely temporary and trivial, while the real life of the soul, which underlies it all, stifled and subdued, pent-up uneasily and cramped unkindly like a bright spring of water under the superincumbent earth, finds its way at last to the light.

On earth we awkwardly divide this impulse; we speak of the relation of the soul to others and of the relation of the soul to God as two separate things. We pass over the words of Christ in the Gospel, which directly contradict this, and which make the one absolutely dependent on, and conditional on, the other. We speak of human affection as a thing which may come in between the soul and God, while it is in reality the swiftest access thither. We speak as though ambition were itself made more noble, if it sternly abjures all multiplication of human tenderness. We speak of a life which sacrifices material success to emotion as a failure and an irresponsible affair. The truth is the precise opposite. All the ambitions which have their end in personal prestige are wholly barren; the ambitions which aim at social amelioration have a certain nobility about them, though they substitute a tortuous by-path for a direct highway. And the plain truth is that all social amelioration would grow up as naturally and as fragrantly as a flower, if we could but refine and strengthen and awaken our slumbering emotions, and let them grow out freely to gladden the little circle of earth in which we live and move.

20

It was at this time that I had a memorable interview with the Master of the College. He appeared very little among us, though he occasionally gave us a short instruction, in which he summed up the teaching on a certain point. He was a man of extraordinary impressiveness, mainly, I think, because he gave the sense of being occupied in much larger and wider interests. I often pondered over the question why the short, clear, rather dry discourses which fell from his lips appeared to be so far more weighty and momentous than anything else that was ever said to us. He used no arts of exhortation, showed no emotion, seemed hardly conscious of our presence; and if one caught his eye as he spoke, one became aware of a curious tremor of awe.

He never made any appeal to our hearts or feelings: but it always seemed as if he had condescended for a moment to put aside far bigger and loftier designs in order to drop a fruit of ripened wisdom in our way. He came among us, indeed, like a statesman rather than like a teacher. The brief interviews we had with him were regarded with a sort of terror, but produced, in me at least, an almost fanatical respect and admiration. And yet I had no reason to suppose that he was not, like all of us, subject to the law of life and pilgrimage, though one could not conceive of him as having to enter the arena of life again as a helpless child!

On this occasion I was summoned suddenly to his presence, I found him, as usual, bent over his work, which he did not intermit, but merely motioned me to be seated. Presently he put away his papers from him, and turned round upon me. One of the disconcerting things about him was the fact that his thought had a peculiarly compelling tendency, and that while he read one's mind in a flash, his own thoughts remained very nearly impenetrable. On this occasion he commended me for my work and my relations with my fellow-students, adding that I had made rapid progress. He then said, "I have two questions to ask you. Have you any special relations, either with any one whom you have left behind you on earth, or with any one with whom you have made acquaintance since you quitted it, which you desire to pursue?"

I told him, which was the truth, that since my stay in the College I had become so much absorbed in the studies of the place that I seemed to have become strangely oblivious of my external friends, but that it was more a suspension than a destruction of would-be relations.

"Yes," he said, "I perceive that that is your temperament. It has its effectiveness, no doubt, but it also has its dangers; and, whatever happens, one ought never to be able to accuse oneself justly of any disloyalty."

He seemed to wait for me to speak, whereupon I mentioned a very dear friend of my days of earth; but I added that most of those whom I had loved best had predeceased me, and that I had looked forward to a renewal of our intercourse. I also mentioned the names of Charmides and Cynthia, the latter of whom was in memory strangely near to my heart.

He seemed satisfied with this. Then he said, "It is true that we have to multiply relationships with others, both in the world and out of it; but we must also practise economy. We must not abandon ourselves to passing fancies, or be subservient to charm, while if we have made an emotional mistake, and have been disappointed with one whom we have taken the trouble to win, we must guard such conquests with a close and peculiar tenderness. But enough of that, for I have to ask you if there is any special work for which you feel yourself disposed. There is a great choice of employment here.

"You may choose, if you will, just to live the spiritual life and discharge whatever duties of citizenship you may be called upon to perform. That is what most spirits do. I need not perhaps tell you "—here he smiled—"that freedom from the body does not confer upon any one, as our poor brothers and sisters upon earth seem to think, a heavenly vocation. Neither of course is the earthly fallacy about a mere absorption in worship a true one—only to a very few is that conceded.

Still less is this a life of leisure. To be leisurely here is permitted only to the wearied, and to those childish creatures with whom you have spent some time in their barren security.

"I do not think you are suited for the work of recording the great scheme of life, nor do I think you are made for a teacher. You are not sufficiently impartial! For mere labour you are not suited; and yet I hardly think you would be fit to adopt the most honourable task which your friend Amroth so finely fulfils—a guide and messenger. What do you think?"

I said at once that I did not wish to have to make a decision, but that I preferred to leave it to him. I added that though I was conscious of my deficiencies, I did not feel conscious of any particular capacities, except that I found character a very fascinating study, especially in connection with the circumstances of life upon earth.

"Very well," he said, "I think that you may perhaps be best suited to the work of deciding what sort of life will best befit the souls who are prepared to take up their life upon earth again. That is a task of deep and infinite concern; it may surprise you," he added, "to learn that this is left to the decision of other souls. But it is, of course, the goal at which all earthly social systems are aiming, the right apportionment of circumstances to temperament, and you must not be surprised to find that here we have gone much further in that direction, though even here the system is not perfected; and you cannot begin to apprehend that fact too soon. It is unfortunate that on earth it is commonly believed, owing to the deadening influence of material causes, that beyond the grave everything is done with a Divine unanimity. But of course, if that were so, further growth and development would be impossible, and in view of infinite perfectibility there is yet very much that is faulty and incomplete.

"But I am not sure what lies before you; there is something in your temperament which a little baffles me, and our plans may have to be changed. Your very absorption in your work, your quick power of forgetting and throwing off impressions has its dangers. But I will bear in mind what you have said, and you may for the present resume your studies, and I will once more commend you; you have done well hitherto, and I will say frankly that I regard you as capable of useful and honourable work."

He bowed in token of dismissal, and I went back to my work with unbounded gratitude and enthusiasm.

21

Sometime after this I was surprised one morning at the sudden entrance of Amroth into my cell. He came in with a very bright and holiday aspect, and, assuming a paternal air, said that he had heard a very creditable account of my work and conduct, and that he had obtained leave for me to have an exeat I suppose that I showed signs of impatience at the interruption, for he broke into a laugh, and said, "Well, I am going to insist. I believe you are working too hard, and we must not overstrain our faculties. It was bad enough in the old days, but then it was generally the poor body which suffered first. But indeed, it is quite possible to overwork here, and you have the dim air of the pale student. Come," he said, "whatever happens, do not become priggish. Not to want a holiday is a sign of spiritual pride. Besides, I have some curious things to show you."

I got up and said that I was ready, and Amroth led the way like a boy out for a holiday. He was brimming over with talk, and told me some stories about my friends in the land of delight, interspersing them with imitation of their manner and gesture, which made me giggle—Amroth was an admirable mimic. "I had hopes of Charmides," he said; "your stay there aroused his curiosity. But he has gone back to his absurd tones and half-tones, and is nearly insupportable. Cynthia is much more sensible, but Lucius is a nuisance, and Charmides, by the way, has become absurdly jealous of him. They really are very silly; but I have a pleasant plot, which I will unfold to you."

As we went down the interminable stairs, I said to Amroth, "There is a question I want to ask you. Why do we have to go and come, up and down, backwards and forwards, in this absurd way, as if we were still in the body? Why not just slip off the leads, and fly down over the crags like a pair of pigeons? It all seems to me so terribly material."

Amroth looked at me with a smile. "I don't advise you to try," he said. "Why, little brother, of course we are just as limited here in these ways. The material laws of earth are only a type of the laws here. They all have a meaning which remains true."

"But," I said, "we can visit the earth with incredible rapidity?"

"How can I explain?" said Amroth. "Of course, we can do that, because the material universe is so extremely small in comparison. All the stars in the world are here but as a heap of sand, like the motes which dance in a sunbeam. There is no question of size, of course! But there is such a thing as spiritual nearness and spiritual distance for all that. The souls who do not return to earth are very far off, as you will sometime see. But we messengers have our short cuts, and I shall take advantage of them today."

We went out of the great door of the fortress, and I felt a sense of relief. It was good to put it all behind one. For a long time, I talked to Amroth about all my doings. "Come," he said at last, "this will never do! You are becoming something of a bore! Do you know that your talk is very provincial? You seem to have forgotten about everyone and everything except your Philips and Annas—very worthy creatures, no doubt—and the Master, who is a very able man, but not the little demigod you believe. You are hypnotised! It is indeed time for you to have a holiday. Why, I believe you have half forgotten about me, and yet you made a great fuss when I quitted you."

I smiled, frowned, blushed. It was indeed true. Now that he was with me I loved him as well, indeed better than ever; but I had not been thinking very much about him.

We went over the moorlands in the keen air, Amroth striding cleanly and lightly over the heather. Then we began to descend into the valley, through a fine forest country, somewhat like the chestnut-woods of the Apennines. The view was of incomparable beauty and width. I could see a great city far out in the plain, with a river entering it and leaving it, like a ribbon of silver. There were rolling ridges beyond. On the left rose huge, shadowy, snow-clad hills, rising to one tremendous dome of snow.

"Where are you going to take me?" I said to Amroth.

"Never mind," said he; "it's my day and my plan for once. You shall see what you shall see, and it will amuse me to hear your ingenuous conjectures."

We were soon on the outskirts of the city we had seen, which seemed a different kind of place from any I had yet visited. It was built, I perceived, upon an exactly conceived plan, of a stately, classical kind of architecture, with great gateways and colonnades. There were people about, rather silent and serious-looking, soberly clad, who saluted us as we passed, but made no attempt to talk to us. "This is rather a tiresome place, I always think," said Amroth; "but you ought to see it."

We went along the great street and reached a square. I was surprised at the elderly air of all we met. We found ourselves opposite a great building with a dome, like a church. People were going in under the portico, and we went in with them. They treated us as strangers, and made courteous way for us to pass.

Inside, the footfalls fell dumbly upon a great carpeted floor. It was very like a great church, except that there was no altar or sign of worship. At the far end, under an alcove, was a statue of white marble gleaming white, with head and hand uplifted. The whole place had a solemn and noble air. Out of the central nave there opened a series of great vaulted chapels; and I could now see that in each chapel there was a dark figure, in a sort of pulpit, addressing a standing audience. There were names on scrolls over the doors of the light iron-work screens which separated the chapels from the nave, but they were in a language I did not understand.

Amroth stopped at the third of the chapels, and said, "Here, this will do." We came in, and as before there was a courteous notice taken of us. A man in black came forward, and led us to a high seat, like a pew, near the preacher, from which we could survey the crowd. I was struck with their look of weariness combined with intentness.

The lecturer, a young man, had made a pause, but upon our taking our places, he resumed his speech. It was a discourse, as far as I could make out, on the development of poetry; he was speaking of lyrical poetry. I will not here reproduce it. I will only say that anything more acute, delicate, and discriminating, and, I must add, more entirely val-ueless and pedantic, I do not think I ever heard. It must have required immense and complicated knowledge. He was tracing the develop-ment of a certain kind of dramatic lyric, and what surprised me was that he supplied the subtle intellectual connection, the missing links, so to speak, of which there is no earthly record.

Let me give a single instance. He was accounting for a rather sud-den change of thought in a well-known poet, and he showed that it had been brought about by his making the acquaintance of a certain friend who had introduced him to a new range of subjects, and by his study of certain books. These facts are unrecorded in his published biography, but the analysis of the lecturer, done in a few pointed sen-tences, not only carried conviction to the mind, but just, so to speak, laid the truth bare. And yet it was all to me incredibly sterile and arid. Not the slightest interest was taken in the emotional or psychological side; it was all purely and exactly scientific.

We waited until the end of the address, which was greeted with decorous applause, and the hall was emptied in a moment

We visited other chapels where the same sort of thing was going on in other subjects. It all produced in me a sort of stupefaction, both at the amazing knowledge involved, and in the essential futility of it all.

Before we left the building, we went up to the statue, which represented a female figure, looking upwards, with a pure and delicate beauty of form and gesture that was inexpressibly and coldly lovely.

We went out in silence, which seemed to be the rule of the place.

When we came away from the building we were accosted by a very grave and courteous person, who said that he perceived that we were strangers, and asked if he could be of any service to us, and whether we proposed to make a stay of any duration. Amroth thanked him, and said smilingly that we were only passing through. The gentleman said that it was a pity, because there was much of interest to hear.

"In this place," he said with a deprecating gesture, "we grudge every hour that is not devoted to thought." He went on to inquire if we were following any particular line of study, and as our answers were unsatisfactory, he said that we could not do better than begin by attending the school of literature. "I observed," he said, "that you were listening to our Professor, Sylvanus, with attention. He is devoting himself to the development of poetical form. It is a rich subject. It has generally been believed that poets work by a sort of native inspiration, and that the poetic gift is a sort of heightening of temperament. But Sylvanus has proved—I think I may go so far as to say this—that this is all pure fancy, and what is worse, unsound fancy. It is all merely a matter of heredity, and the apparent accidents on which poetical expression depends can be analysed exactly and precisely into the most commonplace and simple elements. It is only a question of proportion. Now we who value clearness of mind above everything, find this a very refreshing thought.

"The real crown and sum of human achievement, in the intellectual domain, is to see things clearly and exactly, and upon that clearness all progress depends. We have disposed by this time of most illusions; and the same scientific method is being strenuously applied to all other processes of human endeavour. It is even hinted that Sylvanus has practically proved that the imaginative element in literature is purely a taint of barbarism, though he has not yet announced the fact. But many of his class are looking forward to his final lecture on the subject as to a profoundly sensational event, which is likely to set a deep mark upon all our conceptions of literary endeavour.

"So that," he said with a tolerant smile, gently rubbing his hands together, "our life here is not by any means destitute of the elements of excitement, though we most of us, of course, aim at the acquisition of a serene and philosophic temper. But I must not delay you," he add-

ed; "there is much to see and to hear, and you will be welcomed everywhere: and indeed, I am myself somewhat closely engaged, though
in a subject which is not fraught with such polite emollience. I attend
the school of metaphysics, from which we have at last, I hope, eliminated the last traces of that debasing element of psychology, which has
so long vitiated the exact study of the subject."

He took himself off with a bow, and I gazed blankly at Amroth.
"The conversation of that very polite person," I said, "is like a bad
dream! What is this extraordinarily depressing place? Shall I have to
undergo a course here?"

"No, my dear boy," said Amroth. "This is rather out of your depth.
But I am somewhat disappointed at your view of the situation. Surely
these are all very important matters? Your disposition is, I am afraid,
incurably frivolous! How could people be more worthily employed
than in getting rid of the last traces of intellectual error, and in refer-
ring everything to its actual origin? Did not your heart burn within
you at his luminous exposition? I had always thought you a boy of
intellectual promise."

"Amroth," I said, "I will not be made fun of. This is the most dreadful place I have ever seen or conceived of! It frightens me. The dry-
ness of pure science is terrifying enough, but after all that has a kind
of strange beauty, because it deals either with transcendental ideas of
mathematical relation, or with the deducing of principle from accumulated facts. But here the object appears to be to eliminate the human element from humanity. I insist upon knowing where you have
brought me, and what is going on here?"

"Well, then," said Amroth, "I will conceal it from you no longer.
This is the paradise of thought, where meagre and spurious philoso-
phers, and all who have submerged life in intellect, have their reward.
It is, as you say, a very dreary place for children of nature like you and
me. But I do not suppose that there is a happier or a busier place in all
our dominions. The worst of it is that it is so terribly hard to get out
of. It is a blind alley and leads nowhere. Every step has to be retraced.
These people have to get a very severe dose of homely life to do them
any good; and the worst of it is that they are so entirely virtuous.
They have never had the time or the inclination to be anything else.
And they are among the most troublesome and undisciplined of all
our people. But I see you have had enough; and unless you wish to
wait for Professor Sylvanus's sensational pronouncement, we will go
elsewhere, and have some other sort of fun. But you must not be so

much upset by these things."

"It would kill me," I said, "to hear any more of these lectures, and if I had to listen to much of our polite friend's conversation, I should go out of my mind. I would rather fall into the hands of the cragmen! I would rather have a stand-up fight than be slowly stifled with interesting information. But where do these unhappy people come from?"

"A few come from universities," said Amroth, "but they are not as a rule really learned men. They are more the sort of people who subscribe to libraries, and belong to local literary societies, and go into a good many subjects on their own account. But really learned men are almost always more aware of their ignorance than of their knowledge, and recognise the vitality of life, even if they do not always exhibit it. But come, we are losing time, and we must go further afield."

22

We went some considerable distance, after leaving our intellectual friends, through very beautiful wooded country, and as we went we talked with much animation about the intellectual life and its dangers. It had always, I confess, appeared to me a harmless life enough; not very effective, perhaps, and possibly liable to encourage a man in a trivial sort of self-conceit; but I had always looked upon that as an instinctive kind of self-respect, which kept an intellectual person from dwelling too sorely upon the sense of ineffectiveness; as an addiction not more serious in its effects upon character than the practice of playing golf, a thing in which a leisurely person might immerse himself, and cultivate a decent sense of self-importance. But Amroth showed me that the danger of it lay in the tendency to consider the intellect to be the basis of all life and progress.

"The intellectual man," he said, "is inclined to confuse his own acute perception of the movement of thought with the originating impulse of that movement. But of course, thought is a thing which ebbs and flows, like public opinion, according to its own laws, and is not originated but only perceived by men of intellectual ability. The danger of it is a particularly arid sort of self-conceit. It is as if the Lady of Shallot were to suppose that she created life by observing and rendering it in her magic web, whereas her devotion to her task simply isolates her from the contact with other minds and hearts, which is the one thing worth having. That is, of course, the danger of the artist as well as of the philosopher. They both stand aside from the throng, and are so much absorbed in the aspect of thought and emotion that they do not realise that they are separated from it.

"They are consequently spared, when they come here, the punishment which falls upon those who have mixed greedily, selfishly, and cruelly with life, of which you will have a sight before long. But that place of punishment is not nearly so sad or depressing a place as the paradise of delight, and the paradise of intellect, because the sufferers have no desire to stay there, can repent and feel ashamed, and therefore can suffer, which is always hopeful. But the artistic and intellectual have really starved their capacity for suffering, the one by treating all emotion as spectacular, and the other by treating it as a puerile interruption to serious things. It takes people a long time to work their way out of self-satisfaction! But there is another curious place I wish you to visit.

"It is a dreadful place in a way, but by no means consciously unhappy," and Amroth pointed to a great building which stood on a slope of the hill above the forest, with a wide and beautiful view from it Before very long we came to a high stone wall with a gate carefully guarded. Here Amroth said a few words to a porter, and we went up through a beautiful terraced park. In the park we saw little knots of people walking aimlessly about, and a few more solitary figures. But in each case, they were accompanied by people whom I saw to be warders. We passed indeed close to an elderly man, rather fantastically dressed, who looked possessed with a kind of flighty cheerfulness. He was talking to himself with odd, emphatic gestures, as if he were ticking off the points of a speech. He came up to us and made us an effusive greeting, praising the situation and convenience of the place, and wishing us a pleasant sojourn.

He then was silent for a moment, and added, "Now there is a matter of some importance on which I should like your opinion." At this the warder who was with him, a strong, stolid-looking man, with an expression at once slightly contemptuous and obviously kind, held up his hand and said, "You will, no doubt, sir, remember that you have undertaken—"

"Not a word, not a word," said our friend; "of course you are right! I have really nothing to say to these gentlemen."

We went up to the building, which now became visible, with its long and stately front of stone. Here again we were admitted with some precaution, and after a few minutes there came a tall and benevolent-looking man, to whom Amroth spoke at some length. The man then came up to me, said that he was very glad to welcome me, and that he would be delighted to show us the place.

We went through fine and airy corridors, into which many doors, as of cells, opened. Occasionally a man or a woman, attended by a male or a female warder, passed us. The inmates had all the same kind of air—a sort of amused dignity, which was very marked. Presently our companion opened a door with his key and we went in. It was a small, pleasantly-furnished room. Some books, apparently of devotion, lay on the table. There was a little kneeling-desk near the window, and the room had a half-monastic air about it. When we entered, an elderly man, with a very serene face, was looking earnestly into the door of a cupboard in the wall, which he was holding open; there was, so far as I could see, nothing in the cupboard; but the inmate seemed to be struggling with an access of rather overpowering mirth. He bowed to us.

Our conductor greeted him respectfully, and then said, "There is a stranger here who would like a little conversation with you, if you can spare the time."

"By all means," said the inmate, with a very ingratiating smile. "It is very kind of him to call upon me, and my time is entirely at his disposal."

Our conductor said to me that he and Amroth had some brief business to transact, and that they would call for me again in a moment. The inmate bowed, and seemed almost impatient for them to depart. He motioned me to a chair, and the moment they left us he began to talk with great animation. He asked me if I was a new inmate, and when I said no, only a visitor, he looked at me compassionately, saying that he hoped I might someday attain to the privilege.

"This," he said, "is the abode of final and lasting peace. No one is admitted here unless his convictions are of the firmest and most ardent character; it is a reward for faithful service. But as our time is short, I must tell you," he said, "of a very curious experience I have had this very morning—a spiritual experience of the most reassuring character. You must know that I held a high official position in the religious world—I will mention no details—and I found at an early age, I am glad to say, the imperative necessity of forming absolutely impregnable convictions. I went to work in the most business-like way. I devoted some years to hard reading and solid thought, and I found that the sect to which I belonged was lacking in certain definite notes of divine truth, while the freight of evidence pointed in the clearest possible manner to the fact that one particular section of the Church had preserved absolutely intact the primitive faith of the Saints, and was without any shadow of doubt the perfectly logical development of the principles of the Gospel. Mine is not a nature that can admit of compromise; and at considerable sacrifice of worldly prospects I transferred my allegiance, and was instantly rewarded by a perfect serenity of conviction which has never faltered.

"I had a friend with whom I had often discussed the matter, who was much on my way of thinking. But though I showed him the illogical nature of his position, he hung back—whether from material motives or from mere emotional associations I will not now stop to inquire. But I could not palter with the truth. I expostulated with him, and pointed out to him in the sternest terms the eternal distinctions involved. I broke off all relations with him ultimately. And after a life spent in the most solemn and candid denunciation of the fluidity of religious belief, which is the curse of our age, though it involved me in many of the heart-rending suspensions of human intercourse with my nearest and dearest so plainly indicated in the Gospel, I passed at length, in complete tranquillity, to my final rest. The first duty of the sincere believer is inflexible intolerance. If a man will not recognise the truth when it is plainly presented to him, he must accept the eternal consequences of his act—separation from God, and absorption in guilty and awestruck regret, which admits of no repentance.

"One of the privileges of our sojourn here is that we have a strange and beautiful device—a window, I will call it—which admits one to a sight of the spiritual world. I was today contemplating, not without pain, but with absolute confidence in its justice, the sufferings of some of these lost souls, and I observed, I cannot say with satisfaction, but with complete submission, the form of my friend, whom my testimony might have saved, in eternal misery. I have the tenderest heart of any man alive. It has cost me a sore struggle to subdue it—it is more unruly even than the will—but you may imagine that it is a matter of deep and comforting assurance to reflect that on earth the door, the one door, to salvation is clearly and plainly indicated—though few there be that find it—and that this signal mercy has been vouchsafed to me.

"I have then the peace of knowing, not only that my choice was right, but that all those to whom the truth is revealed have the power to choose it. I am a firm believer in the uncovenanted mercies vouchsafed to those who have not had the advantages of clear presentment, but for the deliberately unfaithful, for all sinners against light, the sentence is inflexible."

He closed his eyes, and a smile played over his features.

I found it very difficult to say anything in answer to this monologue; but I asked my companion whether he did not think that some clearer revelation might be made, after the bodily death, to those who for some human frailty were unable to receive it.

"An intelligent question," said my companion, "but I am obliged to answer in the negative. Of course, the case is different for those who have accepted the truth loyally, even if their record is stained by the foulest and most detestable of crimes. It is the moral and intellectual adhesion that matters; that once secured, conduct is comparatively unimportant, if the soul duly recurs to the medicine of penitence and contrition so mercifully provided. I have the utmost indulgence for every form of human frailty. I may say that I never shrank from contact with the grossest and vilest forms of continuous wrong-doing, so long as I was assured that the true doctrines were unhesitatingly and submissively accepted. A soul which admits the supremacy of authority can go astray like a sheep that is lost, but as long as it recognises its fold and the authority of the divine law, it can be sought and found.

"The little window of which I spoke has given me indubitable testimony of this. There was a man I knew in the flesh, who was regarded as a monster of cruelty and selfishness. He ill-treated his wife and misused his children; his life was spent in gross debauchery, and his conduct on several occasions outstepped the sanctions of legality. He was a forger and an embezzler. I do not attempt to palliate his faults, and there will be a heavy reckoning to pay. But he made his submission at the last, after a long and prostrating illness; and I have ocular demonstration of the fact that, after a mercifully brief period of suffering, he is numbered among the blest. That is a sustaining thought."

He then with much courtesy invited me to partake of some refreshment, which I gratefully declined. Once or twice he rose, and opening the little cupboard door, which revealed nothing but a white wall, he drank in encouragement from some hidden sight. He then invited me to kneel with him, and prayed fervently and with some emotion that light might be vouchsafed to souls on earth who were in darkness. Just as he concluded, Amroth appeared with our conductor. The latter made a courteous inquiry after my host's health and comfort. "I am perfectly happy here," he said, "perfectly happy. The attentions I receive are indeed more than I deserve; and I am specially grateful to my kind visitor, whose indulgence I must beg for my somewhat prolonged statement—but when one has a cause much at heart," he added with a smile, "some prolixity is easily excused."

As we re-entered the corridor, our conductor asked me if I would care to pay any more visits. "The case you have seen," he said, "is an extremely typical and interesting one."

"Have you any hope," said Amroth, "of recovery?"

"Of course, of course," said our conductor with a smile. "Nothing is hopeless here; our cures are complete and even rapid; but this is a particularly obstinate one!"

"Well," said Amroth, "would you like to see more?"

"No," I said, "I have seen enough. I cannot now bear any more."

Our conductor smiled indulgently.

"Yes," he said, "it is bewildering at first; but one sees wonderful things here! This is our library," he added, leading us to a great airy room, full of books and reading-desks, where a large number of inmates were sitting reading and writing. They glanced up at us with friendly and contented smiles. A little further on we came to another cell, before which our conductor stopped, and looked at me. "I should like," he said, "if you are not too tired, just to take you in here; there is a patient, who is very near recovery indeed, in here, and it would do him good to have a little talk with a stranger."

I bowed, and we went in. A man was sitting in a chair with his head in his hands. An attendant was sitting near the window reading a book. The patient, at our entry, removed his hands from his face and looked up, half impatiently, with an air of great suffering, and then slowly rose.

"How are you feeling, dear sir?" said our conductor quietly.

"Oh," said the man, looking at us, "I am better, much better. The light is breaking in, but it is a sore business, when I was so strong in my pride."

"Ah," said our guide, "it is indeed a slow process; but happiness and health must be purchased; and every day I see clearly that you are drawing nearer to the end of your troubles—you will soon be leaving us! But now I want you kindly to bestir yourself, and talk a little to this friend of ours, who has not been long with us, and finds the place somewhat bewildering. You will be able to tell him something of what is passing in your mind; it will do you good to put it into words, and it will be a help to him."

"Very well," said the man gravely, "I will do my best." And the others withdrew, leaving me with the man. When they had gone, the man asked me to be seated, and leaning his head upon his hand he said, "I do not know how much you know and how little, so I will tell you that I left the world very confident in a particular form of faith, and very much disposed to despise and even to dislike those who did not agree with me. I had lived, I may say, uprightly and purely, and I will confess that I even welcomed all signs of laxity and sinfulness in my opponents, because it proved what I believed, that wrong conduct sprang naturally from wrong belief. I came here in great content, and thought that this place was the reward of faithful living. But I had a great shock. I was very tenderly attached to one whom I left on earth, and the severest grief of my life was that she did not think as I did, but used to plead with me for a wider outlook and a larger faith in the designs of God. She used to say to me that she felt that God had different ways of saving different people, and that people were saved by love and not by doctrine. And this I combated with all my might I used to say, 'Doctrine first, and love afterwards,' to which she often said, 'No, love is first!'

"Well, some time ago I had a sight of her; she had died, and entered this world of ours. She was in a very different place from this, but she thought of me without ceasing, and her desire prevailed. I saw her, though I was hidden from her, and looked into her heart, and discerned that the one thing which spoiled her joy was that I was parted from her.

"And after that I had no more delight in my security. I began to suffer and to yearn. And then, little by little, I began to see that it is love after all which binds us together, and which draws us to God; but my difficulty is this, that I still believe that my faith is true; and if that is true, then other faiths cannot be true also, and then I fall into sad bewilderment and despair." He stopped and looked at me fixedly.

"But," I said, "if I may carry the thought further, might not all be true? Two men may be very unlike each other in form and face and thought—yet both are very man. It would be foolish arguing, if a man were to say, 'I am indeed a man, and because my friend is unlike me—taller, lighter-complexioned, swifter of thought—therefore he cannot be a man.' Or, again, two men may travel by the same road, and see many different things, yet it is the same road they have both travelled; and one need not say to the other, 'You cannot have travelled by the same road, because you did not see the violets on the bank under the wood, or the spire that peeped through the trees at the folding of the valleys—and therefore you are a liar and a deceiver!'

"If one believes firmly in one's own faith, one need not therefore say that all who do not hold it are perverse and wilful. There is no excuse, indeed, for not holding to what we believe to be true, but there is no excuse either for interfering with the sincere belief of another, unless one can persuade him he is wrong. Is not the mistake to think that one holds the truth in its entirety, and that one has no more to learn and to perceive? I myself should welcome differences of faith, because it shows me that faith is a larger thing even than I know. What another sees may be but a thought that is hidden from me, because the truth may be seen from a different angle. To complain that we cannot see it all is as foolish as when the child is vexed because it cannot see the back of the moon. And it seems to me that our duty is not to quarrel with others who see things that we do not see, but to rejoice with them, if they will allow us, and meanwhile to discern what is shown to us as faithfully as we can."

The man heard me with a strange smile. "Yes," he said, "you are certainly right, and I bless the goodness that sent you hither; but when you are gone, I doubt that I shall fall back into my old perplexities, and say to myself that though men may see different parts of the same thing, they cannot see the same thing differently."

"I think," I said, "that even that is possible, because on earth things are often mere symbols, and clothe themselves in material forms; and it is the form which deludes us. I do not myself doubt that grace flows into us by very different channels. We may not deny the claim of any one to derive grace from any source or symbol that he can. The only thing we may and must dare to dispute is the claim that only by one channel may grace flow. But I think that the words of the one whom you loved, of whom you spoke, are indeed true, and that the love of each other and of God is the force which draws us, by whatever rite or symbol or doctrine it may be interpreted. That, as I read it, is the message of Christ, who gave up all things for utter love."

As I said this, our guide and Amroth entered the cell. The man rose up quickly, and drawing me apart, thanked me very heartily and with tears in his eyes; and so, we said farewell. When we were outside, I said to the guide, "May I ask you one question? Would it be of use if I remained here for a time to talk with that poor man? It seemed a relief to him to open his heart, and I would gladly be with him and try to comfort him."

The guide shook his head kindly. "No," he said, "I think not. I recognise your kindness very fully—but a soul like this must find the way alone; and there is one who is helping him faster than any of us can avail to do; and besides," he added, "he is very near indeed to his release."

So, we went to the door, and said farewell; and Amroth and I went forward. Then I said to him as we went down through the terraced garden, and saw the inmates wandering about, lost in dreams, "This must be a sad place to live in, Amroth!"

"No, indeed," said he, "I do not think that there are any happier than those who have the charge here. When the patients are in the grip of this disease, they are themselves only too well content; and it is a blessed thing to see the approach of doubt and suffering, which means that health draws near. There is no place in all our realm where one sees so clearly and beautifully the instant and perfect mercy of God, and the joy of pain." And so, we passed together out of the guarded gate.

23

"Well," said Amroth, with a smile, as we went out into the forest, "I am afraid that the last two visits have been rather a strain. We must find something a little less serious; but I am going to fill up all your time. You had got too much taken up with your psychology, and we must not live too much on theory, and spin problems, like the spider, out of our own insides; but we will not spend too much time in trudging over this country, though it is well worth it. Did you ever see anything more beautiful than those pine-trees on the slope there, with the blue distance between their stems? But we must not make a business of landscape-gazing like our friend Charmides! We are men of affairs, you and I. Come, I will show you a thing. Shut your eyes for a minute and give me your hand. Now!"

A sudden breeze fanned my face, sweet and odorous, like the wind out of a wood. "Now," said Amroth, "we have arrived! Where do you think we are?"

The scene had changed in an instant. We were in a wide, level country, in green water-meadows, with a full stream brimming its grassy banks, in willowy loops. Not far away, on a gently rising ground, lay a long, straggling village, of gabled houses, among high trees. It was like the sort of village that you may find in the pleasant Wiltshire countryside, and the sight filled me with a rush of old and joyful memories.

"It is such a relief," I said, "to realise that if man is made in the image of God, heaven is made in the image of England!"

"That is only how you see it, child," said Amroth. "Some of my own happiest days were spent at Tooting: would you be surprised if I said that it reminded me of Tooting?"

"I am surprised at nothing," I said. "I only know that it is all very considerate!"

We entered the village, and found a large number of people, mostly young, going cheerfully about all sorts of simple work. Many of them were gardening, and the gardens were full of old-fashioned flowers, blooming in wonderful profusion. There was an air of settled peace about the place, the peace that on earth one often dreamed of finding, and indeed thought one had found on visiting some secluded place—only to discover, alas! on a nearer acquaintance, that life was as full of anxieties and cares there as elsewhere. There were one or two elderly people going about, giving directions or advice, or lending a helping hand. The workers nodded blithely to us, but did not suspend their work.

"What surprises me," I said to Amroth, "is to find everyone so much occupied wherever we go. One heard so much on earth about craving for rest, that one grew to fancy that the other life was all going to be a sort of solemn meditation, with an occasional hymn/'

"Yes, indeed," said Amroth, "it was the body that was tired—the soul is always fresh and strong—but rest is not idleness. There is no such thing as unemployment here, and there is hardly time, indeed, for all we have to do. Every one really loves work. The child plays at working, the man of leisure works at his play. The difference here is that work is always amusing—there is no such thing as drudgery here."

We walked all through the village, which stretched far away into the country. The whole place hummed like a beehive on a July morning. Many sang to themselves as they went about their business, and sometimes a couple of girls, meeting in the roadway, would entwine their arms and dance a few steps together, with a kiss at parting. There was a sense of high spirits everywhere. At one place we found a group of children sitting in the shade of some trees, while a woman of middle age told them a story. We stood awhile to listen, the woman giving us a pleasant nod as we approached. It was a story of some pleasant adventure, with nothing moral or sentimental about it, like an old folk-tale. The children were listening with unconcealed delight.

When we had walked a little further, Amroth said to me, "Come, I will give you three guesses. Who do you think, by the light of your psychology, are all these simple people?" I guessed in vain. "Well, I see I must tell you," he said. "Would it surprise you to learn that most of these people whom you see here passed upon earth for wicked and unsatisfactory characters? Yet it is true. Don't you know the kind of boys there were at school, who drifted into bad company and idle ways, mostly out of mere good-nature, went out into the world with a black mark against them, having been bullied in vain by virtuous masters, the despair of their parents, always losing their employments, and often coming what we used to call social croppers—untrustworthy, sensual, feckless, no one's enemy but their own, and yet preserving through it all a kind of simple good-nature, always ready to share things with others, never knowing how to take advantage of anyone, trusting the most untrustworthy people; or if they were girls, getting into trouble, losing their good name, perhaps living lives of shame in big cities—yet, for all that, guileless, affectionate, never excusing themselves, believing they had deserved anything that befell them?

"These were the sort of people to whom Christ was so closely drawn. They have no respectability, no conventions; they act upon instinct, never by reason, often foolishly, but seldom unkindly or selfishly. They give all they have, they never take. They have the faults of children, and the trustful affection of children. They will do anything for anyone who is kind to them and fond of them. Of course, they are what is called hopeless, and they use their poor bodies very ill. In their last stages on earth they are often very deplorable objects, slinking into public-houses, plodding raggedly and dismally along highroads, suffering cruelly and complaining little, conscious that they are universally reprobated, and not exactly knowing why.

"They are the victims of society; they do its dirty work, and are cast away as offscourings. They are really youthful and often beautiful spirits, very void of offence, and needing to be treated as children. They live here in great happiness, and are conscious vaguely of the good and great intention of God towards them. They suffer in the world at the hands of cruel, selfish, and stupid people, because they are both humble and disinterested. But in all our realms I do not think there is a place of simpler and sweeter happiness than this, because they do not take their forgiveness as a right, but as a gracious and unexpected boon. And indeed, the sights and sounds of this place are the best medicine for crabbed, worldly, conventional souls, who are often brought here when they are drawing near the truth."

"Yes," I said, "this is just what I wanted. Interesting as my work has lately been, it has wanted simplicity. I have grown to consider life too much as a series of cases, and to forget that it is life itself that one must seek, and not pathology. This is the best sight I have seen, for it is so far removed from all sense of judgment. The song of the saints may be sometimes of mercy too."

24

"And now," said Amroth, "that we have been refreshed by the sight of this guileless place, and as our time is running short, I am going to show you something very serious indeed. In fact, before I show it you I must remind you carefully of one thing which I shall beg you to keep in mind. There is nothing either cruel or hopeless here; all is implacably just and entirely merciful. Whatever a soul needs, that it receives; and it receives nothing that is vindictive or harsh. The ideas of punishment on earth are hopelessly confused; we do not know whether we are revenging ourselves for wrongs done to us, or safeguarding society, or deterring would-be offenders, or trying to amend and uplift the criminal. We end, as a rule, by making everyone concerned, whether punisher or punished, worse. We encourage each other in vindictiveness and hypocrisy, we cow and brutalise the transgressor. We rescue no one, we amend nothing. And yet we cannot read the clear signs of all this. The milder our methods of punishment become, the less crime is there to punish. But instead of being at once kind and severe, which is perfectly possible, we are both cruel and sentimental. Now, there is no such thing as sentiment here, just as there is no cruelty. There is emotion in full measure, and severity in full measure; no one is either pettishly frightened or mildly forgiven; and the joy that awaits us is all the more worth having, because it cannot be rashly enjoyed or reached by any short cuts; but do not forget, in what you now see, that the end is joy."

He spoke so solemnly that I was conscious of overmastering curiosity, not unmixed with awe. Again, the way was abbreviated. Amroth took me by the hand and bade me close my eyes. The breeze beat upon my face for a moment. When I opened my eyes, we were on a bare hillside, full of stones, in a kind of grey and chilly haze which filled the air. Just ahead of us were some rough enclosures of stone, overlooked by a sort of tower. They were like the big sheepfolds which I have seen on northern wolds, into which the sheep of a whole hillside can be driven for shelter. We went round the wall, which was high and strong, and came to the entrance of the tower, the door of which stood open.

There seemed to be no one about, no sign of life; the only sound a curious wailing note, which came at intervals from one of the enclosures, like the crying of a prisoned beast. We went up into the tower; the staircase ended in a bare room, with four apertures, one in each wall, each leading into a kind of balcony. Amroth led the way into one of the balconies, and pointed downwards. We were looking down into one of the enclosures which lay just at our feet, not very far below. The place was perfectly bare, and roughly flagged with stones. In the corner was a rough thatched shelter, in which was some straw. But what at once riveted my attention was the figure of a man, who half lay, half crouched upon the stones, his head in his hands, in an attitude of utter abandonment.

He was dressed in a rough, weather-worn sort of cloak, and his whole appearance suggested the basest neglect; his hands were muscular and knotted; his ragged grey hair streamed over the collar of his cloak. While we looked at him, he drew himself up into a sitting posture, and turned his face blankly upon the sky. It was, or had been, a noble face enough, deeply lined, and with a look of command upon it; but anything like the hopeless and utter misery of the drawn cheeks and staring eyes I had never conceived. I involuntarily drew back, feeling that it was almost wrong to look at anything so fallen and so wretched. But Amroth detained me.

"He is not aware of us," he said, "and I desire you to look at him."

Presently the man rose wearily to his feet, and began to pace up and down round the walls, with the mechanical movements of a caged animal, avoiding -the posts of the shelter without seeming to see them, and then cast himself down again upon the stones in a paroxysm of melancholy. He seemed to have no desire to escape, no energy, except to suffer. There was no hope about it all, no suggestion of prayer, nothing but blank and unadulterated suffering.

Amroth drew me back into the tower, and motioned me to the next balcony. Again, I went out. The sight that I saw was almost more terrible than the first, because the prisoner here, penned in a similar enclosure, was more restless, and seemed to suffer more acutely. This was a younger man, who walked swiftly and vaguely about, casting glances up at the wall which enclosed him. Sometimes he stopped, and seemed to be pursuing some dreadful train of solitary thought; he gesticulated, and even broke out into mutterings and cries—the cries that I had heard from without. I could not bear to look at this sight, and coming back, besought Amroth to lead me away.

Amroth, who was himself, I perceived, deeply moved, and stood with lips compressed, nodded in token of assent. We went quickly down the stairway, and took our way up the hill among the stones, in silence. The shapes of similar enclosures were to be seen everywhere, and the indescribable blankness and grimness of the scene struck a chill to my heart.

From the top of the ridge we could see the same bare valleys stretching in all directions, as far as the eye could see. The only other building in sight was a great circular tower of stone, far down in the valley, from which beat the pulse of some heavy machinery, which gave the sense, I do not know how, of a ghastly and watchful life at the centre of all.

"That is the Tower of Pain," said Amroth, "and I will spare you the inner sight of that. Only our very bravest and strongest can enter there and preserve any hope. But it is well for you to know it is there, and that souls have to enter it. It is thence that all the pain of countless worlds emanates and vibrates, and the governor of the place is the most tried and bravest of all the servants of God. Thither we must go, for you shall have sight of him, though you shall not enter."

We went down the hill with all the speed we might, and, I will confess it, with the darkest dismay I have ever experienced tugging at my heart. We were soon at the foot of the enormous structure. Amroth knocked at the gate, a low door, adorned with some vague and ghastly sculptures, things like worms and huddled forms drearily intertwined. The door opened, and revealed a fiery and smouldering light within. High up in the tower a great wheel whizzed and shivered, and moving shadows crossed and recrossed the firelit walls.

But the figure that came out to us—how shall I describe him? It was the most beautiful and gracious sight of all that I saw in my pilgrimage. He was a man of tall stature, with snow-white, silvery hair and beard, dressed in a dark cloak with a gleaming clasp of gold. But for all his age he had a look of immortal youth. His clear and piercing eye had a glance of infinite tenderness, such as I had never conceived. There were many lines upon his brow and round his eyes, but his complexion was as fresh as that of a child, and he stepped as briskly as a youth. We bowed low to him, and he reached out his hands, taking Amroth's hand and mine in each of his. His touch had a curious thrill, the hand that held mine being firm and smooth and wonderfully warm.

"Well, my children," he said in a clear, youthful voice, "I am glad to see you, because there are few who come hither willingly; and the old and weary are cheered by the sight of those that are young and strong. Amroth I know. But who are you, my child? You have not been among us long. Have you found your work and place here yet?"

I told him my story in a few words, and he smiled indulgently. "There is nothing like being at work," he said. "Even my business here, which seems sad enough to most people, must be done; and I do it very willingly. Do not be frightened, my child," he said to me sudden- ly, drawing me nearer to him, and folding my arm beneath his own. "It is only on earth that we are frightened of pain; it spoils our poor plans, it makes us fretful and miserable, it brings us into the shadow of death. But for all that, as Amroth knows, it is the best and most fruitful of all the works that the Father does for man, and the thing dearest to His heart. We cannot prosper till we suffer, and suffering leads us very swiftly into joy and peace. Indeed, this Tower of Pain, as it is called, is in fact nothing but the Tower of Love.

"Not until love is touched with pain does it become beautiful, and the joy that comes through pain is the only real thing in the world. Of course, when my great engine here sends a thrill into a careless life, it comes as a dark surprise; but then follow courage and patience and wonder, and all the dear tendance of Love. I have borne it all myself a hundred times, and I shall bear it again if the Father wills it. But when you leave me here, do not think of me as of one who works, grim and indifferent, wrecking lives and destroying homes. It is but the burning of the weeds of life; and it is as needful as the sunshine and the rain. Pain does not wander aimlessly, smiting down by mischance and by accident; it comes as the close and dear intention of the Father's heart, and is to a man as a trumpet-call from the land of life, not as a knell from the land of death. And now, dear children, you must leave me, for I have much to do. And I will give you," he added, turning to me, "a gift which shall be your comfort, and a token that you have been here, and seen the worst and the best that there is to see."

He drew from under his cloak a ring, a circlet of gold holding a red stone with a flaming heart, and put it on my finger. There pierced through me a pang intenser than any I had ever experienced, in which all the love and sorrow I had ever known seemed to be suddenly min- gled, and which left behind it a perfect and intense sense of joy.

"There, that is my gift," he said, "and you shall have an old man's loving blessing too, for it is that, after all, that I live for." He drew me to him and kissed me on the brow, and in a moment, he was gone.

We walked away in silence, and for my part with an elation of spirit which I could hardly control, a desire to love and suffer, and do and be all that the mind of man could conceive. But my heart was too full to speak.

"Come," said Amroth presently, "you are not as grateful as I had hoped—you are outgrowing me! Come down to my poor level for an instant, and beware of spiritual pride!" Then altering his tone he said, "Ah, yes, dear friend, I understand. There is nothing in the world like it, and you were most graciously and tenderly received—but the end is not yet."

"Amroth," I said, "I am like one intoxicated with joy. I feel that I could endure anything and never make question of anything again. How infinitely good he was to me—like a dear father!"

"Yes," said Amroth, "he is very like the Father"—and he smiled at me a mysterious smile.

"Amroth," I said, bewildered, "you cannot mean—?"

"No, I mean nothing," said Amroth, "but you have today looked very far into the truth, farther than is given to many so soon; but you are a child of fortune, and seem to please everyone. I declare that a little more would make me jealous."

Presently, catching sight of one of the enclosures hard by, I said to Amroth, "But there are some questions I must ask. What has just happened had put it mostly out of my head. Those poor suffering souls that we saw just now—it is well, with them, I am sure, so near the Master of the Tower—he does not forget them, I am sure—but who are they, and what have they done to suffer so?"

"I will tell you," said Amroth, "for it is a dark business. Those two that you have seen—well, you will know one of them by name and fame, and of the other you may have heard. The first, that old shaggy-haired man, who lay upon the stones, that was——"

He mentioned a name that was notorious in Europe at the time of my life on earth, though he was then long dead; a ruthless and ambitious conqueror, who poured a cataract of life away, in wars, for his own aggrandisement Then he mentioned another name, a statesman who pursued a policy of terrorism and oppression, enriched himself by barbarous cruelty exercised in colonial possessions, and was famous for the calculated libertinism of his private life.

"They were great sinners," said Amroth, "and the sorrows they made and flung so carelessly about them, beat back upon them now in a surge of pain. These men were strangely affected, each of them, by the smallest sight or sound of suffering—a tortured animal, a crying child; and yet they were utterly ruthless of the pain that they did not see. It was a lack, no doubt, of the imagination of which I spoke, and which makes all the difference. And now they have to contemplate the pain which they could not imagine; and they have to learn submission and humility. It is a terrible business in a way—the loneliness of it! There used to be an old saying that the strongest man was the man that was most alone. But it was just because these men practised loneliness on earth that they have to suffer so.

"They used others as counters in a game, they had neither friend nor beloved, except for their own pleasure. They depended upon no one, needed no one, desired no one. But there are many others here who did the same on a small scale—selfish fathers and mothers who made homes miserable; boys who were bullies at school and tyrants in the world, in offices, and places of authority. This is the place of discipline for all base selfishness and vile authority, for all who have oppressed and victimised mankind."

"But," I said, "here is my difficulty. I understand the case of the oppressors well enough; but about the oppressed, what is the justice of that? Is there not a fortuitous element there, an interruption of the Divine plan? Take the case of the thousands of lives wasted by some brutal conqueror. Are souls sent into the world for that, to be driven in gangs, made to fight, let us say, for some abominable cause, and then recklessly dismissed from life?"

"Ah," said Amroth, "you make too much of the dignity of life! You do not know how small a thing a single life is, not as regards the life of mankind, but in the life of one individual. Of course, if a man had but one single life on earth, it would be an intolerable injustice; and that is the factor which sets all straight, the factor which most of us, in our time of bodily self-importance, overlook. These oppressors have no power over other lives except what God allows, and bewildered humanity concedes. Not only is the great plan whole in the mind of God, but every single minutest life is considered as well.

"In the very case you spoke of, the little conscript, torn from his home to fight a tyrant's battles, hectored and ill-treated, and then shot down upon some crowded battlefield, that is precisely the discipline which at that point of time his soul needs, and the blessedness of which he afterwards perceives; sometimes discipline is swift and urgent, sometimes it is slow and lingering: but all experience is exactly apportioned to the quality of which each soul is in need. The only reason why there seems to be an element of chance in it, is that the whole thing is so inconceivably vast and prolonged; and our happiness and our progress alike depend upon our realising at every moment that the smallest joy and the most trifling pleasure, as well as the tiniest ailment or the most subtle sorrow, are just the pieces of experience which we are meant at that moment to use and make our own. No one, not even God, can force us to understand this; we have to perceive it for ourselves, and to live in the knowledge of it."

"Yes," I said, "it is true, all that. My heart tells me so; but it is very wonderful and mysterious, all the same. But, Amroth, I have seen and heard enough. My spirit desires with all its might to be at its own work, hastening on the mighty end. Now, I can hold no more of wonders. Let me return."

"Yes," said Amroth, "yon are right! These wonders are so familiar to me that I forget, perhaps, the shock with which they come to minds unused to them. Yet there are other things which you must assuredly see, when the time comes; but I must not let you bite off a larger piece than you can swallow."

He took me by the hand; the breeze passed through my hair; and in an instant we were back at the fortress-gate, and I entered the beloved shelter, with a grateful sense that I was returning home.

25

I returned, as I said, with a sense of serene pleasure and security to my work; but that serenity did not last long. What I had seen with Amroth, on that day of wandering, filled me with a strange restlessness, and a yearning for I knew not what. I plunged into my studies with determination rather than ardour, and I set myself to study what is the most difficult problem of all—the exact limits of individual responsibility. I had many conversations on the point with one of my teachers, a young man of very wide experience, who combined in an unusual way a close scientific knowledge of the subject with a peculiar emotional sympathy.

He told me once that it was the best outfit for the scientific study of these problems, when the heart anticipated the slower judgment of the mind, and set the mind a goal, so to speak, to work up to; though he warned me that the danger was that the mind was often reluctant to abandon the more indulgent claims of the heart; and he advised me to mistrust alike scientific conclusions and emotional inferences.

I had a very memorable conversation with him on the particular question of responsibility, which I will here give.

"The mistake," I said to him, "of human moralists seems to me to be, that they treat all men as more or less equal in the matter of moral responsibility. How often," I added, "have I heard a school preacher tell boys that they could not all be athletic or clever or popular, but that high principle and moral courage were things within the reach of all. Whereas the more that I studied human nature, the more did the power of surveying and judging one's own moral progress, and the power of enforcing and executing the dictates of the conscience, seem to me faculties, like other faculties. Indeed, it appears to me," I said, "that on the one hand there are people who have a power of moral discrimination, when dealing with the retrospect of their actions, but no power of obeying the claims of principle, when confronted with a situation involving moral strain; while on the other hand there seem to me to be some few men with a great and resolute power of will, capable of swift decision and firm action, but without any instinct for morality at all."

"Yes," he said, "you are quite right. The moral sense is in reality a high artistic sense. It is a power of discerning and being attracted by the beauty of moral action, just as the artist is attracted by form and colour, and the musician by delicate combinations of harmonies and the exquisite balance of sound. You know," he said, "what a suspension is in music—it is a chord which in itself is a discord, but which depends for its beauty on some impending resolution. It is just so with moral choice.

The imagination plays a great part in it. The man whose morality is high and profound sees instinctively the approaching contingency, and his act of self-denial or self-forgetfulness depends for its force upon the way in which it will ultimately combine with other issues involved, even though at the moment that act may seem to be unnecessary and even perverse."

"But," I said, "there are a good many people who attain to a sensible, well-balanced kind of temperance, after perhaps a few failures, from a purely prudential motive. What is the worth of that?"

"Very small indeed," said my teacher. "In fact, the prudential morality, based on motives of health and reputation and success, is a thing that has often to be deliberately unlearnt at a later stage. The strange catastrophes which one sees so often in human life, where a man by one act of rashness, or moral folly, upsets the tranquil tenor of his life—a desperate love affair, a passion of unreasonable anger, a piece of quixotic generosity—are often a symptom of a great effort of the soul to free itself from prudential considerations. A good thing done for a low motive has often a singularly degrading and deforming influence on the soul. One has to remember how terribly the heavenly values are obscured upon earth by the body, its needs and its desires; and current morality of a cautious and sensible kind is often worse than worthless, because it produces a kind of self-satisfaction, which is the hardest thing to overcome."

"But," I said, "in the lives of some of the greatest moralists, one so often sees, or at all events hears it said, that their morality is useless because it is unpractical, too much out of the reach of the ordinary man, too contemptuous of simple human faculties. What is one to make of that?"

"It is a difficult matter," he replied; "one does indeed, in the lives of great moralists, see sometimes that their work is vitiated by perverse and fantastic preferences, which they exalt out of all proportion to their real value. But for all that, it is better to be on the side of the saints; for they are gifted with the sort of instinctive appreciation of the beauty of high morality of which I spoke. Unselfishness, purity, peacefulness seem to them so beautiful and desirable that they are constrained to practise them. While controversy, bitterness, cruelty, meanness, vice, seem so utterly ugly and repulsive that they cannot for an instant entertain even so much as a thought of them."

"But if a man sees that he is wanting in this kind of perception," I said, "what can he do? How is he to learn to love what he does not admire and to abhor what he does not hate? It all seems so fatalistic, so irresistible."

"If he discerns his lack," said my teacher with a smile, "he is probably not so very far from the truth. The germ of the sense of moral beauty is there, and it only wants patience and endeavour to make it grow. But it cannot be all done in any single life, of course; that is where the human faith fails, in its limitations of a man's possibilities to a single life."

"But what is the reason," I said, "why the morality, the high austerity of some persons, who are indubitably high-minded and pure-hearted, is so utterly discouraging and even repellent?"

"Ah," he said, "there you touch on a great truth. The reason of that is that these have but a sterile sort of connoisseurship in virtue. Virtue cannot be attained in solitude, nor can it be made a matter of private enjoyment. The point is, of course, that it is not enough for a man to be himself; he must also give himself; and if a man is moral because of the delicate pleasure it brings him—and the artistic pleasure of asceticism is a very high one—he is apt to find himself here in very strange and distasteful company. In this, as in everything, the only safe motive is the motive of love.

"The man who takes pleasure in using influence, or setting a lofty example, is just as arid a dilettante as the musician who plays, or the artist who paints, for the sake of the applause and the admiration he wins; he is only regarding others as so many instruments for registering his own level of complacency. Everyone, even the least complicated of mankind, must know the exquisite pleasure that comes from doing the simplest and humblest service to one whom he loves; how such love converts the most menial office into a luxurious joy; and the higher that a man goes, the more does he discern in every single human being with whom he is brought into contact a soul whom he can love and serve. Of course, it is but an elementary pleasure to enjoy pleasing those whom we regard with some passion of affection, wife or child or friend, because, after all, one gains something oneself by that. But the purest morality of all discerns the infinitely lovable quality which is in the depth of every human soul, and lavishes its tenderness and its grace upon it, with a compassion that grows and increases, the more unthankful and clumsy and brutish is the soul which it sets out to serve."

"But," I said, "beautiful as that thought is—and I see and recognise its beauty—it does limit the individual responsibility very greatly. Surely a prudential morality, the morality which is just because it fears reprisal, and is kind because it anticipates kindness, is better than none at all? The morality of which you speak can only belong to the noblest human creatures."

"Only to the noblest," he said; "and I must repeat what I said before, that the prudential morality is useless, because it begins at the wrong end, and is set upon self throughout. I must say deliberately that the soul which loves unreasonably and unwisely, which even yields itself to the passion of others for the pleasure it gives rather than for the pleasure it receives—the thriftless, lavish, good-natured, affectionate people, who are said to make such a mess of their lives—are far higher in the scale of hope than the cautiously respectable, the prudently kind, the selfishly pure. There must be no mistake about this.

"One must somehow or other give one's heart away, and it is better to do it in error and disaster than to treasure it for oneself. Of course, there are many lives on earth—and an increasing number as the world develops—which are generous and noble and unselfish, without any sacrifice of purity or self-respect. But the essence of morality is giving, and not receiving, or even practising; the point is free choice, and not compulsion; and if one cannot give because one loves, one must give until one loves,"

<h2 style="text-align:center">26</h2>

But all my speculations were cut short by a strange event which happened about this time. One day, without any warning, the thought of Cynthia darted urgently and irresistibly into my mind. Her image came between me and all my tasks; I saw her in innumerable positions and guises, but always with her eyes bent on me in a pitiful entreaty. After endeavouring to resist the thought for a little as some kind of fantasy, I became suddenly convinced that she was in need of me, and in urgent need.

I asked for an interview with our Master, and told him the story; he heard me gravely, and then said that I might go in search of her; but I was not sure that he was wholly pleased, and he bent his eyes upon me with a very inquiring look. I hesitated whether or not to call Amroth to my aid, but decided that I had better not do so at first. The question was how to find her; the great crags lay between me and the land of delight; and when I hurried out of the college, the thought of the descent and its dangers fairly unmanned me. I knew, however, of no other way. But what was my surprise when, on arriving at the top, not far from the point where Amroth had greeted me after the ascent, I saw a little steep path, which wound itself down into the gulleys and chimneys of the black rocks.

I took it without hesitation, and though again and again it seemed to come to an end in front of me, I found that it could be traced and followed without serious difficulty. The descent was accomplished with a singular rapidity, and I marvelled to find myself at the crag-base in so brief a time, considering the intolerable tedium of the ascent. I rapidly crossed the intervening valley, and was very soon at the gate of the careless land. To my intense joy, and not at all to my surprise, I found Cynthia at the gate itself, waiting for me with a look of expectancy. She came forwards, and threw herself passionately into my arms, murmuring words of delight and welcome, like a child.

"I knew you would come," she said. "I am frightened—all sorts of dreadful things have happened. I have found out where I am—and I seem to have lost all my friends. Charmides is gone, and Lucius is cruel to me—he tells me that I have lost my spirits and my good looks, and am tiresome company."

I looked at her—she was paler and frailer-looking than when I left her; and she was habited very differently, in simpler and graver dress. But she was to my eyes infinitely more beautiful and dearer, and I told her so. She smiled at that, but half tearfully; and we seated ourselves on a bench hard by, looking over the garden, which was strangely and luxuriantly beautiful.

"You must take me away with you at once," she said. "I cannot live here without you. I thought at first, when you went, that it was rather a relief not to have your grave face at my shoulder,"—here she took my face in her hands—"always reminding me of something I did not want, and ought to have wanted—but oh, how I began to miss you! and then I got so tired of this silly, lazy place, and all the music and jokes and compliments. But I am a worthless creature, and not good for anything. I cannot work, and I hate being idle. Take me anywhere, make me do something, beat me if you like, only force me to be different from what I am."

"Very well," I said. "I will give you a good beating presently, of course, but just let me consider what will hurt you most, silly child!"

"That is it," she said. "I want to be hurt and bruised, and shaken as my nurse used to shake me, when I was a naughty child. Oh dear, oh dear, how wretched I am!" and poor Cynthia laid her head on my shoulder and burst into tears.

"Come, come," I said, "you must not do that—I want my wits about me; but if you cry, you will simply make a fool of me—and this is no time for love-making."

"Then you do really care," said Cynthia in a quieter tone. "That is all I want to know! I want to be with you, and see you every hour and every minute. I can't help saying it, though it is really very undignified for me to be making love to you. I did many silly things on earth, but never anything quite so feeble as that!"

I felt myself fairly bewildered by the situation. My psychology did not seem to help me; and here at least was something to love and rescue. I will say frankly that, in my stupidity and superiority, I did not really think of loving Cynthia in the way in which she needed to be loved. She was to me, with all my grave concerns and problems, as a charming and intelligent child, with whom I could not even speak of half the thoughts which absorbed me. So, I just held her in my arms, and comforted her as best I could; but what to do and where to bestow her I could not tell. I saw that her time to leave the place

111

of desire had come, but what she could turn to I could not conceive.

Suddenly I looked up, and saw Lucius approaching, evidently in a very angry mood.

"So, this is the end of all our amusement?" he said, as he came near. "You bring Cynthia here in your tiresome, condescending way, you live among us like an almighty prig, smiling gravely at our fun, and then you go off when it is convenient to yourself; and then, when you want a little recreation, you come and sit here in a corner and hug your darling, when you have never given her a thought of late. You know that is true," he added menacingly.

"Yes," I said, "it is true! I went of my own will, and I have come back of my own will; and you have all been out of my thoughts, because I have had much work to do. But what of that? Cynthia wants me and I have come back to her, and I will do whatever she desires. It is no good threatening me, Lucius—there is nothing you can do or say that will have the smallest effect on me."

"We will see about that," said Lucius. "None of your airs here! We are peaceful enough when we are respectfully and fairly treated, but we have our own laws, and no one shall break them with impunity. We will have no half-hearted fools here. If you come among us with your damned missionary airs, you shall have what I expect you call the crown of martyrdom."

He whistled loud and shrill. Half-a-dozen men sprang from the bushes and flung themselves upon me. I struggled, but was overpowered, and dragged away. The last sight I had was of Lucius standing with a disdainful smile, with Cynthia clinging to his arm; and to my horror and disgust she was smiling too.

27

I had somehow never expected to be used with positive violence in the world of spirits, and least of all in that lazy and good-natured place. Considering, too, the errand on which I had come, not for my own convenience but for the sake of another, my treatment seemed to me very hard. What was still more humiliating was the fact that my spirit seemed just as powerless in the hands of these ruffians as my body would have been on earth. I was pushed, hustled, insulted, hurt. I could have summoned Amroth to my aid, but I felt too proud for that; yet the thought of the crag-men, and the possibility of the second death, did visit my mind with dismal iteration.

I did not at all desire a further death; I felt very much alive, and full of interest and energy. Worst of all was my sense that Cynthia had gone over to the enemy. I had been so loftily kind with her, that I much resented having appeared in her sight as feeble and ridiculous. It is difficult to preserve any dignity of demeanour or thought, with a man's hand at one's neck and his knee in one's back: and I felt that Lucius had displayed a really Satanical malignity in using this particular means of degrading me in Cynthia's sight, and of regaining his own lost influence.

I was thrust and driven before my captors along an alley in the garden, and what added to my discomfiture was that a good many people ran together to see us pass, and watched me with decided amusement. I was taken finally to a little pavilion of stone, with heavily barred windows, and a flagged marble floor. The room was absolutely bare, and contained neither seat nor table. Into this I was thrust, with some obscene jesting, and the door was locked upon me.

The time passed very heavily. At intervals I heard music burst out among the alleys, and a good many people came to peep in upon me with an amused curiosity. I was entirely bewildered by my position, and did not see what I could have done to have incurred my punishment. But in the solitary hours that followed I began to have a suspicion of my fault. I had found myself hitherto the object of so much attention and praise, that I had developed a strong sense of complacency and self-satisfaction. I had an uncomfortable suspicion that there was even more behind, but I could not, by interrogating my mind and searching out my spirits, make out clearly what it was; yet I felt I was having a sharp lesson; and this made me resolve that I would ask for no kind of assistance from Amroth or any other power, but that I would try to meet whatever fell upon me with patience, and extract the full savour of my experience.

I do not know how long I spent in the dismal cell. I was in some discomfort from the handling I had received, and in still greater dejection of mind. Suddenly I heard footsteps approaching. Three of my captors appeared, and told me roughly to go with them. So, a pitiable figure, I limped along between two of them, the third following behind, and was conducted through the central *piazza* of the place, between two lines of people who gave way to the most undisguised merriment, and even shouted opprobrious remarks at me, calling me spy and traitor and other unpleasant names. I could not have believed that these kind-mannered and courteous persons could have exhibited, all of a sudden, such frank brutality, and I saw many of my own acquaintance among them, who regarded me with obvious derision.

I was taken into a big hall, in which I had often sat to hear a concert of music. On the dais at the upper end were seated a number of dignified persons, in a semicircle, with a very handsome and stately old man in the centre on a chair of state, whose face was new to me. Before this Court I was formally arraigned; I had to stand alone in the middle of the floor, in an open space. Two of my captors stood on each side of me; while the rest of the court was densely packed with people, who greeted me with obvious hostility.

When silence was procured, the President said to me, with a show of great courtesy, that he could not disguise from himself that the charge against me was a serious one; but that justice would be done to me, fully and carefully. I should have ample opportunity to excuse myself. He then called upon one of those who sat with him to state the case briefly, and call witnesses; and after that he promised I might speak for myself.

A man rose from one of the seats, and, pleading somewhat rhetorically, said that the object of the great community, to which so many were proud to belong, was to secure to all the utmost amount of innocent enjoyment, and the most entire peace of mind; that no pressure was put upon any one who decided to stay there, and to observe the quiet customs of the place; but that it was always considered a heinous and ill-disposed thing to attempt to unsettle any one's convictions, or to attempt, by using undue influence, to bring about the migration of any citizen to conditions of which little was known, but which there was reason to believe were distinctly undesirable.

"We are, above all," he said, "a religious community; our rites and our ceremonies are privileges open to all; we compel no one to attend them; all that we insist is that no one, by restless innovation or cynical contempt, should attempt to disturb the emotions of serene contemplation, distinguished courtesy, and artistic feeling, for which our society has been so long and justly celebrated."

This was received with loud applause, indulgently checked by the President. Some witnesses were then called, who testified to the indifference and restlessness which I had on many occasions manifested. It was brought up against me that I had provoked a much-respected member of the community, Charmides, to utter some very treasonous and unpleasant language, and that it was believed that the rash and unhappy step, which he had lately taken, of leaving the place, had been entirely or mainly the result of my discontented and ill-advised suggestion.

Then Lucius himself, wearing an air of extreme gravity and even despondency, was called, and a murmur of sympathy ran through the audience. Lucius, apparently struggling with deep emotion, said that he bore me no actual ill-will; that on my first arrival he had done his best to welcome me and make me feel at home; that it was probably known to all that I had been accompanied by an accomplished and justly popular lady, whom I had openly treated with scanty civility and undisguised contempt. That he had himself, under the laws of the place, contracted a close alliance with my unhappy *protégée*, and that their union had been duly accredited; but that I had lost no opportunity of attempting to undermine his happiness, and to maintain an unwholesome influence over her. That I had at last left the place myself, with a most uncivil abruptness; during the interval of absence my occupations were believed to have been of the most dubious character: it was more than suspected, indeed, that I had penetrated to places, the very name of which could hardly be mentioned without shame and consternation.

That my associates had been persons of the vilest character and the most brutal antecedents; and at last, feeling in need of distraction, I had again returned with the deliberate intention of seducing his unhappy partner into accompanying me to one or other of the abandoned places I had visited. He added that Cynthia had been so much overcome by her emotion, and her natural compassion for an old acquaintance, that he had persuaded her not to subject herself to the painful strain of an appearance in public; but that for this action he threw himself upon the mercy of the Court, who would know that it was only dictated by chivalrous motives.

At this there was subdued applause, and Lucius, after adding a few broken words to the effect that he lived only for the maintenance of order, peace, and happiness, and that he was devoted heart and soul to the best interests of the community, completely broke down, and was assisted from his place by friends.

The whole thing was so malignant and ingenious a travesty of what had happened, that I was entirely at a loss to know what to say. The President, however, courteously intimated that though the case appeared to present a good many very unsatisfactory features, yet I was entirely at liberty to justify myself if I could, and, if not, to make submission; and added that I should be dealt with as leniently as possible.

I summoned up my courage as well as I might. I began by saying

115

that I claimed no more than the liberty of thought and action which I knew the Court desired to concede. I said that my arrival at the place was mysterious even to myself, and that I had simply acted under orders in accompanying Cynthia, and in seeing that she was securely bestowed. I said that I had never incited any rebellion, or any disobedience to laws of the scope of which I had never been informed. That I had indeed frankly discussed matters of general interest with any citizen who seemed to desire it; that I had been always treated with marked consideration and courtesy; and that, as far as I was aware, I had always followed the same policy myself. I said that I was sincerely attached to Cynthia, but added that, with all due respect, I could no longer consider myself a member of the community.

I had transferred myself elsewhere under direct orders, with my own entire concurrence, and that I had since acted in accordance with the customs and regulations of the community to which I had been allotted. I went on to say that I had returned under the impression that my presence was desired by Cynthia, and that I must protest with all my power against the treatment I had received. I had been arrested and imprisoned with much violence and contumely, without having had any opportunity of hearing what my offence was supposed to have been, or having had any semblance of a trial, and that I could not consider that my usage had been consistent with the theory of courtesy, order, or justice so eloquently described by the President.

This onslaught of mine produced an obvious revulsion in my favour. The President conferred hastily with his colleagues, and then said that my arrest had indeed been made upon the information of Lucius, and with the cognisance of the Court; but that he sincerely regretted that I had any complaint of unhandsome usage to make, and that the matter would be certainly inquired into. He then added that he understood from my words that I desired to make a complete submission, and that in that case I should be acquitted of any evil intentions. My fault appeared to be that I had yielded too easily to the promptings of an ill-balanced and speculative disposition, and that if I would undertake to disturb no longer the peace of the place, and to desist from all further tampering with the domestic happiness of a much-respected pair, I should be discharged with a caution, and indeed be admitted again to the privileges of orderly residence.

"And I will undertake to say," he added, "that the kindness and courtesy of our community will overlook your fault, and make no further reference to a course of conduct which appears to have been misguided rather than deliberately malevolent. We have every desire not to disturb in way the tranquillity which it is, above all things, our desire to maintain. May I conclude, then, that this is your intention?"

"No, sir," I said, "certainly not! With all due respect to the Court, I cannot submit to the jurisdiction. The only privilege I claim is the privilege of an alien and a stranger, who in a perfectly peaceful manner, and with no seditious intent, has re-entered this land, and has thereupon been treated with gross and unjust violence. I do not for a moment contest the right of this community to make its own laws and regulations, but I do contest its right to fetter the thought and the liberty of speech of all who enter it. I make no submission. The Lady Cynthia came here under my protection, and if any undue influence has been used, it has been used by Lucius, whom I treated with a confidence he has abused. And I here appeal to a higher power and a higher court, which may indeed permit this unhappy community to make its own regulations, but will not permit any gross violation of elementary justice."

I was carried away by great indignation in the course of my words, which had a very startling effect. A large number of the audience left the hall in haste. The judge grew white to the lips, whether with anger or fear I did not know, said a few words to his neighbour, and then with a great effort to control himself, said to me:

"You put us, sir, by your words, in a very painful position. You do not know the conditions under which we live—that is evident—and intemperate language like yours has before now provoked an invasion of our peace of a most undesirable kind. I entreat you to calm yourself, to accept the apologies of the Court for the incidental and indeed unjustifiable violence with which you were treated. If you will only return to your own community, the nature of which I will not now stay to inquire, you may be assured that you will be conducted to our gates with the utmost honour. Will you pledge yourself as a gentleman, and, as I believe I am right in saying, as a Christian, to do this?"

"Yes," I said, "upon one condition: that I may have an interview with the Lady Cynthia, and that she may be free to accompany me, if she wishes."

The President was about to reply, when a sudden and unlooked-for interruption occurred. A man in a pearly-grey dress, with a cloak clasped with gold, came in at the end of the hall, and advanced with rapid steps and a curiously unconcerned air up the hall. The judges rose in their places with a hurried and disconcerted look. The stranger came up to me, tapped me on the shoulder, and bade me presently follow him. Then he turned to the President, and said in a clear, peremptory voice:

"Dissolve the Court! Your powers have been grossly and insolently exceeded. See that nothing of this sort occurs again!" and then, ascending the dais, he struck the President with his open hand hard upon the cheek.

The President gave a stifled cry and staggered in his place, and then, covering his face with his hands, went out at a door on the platform, followed by the rest of the Council in haste. Then the man came down again, and motioned me to follow him. I was not prepared for what happened. Outside in the square was a great, pale, silent crowd, in the most obvious and dreadful excitement and consternation. We went rapidly, in absolute stillness, through two lines of people, who watched us with an emotion I could not quite interpret, but it was something very like hatred.

"Follow me quickly," said my guide; "do not look round!" and, as we went, I heard the crowd closing up in a menacing way behind us. But we walked straight forward, neither slowly nor hurriedly but at a deliberate pace, to the gateway which opened on the cliffs. At this point I saw a confusion in the crowd, as though some one were being kept back, and in the forefront of the throng, gesticulating and arguing, was Lucius himself, with his back to us. Just as we reached the gate I heard a cry; and from the crowd there ran Cynthia, with her hair unbound, in terror and faintness.

Our guide opened the gate, and motioned us swiftly through, turning round to face the crowd, which now ran in upon us. I saw him wave his arm; and then he came quickly through the gate and closed it. He looked at us with a smile. "Don't be afraid," he said; "that was a dangerous business. But they cannot touch us here." As he said the word, there burst from the gardens behind us a storm of the most hideous and horrible cries I had ever heard, like the howling of wild beasts. Cynthia clung to me in terror, and nearly swooned in my arms. "Never mind," said the guide; "they are disappointed, and no wonder. It was a near thing; but, poor creatures, they have no initiative; their life is not a fortifying one; and besides, they will have forgotten all about it tomorrow. But we had better not stop here. There is no use in facing disagreeable things, unless one is obliged," And he led the way down the valley.

When we had got a little farther off, our guide told us to sit down and rest. Cynthia was still very much frightened, speechless with excitement and agitation, and, like all impulsive people, regretting her decision. I saw that it was useless to say anything to her at present. She sat wearily enough, her eyes closed, and her hands clasped. Our guide looked at me with a half-smile, and said:

"That was rather an unpleasant business! It is astonishing how excited those placid and polite people can get if they think their privileges are being threatened. But really that Court was rather too much. They have tried it before with some success, and it is a clever trick. But they have had a lesson today, and it will not need to be repeated for a while."

"You arrived just at the right moment," I said, "and I really cannot express how grateful I am to you for your help."

"Oh," he said, "you were quite safe. It was just that touch of temper that saved you; but I was hard by all the time, to see that things did not go too far."

"May I ask," I said, "exactly what they could have done to me, and what their real power is?"

"They have none at all," he said. "They could not really have done anything to you, except imprison you. What helps them is not their own power, which is nothing, but the terror of their victims. If you had not been frightened when you were first attacked, they could not have overpowered you. It is all a kind of playacting, which they perform with remarkable skill. The Court was really an admirable piece of drama—they have a great gift for representation."

"Do you mean to say," I said, "that they were actually aware that they had no sort of power to inflict any injury upon me?"

"They could have made it very disagreeable for you," he said, "if they had frightened you, and kept you frightened. As long as that lasted, you would have been extremely uncomfortable. But as you saw, the moment you defied them they were helpless. The part played by Lucius was really unpardonable. I am afraid he is a great rascal."

Cynthia faintly demurred to this. "Never mind," said the guide soothingly, "he has only shown you his good side, of course; and I don't deny that he is a very clever and attractive fellow. But he makes no progress, and I am really afraid that he will have to be transferred elsewhere; though there is indeed one hope for him."

"Tell me what that is," said Cynthia faintly.

"I don't think I need do that," said our friend, "you know better than I; and some day, I think, when you are stronger, you will find the way to release him."

"Ah, you don't know him as I do," said Cynthia, and relapsed into silence; but did not withdraw her hand from mine.

"Well," said our guide after a moment's pause, "I think I have done all I can for the time being, and I am wanted elsewhere."

"But will you not advise me what to do next?" I said. "I do not see my way clear."

"No," said the guide rather drily, "I am afraid I cannot do that. That lies outside my province. These delicate questions are not in my line. I will tell you plainly what I am. I am just a messenger, perhaps more like a policeman," he added, smiling, "than anything else. I just go and appear when I am wanted, if there is a row or a chance of one. Don't misunderstand me!" he said more kindly. "It is not from any lack of interest in you or our friend here. I should very much like to know what step you will take, but it is simply not my business: our duties here are very clearly defined, and I can just do my job, and nothing more."

He made a courteous salute, and walked off without looking back, leaving on me the impression of a young military officer, perfectly courteous and reliable, not inclined to cultivate his emotions or to waste words, but absolutely effective, courageous, and dutiful.

"Well," I said to Cynthia with a show of cheerfulness, "what shall we do next? Are you feeling strong enough to go on?"

"I am sure I don't know," said Cynthia wearily. "Don't ask me. I have had a great fright, and I begin to wish I had stayed behind. How uncomfortable everything is! Why can one never have a moment's peace? There," she said to me, "don't be vexed, I am not blaming you; but I hated you for not showing more fight when those men set on you, and I hated Lucius for having done it; you must forgive me! I am sure you only did what was kind and right—but I have had a very trying time, and I don't like these bothers. Let me alone for a little, and I daresay I shall be more sensible."

I sat by her in much perplexity, feeling singularly helpless and ineffective; and in a moment of weakness, not knowing what to do, I wished that Amroth were near me, to advise me; and to my relief saw him approaching, but also realised in a flash that I had acted wrongly, and that he was angry, as I had never seen him before.

He came up to us, and bending down to Cynthia with great tenderness, took her hand, and said, "Will you stay here quietly a little, Cynthia, and rest? You are perfectly safe now, and no one will come near you. We two shall be close at hand; but we must have a talk together, and see what can be done."

Cynthia smiled and released me. Amroth beckoned me to withdraw with him. When we had got out of earshot, he turned upon me very fiercely, and said, "You have made a great mess of this business."

"I know it," I said feebly, "but I cannot for the life of me see where I was wrong."

"You were wrong from beginning to end," he said. "Cannot you see that, whatever this place is, it is not a sentimental place? It is all this wretched sentiment that has done the mischief. Come," he added, "I have an unpleasant task before me, to unmask you to yourself. I don't like it, but I must do it. Don't make it harder for me."

"Very good," I said, rather angrily too. "But allow me to say this first. This is a place of muddle. One is worked too hard, and shown too many things, till one is hopelessly confused. But I had rather have your criticism first, and then I will make mine."

"Very well!" said Amroth facing me, looking at me fixedly with his blue eyes, and his nostrils a little distended. "The mischief lies in your temperament. You are precocious, and you are volatile. You have had special opportunities, and in a way, you have used them well, but your head has been somewhat turned by your successes. You came to that place yonder, with Cynthia, with a sense of superiority. You thought yourself too good for it, and instead of just trying to see into the minds and hearts of the people you met, you despised them; instead of learning, you tried to teach. You took a feeble interest in Cynthia, made a pet of her; then, when I took you away, you forgot all about her. Even the great things I was allowed to show you did not make you humble. You took them as a compliment to your powers. And so, when you had your chance to go back to help Cynthia, you thought out no plan, you asked no advice. You went down in a very self-sufficient mood, expecting that everything would be easy."

"That is not true," I said. "I was very much perplexed."

"It is only too true," said Amroth; "you enjoyed your perplexity; I daresay you called it faith to yourself! It was that which made you weak. You lost your temper with Lucius, you made a miserable fight of it—and even in prison you could not recognise that you were in fault. You did better at the trial—I fully admit that you behaved well there—but the fault is in this, that this girl gave you her heart and her confidence, and you despised them. Your mind was taken up with other things; a very little more, and you would be fit for the intellectual paradise. There," he said, "I have nearly done! You may be angry if you will, but that is the truth. You have a wrong idea of this place. It is not plain sailing here. Life here is a very serious, very intricate, very difficult business. The only complications which are removed are the complications of the body; but one has anxious and trying responsibilities all the same, and you have trifled with them.

"You must not delude yourself. You have many good qualities. You have some courage, much ingenuity, keen interests, and a good deal of conscientiousness; but you have the makings of a dilettante, the readiness to delude yourself that the particular little work you are engaged in is excessively and peculiarly important. You have got the proportion all wrong."

I had a feeling of intense anger and bitterness at all this; but as he spoke, the scales seemed to fall from my eyes, and I saw that Amroth was right. I wrestled with myself in silence.

Presently I said, "Amroth, I believe you are right, though I think at this moment that you have stated all this rather harshly. But I do see that it can be no pleasure to you to state it, though I fear I shall never regain my pleasure in your company."

"There," said Amroth, "that is sentiment again!"

This put me into a great passion.

"Very well," I said, "I will say no more. Perhaps you will just be good enough to tell me what I am to do with Cynthia, and where I am to go, and then I will trouble you no longer."

"Oh," said Amroth with a sneer, "I have no doubt you can find some very nice semi-detached villas hereabouts. Why not settle down, and make the poor girl a little more worthy of yourself?"

At this I turned from him in great anger, and left him standing where he was. If ever I hated anyone, I hated Amroth at that moment. I went back to Cynthia.

"I have come back to you, dear," I said. "Can you trust me and go with me? No one here seems inclined to help us, and we must just help each other."

At which Cynthia rose and flung herself into my arms.

"That was what I wanted all along," she said, "to feel that I could be of use too. You will see how brave I can be. I can go anywhere with you and do anything, because I think I have loved you all the time."

"And you must forgive me, Cynthia," I said, "as well. For I did not know till this moment that I loved you, but I know it now; and I shall love you to the end."

As I said these words I turned, and saw Amroth smiling from afar;

then with a wave of the hand to us, he turned and passed out of our sight

28

Left to ourselves, Cynthia and I sat awhile in silence, hand in hand, like children, she looking anxiously at me. Our talk had broken down all possible reserve between us; but what was strange to me was that I felt, not like a lover with any need to woo, but as though we two had long since been wedded, and had just come to a knowledge of each other's hearts. At last we rose; and strange and bewildering as it all was, I think I was perhaps happier at this time than at any other time in the land of light, before or after.

And let me here say a word about these strange unions of soul that take place in that other land. There is there a whole range of affections, from courteous tolerance to intense passion. But there is a peculiar bond which springs up between pairs of people, not always of different sex, in that country. My relation with Amroth had nothing of that emotion about it. That was simply like a transcendental essence of perfect friendship; but there was a peculiar relation, between pairs of souls, which seems to imply some curious duality of nature, of which earthly passion is but a symbol. It is accompanied by an absolute clearness of vision into the inmost soul and being of the other.

Cynthia's mind was as clear to me in those days as a crystal globe might be which one could hold in one's hand, and my mind was as clear to her. There is a sense accompanying it almost of identity, as if the other nature was the exact and perfect complement of one's own; I can explain this best by an image. Think of a sphere, let us say, of alabaster, broken into two pieces by a blow, and one piece put away or mislaid. The first piece, let us suppose, stands in its accustomed place, and the owner often thinks in a trivial way of having it restored. One day, turning over some lumber, he finds the other piece, and wonders if it is not the lost fragment. He takes it with him, and sees on applying it that the fractures correspond exactly, and that joined together the pieces complete the sphere.

Even so did Cynthia's soul fit into mine. But I grew to understand later the words of the Gospel—"*they neither marry nor are given in marriage.*" These unions are not permanent, any more than they are really permanent on earth. On earth, owing to material considerations such as children and property, a marriage is looked upon as indissoluble. But this takes no account of the development of souls; and indeed, many of the unions of earth, the passion once over, do grow into a very noble and beautiful friendship. But sometimes, even on earth, it is the other way; and passion once extinct, two natures often realise their dissimilarities rather than their similarities; and this is the cause of much unhappiness.

But in the other land, two souls may develop in quite different ways and at a different pace. And then this relation may also come quietly and simply to an end, without the least resentment or regret, and is succeeded invariably by a very tender and true friendship, each being sweetly and serenely content with all that has been given or received; and this friendship is not shaken or fretted, even if both of the lovers form new ties of close intimacy. Some natures form many of these ties, some few, some none at all. I believe that, as a matter of fact, each nature has its counterpart at all times, but does not always succeed in finding it. But the union, when it comes, seems to take precedence of all other emotions and all other work. I did not know this at the time; but I had a sense that my work was for a time over, because it seemed quite plain to me that as yet Cynthia was not in the least degree suited to the sort of work which I had been doing.

We walked on together for some time, in a happy silence, though quiet communications of a blessed sort passed perpetually between us without any interchange of word. Our feet moved along the hillside, away from the crags, because I felt that Cynthia had no strength to climb them; and I wondered what our life would be.

Presently a valley opened before us, folding quietly in among the hills, full of a golden haze; and it seemed to me that our further way lay down it. It fell softly and securely into a further plain, the country being quite unlike anything I had as yet seen—a land of high and craggy mountains, the lower parts of them much overgrown with woods; the valley itself widened out, and passed gently among the hills, with here and there a lake. Dotted all about the mountain-bases, at the edges of the woods, were little white houses, stone-walled and stone-tiled, with small gardens; and then the place seemed to become strangely familiar and homelike; and I became aware that I was coming home: the same thought occurred to Cynthia; and at last, when we turned a corner of the road, and saw lying a little back from the road a small house, with a garden in front of it, shaded by a group of sycamores, we darted forwards with a cry of delight to the home that was indeed our own. The door stood open as though we were certainly expected. It was the simplest little place, just a pair of rooms very roughly and plainly furnished. And there we embraced with tears of joy.

29

The time that I spent in the valley home with Cynthia is the most difficult to describe of all my wanderings; because, indeed, there is nothing to describe. We were always together. Sometimes we wandered high up among the woods, and came out on the bleak mountain-heads. Sometimes we sat within and talked; and by a curious provision there were phenomena there that were more like changes of weather, and interchange of day and night, than at any other place in the heavenly country. Sometimes the whole valley would be shrouded with mists, sometimes it would be grey and overcast, sometimes the light was clear and radiant, but through it all there beat a pulse of light and darkness; and I do not know which was the more desirable—the hours when we walked in the forests, with the wind moving softly in the leaves overhead like a falling sea, or those calm and silent nights when we seemed to sleep and dream, or when, if I waked, I could hear Cynthia's breath coming and going evenly as the breath of a tired child. It seemed like the essence of human passion, the end that lovers desire, and discern faintly behind and beyond the accidents of sense and contact, like the sounding of a sweet chord, without satiety or fever of the sense.

I learnt many strange and beautiful secrets of the human heart in those days: what the dreams of womanhood are—how wholly different from the dreams of man, in which there is always a combative element. The soul of Cynthia was like a silent cleft among the hills, which waits, in its own still content, until the horn of the shepherd winds the notes of a chord in the valley below; and then the cleft makes answer and returns an airy echo, blending the notes into a harmony of dulcet utterance. And she too, I doubt not, learnt something from my soul, which was eager and inventive enough, but restless and fugitive of purpose. And then there came a further joy to us. That which is fatherly and motherly in the world below is not a thing that is lost in heaven; and just as the love of man and woman can draw down and imprison a soul in a body of flesh, so in heaven the dear intention of one soul to another brings about a yearning, which grows day by day in intensity, for some further outlet of love and care.

It was one quiet misty morning that, as we sat together in tranquil talk, we heard faltering steps within our garden. We had seen, let me say, very little of the other inhabitants of our valley. We had sometimes

125

seen a pair of figures wandering at a distance, and we had even met neighbours and exchanged a greeting. But the valley had no social life of its own, and no one ever seemed, so far as we knew, to enter any other dwelling, though they met in quiet friendliness. Cynthia went to the door and opened it; then she darted out, and, just when I was about to follow, she returned, leading by the hand a tiny child, who looked at us with an air, of perfect contentment and simplicity.

"Where on earth has this enchanting baby sprung from?" said Cynthia, seating the child upon her lap, and beginning to talk to it in a strangely unintelligible language, which the child appeared to understand perfectly,

I laughed. "Out of our two hearts, perhaps," I said. At which Cynthia blushed, and said that I did not understand or care for children. She added that men's only idea about children was to think how much they could teach them.

"Yes," I said, "we will begin lessons tomorrow, and go on to the Latin Grammar very shortly."

At which Cynthia folded the child in her arms, to defend it, and reassured it in a sentence which is far too silly to set down here.

I think that sometimes on earth the arrival of a first child is a very trying time for a wedded pair. The husband is apt to find his wife's love almost withdrawn from him, and to see her nourishing all kinds of jealousies and vague ambitions for her child. Paternity is apt to be a very bewildered and often rather dramatic emotion. But it was not so with us. The child seemed the very thing we had been needing without knowing it. It was a constant source of interest and delight; and in spite of Cynthia's attempts to keep it ignorant and even fatuous, it did develop a very charming intelligence, or rather, as I soon saw, began to perceive what it already knew. It soon overwhelmed us with questions, and used to patter about the garden with me, airing all sorts of delicious and absurd fancies. But, for all that, it did seem to make an end of the first utter closeness of our love.

Cynthia after this seldom went far afield, and I ranged the hills and woods alone; but it was all absurdly and continuously happy, though I began to wonder how long it could last, and whether my faculties and energies, such as they were, could continue thus unused. And I had, too, in my mind that other scene which I had beheld, of how the boy was withdrawn from the two old people in the other valley. Was it always thus, I wondered? Was it so, that souls were drawn upwards in ceaseless pilgrimage, loving and passing on, and leaving in the hearts of

those who stayed behind a longing unassuaged, which was presently
to draw them onwards from the peace which they loved perhaps too
well?

30

The serene life came all to an end very suddenly, and with no
warning. One day I had been sitting with Cynthia, and the child was
playing on the floor with some little things—stones, bits of sticks,
nuts—which it had collected. It was a mysterious game too, accompanied with much impressive talk and gesticulations, much emphatic
lecturing of recalcitrant pebbles, with interludes of unaccountable
laughter. We had been watching the child, when Cynthia leaned across
to me and said:

"There is something in your mind, dear, which I cannot quite see
into. It has been there for a long time, and I have not liked to ask you
about it. Won't you tell me what it is?"

"Yes, of course," I said; "I will tell you anything I can."

"It has nothing to do with me," said Cynthia, "nor with the child;
it is about yourself, I think; and it is not altogether a happy thought."

"It is not unhappy," I said, "because I am very happy and very well-
content. It is just this, I think. You know, don't you, how I was being
employed, before I came back, God be praised, to find you? I was being trained, very carefully and elaborately trained, I won't say to help
people, but to be of use in a way. Well, I have been wondering why all
that was suspended and cut short, just when I seemed to be finishing
my training. I have been much happier here than I ever was before, of
course. Indeed, I have been so happy that I have sometimes thought
it almost wrong that any one should have so much to enjoy. But I am
puzzled, because the other work seems thrown away. If you wonder
whether I want to leave our life here and go back to the other, of
course I do not; but I have felt idle, and like a boy turned down from
a high class at school to a low one."

"That is not very complimentary to me!" said Cynthia, laughing.
"Suppose we say a boy who has been working too hard for his health,
and has been given a long holiday?"

"Yes," I said, "that is better. It is as if a clerk was told that he need
not attend his office, but stay at home; and though it is pleasant enough,
he feels as if he ought to be at his work, that he appreciates his home
all the more when he can't sit reading the paper all the morning, and
that he does not love his home less, but rather more, because he is

away all the day."

"Yes," said Cynthia, "that is sensible enough; and I am amazed sometimes that you can be so good and patient about it all—so content to be so much with me and baby here; but I don't think it is quite—what shall I say?—quite healthy either!"

"Well," I said, "I have no wish to change; and here, I am glad to think, there is never any doubt about what one is meant to do."

And so, the subject dropped.

How little I thought then that this was to be the end of the old scene, and that the curtain was to draw up so suddenly upon a new one.

But the following morning I had been wandering contentedly enough in the wood, watching the shafts of light strike in among the trees, upon the glittering fronds of the ferns, and thinking idly of all my strange experiences. I came home, and to my surprise, as I came to the door, I heard talk going on inside. I went hastily in, and saw that Cynthia was not alone. She was sitting, looking very grave and serious, and wonderfully beautiful—her beauty had grown and increased in a marvellous way of late. And there were two men, one sitting in a chair near her and regarding her with a look of love; it was Lucius; and I saw at a glance that he was strangely changed. He had the same spirited and mirthful look as of old, but there was something there which I had never seen before—the look of a man who had work of his own, and had learned something of the perplexity and suffering of responsibility. The other was Amroth, who was looking at the two with an air of irrepressible amusement. When I entered, Lucius rose, and Amroth said to me:

"Here I am again, you see, and wondering whether you can regain the pleasure you once were kind enough to take in my company?"

"What nonsense!" I said rather shamefacedly. "How often have I blushed in secret to think of that awful remark. But I was rather harried, you must admit."

Amroth came across to me and put his arm through mine.

"I forgive you," he said, "and I will admit that I was very provoking; but things were in a mess, and, besides, it was very inconvenient for me to be called away at that moment from my job!"

But Lucius came up to me and said:

"I have come to apologise to you. My behaviour was hideous and horrible. I won't make any excuses, and I don't suppose you can ever forget what I did. I was utterly and entirely in the wrong."

"Thank you, Lucius," I said. "But please say no more about it. My own behaviour on that occasion was infamous too. And really, we need not go back on all that. The whole affair has become quite an agreeable reminiscence. It is a pleasure, when it is all over, to have been thoroughly and wholesomely shown up, and to discover that one has been a pompous and priggish ass. And you and Amroth between you did me that blessed turn. I am not quite sure which of you I hated most. But I may say one thing, and that is that I am heartily glad to see you have left the land of delight."

"It was a tedious place really," said Lucius, "but one felt bound in honour to make the best of it. But indeed, after that day it was horrible. And I wearied for a sight of Cynthia! But you seem to have done very well for yourselves here. May I venture to say frankly how well she is looking, and you too? But I am not going to interrupt you. I have got my billet, I am thankful to say. It is not a very exalted one, but it is better than I deserve; and I shall try to make up for wasted time."

"Hear, hear!" said Amroth; "a very creditable sentiment, to be sure!"

Lucius smiled and blushed. Then he said:

"I never was much of a hand at expressing myself correctly; but you know what I mean. Don't take the wind out of my sails!"

And then Amroth turned to me, and said suddenly:

"And now I have something else to tell you, and not wholly good news; so, I will just say it at once, without beating about the bush. You are to come with us too."

Cynthia looked up suddenly with a glance of pale inquiry. Amroth took her hand.

"No, dear child," he said, "you are not to accompany him. You must stay here awhile, until the child is grown. But don't look like that! There is no such thing as separation here, or anywhere. Don't make it harder for us all. It is unpleasant of course; but, good heavens, what would become of us all if it were not for that! How dull we should be without suffering!"

"Yes, yes," said Cynthia, "I know—and I will say nothing against it. But—"and she burst into tears.

"Come, come," said Amroth cheerfully, "we must not go back to the old days, and behave as if there were partings and funerals. I will give you five minutes alone to say goodbye. Lucius, we must start," and, turning to me, he said, "Meet us in five minutes by the oak-tree in the road."

They went out, Lucius kissing Cynthia's hand in silence.

Cynthia came up to me and put her arms round my neck and her cheek to mine. We sobbed, I fear, like two children.

"Don't forget me, dearest," she said.

"My darling, what a word!" I said.

"Oh, how happy we have been together!" she said.

"Yes, and shall be happier still," I said.

And then with more words and signs of love, too sacred even to be written down, we parted. It was over. I looked back once, and saw my darling gather the child to her heart, and look up once more at me. Then I closed the door; something seemed to surge up in my heart and overwhelm me; and then the ring on my finger sent a sharp pang through my whole frame, which recalled me to myself. And I say it with all the strength of my spirit, I saw how joyful a thing it was to suffer and grieve. I came down to the oak. The two were waiting in silence, and Lucius seemed to be in tears. Amroth put his arm through mine.

"Come, brother," he said, "that was a bad business; I won't pretend otherwise; but these things had better come swiftly."

"Yes," said Lucius, "but it is a cruel affair, and I can't say otherwise. Why cannot God leave us alone?"

"Lucius," said Amroth very gravely, "here you may say and think as you will—and the thoughts of the heart are best uttered. But one must not blaspheme."

"No, no," said Lucius, "I was wrong, I ought not to have spoken so. And indeed, I know in my heart that somehow, far off, it is well. But I was thinking," he said, turning to me, and grasping my hand in both of his own, "not of you, but of Cynthia, I am glad with all my heart that you took her from me, and have made her happy. But what miserable creatures we all are; and how much more miserable we should be if we were not miserable!"

And then we started. It was a dreary hour that, full of deep and gnawing pain. I pictured to myself Cynthia at every moment, what she was doing and thinking; how swiftly the good days had flown; how perfectly happy I had been; and so my wretched silent reverie went on.

"I must say," said Amroth at length, breaking a dismal silence, "that this is very tedious. Can't you take some interest? I have very disagreeable things to do, but that is no reason why I should be bored as well!" And he then set himself to talk with much zest of all my old friends and companions, telling me how each was faring. Charmides, it seemed, had become a very accomplished architect and designer; Philip was a teacher at the College. And he went on until, in spite of my heaviness, I felt the whole of life beginning to widen and vibrate all about me, and a sense almost of shame creeping into my mind that I had become so oblivious of all the other friendships and relations I had formed. I forced myself to talk and to ask questions, and found myself walking more briskly. It was not very long before we parted with Lucius. He was left at the doors of a great barracklike building, and Amroth told me he was to be employed as an officer, very much in the same way as the young man who was sent to conduct me away from the trial; and I felt what a good officer Lucius would make— smart, prompt, polite, and not in the least sentimental.

So we went on together rather gloomily; and then Amroth let me look for a little deep into his heart; and I saw that it was filled with a kind of noble pity for me in my suffering; but behind the pity lay that blissful certainty which made Amroth so light-hearted, that it was just so, through suffering, that one became wise; and he could no more think of it as irksome or sad than a jolly undergraduate thinks of the training for a race or the rowing in the race as painful, but takes it all with a kind of high-hearted zest, and finds even the nervousness an exciting thing, life lived at high pressure in a crowded hour.

31

And thus, we came ourselves to a new place, though I took but little note of all we passed, for my mind was bent inward upon itself and upon Cynthia. The place was a great solid stone building, in many courts, with fine tree-shaded fields all about; a school, it seemed to me, with boys and girls going in and out, playing games together, Amroth told me that children were bestowed here who had been of naturally fine and frank dispositions, but who had lived their life on earth under foul and cramped conditions, by which they had been fretted rather than tainted. It seemed a very happy and busy place. Amroth took me into a great room that seemed a sort of library or common-room.

There was no one there, and I was glad to sit and rest; when suddenly the door opened, and a man came in with outstretched hands and a smile of welcome. I looked up, and it was none but the oldest and dearest friend of my last life, who had died before me. He had been a teacher, a man of the simplest and most guileless life, whose whole energy and delight was given to teaching and loving the young. The surprising thing about him had always been that he could meet one, after a long silence or a suspension of intercourse, as simply and easily as if one had but left him the day before; and it was just the same here. There was no effusiveness of greeting—we just fell at once into the old familiar talk.

"You are just the same," I said to him, looking at the burly figure, the big, almost clumsy, head, and the irradiating smile. His great charm had always been an entire unworldliness and absence of ambition.

He smiled at this and said:

"Yes, I am afraid I am too easy-going." He had never cared to talk about himself, and now he said, "Well, yes, I go along in my old prosy way. It is just like the old schooldays, with half the difficulties gone. Of course, the children are not always good, but that makes it the more amusing; and one can see much more easily what they are thinking of and dreaming about."

I found myself telling him my adventures, which he heard with the same quiet attention; and I was sure that he would never forget a single point—he never forgot anything in the old days.

"Yes," he said at the end, "that's a wonderful story. You always had the trouble of the adventures, and I had the fun of hearing them."

He asked me what I was now going to do, and I said that I had not the least idea.

"Oh, that will be all right," he said.

It was all so comfortable and simple, so obvious indeed, that I laughed to think of the bitter and miserable reveries I had indulged in when he was taken from me, and when the stay of my life seemed gone. The whole incident seemed to give me back a touch of the serenity which I had lost, and I saw how beautifully this joy of meeting had been planned for me, when I wanted it most. Presently he said that he must go off for a lesson, and asked me to come with him and see the children. We went into a big classroom, where some boys and girls were assembling. Here he was exactly the same as ever; no sentiment, but just a kind of bluff paternal kindness.

The lesson was most informal—a good deal of questioning and answering; it was a biographical lecture, but devoted, I saw, in a simple way, to tracing the development of the hero's character. "What made him do that?" was a constant question. The answers were most ingenious and extraordinarily lively; but the order was perfect. At the end he called up two or three children who had shown some impatience or jealousy in the lesson, and said a few half-humorous words to them, with an air of affectionate interest.

"They are jolly little creatures," he said when they had all gone out.

"Yes," I said, with a sigh, "I do indeed envy you. I wish I could be set to something of the kind."

"Oh, no, you don't," he said; "this is too simple for you! You want something more artistic and more psychological. This would bore you to extinction."

We walked all round the place, saw the games going on, and were presently joined by Amroth, who seemed to be on terms of old acquaintanceship with my friend. I was surprised at this, and he said:

"Why, yes, Amroth had the pleasure of bringing me here too. Things are done here in groups, you know; and Amroth knows all about our lot. It is very well organised, much better than one perceives at first. You remember how you and I drifted to school together, and the set of boys we found ourselves with—my word, what young ruffians some of us were! Well, of course, all that had been planned, though we did not know it."

"What!" said I; "the evil as well as the good?"

The two looked at each other and smiled.

"That is not a very real distinction," said Amroth. "Of course, the poor bodies got in the way, as always; there was some fizzing and some precipitation, as they say in chemistry. But you each of you gave and received just what you were meant to give and receive; though these are complicated matters, like the higher mathematics; and we must not talk of them today. If one can escape the being shocked at things and yet be untainted by them, and, on the other hand, if one can avoid pomposity and yet learn self-respect, that is enough. But you are tired today, and I want you just to rest and be refreshed."

Presently Amroth asked me if I should like to stay there awhile, and I most willingly consented.

"You want something to do," he said, "and you shall have some light employment."

That same day, before Amroth left me, I had a curious talk with him.

I said to him: "Let me ask you one question. I had always had a sort of hope that when I came to the land of spirits, I should have a chance of seeing and hearing something of some of the great souls of earth. I had dimly imagined a sort of reception, where one could wander about and listen to the talk of the men one had admired and longed to see—Plato, let me say, and Shakespeare, Walter Scott, and Shelley—some of the immortals. But I don't seem to have seen anything of them—only just ordinary and simple people."

Amroth laughed.

"You do say the most extraordinarily ingenuous things," he said. "In the first place, of course, we have quite a different scale of values here. People do not take rank by their accomplishments, but by their power of loving. Many of the great men of earth—and this is particularly the case with writers and artists—are absolutely nothing here. They had, it is true, a fine and delicate brain, on which they played with great skill; but half the artists of the world are great as artists, simply because they do not care. They perceive and they express; but they would not have the heart to do it at all, if they really cared. Some of them, no doubt, were men of great hearts, and they have their place and work. But to claim to see all the highest spirits together is as absurd as if you called on a doctor in London at eleven o'clock and expected to meet all the great physicians at his house, intent on general conversation.

"Some of the great people, indeed, you have met, and they were very simple persons on earth. The greatest person you have hitherto seen was a butler on earth—the master of your College. And if it does not shock your aristocratic susceptibilities too much, the President of this place kept a small shop in a country village. But one of the teachers here was actually a marquis in the world! Does that uplift you? He teaches the little girls how to play cricket, and he is a very good dancer. Perhaps you would like to be introduced to him?"

"Don't treat me as a child," I said, rather pettishly.

"No, no," said Amroth, "it isn't that. But you are one of those impressible people; and they always find it harder to disentangle themselves from the old ideas."

I spent a long and happy time in the school. I was given a little teaching to do, and found it perfectly enchanting. Imagine children with everything greedy and sensual gone, with none of the crossness or spitefulness that comes of fatigue or pressure, but with all the interesting passions of humanity, admiration, keenness, curiosity, and even jealousy, emulation, and anger, all alive and active in them. They were not angelic children at all, neither meek nor mild. But they were generous and affectionate, and it was easy to evoke these feelings. The one thing absent from the whole place was any touch of sentimentality, which arises from natural affections suppressed into a giggling kind of secrecy.

They expressed affection loudly and frankly, just as they expressed indignation and annoyance. All the while I kept Cynthia in my heart;

she was ever before me in a thousand sweet postures and with innumerable glances. But I saw much of my sturdy and wholesomeminded old friend; and the sore pain of parting faded away out of my heart, and left me with nothing but the purest and deepest love, which helped me in all I did or said, and made me patient and tenderhearted. And thus, the period sped not unhappily away, though I had my times of agony and despair.

32

I became aware at this time, very gradually and even solemnly, that some crisis of my life was approaching. How the monition came to me I hardly know; I felt like a man wandering in the dark, with eyes strained and hands outstretched, who is dimly aware of some great object, tree or haystack or house, looming up ahead of him, which he cannot directly see, but of which he is yet conscious by the vibration of some sixth sense. The wonder came by degrees to overshadow my thoughts with a sense of expectant awe, and to permeate all the urgent concerns of my life with its shadowy presence. Even the thought of Cynthia, who indeed was always in my mind, became obscured with the dimness of this obscure anticipation.

One day Amroth stood beside me as I worked; he was very grave and serious, but with a joyful kind of courage about him. I pushed my books and papers away, and rose to greet him, saying half-unconsciously, and just putting my thought into words:

"So, it has come!"

"Yes," said Amroth, "it has come! I have known it for some little time, and my thought has mingled with yours. I tell you frankly that I did not quite expect it; but one never knows here. You must come with me at once. You are to see the last mystery; and though I am glad for your sake that it is come, yet I tremble for you, because it is unlike any other experience; and one can never be the same again."

I felt myself oppressed by a sudden terror of darkness, but, half to reassure myself, I answered lightly:

"But it does not seem to have affected you, Amroth! You are always light-hearted and cheerful, and not overshadowed by any dark or gloomy thoughts."

"Yes, yes," said Amroth hurriedly. "It is easy enough, when it is once over. Nothing that is behind one matters; but this is a thing that one cannot jest about. Of course, there is nothing to fear; but to be brought face to face with the greatest thing in the world is not a light matter. Let me say this. I am to be with you all through; and my only word to you is that you must do exactly what I tell you, and at once, without any doubting or flinching. Then all will be well! But we must not delay. Come at once, and keep your mind perfectly quiet."

We went out together; and there seemed to have fallen a sense of gravity over all whom we met. My companions did not speak to me as we walked out, but stood aside to see me pass, and even looked at me, I thought, with an air half of reverence, half of a sort of natural compassion, as one might watch a dear friend go to be tried for his life.

We came out of the door, and found, it seemed to me, an unusual stillness everywhere. The wind, which often blew high on the bare moor, had dropped. We took a path, which I had never seen, which struck off over the hills. We walked for a long time, almost in silence. But I could not bear the strange curiosity which was straining at my heart, and I said presently to Amroth:

"Give me some idea what I am to see or to endure. Is it some judgment which I am to face, or am I to suffer pain? I would rather know the best and the worst of it."

"It is everything," said Amroth; "you are to see God. All is comprised in that."

His words fell with a shocking distinctness in the calm air, and I felt my heart and limbs fail me, and a dizziness came over my mind. Hardly knowing what I did or said, I came to a stop.

"But I did not know that it was possible," I said. "I thought that God was everywhere—within us, about us, beyond us? How can that be?"

"Yes," said Amroth, "God is indeed everywhere, and no place contains Him; neither can any of us see or comprehend Him. I cannot explain it; but there is a centre, so to speak, near to which the unclean and the evil cannot come, where the fire of His thought burns the hottest. . . . Oh," he said, "neither word nor thought is of any use here; you will see what you will see!"

Perhaps the hardest thing I had to bear in all my wanderings was the sight of Amroth's own fear. It was unmistakable. His spirit seemed prepared for it, perfectly courageous and sincere as it was; but there was a shuddering awe upon him, for all that, which infected me with an extremity of terror. Was it that he thought me unequal to the experience? I could not tell. But we walked as men dragging themselves into some fiery and dreadful martyrdom.

Again, I could not bear it, and I cried out suddenly:

"But, Amroth, He is Love; and we can enter without fear into the presence of Love!"

"Have you not yet guessed," said Amroth sternly, "how terrible Love can be? It is the most terrible thing in the world, because it is the strongest. If Death is dreadful, what must that be which is stronger than Death? Come, let us be silent, for we are near the place, and this is no time for words;" and then he added with a look of the deepest compassion and tenderness, "I wish I could speak differently, brother, at this hour; but I am myself afraid."

And at that we gave up all speech, and only our thoughts sprang together and intertwined, like two children that clasp each other close in a burning house, when the smoke comes volleying from the door.

We were coming now to what looked like a ridge of rocks ahead of us; and I saw here a wonderful thing, a great light of incredible pureness and whiteness, which struck upwards from the farther side. This began to light up our own pale faces, and to throw our backs into a dark shadow, even though the radiance of the heavenly day was all about us. And at last we came to the place.

It was the edge of a precipice so vast, so stupendous, that no word can even dimly describe its depth; it was all illuminated with incredible clearness by the light which struck upwards from below. It was absolutely sheer, great, pale cliffs of white stone running downwards into the depth. To left and right the precipice ran, with an irregular outline, so that one could see the cliff-fronts gleam how many millions of leagues below! There seemed no end to it. But at a certain point far down in the abyss the light seemed stronger and purer. I was at first so amazed by the sight that I gazed in silence. Then a dreadful dizziness came over me, and I felt Amroth's hand put round me to sustain me. Then in a faint whisper, that was almost inaudible, Amroth, pointing with his finger downwards, said:

"Watch that place where the light seems clearest."

I did so. Suddenly there came, as from the face of the cliff, a thing like a cloudy jet of golden steam. It passed out into the clear air, shaping itself in strange and intricate curves; then it grew darker in colour, hung for an instant like a cloud of smoke, and then faded into the sky.

"What is that?" I said, surprised out of my terror.

"I may tell you that," said Amroth, "that you may know what you see. There is no time here; and you have seen a universe made, and live its life, and die. You have seen the worlds created. That cloud of whirling suns, each with its planets, has taken shape before your eyes;

life has arisen there, has developed; men like ourselves have lived, have wrestled with evil, have formed states, have died and vanished. That is all but a single thought of God."

Another came, and then another of the golden jets, each fading into darkness and dispersing.

"And now," said Amroth, "the moment has come. You are to make the last sacrifice of the soul. Do not shrink back, fear nothing. Leap into the abyss!"

The thought fell upon me with an infinity and an incredulity of horror that I cannot express in words. I covered my eyes with my hands.

"Oh, I cannot, I cannot," I said; "anything but this! God be merciful; let me go rather to some infinite place of torment where at least I may feel myself alive. Do not ask this of me!"

Amroth made no answer, and I saw that he was regarding me fixedly, himself pale to the lips; but with a touch of anger and even of contempt, mixed with a world of compassion and love. There was something in this look which seemed to entreat me mutely for my own sake and his own to act. I do not know what the impulse was that came to me—self-contempt, trust, curiosity, the yearning of love. I closed my eyes, I took a faltering step, and stumbled, huddling and aghast, over the edge. The air flew up past me with a sort of shriek; I opened my eyes once, and saw the white cliffs speeding past. Then an unconsciousness came over me and I knew no more.

33

I came to myself very gradually and dimly, with no recollection at first of what had happened. I was lying on my back on some soft grassy place, with the air blowing cool over me. I thought I saw Amroth bending over me with a look of extraordinary happiness, and felt his arm about me; but again, I became unconscious, yet all the time with a blissfulness of repose and joy, far beyond what I had experienced at my first waking on the sunlit sea. Again, life dawned upon me. I was there, I was myself. What had happened to me? I could not tell. So, I lay for a long-time half dreaming and half swooning; till at last life seemed to come back suddenly to me, and I sat up. Amroth was holding me in his arms close to the spot from which I had sprung.

"Have I been dreaming?" I said. "Was it here? and when? I cannot remember. It seems impossible, but was I told to jump down? What has happened to me? I am confused."

"You will know presently," said Amroth, in a tone from which all the fear seemed to have vanished. "It is all over, and I am thankful. Do not try to recollect; it will come back to you presently. Just rest now; you have been through strange things."

Suddenly a thought began to shape itself in my mind, a thought of perfect and irresistible joy.

"Yes," I said, "I remember now. We were afraid, both of us, and you told me to leap down. But what was it that I saw, and what was it that was told me? I cannot recall it. Oh," I said at last, "I know now; it comes back to me. I fell, in hideous cowardice and misery. The wind blew shrill. I saw the cliffs stream past; then I was unconscious, I think. I seem to have died; but part of me was not dead. My flight was stayed, and I floated out somewhere. I was joined to something that was like both fire and water in one. I was seen and known and understood and loved, perfectly and unutterably and for ever. But there was pain, somewhere, Amroth! How was that? I am sure there was pain."

"Of course, dear child," said Amroth, "there was pain, because there was everything."

"But," I said, "I cannot understand yet; why was that terrible leap demanded of me? And why did I confront it with such abject cowardice and dismay? Surely one need not go stumbling and cowed into the presence of God?"

"There is no other way," said Amroth; "you do not understand how terrible perfect love is. It is because it is perfect that it is terrible. Our own imperfect love has some weakness in it. It is mixed with pleasure, and then it is not a sacrifice; one gives as much of oneself as one chooses; one is known just so far as one wishes to be known. But here with God there must be no concealment—though even there a man can withhold his heart from God—God never uses compulsion; and the will can prevail even against Him. But the reason of the leap that must be taken is this: it is the last surrender, and it cannot be made on our terms and conditions; it must be absolute. And what I feared for you was not anything that would happen if you did commit yourself to God, but what would happen if you did not; for, of course, you could have resisted, and then you would have had to begin again."

I was silent for a little, and then I said: "I remember now more clearly, but did I really see Him? It seems so absolutely simple. Nothing happened. I just became one with the heart and life of the world; I came home at last Yet how am I here? How is it I was not merged in light and life?"

"Ah," said Amroth, "it is the new birth. You can never be the same again. But you are not yet lost in Him. The time for that is not yet. It is a mystery; but as yet God works outward, radiates energy and force and love; the time will come when all will draw inward again, and be merged in Him. But the world is as yet in its dawning. The rising sun scatters light and heat, and the hot and silent noon is yet to come; then the shadows move eastward, and after that comes the waning sunset and the evening light, and last of all the huge and starlit peace of the night."

"But," I said, "if this is really so, if I have been gathered close to God's heart, why is it that instead of feeling stronger, I only feel weak and unstrung? I have indeed an inner sense of peace and happiness, but I have no will or purpose of my own that I can discern."

"That," said Amroth, "is because you have given up all. The sense of strength is part of our weakness. Our plans, our schemes, our ambitions, all the things that make us enjoy and hope and arrange, are but signs of our incompleteness. Your will is still as molten metal, it has borne the fierce heat of inner love; and this has taken all that is hard and stubborn and complacent out of you—for a time. But when you return to the life of the body, as you will return, there will be this great difference in you. You will have to toil and suffer, and even sin. But there will be one thing that you will not do: you will never be complacent or self-righteous, you will not judge others hardly. You will be able to forgive and to make allowances; you will concern yourself with loving others, not with trying to improve them up to your own standard.

"You will wish them to be different, but you will not condemn them for being different; and hereafter the lives you live on earth will be of the humblest You will have none of the temptations of authority, or influence, or ambition again—all that will be far behind you. You will live among the poor, you will do the most menial and commonplace drudgery, you will have none of the delights of life. You will be despised and contemned for being ugly and humble and serviceable and meek. You will be one of those who will be thought to have no spirit to rise, no power of making men serve your turn. You will miss what are called your chances, you will be a failure; but you will be trusted and loved by children and simple people; they will depend upon you, and you will make the atmosphere in which you live one of peace and joy. You will have selfish employers, tyrannical masters, thankless children perhaps, for whom you will slave lovingly.

140

"They will slight you and even despise you, but their hearts will turn to you again and again, and yours will be the face that they will remember when they come to die, as that of the one person who loved them truly and unquestioningly. That will be your destiny; one of utter obscurity and nothingness upon earth. Yet each time, when you return hither, your work will be higher and holier, and nearer to the heart of God. And now I have said enough; for you have seen God, as I too saw Him long ago; and our hope is henceforward the same."

"Yes," I said to Amroth, "I am content. I had thought that I should be exalted and elated by my privileges; but I have no thought or dream of that I only desire to go where I am sent, to do what is desired of me. I have laid my burden down."

34

Presently Amroth rose, and said that we must be going onward.

"And now," he said, "I have a further thing to tell you, and that is that I have very soon to leave you. To bring you hither was the last of my appointed tasks, and my work is now done. It is strange to remember how I bore you in my arms out of life, like a little sleeping child, and how much we have been together."

"Do not leave me now," I said to Amroth. "There seems so much that I have to ask you. And if your work with me is done, where are you now going?"

"Where am I going, brother?" said Amroth. "Back to life again, and immediately. And there is one thing more that is permitted, and that is that you should be with me to the last. Strange that I should have attended you here, to the very crown and sum of life, and that you should now attend me where I am going! But so, it is."

"And what do you feel about it?" I said.

"Oh," said Amroth, "I do not like it, of course. To be so free and active here, and to be bound again in the body, in the close, suffering, ill-savoured house of life! But I have much to gain by it. I have a sharpness of temper and a peremptoriness—of which indeed," he said, smiling, "you have had experience. I am fond of doing things in my own way, inconsiderate of others, and impatient if they do not go right. I am hard, and perhaps even vulgar. But now I am going like a board to the carpenter, to have some of my roughness planed out of me, and I hope to do better."

"Well," I said, "I am too full of wonder and hope just now to be alarmed for you. I could even wish I were myself departing. But I have a desire to see Cynthia again."

"Yes," said Amroth, "and you will see her; but you will not be long after me, brother; comfort yourself with that!"

We walked a little farther across the moorland, talking softly at intervals, till suddenly I discerned a solitary figure which was approaching us swiftly.

"Ah," said Amroth, "my time has indeed come. I am summoned."

He waved his hand to the man, who came up quickly and even breathlessly, and handed Amroth a sealed paper. Amroth tore it open, read it smilingly, gave a nod to the officer, saying "Many thanks." The officer saluted him; he was a brisk young man, with a fresh air; and he then, without a word, turned from us and went over the moorland.

"Come," said Amroth, "let us descend. You can do this for yourself now; you do not need my help." He took my hand, and a mist enveloped us. Suddenly the mist broke up and streamed away. I looked round me in curiosity.

We were standing in a very mean street of brick-built houses, with slated roofs; over the roofs we could see a spire, and the chimneys of mills, spouting smoke. The houses had tiny smoke-dried gardens in front of them. At the end of the street was an ugly, ill-tended field, on which much rubbish lay. There were some dirty children playing about, and a few women, with shawls over their heads, were standing together watching a house opposite. The window of an upper room was open, and out of it came cries and moans.

"It's going very badly with her," said one of the women, "poor soul; but the doctor will be here soon. She was about this morning too. I had a word with her, and she was feeling very bad. I said she ought to be in bed, but she said she had her work to do first."

The women glanced at the window with a hushed sort of sympathy. A young woman, evidently soon to become a mother, looked pale and apprehensive.

"Will she get through?" she said timidly.

"Oh, don't you fear, Sarah," said one of the women, kindly enough. "She will be all right Bless you, I've been through it five times myself, and I am none the worse. And when it's over she'll be as comfortable as never was. It seems worth it then."

A man suddenly turned the corner of the street; he was dressed in a shabby overcoat with a bowler hat, and he carried a bag in his hand. He came past us. He looked a busy, overtried man, but he had a good-humoured air. He nodded pleasantly to the women. One said:

"You are wanted badly in there, doctor."

"Yes," he said cheerfully, "I am making all the haste I can. Where's John?"

"Oh, he's at work," said the woman. "He didn't expect it today. But he's better out of the way: he'd be no good; he'd only be interfering and grumbling; but I'll come across with you, and when it's over, I'll just run down and tell him."

"That's right," said the doctor, "come along—the nurse will be round in a minute; and I can make things easy meantime."

Strange to say, it had hardly dawned upon me what was happening. I turned to Amroth, who stood there smiling, but a little pale, his arm in mine; fresh and upright, with his slim and graceful limbs, his bright curled hair, a strange contrast to the slatternly women and the heavily-built doctor.

"So, this," he said, "is where I am to spend a few years; my new father is a hardworking man, I believe, perhaps a little given to drink but kind enough; and I daresay some of these children are my brothers and sisters. A score of years or more to spend here, no doubt! Well, it might be worse. You will think of me while you can, and if you have the time, you may pay me a visit, though I don't suppose I shall recognise you."

"It seems rather dreadful to me," said I, "I must confess! Who would have thought that I should have forgotten my visions so soon? Amroth, dear, I can't bear this—that you should suffer such a change."

"Sentiment again, brother," said Amroth. "To me it is curious and interesting, even exciting. Well, goodbye; my time is just up, I think."

The doctor had gone into the house, and the cries died away. A moment after a woman in the dress of a nurse came quickly along the street, knocked, opened the door, and went in. I could see into the room, a poorly furnished one. A girl sat nursing a baby by the fire, and looked very much frightened. A little boy played in the corner. A woman was bustling about, making some preparations for a meal.

"Let me do you the honours of my new establishment," said Amroth with a smile. "No, dear man, don't go with me any farther. We will part here, and when we meet again we shall have some new stories to tell. Bless you." He took his hand from my arm, caught up my hand, kissed it, said, "There, that is for you," and disappeared smiling into the house.

A moment later there came the cry of a new-born child from the window above. The doctor came out and went down the street; one of the women joined him and walked with him. A few minutes later she returned with a young and sturdy workman, looking rather anxious.

"It's all right," I heard her say, "it's a fine boy, and Annie is doing well—she'll be about again soon enough."

They disappeared into the house, and I turned away.

35

It is difficult to describe the strange emotions with which the departure of Amroth filled me. I think that, when I first entered the heavenly country, the strongest feeling I experienced was the sense of security—the thought that the earthly life was over and done with, and that there remained the rest and tranquillity of heaven. What I cannot even now understand is this. I am dimly aware that I have lived a great series of lives, in each of which I have had to exist blindly, not knowing that my life was not bounded and terminated by death, and only darkly guessing and hoping, in passionate glimpses, that there might be a permanent life of the soul behind the life of the body.

And yet, at first, on entering the heavenly country, I did not remember having entered it before; it was not familiar to me, nor did I at first recall in memory that I had been there before. The earthly life seems to obliterate for a time even the heavenly memory. But the departure of Amroth swept away once and for all the sense of security. One felt of the earthly life, indeed, as a busy man may think of a troublesome visit he has to pay, which breaks across the normal current of his life, while he anticipates with pleasure his return to the usual activities of home across the interval of social distraction, which he does not exactly desire, but yet is glad that it should intervene, if only for the heightened sense of delight with which he will resume his real life.

I had been happy in heaven, though with periods of discontent and moments of dismay. But I no longer desired a dreamful ease; I only wished passionately to be employed. And now I saw that I must resign all expectation of that. As so often happens, both on earth and in heaven, I had found something of which I was not in search, while the work which I had estimated so highly, and prepared myself so ardently for, had never been given to me to do at all.

But for the moment I had but one single thought. I was to see Cynthia again, and I might then expect my own summons to return to life. What surprised me, on looking back at my present sojourn, was the extreme apparent fortuitousness of it. It had not been seemingly organised or laid out on any plan; and yet it had shown me this, that my own intentions and desires counted for nothing. I had meant to work, and I had been mostly idle; I had intended to study psychology, and I had found love. How much wiser and deeper it had all been than anything which I had designed!

Even now I was uncertain how to find Cynthia. But recollecting that Amroth had warned me that I had gained new powers which I might exercise, I set myself to use them. I concentrated myself upon the thought of Cynthia; and in a moment, just as the hand of a man in a dark room, feeling for some familiar object, encounters and closes upon the thing he is seeking, I seemed to touch and embrace the thought of Cynthia. I directed myself thither. The breeze fanned my hair, and as I opened my eyes I saw that I was in an unfamiliar place—not the forest where I had left Cynthia, but in a terraced garden, under a great hill, wooded to the peak. Stone steps ran up through the terraces, the topmost of which was crowned by a long irregular building, very quaintly designed. I went up the steps, and, looking about me, caught sight of two figures seated on a wooden seat at a little distance from me, overlooking the valley. One of these was Cynthia. The other was a young and beautiful woman; the two were talking earnestly together. Suddenly Cynthia turned and saw me, and rising quickly, came to me and caught me in her arms.

"I was sure you were somewhere near me, dearest," she said; "I dreamed of you last night, and you have been in my thoughts all day."

My darling was in some way altered. She looked older, wiser, and calmer, but she was in my eyes even more beautiful. The other girl, who had looked at us in surprise for a moment, rose too and came shyly forwards. Cynthia caught her hand, and presented her to me, adding, "And now you must leave us alone for a little, if you will forgive me for asking it, for we have much to ask and to say."

The girl smiled and went off, looking back at us, I thought, half-enviously.

We went and sat down on the seat, and Cynthia said:

"Something has happened to you, dear one, I see, since I saw you last—something great and glorious."

"Yes," I said, "you are right; I have seen the beginning and the end; and I have not yet learned to understand it. But I am the same, Cynthia, and yours utterly. We will speak of this later. Tell me first what has happened to you, and what this place is. I will not waste time in talking; I want to hear you talk and to see you talk. How often have I longed for that!"

145

Cynthia took my hand in both of her own, and then unfolded to me her story. She had lived long in the forest, alone with the child, and then the day had come when the desire to go farther had arisen in his mind, and he had left her, and she had felt strangely desolate, till she too had been summoned.

"And this place—how can I describe it?" she said. "It is a home for spirits who have desired love on earth, and who yet, from some accident of circumstance, have never found one to love them with any intimacy of passion. How strange it is to think," she went on, "that I, just by the inheritance of beauty, was surrounded with love and the wrong sort of love, so that I never learned to love rightly and truly; while so many, just from some lack of beauty, some homeliness or ungainliness of feature or carriage, missed the one kind of love that would have sustained and fed them—have never been held in a lover's arms, or held a child of their own against their heart.

"And so," she went on smiling, "many of them lavished their tenderness upon animals or crafty servants or selfish relations; and grew old and fanciful and petulant before their time. It seems a sad waste of life that! Because so many of them are spirits that could have loved finely and devotedly all the time. But here," she said, "they unlearn their caprices, and live a life by strict rule—and they go out hence to have the care of children, or to tend broken lives into tranquillity—and some of them, nay most of them, find heavenly lovers of their own. They are odd, fractious people at first, curiously concerned about health and occupation; and one can often do nothing but listen to their complaints. But they find their way out in time, and one can help them a little, as soon as they begin to desire to hear something of other lives but their own. They have to learn to turn love outwards instead of inwards; just as I," she added laughing, "had to turn my own love inwards instead of outwards."

Then I told Cynthia what I could tell of my own experiences, and she heard them with astonishment Then I said:

"What surprises me about it, is that I seem somehow to have been given more than I can hold. I have a very shallow and trivial nature, like a stream that sparkles pleasantly enough over a pebbly bottom, but in which no boat or man can swim. I have always been absorbed in the observation of details and in the outside of things. I spent so much energy in watching the faces and gestures and utterances and tricks of those about me that I never had the leisure to look into their hearts. And now these great depths have opened before me, and I feel more childish and feeble than ever, like a frail glass which holds a most precious liquor, and gains brightness and glory from the hues of the wine it holds, but is not like the gem, compact of colour and radiance."

Cynthia laughed at me.

"At all events, you have not forgotten how to make metaphors," she said.

"No," said I, "that is part of the mischief, that I see the likenesses of things and not their essences." At which she laughed again more softly, and rested her cheek on my shoulder.

Then I told her of the departure of Amroth.

"That is wonderful," she said.

And then I told her of my own approaching departure, at which she grew sad for a moment. Then she said, "But come, let us not waste time in forebodings. Will you come with me into the house to see the likenesses of things, or shall we have an hour alone together, and try to look into essences?"

I caught her by the hand.

"No," I said, "I care no more about the machinery of these institutions. I am the pilgrim of love, and not the student of organisations. If you may quit your task, and leave your ladies to regretful memories of their lap-dogs, let us go out together for a little, and say what we can—for I am sure that my time is approaching."

Cynthia smiled and left me, and returned running; and then we rambled off together, up the steep paths of the woodland, to the mountain-top, from which we had a wide prospect of the heavenly country, a great blue well-watered plain lying out for leagues before us, with the shapes of mysterious mountains in the distance. But I can give no account of all we said or did, for heart mingled with heart, and there was little need of speech. And even so, in those last sweet hours, I could not help marvelling at how utterly different Cynthia's heart and mind were from my own; even then it was a constant shock of surprise that we should understand each other so perfectly, and yet feel so differently about so much. It seemed to me that, even after all I had seen and suffered, my heart was still bent on taking and Cynthia's on giving. I seemed to see my own heart through Cynthia's, while she appeared to see mine but through her own. We spoke of our experiences, and of our many friends, now hidden from us—and at last we spoke of Lucius. And then Cynthia said:

"It is strange, dearest, that now and then there should yet remain any doubt at all in my mind about your wish or desire; but I must speak; and before I speak, I will say that whatever you desire, I will do. But I think that Lucius has need of me, and I am his, in a way which I cannot describe. He is halting now in his way, and he is unhappy because his life is incomplete. May I help him?"

At this there struck through me a sharp and jealous pang; and a dark cloud seemed to float across my mind for a moment. But I set all aside, and thought for an instant of the vision of God. And then I said:

"Yes, Cynthia! I had wondered too; and it seems perhaps like the last taint of earth, that I would, as it were, condemn you to a sort of widowhood of love when I am gone. But you must follow your own heart, and its pure and sweet advice, and the Will of Love; and you must use your treasure, not hoard it for me in solitude. Dearest, I trust you and worship you utterly and entirely. It is through you and your love that I have found my way to the heart of God; and if indeed you can take another heart thither, you must do it for love's own sake." And after this we were silent for a long space, heart blending wholly with heart.

Then suddenly I became aware that someone was coming up through the wood, to the rocks where we sat: and Cynthia clung close to me, and I knew that she was sorrowful to death. And then I saw Lucius come up out of the wood, and halt for a moment at the sight of us together. Then he came on almost reverently, and I saw that he carried in his hand a sealed paper like that which had been given to Amroth; and I read it and found my summons written.

Then while Lucius stood beside me, with his eyes upon the ground, I said:

"I must go in haste; and I have but one thing to do. We have spoken, Cynthia and I, of the love you have long borne her; and she is yours now, to comfort and lead you as she has led and comforted me. This is the last sacrifice of love, to give up love itself; and this I do very willingly for the sake of Him that loves us: and here," I said, "is a strange thing, that at the very crown and summit of life, for I am sure that this is so, we should be three hearts, so full of love, and yet so sorrowing and suffering as we are. Is pain indeed the end of all?"

"No," said Cynthia, "it is not the end, and yet only by it can we measure the depth and height of love. If we look into our hearts, we know that in spite of all we are more than rewarded, and more than conquerors."

Then I took Cynthia's hand and laid it in the hand of Lucius; and I left them there upon the peak, and turned no more. And no more woeful spirit was in the land of heaven that day than mine as I stumbled wearily down the slope, and found the valley. And then, for I did not know the way to descend, I commended myself to God; and He took me.

36

I saw that I was standing in a narrow muddy road, with deep ruts, which led up from the bank of a wide river—a tidal river, as I could see, from the great mudflats fringed with sea-weed. The sun blazed down upon the whole scene. Just below was a sort of landing-place, where lay a number of long, low boats, shaded with mats curved like the hood of a waggon; a little farther out was a big quaint ship, with a high stern and yellow sails. Beyond the river rose great hills, thickly clothed with vegetation.

In front of me, along the roadside, stood a number of mud-walled huts, thatched with some sort of reeds; beyond these, on the left, was the entrance of a larger house, surrounded with high walls, the tops of trees, with a strange red foliage, appearing over the enclosure, and the tiled roofs of buildings. Farther still were the walls of a great town, huge earthworks crowned with plastered fortifications, and a gate, with a curious roof to it, running out at each end into horns carved of wood. At some distance, out of a grove to the right, rose a round tapering tower of mouldering brickwork. The rest of the nearer country seemed laid out in low plantations of some green-leaved shrub, with rice-fields interspersed in the more level ground.

There were only a few people in sight. Some men with arms and legs bare, and big hats made of reeds, were carrying up goods from the landing-place, and a number of children, pale and small-eyed, dirty and half-naked, were playing about by the roadside. I went a few paces up the road, and stopped beside a house, a little larger than the rest, with a rough verandah by the door. Here a middle-aged man was seated, plaiting something out of reeds, but evidently listening for sounds within the house, with an air half-tranquil, half-anxious; by him on a slab stood something that looked like a drum, and a spray of azalea flowers. While I watched, a man of a rather superior rank, with a dark flowered jacket and a curious hat, looked out of a door which opened on the verandah and beckoned him in; a sound of low subdued wailing came out from the house, and I knew that my time was hard at hand.

It was strange and terrible to me at the moment to realise that my life was to be bound up, I knew not for how long, with this remote place; but I was conscious too of a deep excitement, as of a man about to start upon a race on which much depends. There came a groan from the interior of the house, and through the half-open door I could see two or three dim figures standing round a bed in a dark and ill-furnished room. One of the figures bent down, and I could see the face of a woman, very pale, the eyes closed, and the lips open, her arms drawn up over her head as in an agony of pain. Then a sudden dimness came over me, and a deadly faintness. I stumbled through the verandah to the open door.

The darkness closed in upon me, and I knew no more.

The Uttermost Farthing

1

Yes, Hebden Hill was the next station, the porter told me, and as the dowdy little train puffed sturdily across the wide green flat, intersected by dykes, which had once been a great bay of the sea, I watched with pleasure the low shapely bluffs, like miniature sea cliffs, but now covered with thickets and copses, which bounded the plain to the west half a mile away, and thought how like it was to the background of an old Italian picture. It was a warm summer evening, not oppressive, as there was a fresh breeze from the sea, along which white clouds sailed lazily landward. I could see far out in the plain hamlets and solitary farms nestling among trees; and it was pleasant to see the birds, crested plovers and pearly-grey gulls, that stood motionless, all facing up the wind in the pastures; and a lean grey heron by the old sluice-gate, poring upon the water.

And then I began to wonder how it was

that I was going on so vaguely defined a visit to Hector Bendyshe, whom I knew so slightly. What exactly *did* I know about him? He was just an agreeable man, whom one was never surprised to meet at dinner, and whose talk, mildly interesting, seldom flagged. He had been at Winchester and at Oxford; he had been perhaps in the diplomatic service, and had certainly travelled a good deal. He was clearly wealthy, for he had a flat in town, and a house understood to be of an attractive kind in Sussex, at Hebden Hill. But he had done nothing particular for twenty years—he was a man of fifty—he read a good many books, he was fond of music, he was something of a connoisseur.

But the more I reflected the less I seemed to know. He had no relations that I had ever heard of, and no intimate friends, though a host of acquaintances; he went everywhere and got on with everybody. He did not seem mysterious or secretive in any way; he talked easily

151

and frankly about his own concerns and pursuits, and indeed on most topics of general interest.

How then had my visit come about? I was myself a so-called literary man, who lived, not very prosperously, in rooms in town, reviewing, writing literary articles, putting together an occasional book, and enabled by my small earnings and a little private income to exist in tolerable comfort. I was just over forty, and the artistic ambitions I had once had, had long vanished; but I was more than content with my life, and my interest in other people was stronger than ever. The unexpected things that happened, the strange contrasts and contradictions of character, the amazing inconsistency of human beings and their intricate relations, so utterly different from and so much richer than the helpless conventional traditions of fiction—all this had kept alive in me a sense of romance in life which amply atoned for a career which had been disappointing and even humiliating.

I had met Bendyshe at dinner sometime in May. I had walked away with him, and he had asked me to his rooms. They were well furnished and comfortable, but with a certain austerity that took my fancy. Our talk had turned somehow on psychical things, in which I was a good deal interested; and before we had talked ten minutes I became aware that Bendyshe had dropped the mask of amiable levity which characterised his habitual conversation, and was speaking seriously and drily, but with a profound sense of conviction, which was quite unlike anything I had ever heard from him.

Suddenly he turned to me, a little sternly, I thought, and said, "But perhaps you are not interested in these things?"

"Yes and no," I said, "but to tell the truth, I am a little surprised to find that *you* are."

"Well," he said, "I don't wonder at that. You see, it has become of late rather a hobby of mine. I will tell you why some day, if you care to know. But tell me one thing: why do you say 'Yes and no'?"

"Because," I said, "in the first place I think that ordinary talk about psychical things is such fearful twaddle. It seems to me a scientific affair; but when foolish people talk about it, it's all a mixture of feeble sentiment and weak imagination."

"That's so," he said;" but if you feel about it like that, why don't you look into it?"

"Because the sort of experiments people try," I said," such as seances and trances and automatic writing, seem to me more sickening still, like drugtaking; it's like deliberately playing with the ugliest part of one's mind, the part that deals in fear. I don't want to wake that up—I want to think it is not there; and, moreover, I am so much interested in people as I see and know them that I don't want to explore the unknown."

"You want to live in a fool's paradise, in fact," said Bendyshe; and I could see from the pallor of his face and his distended nostrils that I had angered him; but he controlled himself. "No," he added, "I ought not to say that—it was rude and stupid! I apologise."

"No, please don't do that," I said; "it was my fault. What I said was very crude; it was like talking to a man of science about 'stinks' or to an actor about his 'patter'—the insolence of the amateur: that's unpardonable."

"Well, but I *really* want to know," he said rather gravely. "I agreed with you up to a certain point; but what you said amounted to this, that you are so much interested in people when they are alive that you don't take any interest in what happens to them after they are dead?"

"Yes," I said, "that is quite fair. I am immensely interested in what I can see and observe and infer in people. It seems to me dramatic, exciting, sometimes very beautiful. But I'm a homeless man and a bachelor, and I don't get very near to them. I only see the polite side of life; and when people disappear, as they unhappily do, and I can't follow them further, why, I turn back to what I can see and know."

"I understand perfectly," he said;" but it's just the other way with me. People seem to me so amazing, so incredibly fine at times and so unutterably low at others, that I can't believe it all begins and ends here, and I find myself consumed by the most intense curiosity, to use rather a feeble word, to know what the next act is. It seems to me all like a big rehearsal for something, full of trivial, grotesque, and annoying things—two people playing nap, a girl eating a sandwich as she waits for her cue—but the play is going on all the time, and everybody has his part. I feel that I *must* know what is behind it all, if it can be known. I'm not exaggerating when I say that I have thought many times of putting a pistol to my head in order to find out what does happen; but I doubt if it can be found out that way."

He was silent for a little; musing inwardly.

I watched him as he sat. He was a tall lean man, finely formed and modelled. He had close, crisply curling black hair, a little grizzled. His forehead was high, his eyebrows black, and he had large dark eyes which it seemed to me I had never seen fully opened before. He was clean-shaven, and his nose, straight and clean-cut, came down on a

153

short upper lip; but the under-lip was full, and the chin perhaps a little large for symmetry. He had a slightly worn air, but his face, which was hardly marked by wrinkles, had a fresh colour like that of a man who lived much in the open air.

If anything, his expression was little judicial; but when I had seen him on previous occasions, his prevailing expression was one of tolerant good-humour and friendliness. It had never occurred to me that he could be formidable, and indeed my impression had been that, if anything, he over-valued serenity and equanimity. There was nothing ascetic or scholarly about him. His hands were large and mobile, and had, I thought, more expression than his face; and his dress had a touch of negligence about it which became him well.

I had never thought him a particularly interesting man, because he never gave himself away or appeared to have any preferences. But now I had seen something very different, something alert, passionate, even terrifying.

But when he began to talk again, his mood had changed, and he was his old wary and kindly self.

"By the way," he said, "what do you generally do in the summer?"

"Oh, I stay about a little," I said; "but I have to stick pretty close to my work, you know. I'm a literary hack, and I have to be waiting on the stand in case of a call. If I happen to be in funds, I go to a quiet hotel somewhere—I rather like exploring the country; old houses and churches are the next most interesting things to people. But I generally end by being a little bored."

"I wish you would come down and stay with me for a week or two," he said. "I have got rather a nice old house in Sussex, and it is a pleasant country. It is very quiet, and you could work if you wanted to, or wander about. I should like to talk this matter over with you."

"Thank you very much," I said; "I should enjoy it immensely. Where did you say it was?"

"Hebden Hill," he said. "Not very far from Ashford—it's a biggish village. I'll drop you a line."

2

That was at the end of May. I heard nothing more for a month and began to think he had forgotten all about it, or that he was perhaps sorry that he had shown me the inner side of himself. But at the end of June I had a note asking me to go down on July the 7th, and an hour or two later a wire.

Am unexpectedly alone, and should be glad to see you tomorrow Thursday if you can manage it but don't alter arrangements. Would meet the train arriving 6.30. Hope you can stay a fortnight.

It seemed to me a little peremptory perhaps? No, I had no engagements, and I was glad to get out of the heat of London, so I wired an acceptance, packed my books and papers, and went; and now that I was embarked I began to have a curious feeling that I was in for an adventure of some kind, not very pleasant.

However, I arrived in the summer twilight. Bendyshe was on the platform to meet me, and I could see from the civility of the officials that he was not only an important personage, but a highly popular one. He had a pleasant word for everybody, and he introduced me formally to the stationmaster, saying gravely, "It's very important that my friend Mr. Hartley should form a good impression of the place; you know, he writes in all the papers, and could make our fortunes by a paragraph."

"Indeed, sir?" said the delighted stationmaster. "I'm sure you're very welcome to Hebden Hill, sir. We're old-fashioned, but going ahead a bit nowadays."

Bendyshe had a good car waiting. The station was at the bottom of the hill; and he motored me swiftly up a steep irregular street of red-brick and timbered houses with pleasant gardens—a most comfortable and homely place. At the top of the hill we turned into a small square or *piazza*, with five or six substantial eighteenth-century houses. Fronting the west end of the church was a long mellow brick wall with big gate posts and a gate of fine ironwork. Behind this there appeared a handsome *façade*; a brick Georgian mansion with a pediment, a solid pillared doorway, seven windows above and three on each side of the door, and a round window in the pediment. It was evidently the chief mansion of the village. The windows had old heavy casements painted white, and the house was flanked at each end by fine old sycamores.

"Here we are," said Bendyshe. "It's called the Manor-house, but it's not my idea of a manor-house at all!"

Inside appeared a white-painted, marbleflagged hall, heavily panelled and pillared, with two mahogany doors on each side and a broad balustraded staircase ascending under an arch at the end. It was all a little bare. There were a few portraits and some solid Chippendale chairs. A venerable and portly butler met us.

"Perhaps you would like to stroll round before you go and dress?" said Bendyshe. "It's a good thing to get one's bearings clear at once."

He showed me first a room to the left of the front door, a small dining-room panelled with dark oak. Here there were more portraits, and a fine Italian bust of a young man in red porphyry, evidently a masterpiece. The next room was a little library almost lined with books, with a big French window which opened on to the garden. "This is *your* room," said Bendyshe, "and you can have it entirely to yourself to work in. My own study is upstairs."

The door to the right of the front door led to a smoking-room, a comfortable place with a few red leather armchairs and some old dark landscape pictures in oil. "This is everybody's room," said Bendyshe. "That other door leads to the back regions; but now we'll have a look at the garden."

We went out through a door under the stairs. I could not restrain an exclamation of delight. We came out into a portico supported by pillars extending along the whole centre of the house, between two flanking shallow wings; it was paved with black-and-white marble, and furnished with some comfortable oak seats and tables.

The garden was not large, but beautifully designed. On each side it was walled, and shielded from intrusive eyes by a row on either hand of sycamores, fine old trees. The lawn was perfectly plain, but for a fine leaden statue of a youth with clasped hands looking upwards towards the house—a most enchanting piece of work. At the far end, sheltered by a low wall, was a great flower-border, blazing with colour; and as we drew near, I could see that the ground fell rapidly—to a tiny park with clumps of trees on either hand, and beyond, a magnificent view of a great green plain with low wooded ridges and blue shadowy hills to the right, while a mile or two to the left we could see a wide expanse of sea.

I said something feeble about the wonderful beauty of the place, and its magnificence.

"Well, that's rather a tall word," said Bendyshe. "It isn't a big house really, and the domain extends to about fifty acres. But it is cleverly designed, and makes the best use of every inch of earth and sky."

"Has it been long in your family?" I said.

"No, indeed," said Bendyshe; "I bought it just as it stands, furniture and all, from the last member of an old family—the Faulkners—that had come to hopeless grief. It was in an awful state—the house almost ruinous, the park full of weeds and thorn bushes. No one would look at it. But I heard of it by what we call accident, just when I wanted a house, about fifteen years ago, and saw its possibilities. I got it very cheap, and I really have not spent much money upon it. But I have got uncommonly fond of it, and feel as if I had lived here all my life, and a little more."

The light was beginning to fade as we went back to the house, which I found was all lit by electric light, carefully subdued and shaded. We went upstairs. There was a corridor above the hall, only not so wide, with three doors on either side, and one to the right, close to the head of the stairs; and these I must describe with some particularity.

The first door on the left as we came up—the staircase had turned round to the right, so that we were facing in the direction of the front door—led to two staircases, one going up to the attics and one descending to the offices. The second door on the left led to Bendyshe's bedroom, a very bare place, with a press or two and a few books; then came a bathroom with a door from the bedroom, and opposite the door, another door led into Bendyshe's study, which communicated with the corridor by what was the third door on the left.

The study was entirely filled with books, had a big table covered with papers, and two very uncompromising oak writing-chairs. A room less luxurious I have seldom seen. It had no ornament but a single picture, a very beautiful portrait of a girl, fair-haired and blue-eyed, with an expression of the most perfect naturalness and simplicity, and full of animation and delight. The room had two windows, one looking out to the church, the other down towards the village.

We went out again into the corridor. The door opposite Bendyshe's study was my bedroom, one window of which looked towards the church, and the other out on the great sycamore by the corner of the house. A little bathroom was attached. The room was furnished with great comfort, and had some fine water-colours. Returning down the corridor, the two other doors opened into bedrooms similar to mine, each with a bathroom, and at the end, close to the head of the stairs, the remaining door led into another bedroom, which looked out on to the garden. But this room was wholly unfurnished, just a bare-boarded, white-panelled place, with that peculiar and unpleasant staleness that develops in an unventilated sun-baked room.

"I don't like this room," said Bendyshe. "It was the room, to tell you the truth, in which the scoundrel from whose heirs I bought the property came to his miserable end. It's a squalid story; and as for the room, well, I think there is something sinister about it. What do you feel? Yet it's a pity not to use it, because it has the finest view in the house!"

"I don't know," said I; "I think that the best way to exorcise disagreeable associations is not to fasten things up, but to let in a new current of pleasant usage."

"Yes," said Bendyshe; "if I had children, I should make this their schoolroom—then it would be all right!"

An hour later we dined—a well-appointed meal, though a simple one, very promptly served.

"I don't know what you feel," he said to me, "but it always seems to me rather uncivilised to dawdle over food."

He himself ate rapidly, but with appetite, and drank a glass or two of wine. After dinner we withdrew to the smoking-room. Bendyshe was in his familiar mood, full of little anecdotes and reminiscences.

When we had established ourselves with coffee and cigars, he said, "Now let me first say how glad I am to see you here. I have a notion that we agree, more than perhaps appeared the other night, about that matter we spoke of; and I think you can help me very much, if you are disposed to do so. I think you are a fair-minded man and impartial. Would you mind telling me exactly where you stand? Or perhaps you are tired and would like to defer it? Tomorrow night, I ought to say, the parson, Fortescue by name, is coming to dine, a very interesting and remarkable man, so that if you would like to leave it alone, we must wait till the day after tomorrow—the evening is the only time to talk seriously about things."

"I should like to start at once," I said. "But tell me, what did you mean by saying I could be of use to you?"

"Why," said Bendyshe, "living alone, as I do, and with but few people to talk things over with, one gets into a tangle. I generally have a visitor or two here, because solitude unadulterated is not a wholesome thing. But they are not the sort of people I can really talk to; and just now I have got hold of some new material—I am always collecting materials—and it doesn't seem to fit in with my ideas. But the point is this—how much and how little do you believe?"

"Oh," I said, "my position is a simple one. It's all just a question of evidence. Any materials ought to be rigidly scrutinised—one mustn't either accept or dismiss evidence summarily—and then one may begin to draw conclusions."

"Yes," said Bendyshe; "that's very much what I believe. But it's uncommonly hard to trace these psychical stories to their source. I have tried to unravel a good many, and it gives one a deplorable opinion of the value of human evidence. But," he went on, "before we begin, I must tell you in as few words as I can how I came to set to work. I don't like to talk about it—it's like tearing open an old wound—but I must make this plain. Some twenty-five years ago I became engaged to a girl, the daughter of a parson; you saw her picture, perhaps, in my room. You must take it on trust from me that she was a wonderful creature, and gave me not only a new view of life, but something to live for.

"We arranged everything. We were to have lived in London, and I was actually thinking of standing for Parliament, when just a month before our marriage she caught diphtheria and died within the week. I can't tell you what an appalling catastrophe it was for me. It had seemed to me that her love was the one thing I had been waiting for all my life, the one thing that had given me a reason for living. You see, I was an only son, entirely trusted a d indulged by my parents, and with plenty of money about and no motive for exerting myself.

"The thing very nearly drove me mad. A week before she had been with me, answering every question I had asked of life, and giving me the very water of life to drink. And now she was gone without a word. The last time I saw her she didn't even know me. She was in torture and half-unconscious. And there was nothing left, not a glance or a sign or the faintest message to me whom she loved best, or to any other human being—and there were many that loved her. It was so utterly unlike her, and yet there it was. Her parents were what is called 'wonderful.' They had a strong religious faith, and it helped them through."

Bendyshe stopped with a kind of gasp, gripped the arms of his chair, and abandoned himself for a minute to a paroxysm of misery. "It all comes over me again," he said. "Don't look at me—I shall be all right in a minute."

Presently he went on in a low voice: "I hardly know what I did. I travelled, I did some exploration, I courted death, but it never came near me. But I never had the smallest sense of contact with her, or even of any thought coming from beyond.

"Then I came back and tried to occupy myself in many ways— what is called social service. But I'm a hopeless individualist, and I don't care about my fellowmen simply as such, and I was taken in many times.

"Then I started this work, and it began to seem to me the one thing worth doing—to find out, if I could, whether there was any possible contact with the spirits of the dead, whether they existed at all. I had all kinds of sickening experiences, but could find nothing definite.

"And I never could cross the threshold, though I came to believe that, under certain obscure conditions, living minds could communicate direct with each other, apart from material agencies. And then the case seemed worse to me than ever, because it all seemed to depend upon material existence as a necessary condition."

Then after a moment's pause, he went on slowly and rather wearily:

"And what makes things even worse is this. There are a good many stories of appearances which seem to have some element of truth about them. But most of these are connected with horrible and tragic occurrences——crimes, murders, solitary imprisonments, as if (supposing for a moment the things to be true) it were a punishment of some kind to have to return to the earth and to re-enact the scenes of desperation and wickedness. And even the unhappy victims of such outrages seem condemned to the same fate; as if the only motive force that could bring one back were fear and indelible horror, reconstructing incidents which one would give anything to forget, but cannot.

"If there were stories of spirits returning to earth to revive gratefully scenes of happiness and love, delightful experiences of youth and friendship and ingenuous aspiration, when the heart was full of hope and joy, it would be different; but no spirits ever seem to think of this. Are they ungrateful? Have they forgotten?"

"Religious people would perhaps say," I said," that the happiness of the farther world was so great, that a blest spirit would never care to return to these half-lit skies, and to the memory of joys that were always shadowed by some fear of loss and separation."

"But this is an utterly selfish and indifferent business," said Bendyshe. "We should despise it in a living human being. And even if it were so, have they no wish to comfort the hearts that ache with the memories of perished happiness? No; if the spirits of even the blest are so drugged and intoxicated with delight that they have no room for remembrance or tenderness, it is a more ghastly business still."

We sat for a little while in silence. "I expect it's about time to go to bed?" he said. "I ought not to go on soliloquising like this." He escorted me to my room, and said another friendly word about my visit,

160

adding, "Breakfast at nine—please ask for anything you want. Hope you'll sleep well; and you will find some good bedside-books there if you want them."

I was soon in bed, and I fell asleep in a mood of pleasurable antici-pation. This was going to be a novel experience, I felt sure, and Bendy-she's theories interested me; and almost immediately, so it seemed, I woke from a dreamless sleep, with old Bartlett the butler in my room, coughing deferentially, and asking if I would have a cup of tea, and whether I would have a hot or cold bath, and if there was anything else I required.

3

That morning at breakfast I found Bendyshe in a cheerful and eminently commonplace mood. He told me stories about the village and the people and the countryside. I asked some questions about one of the portraits, an old, rugged-looking man with prominent eyes and upstanding hair.

"'*What the dickens!*' I call him," said Bendyshe, smiling. "But we'll leave all that to the vicar, who is coming to dinner this evening—he knows far more about the house and the family than I do. He has been here thirty years—in fact his wife, now dead, was connected in some way with the Faulkners."

After breakfast I went off to do some writing, but I did very little, and my mind ran with curious persistency on what Bendyshe had told me on the previous night. He did not look like a man who had ever had a great shock or had passed through tragic experiences; indeed, his preoccupation with psychical matters seemed to me still a little unaccountable, and inconsistent with the fact that he evidently lived a busy and active life, and took a considerable share in local business.

He came and fetched me out about noon, and we strolled to the church and village. He had a word for all the people he met; he called the boys and girls by their Christian names; his hat went off to any woman. We met an old man hobbling along with two sticks.

"Why, Mr. Barry," said Bendyshe, "I'm glad to see you about again. Feeling better? You look quite your old self again."

"Thank you kindly, sir—yes, I'm better, Mr. Bendyshe, but feeling powerful giddy at times!"

"Ah, that'll soon pass off in the open air," said Bendyshe. "Now, shall I step in this evening for a bit of a gossip, Mr. Barry? I always get the news of the place from you. Hartley, this is Mr. Barry; I call him the father of the place. He will be a hundred and one years old in January next—isn't that so?"

Mr. Barry chuckled. "Don't you believe Mr. Bendyshe, sir," he said to me with a smile. "He will have his joke; 'tis only eighty-eight I am, last Febbery!"

So Bendyshe went on—but not for a moment did it seem an assumed heartiness, rather the natural overflowing of a neighbourly geniality; while a word of sympathy which he said to an old lady in rusty black was both tender and straightforward. With the children he was entirely delightful, with mysterious jests and allusions.

I said something about this. "Oh, yes," he said, "a child likes to share a secret with a grownup person, a secret which no one else knows. I'm not sure we don't all like it," he added with a smile; "a secret's rather an explosive thing."

We went to the church, a fine, ancient place which had evidently been carefully restored; one aisle was full of monuments to the Faulkner family, from a knight in armour in a canopied niche to a weeping nymph by Chantrey. "Fancy throwing away an inheritance like that," he said, as we looked at the old tombs; "but the whole history of the family is a steady process of climbing down. I'll show you the remains of their old mansion, about half a mile away, one of these days. The vicar thinks it is the doom of sacrilege, but that's rather too business-like a view for me!"

I grew more astonished as the day went on to find the polite and solitary diner-out transformed here into so bustling and genial a squire. I could not fit the puzzle together; and still less did he seem to me a man who carried about, hidden in his mind, so strange and haunting an aspiration.

In the afternoon it was very hot; we went round the house and looked at the portraits.

They were not particularly good, but the family likeness was strong; and the picture of the last of the Faulkner race, as a boy of sixteen, was a graceful and beautiful thing. It represented him in riding-dress standing beside a pony, slender, blue-eyed and light-haired, with a gentle, rather wistful ex pression. Next to the picture was one of his mother—a woman of rare beauty and charm—and a rather commonplace portrait on the other side of his father, a burly country squire.

"It's all rather an enigma," said Bendyshe, looking thoughtfully at the portraits. "Up till that time, you see, they had been very ordinary people, moderately prosperous, but not very successful, and quite unadventurous. There doesn't seem to have been a single instance of a man of any eminence among them, not even a soldier or a bishop. One of them was an M.P., but unseated for bribery. And then just when a strain of beauty comes into the family and a touch of romance, that minute the devil comes too. It looks as if there were something in the old idea of Nemesis, as if the way to be happy was not to attract the attention of the powers above. That pretty woman was an heiress, and the boy was born wealthy; and he was certainly charming, and I believe clever too—the vicar shall tell us all about him this evening."

I was somewhat struck by the interest which Bendyshe seemed to take in the old family. As a rule, the last thing that a new proprietor is interested in is the history of the family he has ousted. But Bendyshe seemed to wish to bring me into touch with the personalities of his predecessors, as though he desired me to draw some inference or to solve some problem. Indeed, when later in the afternoon he took me out and showed me the relics of the old Faulkner mansion, an octagonal turret and a crow-stepped gable, with a fine chimneystack of moulded bricks, and a great dovecot, all forming part of a rather ramshackle farm, I became even more sure of this, and commented on it.

Bendyshe laughed a short laugh, as though partly pleased and partly disconcerted, and said, "Yes, don't you think it would all make rather a picturesque article?" adding with a smile, "You see, if I take you away from your work, I ought to give you some copy in exchange. But don't let me bore you. I am afraid it is rather a tiresome fancy of mine, to speculate about my predecessors."

"Oh, I'm not bored," I said—"quite the reverse. What I feel is rather that you have some idea in your mind, which you want me to perceive for myself, and that you were, so to speak, inoculating me!" Bendyshe looked at me sharply, but I somehow saw that he was not displeased.

After tea I read and wrote a little in the library. I felt rather drowsy after a day in the open air, and fell asleep in my chair, but awakened suddenly with a start, and with a strong impression that someone had entered the room softly, and as softly withdrawn. I had, too, a sensation of something chilly in the air, and a faint earthy odour such as one connects with stone-built, underground, airless places. But it was all a momentary fancy; the flower—scented air was blowing in from the garden, and the bell of the church was ringing for Vespers. I got up and went out into the hall, and found Bendyshe with his hat on just going out of the front-door. "Was it you who caught me napping just now?" I said.

Bendyshe gave me one of his quick glances, and said, "Well, I thought you might be having forty winks"—and then added, a little shamefacedly, "The fact is, I'm going to church—the vicar is very good about services and doesn't get much of a congregation; besides, it makes me feel cosy, as Mrs. Carlyle said of the glass of port. Do you care to come?"

"It isn't very much in my line," I said lightly, "but I'll come with pleasure—it's all part of the atmosphere; and besides, I shall get into the vicar's good graces."

We sat in the chancel. There were only two other people present, both women. The vicar, a big, sanguine—faced man with a fine head of silky white hair, read evening prayer with great rapidity but with extreme reverence; and I was pleased to see never once looked in our direction. His reading of the lessons was strangely impressive; the second lesson was a chapter from the Gospel. "*When the evil spirit is gone out of a man, he walketh through dry places, seeking rest, and finding none.*" He had lowered his voice, and read as though it was a thing almost too terrible to be mentioned, except from a sense of duty. Just before the end of the passage he shut his book and made a slight pause; and then, as though it was his own comment, looking round at us, he added, "So the last state of that man is worse than the first." And then he began the *Nunc Dimittis* in a tone of unmistakable relief.

When I got down before dinner, the vicar and Bendyshe were sitting in the hall, talking in low tones. The vicar got briskly up, and shook hands with me with great cordiality. His face was full of animation and benevolence. Bendyshe had said something to me about his being much of a mystic; but anything less mystical I had never seen. He was alive to the fingertips. We had an amusing evening. The vicar made a remarkably good meal, and told a few excellent stories of a local kind, crisply and shortly, in response to a direct request from Bendyshe. I indulged in some literary gossip, and the vicar listened to stories about some of the well-known writers of the day with childish avidity and hearty laughter. "Excellent, excellent!" I remember his saying. "I have never been able to get on with his books—rather precious, I think?—but I'll give them another try; I didn't know the old man had so much blood in him!"

4

We settled ourselves after dinner in the smoking-room, and as soon as we were alone, Bendyshe said to the vicar, "Now I want you to tell

Hartley something about Hugh Faulkner" —adding to me, "that is the man whose portrait as a boy I showed you—and what happened when you came here. I always think it is an extraordinary story. Hartley won't make capital out of it, you know—he is quite discreet!"

"Well, then," said the vicar, "I'll tell you. It was over thirty years ago that Hugh Faulkner—he was a distant cousin of my dear wife—offered me the living through his lawyer. I came down and looked round, but Mr. Faulkner was ill, and I could not see him. I was just thirty then, and working in a quiet country curacy; and this gave me exactly what I wanted: more work, and a chance of really getting a hold on a place—and a beautiful church too—and I won't pretend that a larger income wasn't some inducement.

"Well, we settled here; and then bit by bit became aware that things were very wrong indeed in this house. Hugh Faulkner was about forty. His father and mother were both dead. He had been in the Guards, and he had done a good many wild things, and when at last he did something so outrageous that he was summarily told to send in his papers, he came down here. A less courageous man—he had plenty of courage—would have gone abroad for a bit, and waited for the thing to blow over. But he wasn't that sort. He came down here, and tried to brazen it out. But everyone knew about the scandal, and it was no use. People simply would not meet him, and were out when he called. He was cut and cold-shouldered everywhere.

"A few of the village people were civil to him; but he couldn't get servants, no one would accept his invitations. I've seen people in the street turn back rather than meet him. He stuck to it for weeks and months; and I tell you, Mr. Hartley, my heart bled for that man, though one could neither like him nor trust him: but I couldn't help admiring him. He generally took no notice, but once or twice he lost his temper. I saw him with my own eyes stop and say something civil to a farmer—Pratt, by name—in the street, and the man pushed by: Faulkner went after him and screamed something into his ear—Pratt wasn't a very exemplary person, either—and the man went on white and shaking.

"One day he came to the vicarage. I should say that I and my wife did see something of him; we went to dine there occasion ally, but it was quite intolerable. He used to tell unpleasant stories, not anything to which you could take open exception, but one saw what he meant; and he had an old soldier—servant, a real ruffian, who used to giggle at the sideboard. One day he had come in to tea at the vicarage, and he looked tired to death. While we were at tea, a neighbouring parson and his wife called. I mentioned Faulkner's name; they made hasty excuses—they couldn't stay for tea—they had only looked in. They didn't say a word to Faulkner, who stood there with his teacup looking as if he was on fire within. Then he went up to the parson as he was leaving the room, and said to him in a low voice, 'So this is what you do for sinners, Mr. Hale? What is your tone with the publicans?' What made it worse was that old Hale had the reputation of being rather too good a judge of wine.

"Then he said goodbye to us and marched out. I went back with him afterwards and did my best to talk to him. We parsons see some bad things, Mr. Hartley, but I never had a worse hour. The man was possessed by devils, not by one only. He was not violent or obscene; he was simply desperate. And he told me, sitting in this very room, what some of his performances had been, and such a catalogue I never heard. However, that is all *sub sigillo,* you know. He said, I remember, that he had carefully considered whether he could have helped behaving so, and he had decided that he could not help it, and would do just the same again under the same conditions. 'You see, I didn't make myself,' he said.

"Then he went on to say that once he had left the army he had kept clear of it all, except in one respect; but that the more he put the pillow on his desires, the more they peeped round the corner of it. He was quoting Martin Chuzzlewit, I believe?—he was a great reader, I should say—and then he asked me to tell him plainly if I thought he had a chance of putting things straight—'I'm really rather a goodnatured man,' he said, with a sort of pathos. 'I hardly expect to be liked—but I want to live on decent terms with my neighbours.' I said that it would take time, and it would depend on how he behaved—but that if he spoke to people as he had spoken to Hale at the vicarage it was of no use expecting things to go better. 'But the man was damnably insolent!' he said, ' and I won't take that from anyone.'

"Well, we argued on, and then I tried to go a step farther—that's my trade, you know—and I wanted to see if the man felt any kind of regret for any of the things he had done. He was quieter by that time, but he told me plainly to remember that I was not in my Sunday school. I nearly lost my temper at that, but I saw that it wouldn't do to back out. So, I said that I was there to help him if I could, but that I could do nothing unless I knew more or less what his feeling was. 'It's like calling in a doctor,' I said, 'and then keeping back some of your symptoms.'

"And then, Mr. Hartley, I had a look for the first and last time of my life into the soul of a very bad man. He told me that he regretted it, in a way, because he didn't like the consequences. But that if there were no consequences, he would not even regret it. One phrase of his I remember, 'Why, I think no more of doing this and that than you think about taking a cup of tea!' He went on to say that when certain temptations came to him, he had no choice—'I really don't think I am quite responsible,' he said; 'there is nothing in my mind that even wishes to resist.' And as to feeling the need of forgiveness either from the people he had wronged or Almighty God, the idea seemed simply laughable to him; and I will only say this, that for the first and only time in my life I felt like doubting the power of God. And then at last I got away. I may add that for a month or two afterwards I was really ill. I could not sleep; I could not get the man's face out of my mind.

"And then there came a worse complication. Pratt, the farmer to whom Faulkner had spoken in the street, had an accident and was thrown out of his dog-cart; and Hale had a sort of stroke and was ill for a long time. And this I think made matters hopeless. You know what sort of things people say, and underneath all our civilisation there's a great deal of the ugliest old superstition left.

"After that Faulkner shut himself up al together, except that he would ride or walk in the early summer mornings before people were about. In winter he hardly ever left the house; and what went on here I don't know—I don't like to think. He read a great deal, he did some gardening. I went to s.ee him from time to time, but he would never talk freely again. He used to ask a few questions, and sometimes told me stories about his boyhood, things his mother had said to him—he had a curious kind of affection for her—the tricks he had played on his father; he seemed to me like a man in a dream. He also took to speculating on the Stock Exchange, and lost a lot of money. The only person who stuck to him was the old soldier-servant. They lived in three or four rooms, did their own cooking, smoked and drank together, and the house got into a filthy state.

"But nothing happened: he didn't die, he was never ill, he simply lived on. Once or twice old friends came to see him; and I remember one man—a retired colonel, I believe—whom I met, leaving the house in haste, looking very much perturbed. He came up and spoke to me, said he had been to see his old friend Faulkner—they had been subalterns together—and he had been very much shocked, 'though

I'm not very particular,' he added. Then he suddenly said, 'Tell me, is he mad?'

"'Not in the least,' I said.

"'Then, good God,' said the colonel, 'why doesn't the man shoot himself?'—and he went off straight to the station.

"Now, for more than ten years things went on—think what that means—the garden was all overgrown with bushes and brambles, with a path through to plot where they grew vegetables; and in front the shrubs grew over the lower windows, and most of the upper windows were broken. But it shows what a strange thing human nature is, Mr. Hartley, for I believe the people here were rather proud of it than otherwise, though there was once an ugly demonstration. The old soldier-servant used to be seen about—he did the shopping, and he was rather a feature of the place. And strange to say, I got rather to like the man. He had been a real ruffian, I expect, but the way that man stuck to poor Hugh—it was heroic. There was nothing he wouldn't have done for him, and he simply worshipped him. I used to wonder what would happen to Hugh if he died.

"I still went in at times to see Hugh, and I believe he was glad to see me, though when he was in a bad mood he used to ask me all kinds of ingenious and bewildering questions about religious matters which I could not answer; but as a rule, I don't think he was even very consciously unhappy. They lived by a routine, and Hugh used to talk mysteriously of his experiments—I never quite knew what he meant, but nothing very good, I fear. And then there were stories—at one time the garden was thought to be full of great black birds; and at another there were supposed to be creatures which grunted and snorted about among the bushes, and screamed out sharply at night. There were said to be curious mounds in the garden, like earth thrown out from burrows. Sometimes the windows were lighted up, and music was heard; and a man was said to have been seen going up the wall at the back like a fly. But I never saw anything myself, except for the fact that the house seemed to me sometimes to be full of smells—bitter, suffocating smells, like nothing on earth; and at times appeared full of shadows, gliding blacknesses, like mist or smoke. But I daresay all these things had some explanation.

"But I must bring my story to an end—and I must add that though I never quite gave up trying to get hold of something in Hugh's mind and heart that I could pull on, and though I said many prayers for him, it all was a total failure; but I somehow became aware of a change of atmosphere about the house, about Hugh himself. I had generally had the feeling as if some struggle was going on somewhere out of sight, or even as though one were watched by something that would like to make a spring if it dared. Hugh himself was less violent and quieter; it seemed like exhaustion.

"One night, about the end of April (I was alone then, for my dear wife had died the year before; and I must tell you that in one of the last talks we had, she said to me, 'Don't give Hugh up—I think there is something coming to him,' but she could not explain), I was working late when I heard someone tapping at the door, quietly and insistently; and I found it was Hugh's servant. He wanted me to come and see Hugh at once. 'Did he send for me?' I said. 'No, sir—but I'm frightened about him. He doesn't eat, he doesn't sleep—he sits watching something.' The man kept moistening his lips as he spoke and then broke out, 'Come and see if you can help him.'

"I went off at once; and when we got into the house I knew that there· was something very wrong indeed. There was a silence that appalled me—I have never experienced such a silence; and though it was a warm night, the house was deadly cold. But worse still, there seemed something holding us back which required pushing into. I fought my way upstairs; but the old servant gave up, sate down on the bottom step and watched me. There was one solitary candle in the hall, which flickered and cast hideous shadows.

"I went straight into Hugh's room—the room at the top of the stairs. I found him stretched fully dressed upon his bed, his eyes closed, and making motions with his hands as if he were trying to thrust something away. His brow was horribly puckered and his face seemed swollen and congested. I went up and took his hand, and he gave a kind of moan or wail—the sort of cry a hare gives when a keeper takes hold of it. 'Don't be afraid,' I said; 'it's only me. John, you know!'

"At this he sate up and opened his eyes. 'The dream,' he said, 'the dream—it's closing in on me!' Then he said to me in a faint voice, 'Surely it's enough?—it's all empty and dark—it's draining my life away!' Then he turned to me and said, 'Where have I been?' I knew well enough. It isn't only a name, Mr. Hartley, it's a very real thing—the most real thing but one in the world. Then he said to me, 'Fifteen years of hell, John—does anything deserve that?' I hardly knew what I was saying then, for the cold that I had felt on the stairs was gathering in, thicker than ever.

"But I said—the words were given me somehow, 'Perhaps you

have done your punishment, Hugh; it's over and done.' He shook his head and lay down again; and I just knelt down and said the last prayers, and in the middle he gave one shudder, which went through him from head to foot, and I knew he was gone.

"Yes, I know what you would like to ask me, Mr. Hartley, and my answer is that I don't know. He was gone, but something else was gone too. The servant came running up the stairs, and looked in. I beckoned to him. He came and knelt down by me, and I finished the prayers; and when I had finished, he took my hand and pressed it; and then he took Hugh in his arms and stroked his face. I left them there, and went away a wiser man, I hope.

"The family lawyer came down, and he and I made a search for documents to no purpose. He had kept some papers in a despatch box that was always near him; but this was missing, and could not be found. There was nothing to throw light on the matter, except that the servant said that he had lately been strange in manner and apathetic, and that he had lost his appetite; and I will only add that there was an inquest. I told my tale with reservations, and they called it natural death. I didn't hesitate to bury him in the churchyard, and there he lies; but no one came to the funeral.

"And the bishop sent for me to enquire into the circumstances; but when I had finished the story, as much as it was fit for a bishop to hear, he told me frankly that he had meant to suggest to me to resign my living, but that now he had altered his mind, and that I must on no account leave the place. I never saw a man in such a state of what we will call godly embarrassment. And the next Sunday I made my flock a little sermon on *Judge not, that ye be not judged*, and gave them a bit of my mind. And, strange to say, I have never had any trouble to speak of since."

The vicar made a long pause, and shook his head. I could see that there was something further in his mind which he had decided not to mention. I confess that this strange and tragic story produced an extra ordinary effect upon me. For one thing, it was all so darkly mysterious, so full of un explained hints and suggestions of evil, that it aroused in me a vague terror which made me wish that I had never listened to it. Not so Bendyshe; he was sitting back in his chair, his hands clasped together, looking at the vicar with gleaming eyes, like a man on the brink of a great discovery.

Then the vicar turned to me, and said, "There, Mr. Hartley, I have told you the story at Mr. Bendyshe's request. You may be thinking that it is the sort of tale that had better not be told, and that such a collection of shocking incidents is better forgotten and buried in oblivion. But I have two reasons for telling you. In the first place, the outline of the story, only greatly exaggerated, is known to and repeated by a good many people in this place, and I should wish you to have a more accurate version of what happened—anything is better than secrecy about such things; and Mr. Bendyshe tells me he has a special reason for asking me to relate it to you, which you no doubt know, and of which I approve. I think it ought to be seriously investigated.

"And then, too, I have a further reason. There are very dark corners in this world of ours, and facts of our existence, which seem inconsistent with any faith in a beneficent and Almighty Creator; and I don't think it right to ignore them. My own belief—I will speak frankly—is that God is slowly and patiently making a conquest of a world in which there exists—how originated I cannot even guess—a strong element of something atrocious and horrible, which defies Him, and seizes every opportunity of undoing His work.

"And to my mind, the horror of this story is that it seems like a deliberate attempt to focus this evil power, an attempt which failed, because this malignant influence, as I interpret it, is essentially what is called stupid. It has no principle; it works at details with a laborious persistency—that is where its essential weakness lies; but it ought not to be ignored; it must be met by anyone who comes across it with courage and intelligence. I don't think that Hugh Faulkner did any very serious or deep-seated harm here, and he certainly did not succeed in making evil attractive. He may have struck a blow at individuals, and I believe that he certainly did but that is all.

"And now I must ask you to excuse me, if I say goodnight. May I have the pleasure of seeing you at the vicarage, Mr. Hartley? You may have some questions to ask about what I have told you. But I have nothing to add, and I may not be in a position to give you an answer."

The vicar took his leave, and left on my mind the impression of great simplicity and goodness. He and Bendyshe went to the door together, and stood talking for some little time in low tones.

When Bendyshe came back, he said to me with a curious look, "Now what do you think of all that?"

"I don't know what to make of it," I said—"at present I'm simply rather stupefied. One goes along making the best of life and thinking the world on the whole a satisfactory and wholesome place; and then comes a tale like this, and one wonders if one has any real idea of what is going on, or of what may be hidden away in the minds of men and women. I wish I had never heard the story."

"Oh, come," said Bendyshe, "don't say that—it seems to me to have all the elements of a big adventure. I would give anything to get a little more information; but here one only gets the wildest and silliest gossip. I may tell you that I have tried to get on the track of Faulkner's servant, but I can't find a trace of him."

"I expect he is dead by this time," I said.

"No," said Bendyshe; "he is not dead. I can say that quite confidently—I have my reasons."

We sate for some little time together, and I asked Bendyshe one or two disjointed questions. I said, "There was one point in what the vicar said which I did not quite understand. He spoke of Faulkner doing harm to individuals. What did he mean by that?

"Well," said Bendyshe, "he meant Hale and Farmer Pratt in the first place; and there are some other cases too, if you care to hear them."

"No, I don't want to hear them," I said; "but tell me this. Do you, and does the vicar, really believe that Faulkner had the power of inflicting bodily damage upon these unfortunate men, without using some known human agency? Of course, it might be that some mental shock and physical deterioration followed from a fright which——"

But Bendyshe interrupted me. "Do I believe it?" he said. "Why, I *know* it. Faulkner was just as much responsible for their illness as if he had fired a gun at them."

"But how is it possible?" I said.

"Ah, I don't know that," said Bendyshe; "but that he had the power of doing that sort of thing—at all events in the case, let us say, of people whose moral force was weakened by some indulgence—is incontestable. He didn't use it often, I admit; he was afraid to do so; but in both of these cases, and in others which I could tell you, he lost all control of himself, and I believe that he let loose against them an undiluted current of evil; and the vicar believes it too."

"But it isn't rational," I said; "we don't believe in witchcraft in the twentieth century."

"Perhaps it would be better if we did," said Bendyshe grimly. "We can't get rid of facts by calling them irrational."

I saw that he was getting nettled by the discussion, so I said, "Well, I must have time to let all this settle down."

In a moment the other Bendyshe appeared. "Yes," he said; "we mustn't let this visit of yours degenerate into a series of shocks and explosions. I've no right to do that, and if you give me a hint, I will drop my theory for a bit. But I very much hope you will help me to look into the matter. We'll have an easy day tomorrow."

He accompanied me to my room and said, "I hope the story to-night hasn't made you nervous? Perhaps this will reassure you." He showed me, let in beneath the dadocornice, in the corner by my bed, a little circle looking like the top of a wooden peg, and painted white like the rest of the room. "That's a fancy of mine. My butler, Bartlett, doesn't sleep in the house—he has a house in the village. And this bell rings in my room—both the other spare bedrooms have it. I put it up when old Ford was staying here, and was taken ill in the night and couldn't make anyone hear. If you press on that, I'll be with you in a minute. I'm a very light sleeper!"

"Oh, I'm not nervous," I said. "I'm a sound sleeper, and then I'm a rational man."

Bendyshe smiled at this and said, "Yes; that's just why I want your help. Goodnight, old man."

5

Left to myself that night, I went slowly and deliberately to bed. I felt curiously tired and drowsy after the cataract of varied impressions which I had received during the day; and I was conscious, too, of a growing excitement. The vicar's story had done more to arouse this than any of Bendyshe's semi-scientific theories. The vicar, I felt, was a man without an axe to grind, and with a certain duty to perform in the world, a desire to illumine the darkness, to extinguish evil. He did not turn his back upon it or ignore it, and his aim was a practical one. Bendyshe, on the other hand, was like a man engaged in research; he simply wanted to arrive at facts. Indeed, there had been moments in the day when I had suspected him of being something very like a monomaniac; but his friendliness was engaging, and the appeal he had made to me for help had touched me. But help in what? That I could not say.

Just, I imagine, before I slept, I had a curious sensation of some-thing vague and restless in the house, something that faintly jarred my drowsy nerves; it was all a fancy, but I thought dimly that some-one, sleeplessly and wearily, was engaged in pacing about, and search-ing for a thing both secret and momentous, which had been mislaid or hidden.   I wondered vaguely if the inquisitive brain of Bendy-she, weighing, considering, discriminating, was having a sort of telepathic effect on my own. The house was absolutely still; the church clock struck two with a murmur sweet as honey; and then, curiously enough, I had a sensation of great mental ease. If anything was going forward, I was at least in no way concerned in it; the searcher did not wish me ill—my presence there was nothing to him. And then, I suppose, I passed into sleep.

While I dressed in the morning, I could see Bendyshe pacing in the narrow strip of garden that lay beneath my windows, lost in thought. He greeted me when I came downstairs with much effusion. "Slept well?" he said. "That's right. You look very fit and spry. We'll have a good spin today—we might go to Canterbury perhaps?"

And yet, strange to say, I had an indefinable sense that Bendyshe was in some way disappointed.

Our run was uneventful enough. Bendyshe made no allusion to the narrative of the previous evening. I thought, indeed, that he was a little conscience-stricken for having plunged me, so to speak, up to the neck in these dark matters. In fact, I do not think he had intended to do so, but his own overpowering interest, in the company of some one whom he thought sympathetic, had run away with him. I felt in a singularly placid mood, and the summer fields, the woodland corners, the hop-gardens, the hamlets through which we went, worked upon me like some gentle anodyne. We ate our luncheon on the shoulder of a high, upstanding ridge along which the road passed; and I was amazed at Bendyshe's knowledge of the country. There was hardly a church-tower visible that he could not name, and he was full of local and personal anecdotes which beguiled the time very pleasantly.

We got back for tea, and I then experienced something of a reaction. In spite of the beauty and comfort of the house, there came on me a sense of lurking dreariness which I could not analyse; something was going on there, in the cool rooms, the panelled corridors, which I could not penetrate. I tried to work, I tried to read—Bendyshe had gone off to the village on some friendly errand and I became aware that I did not wish to be alone. When the dressing-gong sounded, I felt a strong disinclination to leave the room. Ten minutes later I heard the front-door open. Bendyshe's brisk stride was audible in the hall. This was a relief to me; but instead of coming, as I had expected, to the library, he went quickly upstairs.

I decided that I must go too; but just as I got to the head of the stairs, I became aware that someone was coming down the corridor as if from Bendyshe's room. It was beginning to be dusk, and I could not see the figure very plainly. It was a man, carelessly dressed in an old grey suit of clothes, shuffling along very noiselessly, his head hanging down, with a markedly sullen and dejected air. The face looked healthy but careworn, and it came into my mind that it was some petitioner who had come to make a request of Bendyshe, but who had been decisively and perhaps unceremoniously refused.

I said "Good evening" to the man as he passed me, and then I had a real surprise of rather an unpleasant kind, for he took not the slightest notice of me or my salutation, as if he neither heard nor saw me; he shuffled on down the corridor and was swallowed up in the shadow at the head of the stairs. Yet it did not seem to me an intentional rudeness, but rather as if the stranger's preoccupation was so intense that there was no room in his mind for any other impression.

I went and dressed and was downstairs in the smoking-room when Bendyshe appeared. "You've had a busy evening," I said. "And I saw you got caught by a caller on coming in."

Bendyshe looked at me quickly and interrogatively. "Oh, yes," he said, "I have endless visitors—there's nothing I'm not asked to do."

"But I expect you can't always do it," I said. "I passed your friend in the corridor, and I never saw disappointment so legibly written on anyone's face as on his—he hadn't even time to exchange civilities!"

"You spoke to him?" said Bendyshe, adding, "Poor chap, yes, he has no end of troubles. But what the real trouble is I don't quite know. So, he struck you as disappointed, did he?"

"Yes, indeed," I said. "I almost wonder that you had the heart to refuse him. He looked quite worn out, and took no notice whatever· of me. I should like to know his history."

Bendyshe stared at me in silence, and it struck me that I had been impertinent. "I'm sorry," I said, "if I have been too inquisitive."

"Good Lord, it isn't that," said Bendyshe; "but the man doesn't know what he wants, or at least I don't know what he wants—I can't make out, and that's just the difficulty. And when I find out, then—well, then I shall know what to do."

Bendyshe was in a very strange mood that evening—so strange that I more than once thought that my half-formed conjecture of the previous night was true. He seemed to be wrestling against the approach of a secret and triumphant mirth. Our talk turned on the ailments of middle-age, and I confessed to being conscious of the necessity of a regime. "I don't believe in taking care of oneself," he said—"plenty of air, enough exercise, variety, work, plenty of other

175

people's business, not too much eating and drinking and smoking; and most of all, if you think you can't do a particular thing or don't want to, go and do it!"

"That's rather Spartan," I said.

"No," said Bendyshe; "it's simply this—we have all of us got three at least, or even more, people inside us. There's the one that admires and enjoys—he's all right. Then there's the one that criticises and reflects. Then there's the animal, which needs to be sensibly and good—humouredly drilled, like a dog or horse, and he's a patient and serviceable fellow enough. But behind them all, in the little innermost room, there's the one that fears, and he mustn't be listened to for a single instant, or he will run the whole show."

"I never thought of it like that," said I; "yet I'm sure you are right. But which is the one that *wills?*"

"Oh, they all do that," said Bendyshe, laughing; "it's a kind of board. The point is that the right man should have the casting vote." And then he was again overtaken by his tendency to laughter, and laughed unreservedly. I suppose that he detected some annoyance in my face, for he suddenly stopped. "Forgive me," he said; "I have a fit of the giggles sometimes, and it is bad manners. But I have been lucky today. I have made some progress—more than I expected."

After dinner we had a game of piquet, and went up to bed about midnight. As we came out at the head of the stairs, Bendyshe said, "Was it here you met my poor friend? Which way did he go?"

"Down the stairs," said I; "but I lost sight of him."

"Ah, he ought to have gone down the backstairs," said Bendyshe, "but I suppose he forgot. Hullo, what's this?" He turned sharply round. The door leading into the unfurnished bedroom was open, and the moon shone in, showing the boarded floor and the clean-cut panelling. "Who the devil did that?" said Bendyshe very irritably. "Here, come in—let's have a look. Has there been someone prowling about, I wonder?" He led the way into the room, but I felt an insupportable reluctance to enter it. "I must have this place locked up," said Bendyshe, half to himself. "Hullo, this is all quite new."

I followed him into the room, suddenly feeling the need of company. He was bending down, looking at something on the floor. "The wet must have got through," said Bendyshe to himself. I drew nearer, and saw that a quantity of plaster had fallen from the ceiling; up above an irregular square opening appeared; but what, I confess, gave me a shudder of dismay was that the plaster on the floor had a strange resemblance to the shape of a prostrate figure. I saw at once that it was a merely accidental likeness, and even as I looked Bendyshe with his foot swept the debris together.

He took me to my room and said a few friendly words. I saw that he wished to obliterate the· impression caused by his merriment. I went to bed, and, contrary to all my expectations, for the evening baa been an agitating one, I slept profoundly. But before I slept, I half determined that I would not prolong my stay. Bendyshe was behaving very oddly; but then I thought of the vicar, and I decided that as he had asked me to his house, I would go and consult him; and this brought me a sense of relief.

6

The morning turned out insufferably hot. Bendyshe was very cheerful and pleasant at breakfast. He said he had directed that some chairs should be taken out into the shade of the sycamores. "The verandah is a bit stuffy," he said, "when the wind is in the north." He had got down a parcel of books from town, new books which he thought might interest me. And when we went out there was a table, and two chairs, and an irresistible heap of neat volumes of all shapes and sizes. We sate mostly in silence; occasionally Bendyshe went off to the house, and twice at least he was summoned by the butler to see a caller. "I lead a dog's life," he said, laughing—"plenty of fleas!"

I had again become immersed in my book, when a sudden exclamation from Bendyshe, betraying a poignant and acute emotion, made me look up. He was leaning forwards, his gaze bent on the front of the house. At the closed window of the unfurnished bedroom, plainly visible, and indeed made curiously luminous by the sunlight, a man was standing looking out into the garden. He was, so far as I could judge, an elderly man, with a shock of grey hair, and a curiously blurred and puffy face, red and bloated. He was dressed in a sort of apron, dirty white, showing arms bare to the elbow. "Who's that? What's that?" said Bendyshe in indescribable agitation.

It seemed to me so unnecessary and unaccountable an excitement, that I said, "Well, if you ask me, I should say it was the plasterer come to repair the ceiling."

"You're right—you're right," said Bendyshe, with a gesture of intense relief. "Of course, I forgot—I mentioned it to Bartlett—but I didn't expect him today. I imagined—well, I don't know what I did imagine."

He got up from his chair and went hurriedly to the house.

I was by this time very seriously perturbed indeed, about Bendyshe, and began to believe that he was on the brink of insanity. It rushed into my mind that I would go to the vicarage at once. I went back to the house, where all was silent. Old Bartlett was laying the table in the dining-room. I said to him, "'If Mr. Bendyshe asks for me, will you tell him I have just gone into the village, but shall be back in a few minutes?"

He was a comfortable and amiable old fellow. "Certainly, sir," he said; "but it's a terrible hot day for the street—you'll wear your straw, no doubt, sir," and he bustled out to open the door for me.

I arrived at the vicarage—an old substantial house, behind the church—and was shown straight into the study. The vicar greeted me very warmly. "Yes, I had hoped I might see you, Mr. Hartley," he said. "I'm afraid you think you have got into a very strange place here, and I'm not surprised at your coming."

I sate down and told him the incidents of the morning and the previous day. He listened to me very gravely. Then he said: "I can't cast any light, I fear, on what has been happening—indeed, I am under a promise to Mr. Bendyshe not to do so. But the important point is this. You may be absolutely and entirely reassured about his sanity. He is as sane as you are, and a great deal more sane than I am. He is the hardest-headed man I know. Mr. Hartley, I can tell you that that man has gone through experiences which would have sent nine out of ten men crazy. And he is a man of great emotional sensibility too, but he has got infinite courage and inflexible purpose. I cannot tell you how I admire and reverence him. But I must add this: Bendyshe wants your help very much. It is worth your while to give it him, and I think that, so far as I can judge from our short acquaintance, he has made a remarkably shrewd choice. But if, on the other hand, you feel in any way alarmed or repelled by the claim, I will go over to the Manor-house with you, and insist on your being released from any obligation—and he will take my advice."

"No," I said; "once really assured of Bendyshe's sanity, I have no wish to be released. He shall have whatever help I can give him, for as long as I can give it—but I confess I do not quite trust myself."

"Mr. Hartley," said the vicar, "you have chosen the right course, and I am infinitely relieved; and I may add this, that the results may turn out to be of the utmost importance. Please consult me at any time."

Just as I was going, the vicar said, "Would it be troublesome if I asked you to take a note for me to Bendyshe? I will come round at 2. 30 to speak to him about it; but I think he ought to have this news at once."

The vicar scribbled a few words on a beet of writing-paper, enclosed in it an open telegram which was lying on the table, sealed and addressed an envelope, and handed it to me. I returned to find luncheon ready and Bendyshe pacing in the hall, evidently in a state of great suppressed excitement. I handed him the note and gave him the vicar's message. He tore the envelope open, read the enclosure, and a cry of surprise not unmixed with a deep satisfaction escaped from his lips. I thought for a moment that he was going to hand it to me; but he did not, and presently replaced it carefully in the envelope. Then he looked at me, rather a grim and searching look. "So, you went round to see the vicar?" he said. "May I ask what you went to talk about?"

"Yes, certainly," I replied. "I was beginning to feel this morning that I was getting too deep into a rather mysterious business; and I don't feel very sure of myself. You must remember how new and unfamiliar this all is to me—how little, in fact, I know of you beyond a mere acquaintanceship, to speak plainly; and I felt the other night that the vicar was a man I could trust, so I went round to ask him a few questions."

Bendyshe put down his knife and fork and drummed with his fingers on the table. "Well," he said in rather a grim tone, "what's the result?"

"He seemed to think," I said, "that you needed my assistance, and he was very insistent that I should give it, if I felt able to do so. And the long and short of it is that I decided to do so."

Bendyshe's face lit up with a smile; he held out his hand to me, and I grasped it, feeling that some compact of a momentous kind was being made. "Well, old man," he added in a tone which showed that he was deeply moved, "I can only say that I am truly grateful and thankful. It's a big business, and I want someone at hand whom I can trust, very badly indeed. Mind," he added, "I'm not afraid of anything that may happen—but I want a perfectly fair-minded man, who isn't afraid either, and that's what I feel you are. Now," he went on, "I'll have no secrets from you. Ask me any questions, and I'll answer them."

"No," I said, "I won't ask for that. I know that you want an impartial observer. I can see that something very queer is going on in this house, but I won't ask questions; I'll draw my own conclusions, and then when you think it best you shall tell me."

"That's right," said Bendyshe, "just what I want, and that's a bargain. If you will keep your ears and eyes open, it's all I ask. You may be surprised—you may even be shocked; but I can assure you that there is nothing to be afraid of—nothing whatever. We will just go our own way for a bit, and see how things turn out. Now, this letter," he went on, slapping his pocket, "is the most important thing that has happened yet. Perhaps you will see the vicar when he comes up, and tell him anything you have noticed, anything in the smallest degree unusual; and then leave us to discuss it—and thank you once again."

While we were smoking, the vicar arrived, and I saw that he looked perturbed. I left the two alone together, and half an hour later Bendyshe came to the library, and said that the vicar and himself were obliged, owing to the news received, to go away on the following day.

"We shall leave immediately after breakfast in my car," he said, "and we shall be back for dinner, unless anything unforeseen occurs. It's very inhospitable, I know," he added, "and I don't feel sure if you will care to be so long alone. Have you anything in town that you want to do? Or you could easily spend the day at the vicarage—that could be arranged. I'm afraid it is absolutely imperative for us to go."

"Oh, don't bother about me," I said. "I will do what I am very fond of doing—go out for a long vague walk, get some food at a village inn, and be back in good time in the evening. It will do me good; and I can think over things a bit."

"It's very good of you," said Bendyshe, looking decidedly relieved.

The rest of the day passed quietly enough. We sat in the garden, and the only event that struck me was that one of the gardeners and the chauffeur, in the course of the afternoon, brought a ladder across the lawn and got it into the house with some difficulty.

Bendyshe was thoughtful and cheerful. We played a game after dinner, and he proposed an early adjournment.

I was glad to go to bed—the day had been one of some agitation. But when I had got to bed I could not sleep. I was seized with a kind of detective fever, and found myself speculating as to what the whole mystery could be. I did not believe very firmly in its supernatural character, and as for the occult side of it all, I may say I was frankly sceptical. It seemed to me that the vicar and Bendyshe were probably affected by the tragic fate of Faulkner, and were perhaps inclined to attribute significance to circumstances of no great importance, but there were evidently things which had yet to be told me. While I was pursuing this train of thought—it was now nearly one—I distinctly heard soft footsteps in the corridor. I went to the door, opened it very quietly, and looked out.

I saw Bendyshe, in his shirt and trousers, carrying in his hand a lantern, walking very gently, his back to me, towards the staircase. He came to the door of the unfurnished room, drew a key from his pocket, unlocked the door, and went in, closing it with great precaution. I had a strong impulse to follow him, but thought that he might be annoyed at my intrusion; so, I left my door half-open, and feeling restless and anxious, I put on some clothes, sat down in an armchair near the door, prepared to rise and close it the moment I heard the door of the unfurnished room open. I will admit that I was far from easy in my mind about this solitary exploration, but I had by this time a robust confidence in Bendyshe's strength of will. For a time, I heard nothing; but then I began to perceive very faint muffled sounds overhead, as though Bendyshe (I supposed) was moving about slowly and cautiously, and perhaps searching for something that was not easily to be discovered—for there were long pauses between the sounds, as if the searcher were standing still.

I suddenly perceived what was happening.

The ladder had no doubt been brought upstairs and put in the unfurnished room. Bendyshe was certainly using it to obtain access through the hole in the ceiling to some room or loft overhead, and was quietly investigating it at night, so as to be secure against interruption. I confess that the nerve which would be required for such a proceeding fairly amazed me, particularly when I thought of the supernatural influences which Bendyshe clearly believed to be at work in the house.

I suppose that half an hour had passed thus, when suddenly I became aware that a very alarming interruption had happened overhead. Heavy footsteps stamped and rushed in the loft above me, then grew fainter, and then I heard the sound of a fall and a half-stifled cry from the direction of the unfurnished room. I rose and hurried down the corridor, flung open the door of the room and saw a sight which horrified me. The moonlight streamed in at the open window. Bendyshe was sitting on the ground with his hands clasped on his forehead; beside him lay the extinguished lantern.

"What has happened, Bendyshe?" I said, hastening to his side. He unclasped his hands and looked at me, and I could see that blood was flowing on to his shirt.

"I have had an accident, old man," said Bendyshe in rather a husky tone, "but I'm not much the worse, I think. No, don't ask questions—just help me up." I held out a hand and lifted him to his feet. He looked dizzily round. "Good God, what a fool I was!" he said. "I might have known it wouldn't do—here, Hartley, pick up that lantern, there's a good fellow, and come to my room with me. I don't think I'm much amiss, after all. I only hope to God that no one else heard. How did you know I was here? You came like lightning."

"I saw you go in here," I said, "and I heard you overhead—and I had a feeling that I might be wanted."

We went into the passage; I passed my arm through his, and he seemed glad of the support. He turned on the electric light in his room and I followed him into the bathroom. He was very pale, his hair disordered; the wound turned out to be at the base of his throat, a scratch or cut, torn and lacerated. He bathed it, and it proved not to be very deep. "I must have caught my neck on the broken edges of some of the laths," he said. "Well, I'm thankful it's no worse." He came back into his bedroom, and opened a small case which I saw contained some surgical appliances. He soaked a bit of cotton-wool in some disinfectant; and very deftly wrapped a bandage round his neck and under his arms, only asking me to fasten it for him. Then he dropped some liquid into a glass and swallowed it. "Now, old man," he said, "you get to bed and let me have a sleep. I have got a long day tomorrow."

"But you won't go in this condition?" I said.

"Yes, I must go," he said, "but Elton will drive. I shall be all right. I have just had a bit of a shock—I slipped on the ladder, you see, and I'm only thankful I didn't break a limb. Now go and get some sleep yourself," he added—"you look as if you wanted it; and mind, don't be *excited!* Nothing more will happen tonight, you may be sure of that—I've had a lesson, anyhow!"

And so, I left him, but lay long awake, pondering and speculating what had Bendyshe expected to find in the loft; and what had he found or seen that caused him to beat so hasty a retreat. For I knew enough of Bendyshe by this time to know that it must have been something of a very alarming or startling kind to upset him so.

7

I was relieved to find in the morning that Bendyshe showed few signs of the adventure of the previous day. The man was as tough as steel! He limped a little, and the wound in his neck was stiff and uncomfortable; but he was cheerful, not with any assumed cheerfulness, but with the tranquil assurance of the soldier who has come out unexpectedly well from a dangerous affray. I saw that the element of danger, whatever it was, about the whole investigation was a stimulus to him rather than the reverse.

It was a fine cool day, and the vicar and he started about ten o'clock. It was a four-hour drive, Bendyshe told me, and they hoped to be back at seven. "If we are delayed," he said, "we will wire at once; and if you then don't care about staying here alone, the vicar has arranged for his housekeeper to give you a cold supper at the vicarage."

I wrote a letter or two, and telling Bartlett that I should be out for luncheon and probably for tea as well, I went off soon after eleven.

It was astonishing to find how much more cheerful and light— hearted I became on getting clear of the house. I had hardly realised how much the atmosphere of the place was weighing on my spirits. It was not what had actually occurred, for that was trivial enough. It was a feeling of suspense, of hardly knowing from hour to hour what might not happen.

I walked off into the country, delighting in the freshness of the green lanes, the views from higher ground, the pleasant villages and farms I passed through. I got some bread and cheese at an inn. The landlord was a chatty old man, amiably inquisitive. He asked where I had come from, and when I said from Hebden Hill, he brightened up. He knew Hebden well, it seemed, and had some relations living there. Then he asked me if I knew the Manor-house. "You mean the big house opposite the west end of the church?" I said.

"That's it, sir," he said. "Did you ever hear tell of Squire Faulkner?" he went on.

"Yes," I said, "I have heard the name—I think the vicar mentioned it."

"Ah! that would be Mr. Fortescue," he said. "I knew him when I was a young man." Then he went on in a rambling way, telling me about the squire. "They did say he done a murder, or next door to it, and he come out of the army, and he lived all alone at the Manor with an old soldier as had been in his regiment for his servant, and they carried on dreadful. People used to say that they cooked the mice and rats and ate them, and the drink going from morning to night. But there were worse stories than that, sir," the old man went on, dropping his voice. "Folk said the squire had sold himself to you know who, sir, that ain't the one above—and that don't seem hardly worthwhile, do it?

And if the squire had an ill-will to anyone, he could bring all sorts of mischief to pass. I don't know rightly about it, sir, but it wasn't thought hardly safe to cross the squire, and they used to say that the two would catch a cat, as it might be, and burn it alive, and then it would be like poison to the man the squire had an ill-will to.

"And there was one bad story about a poor girl—a pretty girl she was, Annie Rogers by name, who lived with her mother that was a widow, and had a little money of her own. The old sergeant, it seems, took a fancy to her, and wanted her to marry him, but she couldn't abide the sight of him. That was hard enough, but then the squire got wind of it, and thought that if the sergeant married her, he would lose his servant. And they had very high words about it, it was said. But the Squire went secret to work, and first old Mrs. Rogers lost her bit of money and had to go out for jobs; and then she died; and Mr. Fortescue was very good to Annie, and took her as a servant—but she was afraid of meeting the sergeant about the place; and one day the vicar found him at the back door, speaking to Annie and frightening the girl with some nonsense; and the vicar ordered him off, and the sergeant swore and that, and the vicar went after him to the gate.

"There were some people passing by who stopped to look on; and the vicar kept quite cool, and said to the sergeant in a loud voice that he was going to say before them all what he thought of him; and he said he was a dangerous and drunken ruffian—those were his words—and that if he ever annoyed the girl again, he would have him up before the magistrates and they would put him where he would have to hold his tongue.

"The sergeant kept quiet after that for a long time; some of the Hebden men liked him well enough, for he could be very friendly when he chose, and could tell a good story. But poor Annie fell ill after that, and the vicar sent her to the seaside, but she died for all that—they said it was a decline."

The old man stopped for breath.

"But if the squire was like that," I said, "and if the people believed all this about him, did they never show him what they thought of him?"

"Well, not for a long time, sir," said the old man. "You see, he was a cousin of the vicar's, and the vicar used to stand up for him. Some of the men in the place went one day to the vicar and complained about the squire; and the vicar said to them, 'It isn't the squire,' he said, 'as does the harm—it's your fear of him. The worst harm he can do is to make you afraid of him—it's the fear does the rest.' That was a true word, sir. But a little while after that, some of the same men, who had been having a bit of a drink, went up to the Manor, and began shouting under the windows, and beating on cans, and carrying on. And some of them threw stones and broke some of. the windows—the squire would never have them mended afterwards, but boarded them up.

"Someone saw and told the vicar, and he ran down, but before he got there, the big door flung open, and the squire, he marched out, and stood on the steps between the gateposts. 'Here I am,' he says, without turning a hair, and they say his face was dreadful to look upon, all white, with his eyes flaming; and then he called them cowards, brute beasts, and a lot of things that it wouldn't be hardly proper for me to repeat nor for you to hear. And he invited them to do what they liked to him. But no one dare lift a finger. 'There,' said he, 'you daren't so much as speak.' And someone in the crowd piped up at that and called him a hard name. 'Oh, so that's what you think,' said the squire; and if you weren't such a little cur, I'd ask you to step out here, and do you the honour of knocking you down.' And then he stopped short, and said, 'But there's a better way than that!' and he looked about him, they say, like a devil, and then they began to slink away, one by one; and some of them began to run. And that was the end of that evening's work. But would you believe it, sir, Billy Dale—that's the one that spoke—within a week went clean crazy, and was took away; and after that they left the squire alone."

I felt that I had perhaps better not listen to more of these tales. I did not know how much was fact and how much fiction. But it was clear that the squire was a man suspected of unspeakable things, and not without some reason. I began to feel that the best course would be to forget all about them. But then, why was Bendyshe so hot on the scent; and suddenly, like a flash of lightning, the truth, or what seemed the truth, dawned upon me. The evil was not dead; it was alive and active; and Bendyshe was trying to drag it to the light. Evil, of course, was anywhere and everywhere. But had something been done, did something remain in the house, that formed as it were a guarded stronghold of evil? Was there a core of malignant influence which needed to be extirpated? And if so, by what hideous personal agency, what bodiless ministers of fear was it perpetuated?

And then it dawned upon me that if there was any truth in my thoughts, Bendyshe must be exposed to dangers of a kind that defied precaution, and the more courageous he was, the nearer he got to the goal, the more appalling was the danger. I could not quite understand what part the vicar was playing in all this. He was standing by Bendyshe—that was clear; but I thought that his kindly and generous nature might perhaps blind him to the danger, by lead1ng him to believe that things had never been so bad as were supposed. In any case my duty was clear: I must stand by Bendyshe at any risk, and share the danger with him. It was a contest of wills, perhaps; and I could possibly, by throwing. my own will into the scale, turn the current against our adversaries. And in any case, I felt that I must not be left any longer in the dark, but must know exactly what had happened, and what had induced Bendyshe to embark on the quest.

I wandered on in the grip of these thoughts, hardly knowing where I went; I felt for a moment that I ought to return at once to the house—that I was like a sentinel deserting his post; but, on the other hand, I felt that it might be simply foolhardy and reckless to go back and wait in solitude until Bendyshe and the vicar returned, and that some experience might befall me which would mar or damage such effectiveness as I might possess.

I got a cup of tea at an inn which proved to be about five miles from Hebden; and then I strolled quietly back, arriving about seven. To my relief the car caught me up about half a mile out of the village. Both Bendyshe and the vicar looked tired, and were very grave. I talked vaguely about my wanderings, and they gave me but scanty attention.

When we got to the house, I said to Bendyshe, "If the vicar is not too tired, would he come back to dinner?—I have a special reason for asking this. I have something to tell you and some further questions to ask." The vicar assented, and Bendyshe and I entered the house together, while the vicar pledged himself to return at eight.

Bendyshe went to the smoking-room, and flung himself down in a deep chair.

"Any the worse for yesterday?" I said.

"Oh, I'm stiff as a board, and dog-tired," he said rather impatiently, "and just when I had need of all my strength; but we have found what we wanted to know, and it is all as I expected, only worse; and now the whole business is in such a tangle that I hardly know what to do!" Then he added, "Why were you so keen that the vicar should come back? He has had a shock, and seems to me done up."

"I couldn't help it," I said; "today I have thought it all out, and I'll stick to you through thick and thin; but I feel that I must know all, and

186

know at once. If I am to share a danger, I must know what the danger is; I can't be of any use if I am still groping in the dark."

"Yes, you're right," said Bendyshe wearily.

"I have been feeling that too—but I wanted you to form your own opinion."

When we went up to dress, Bendyshe said, looking round, "I don't like the feel of the house tonight, old man. There's mischief brewing of a bad kind—but we'll weather it out!"

I was conscious too myself of a sort of heavy and brooding stillness everywhere; but I saw and heard nothing.

8

At dinner, while the servants were in the room, we did our best to talk of indifferent matters. It was like a bad play, I thought. When we adjourned to the smoking-room, Bendyshe said to the vicar, "Here, vicar, Hartley says that he thinks he had better have the whole story, and I agree with him. He won't be taken by surprise; and it's no use pretending now that it is a mild sort of investigation; it's a battle of a bad kind, and we must be forearmed, if we can. I made a mistake last night by taking the offensive and now hell's loose—— But I'll go ahead.

"It was about three years ago that the thing began," said Bendyshe. "I don't know why it didn't begin before—perhaps it *had* begun; but I had been getting more and more interested in my problem, and I had been, I suppose, training my perceptions without knowing it; and the curtain went up with a run. I ought to say that when I first settled in here, I had taken the unfurnished room for my study. But I could never work there in any peace. There seemed to be something on the move there, and if I sate at the table, I used to feel there was someone behind me; and there were odd noises overhead too. I had the roof examined—the only way in was through a little trapdoor in the ceiling, in the corner where the plaster came down—but above, there was only a long, low loft, lit by a window looking out on the tiles and gutters, with a cistern in it and waterpipes, and the builder said that the noises came from the pipes.

"However, one day I was coming down the corridor, I saw a man standing by the door of the room—the same man, Hartley, I will tell you at once, that you saw up there, the same dress, the same sort of expression. I thought it must be a plumber for a moment; when it suddenly came upon me with a rush that the wall, so to speak, was broken

187

down, and I had seen something that a normal healthy man has no business to see. I said out loud, 'What are you doing there?—who are you?' but he took no notice of me whatever, and continued to stand by the door, like a man who wanted something badly, and had been trying for a long time to get it, but all in vain.

"I didn't think of it as being in any definite and actual way connected with the place—I thought it was an hallucination produced by overtasking my nerves in one direction. I went along to the door, my eyes fixed on the man, and suddenly he was gone. I wasn't exactly frightened, but I felt uneasy about myself. I went up to town and saw a doctor, a friend of mine. He sounded me and questioned me up and down; then he declared me perfectly well in every way. I told him about my studies and he asked me if I had ever seen any such figure in real life, in childhood, or had any fright or shock connected with such a figure. But I couldn't think of anything. He told me at last that he was frankly puzzled, but that he had little doubt that it was an hallucination, and did in some way result from my thinking so much about such phenomena. He gave me the advice to turn to other occupations for a bit, limit my work, have more company in the house—all very sensible.

"I did just what he advised, and had a succession of guests here, who bored me to death; and I took up constitutional history, as the least exciting subject I could find. But a fortnight later I saw the thing again, this time in my study, looking up at the trapdoor. I got up, and walked straight up to him and the same thing happened; he took no notice of me whatever, and when I was within a foot of him, disappeared.

"Then I did what I ought to have done before; I went to the vicar and told him the whole story—and then it came out. The vicar told me, with a good deal of hesitation, that the figure I described was beyond all doubt the figure of Hugh Faulkner himself, just as he looked in his later years. Wasn't that so?"

The vicar nodded. "It was unmistakable, your description! And it gave me a dreadful shock, though I can't say I was exactly surprised." Then the vicar turned to me and said, "Of course, Mr. Hartley, I am a firm believer in the immortality of the spirit; and I believe that we preserve identity and intelligence, and are not much affected or altered by death; but the spirit is, of course, a bodiless thing—a conscious and intelligent influence. I want to make this clear. There was nothing *material* there to see; but I realised that Bendyshe had somehow or other got within the range of Faulkner's thought, and that the figure was evolved out of this thought acting on Bendyshe's mind, just as we evolve figures in our dreams."

"Yes," said Bendyshe, "but I was also aware that Faulkner was not consciously influencing me—in fact, I think he was wholly unaware of my existence then; and this was a great relief to me—I was simply a spectator of what was going on, just as you were when you saw him. In fact, if I may say so, I doubt if it was *his* mind acting on yours which made you see him. I think it was *my* mind. And then," he went on, "I saw the figure pretty often. But never in the presence of anyone else— that seemed an absolute bar, I don't know why. I lost all fear of it, and just accepted it as a fact Once or twice I saw it in the garden, and once or twice downstairs, but almost always in the corridor upstairs, or in the empty room. But I didn't want to run any risks. So, I had the trap- door plastered up, moved the furniture out, and locked the place up.

"Meanwhile I speculated about it, and dis cussed it with the vicar; and we came to the conclusion that there was some particular thing that Faulkner was—I won't say looking for exactly, but trying to trace, some book, perhaps, or manuscript—I couldn't make it out—but we decided at last that it was something which someone else had hidden; but was it in the house at all? Or if so, why couldn't he see it? Or if he could see it, what could he do with it? I don't believe that these spirits have any material powers at all—they can only act through liv- ing brains."

I turned to the vicar. "Did you ever see the figure?" I said.

"No," he said, "I did not—I don't know why. I was nearer to Faulkner than anyone living, except his servant. But I have thought that perhaps Faulkner wished to conceal the very existence of the thing, whatever it is, from me, and was careful not to bring me in."

"But why then did Bendyshe see him?" I asked.

"Oh," said Bendyshe, "I stumbled into it by accident, I believe—it was just a question of my power of perception being heightened." "But let me ask one other thing," I said:

"How do you account for your seeing it only occasionally? If the thing is always in Faulkner's mind, you ought to see it constantly."

"Well," said Bendyshe, "we don't know what his mental occupa- tions may be—I daresay he has other things to think of."

"Yes, indeed," said the vicar, shaking his head;" he was a very self- willed and perverse man—he has much to learn."

Bendyshe gave a grim smile, and went on, "What I believe is this—

that at times the spirit of Faulkner remembers this thing, whatever it is, and believes it to be still in this house. The result is that for a time his thought is occupied with the house and the familiar rooms; and being an abstract essence, it ranges about the well—known scene; and if one comes within the reach of it, one sees the figure automatically."

"But why, then, does the figure disappear when you come close to it?"

"Ah, I don't know everything," said Bendyshe; "indeed, there is much that quite baffles me. But I have thought that it may be in some way obliterated by the proximity of my own consciousness, as the moon obliterates the light of the surrounding stars—but that is only my idea.

"And now," he went on, "we come to the more serious part of the story. Some weeks ago, I became suddenly aware that the spirit of Faulkner had become aware of mine. I suppose I had begun to speculate more closely as to where the lost thing was, and what it might be. And then, too, it had occurred to me that the old sergeant might be still alive—the vicar had told me that he thought he was dead—and I had begun to make some enquiries, and had employed a detective to try to trace the man. We now know that he was alive all the time. Faulkner had given him some money at various times, and after Faulkner's death the sergeant had rented a farm in Hampshire, a little bit of a place; but he had taken to drink, and was in a bad way, nearly at the end of his resources.

"He became aware that he was being tracked, and I daresay there were plenty of other things about which he might have got into trouble. Anyhow, he was frightened. He sold his farm, which was mortgaged, so he only got a few pounds out of it; and he went off on the tramp. The money was spent at last, and he took cold by sleeping in the open air; he was taken to the workhouse at Pentlow, near Horsham, and went to the infirmary with rheumatic fever.

"But I must go back for a moment. While all this was going on, I became aware, as I told you, that I had for some reason or other come within Faulkner's consciousness, and that he realised that someone was on the same scent as himself. His expression seemed to me to change when I saw him, he looked angry and defiant, and as though he was guarding the approach to something. But even so he was not apparently at first conscious of my physical presence. Then he assumed a menacing air, and made gestures of anger and rage. It was at this time that I asked you to join me here, because I began to feel that I *must*

190

have someone with me that I could not be sure of my nerves not failing me; moreover, his appearances became much more frequent.

"And then you came, but instead of telling you everything at once, which would have been by far the best course, I waited, in order to see whether you had any perception of his presence; and when you began to notice certain phenomena, I made excuses and gave explanations—it was all very stupid—in order that you might have your own experiences and draw your own conclusions.

"And then a quite new development occurred. The old sergeant died in the workhouse, and the first intimation of it that I got was the appearance of a new figure at the window, which you also saw. I did not know what to make of this, though I had a strong suspicion; but it happened that they found on the man a letter from someone in the village—one of his old acquaintances—which seemed to show that he had lived here; and then they wired to the vicar to say that an unknown man had died in the workhouse—they gave a brief description of him—who seemed to have once lived at Hebden. The vicar sent the wire on to me, as you know, and I was sure who it was; we went off together to identify him, and the vicar recognised him at once. That is the position of affairs."

"But," I said, "in what way is he connected with these papers, or whatever they are?"

"Do you remember," said Bendyshe, "that the vicar said something about a despatch-box that was missing after Faulkner's death?"

The vicar turned to me. "I ought to have been more explicit," he said. "For some time before his death, I noticed that Faulkner was always writing when I saw him, and that when I came in, he always slipped the papers into an old despatch-box on the table, and locked them up. I remember once asking him what he was writing. 'My memoirs,' he said with an ugly kind of smile—'an interesting book, don't you think?' When he died, I am nearly certain that the box was by his bedside, though I could not swear to it; and we thought—the lawyer who came down to see about the property and I—that there might be papers of importance in it; but when we questioned the sergeant, who knew the box perfectly well, he stuck to it that he hadn't seen the box for the day or two preceding Faulkner's death, and that he was quite certain that Faulkner had hidden it somewhere—and I couldn't be sure that he was not right."

"Yes," said Bendyshe, "and what I conjecture happened was that the sergeant, thinking that the contents of the box might be valuable, or indeed might incriminate himself in some way, had secured it himself, meaning later to remove it. That would explain everything—it would explain why Faulkner did not seem to know where it was, and further it would explain what happened to me there last night."

"What exactly did happen?" I asked.

"I'll tell you," said Bendyshe, looking up at me, "just how it was. I had had a ladder brought up here. Whether the fall of the plaster was purely accidental, I don't know, but anyhow it gave me the idea that the papers had been hidden up in the loft. I didn't like to ask you to join me, Hartley, but I did a very rash and idiotic thing. In the afternoon, I took the ladder into the room, and when the house was all quiet, I went in with a lantern and up into the loft. At first all was quiet, and I hunted about everywhere, but found nothing. Then suddenly I became aware that I was not alone, and I saw two figures standing together in the far corner of the loft looking down at the boarded floor.

"And then I felt no doubt at all that I had got near the hiding-place. I had better have gone away at once, and bided my time; but instead, I was fool enough to go to the place. I don't quite know what happened. They flew at me like two wild beasts. It was not a case of any physical violence—it was just a contest of will and brain; but I had all the terror of being attacked, without the possibility of offering any physical resistance. I simply felt that my mind would give way. I ran down the loft, and tried to get on to the ladder; but I slipped when I was half through the hole, cut my neck, I suppose, on the jagged edges of the broken laths; and you heard my fall!"

"What an appalling business!" I said—and there was a silence for a moment. Then I said, "But why did the sergeant not remove the box after Faulkner's death?"

"Ah! I can explain that," said the vicar. "He had not the time. We had moved Faulkner's body into another room, and we had some talk with the sergeant, Mr. Hartley, and I suppose he was frightened. He had got hold of a certain amount of money, as it was; and I imagine he never dared to come back."

"There are just two things more," I said: "what *are* these papers, after all?"

"Ah! that I don't know," said Bendyshe; "but I imagine that they are what Faulkner called his experiments—an account of what he did, or tried to do, and the devices by which he carried them out. The force he used was fear, and the question is, how can you frighten people purely through the agency of the mind? We must remember that Faulkner was a very able man, and that the sergeant was clever enough in his way too—and that they were both men of remarkable courage and force of character."

"And if we grant that," I said, "what do they want to do with the papers?"

"My belief," said Bendyshe, "is that they just want to guard them—to preserve them somehow. I don't think they have a very clear idea about them. They don't want them to be made public, and yet they want to hand on their secrets to someone who will use them. If any of us three, for instance, were a man inclined to make use of these evil agencies, we should encounter no opposition; but at present they simply know that we are hostile, that we want to find the papers, and perhaps to put an end to them; and this they mean to prevent as well as they can."

"What are we going to do?" I said.

"I am afraid that the question rather is," said Bendyshe, "what are *they* going to do?"

The words were hardly out of his lips when an answer came—a thin high mocking laugh was heard in the air, in the middle of us. I can't say how inexpressibly horrible it was, to feel in the presence of something hostile and derisive, and yet not to know what it could do or might do. The horror was that it was *there*. The silent auditor knew what we had said and what was in our minds; and we could do nothing. It seemed to me for a moment as if I should lose control of myself, and that my brain would give way under the consciousness of this unseen and intangible presence. I looked at Bendyshe; and he was sitting clasping the arms of his chair, looking down and frowning.

The vicar rose unsteadily to his feet, his face very pale. "Merciful God," he said, "here have I been fighting with evil all my days, and trying to think it was weaker than good—and now that I am confronted with it; I can do nothing—nothing."

"No," said Bendyshe, looking up; "that isn't so, vicar! You have a far stronger hold of this business than either Hartley or myself. We are just fighting for ourselves and our sanity, but you have got bigger forces with you. I want to ask you one thing: Hartley and I—or I—must go and find this thing, whatever it *is—and there's no time to be lost!* The longer we put it off, the worse it will be. But will you stay with us, and see the end? Whatever happens, you must not lose faith."

When Bendyshe spoke of the necessity of our going straight to our goal and without delay, I confess that I had an access of fear more terrible than anything I had ever experienced. The blood seemed to stand still in my brain—my strength seemed to ebb from me; but I felt too that the idea of giving up, of turning tail now, would leave even a worse legacy of terror behind. It was not a question of moral courage—there simply was no way out.

The vicar said nothing in reply, but he put his hand out—clasped first Bendyshe's and then mine. And the next minute we were out in the hall. Then Bendyshe took command.

9

We had risen, and stood looking at each other in silence.

"Now, don't hurry," Bendyshe said. "Try just to think of what we are going to do. I shall want something to prize up the boards with. I know!" He went back to the smoking-room, and returned in a moment with an old ice-axe. Its blade was protected by a leathern cover, and Bendyshe slipped it off. Then he strode to the foot of the stairs and went deliberately up; I followed him, and the vicar followed me. In a moment we were on the landing. The house was deathly still, with a brooding stillness, like that of a thunder-cloud. Bendyshe drew out his key, and produced two electric torches from his pocket, and then said, "Now, I go first, because I know where the thing is; and when I am up the ladder—in the loft, Hartley you come up; and, vicar, will you stay in the room, and lend a hand? And mind this—they can do *nothing* so long as we don't fear them; or if we do, we must behave as if we did not."

Then he unlocked the door, and we went into the room. Bendyshe clicked on both the electric torches, and gave one to the vicar. The moon was shining bright, and the shadow of the casements lay dark on the floor.

Then I suddenly became aware of a strange shadow, of an impenetrable blackness, in the corner of the room under the trapdoor. But Bendyshe strode out straight to the foot of the ladder, and seemed to me for a moment engulfed in darkness. I followed close behind; and there was nothing there. "You see," said Bendyshe to me in a low tone—"it will all be like that."

But as we stood together at the foot of the ladder, a stream of ice-cold air came gushing down from the hole in the ceiling, as if coming out of some frozen cave, so cold that I felt my very bones shivering under their covering of flesh. But Bendyshe slipped his hand through the loop of the axe, and then very slowly and deliberately began to ascend the ladder. "Come when I call," he said, "and not before."

I looked round; the vicar was on his knees in prayer; but neither that nor Bendyshe's courage gave me any relief. I just thought of the next thing I had to do. Bendyshe disappeared through the hole, and I heard him step out on the floor of the loft. Then he said, "Now come!" The vicar held his torch up to illuminate the steps of the ladder, and step by step I went slowly up in the icy air.

As soon as my head and shoulders were in the loft, I felt Bendyshe grasp my arm. "Steady," he said, "step carefully." Bendyshe raised his torch, which sent a long stream of light down the loft, and then in the silence came a strange tremor and agitation of the empty air. "Now," said Bendyshe, "it will be all over in a moment! Hold on to the top of the ladder, and keep your eye on me." He walked slowly along the loft, to a place about twenty feet away, looking carefully at the boards and turning the torch down on them. "Now," he said, "come up here slowly and hold the torch for me—this is the place!"

Bendyshe bent his head down, and examined the boards. Then he raised his axe and delivered a tremendous blow at the chink between the boards, and then another. The chips of the broken board flew out on the floor; suddenly from the hole he had made there was protruded a dusky thing. It was the head of a great snake; I could see its dull blinking eyes, the black spots that ran in a chain down its forehead, its flickering tongue, and the greenish pallor of its throat.

Bendyshe struck another blow, and the creature came out, reared itself up as though to strike at us, and then as suddenly darted back into the hole again. Bendyshe again raised the axe, and struck fearlessly again. There was now a considerable hole between the boards, and he reversed the axe, inserted the point under the loose board, and putting his foot on the head of the axe brought it down like a lever; the board cracked and split; Bendyshe dropped the axe, and bending down seized the board and tore it up.

A dreadful sight met my eyes. The whole cavity was filled with snakes, entwining, interlocked, writhing; sometimes a head was put up from the mass, and sometimes half a dozen would detach themselves and wriggle over the floor. I must confess that I was now half frantic with horror. But Bendyshe plunged his hands into the mass of snakes, and drew out an old leather despatch-box covered with dust. "This is it," he said; and I was bending down to look at it, when a thing more dreadful than any of our previous experiences occurred.

The icy air beat upon us, and turning my head, I saw standing beside us, stiff and upright, a corpse, swathed in graveclothes, with pale leaden-coloured hands hanging down; the face was of the same hue, with a fringe of ragged-looking grey hair straggling over the forehead. It had a faint smile, it seemed, on its lips, and its dull eyes, grey like chalcedony, looked fixedly at the opening in the floor; and then a heavy odour of corruption began to spread around us. And then for a moment I wished that I had died rather than have come into this place of horrors. Bendyshe himself turned, and confronted the gaze of the figure. Then he signed to me to pick up the torch and axe, and walked firmly down the loft to the ladder's head.

"Go down first," he said," and I will lower the box to you—don't leave go of it, whatever happens."

And so, I pushed on. It was no time to hesitate. I climbed hastily down the ladder, and on reaching the floor, saw the vicar standing with his back to me, looking out of the window. But I had no time to attend to anything else, and cried out in a cautious tone, "Now, the box"—and it appeared from the orifice. I seized hold of it, and a moment later Bendyshe began to descend the ladder. But when he reached me, I saw that his strength was failing. At that moment the vicar turned round, and came up to me with outstretched hands as if to receive the box. I was about to hand it to him, when Bendyshe cried out in an unsteady voice, "No, no—keep hold of it, I say—don't you see?"

And then I hardly knew for a moment what happened. Something seemed to rush towards me in a passion half of rage, half of entreaty. I was fighting with shadows. The figure that I had thought to be the vicar came nearer and looked me in the face—and it was Faulkner himself, in a fury of baffled rage and despair, such as a human mind can hardly conceive; and while I gazed fascinated, I heard Bendyshe come close beside me; and the vicar himself came forward out of the dark corner of the room, and after that I knew no more.

I awoke not long after from a kind of stupor. I was conscious of having been led and propelled down the corridor. I was in my bedroom, lying on my bed, and the vicar was sitting beside me with a very anxious face.

"How do you feel?" he said in a gentle voice.

"Oh," I said, "I'm all right—in mind, that is; I feel very tired and battered, but not damaged, at least not irretrievably. What I most want is sleep, I think. I suppose I fainted?"

"Yes," said the vicar, "and I was afraid it was worse; but don't let us talk about that now."

"Where is Bendyshe?" I said.

"Oh, he is all right," said the vicar; "he has just gone to get something for you. He will be here in a moment. He is very anxious, and so am I, that we should settle at once, without any delay, about these papers, whatever they are. But he and I disagree; and if you feel up to it, he would like to have your opinion."

"I don't know that my opinion is worth much just now," I said.

But at that moment Bendyshe entered the room with a little cut-glass flask in his hand. He showed few traces of an ordeal—indeed he looked more self-possessed and determined than ever. He carried the box with him, I noticed. He came to my bedside and took my hand. "Well, old man," he said, "this is a good sight! I was afraid . . . well, I won't say what I feared, but I felt that if things had gone wrong, I should never have forgiven myself for bringing you in. How are you feeling—only a faint, you think? Well, I am sure of it—heart, not brain, gave way." He poured something out of the flask, a clear aromatic liquid, and asked me to drink it off. "It is quite harmless," he said. "It will give you an extreme lucidity of mind for about half an hour, and then the best sleep you have ever had in your life."

I drank it, and the other two sat in silence. A few minutes later I sat up and said, "It is very strange—I could not have believed I could have felt like this. I can remember and see quite clearly all that happened yesterday—was it yesterday? But there's no horror about it. I feel extraordinarily happy—something poisonous seems to have cleared away, and I don't think it will come back."

"Yes," said Bendyshe, "I think we have cleared the air somewhat—blown up the wasps' nest, perhaps! But now—do you feel fit to hear two sides of a question? These horrible papers—what is to be done with them? My own view is that I should go through them carefully. They may have immense evidential value. Here is the packet."

He opened the despatch-box—I noticed that he had forced the lid—and took out a small packet of papers, not more than a hundred sheets, I guessed, carefully tied up with black ribbon, and sealed with two large seals. He put the packet in my hands. On the first page was written in a bold handwriting,

A record of experiments made at Hebden Manor-house between the years 1890 and 1903, with the results obtained by

Hugh Faulkner and Harry M'Gee. It is earnestly desired that anyone into whose hands they may come will have them examined by someone of scientific eminence, as they deal with the surprising development of a comparatively unknown psychical force, the results of which have been of an extraordinary character.

It was signed *"Hugh Faulkner."*

"Mind," said Bendyshe, "I will take the entire and sole responsibility for examining the packet; and I will add that if I had been able to find the packet unaided—as I think I should have done—I should have gone through the whole thing with the utmost care."

"Bendyshe," said the vicar, very gravely—and I saw that he was in a state of great depression and exhaustion—"I implore you not to speak like this! If you had attempted to take possession of the packet single-handed, it would have cost you your reason, and perhaps your life. It may be that you would have lost something even more precious than life. And I must say something more, painful though it may be. You are not as strong as you think! You are in greater danger at the moment than you were in either of your two visits to that unholy place up there. My feeling is that the papers should be instantly destroyed. I regard them as I would regard a case which I knew to contain the living germs of all the deadliest diseases known to humanity. For you to read them would be deliberately to introduce into your own spirit the most satanical of all infections."

Bendyshe listened to the vicar's words with a look of ill-concealed impatience, and then turning to me, he said, "Now, Hartley, it is for you to decide. The quest was mine, and it was the vicar's duty to help me; but you are the volunteer, who might have been a martyr, who made the search successful. I leave it in your hands."

"Bendyshe," I said, "you have given me a dreadful task. I see what you feel about it, but I have no sort of doubt that the vicar is right. We have torn the evil out by the roots, with terrible risks; and you would propose to plant it again for the sake of scientific curiosity?"

Bendyshe stood holding the packet in his hands.

"You would destroy knowledge which has been paid for by a man's soul," he said.

"Yes," said the vicar, "because it is the price of blood—and you dare not traffic with that!"

I looked up; and in a flash I saw, a little way from the group, the figure of Faulkner kneeling, his hands clasped and a look of agonised entreaty on his face. I lost control of myself. "It must be destroyed at once," I said, "now and here!"

"Very well," said Bendyshe, "I yield—but I shall regret it all my life!" He said no more, but drew a knife from his pocket, cut the ribbon, drew out a mass of closelywritten sheets, stuffed them loosely into the empty hearth, and set fire to the heap. The little pile flared up, and in five minutes was a glowing lump, the writing standing out in lines of fire; and a moment later it was nothing but ashes. And at that moment Bendyshe and the vicar, who had been gazing at the fire, looked up; and they too saw the figure of Faulkner. But then a strange thing happened, and so swiftly that I can hardly say what it was—a figure in white, young, radiant, smiling, seemed to step up to Faulkner from behind, like a bringer of good tidings.

Bendyshe put his hand before his eyes. The vicar clasped his hands together. "The uttermost farthing!" he said in a tone of intense joy, "and he departs thence—that is the mercy of God."

The Closed Window

The Tower of Nort stood in a deep angle of the downs; formerly an old road led over the hill, but it is now a green track covered with turf; the later highway choosing rather to cross a low saddle of the ridge, for the sake of the beasts of burden. The tower, originally built to guard the great road, was a plain, strong, thick-walled fortress. To the tower had been added a plain and seemly house, where the young Sir Mark de Nort lived very easily and plentifully. To the south stretched the great wood of Nort, but the tower stood high on an elbow of the down, sheltered from the north by the great green hills.

The villagers had an odd ugly name for the tower, which they called the Tower of Fear; but the name was falling into disuse, and was only spoken, and that heedlessly, by ancient men, because Sir Mark was vexed to hear it so called. Sir Mark was not yet thirty, and had begun to say that he must marry a wife; but he seemed in no great haste to do so, and loved his easy, lonely life, with plenty of hunting and hawking on the down. With him lived his cousin and heir, Roland Ellice, a heedless good-tempered man, a few years older than Sir Mark; he had come on a visit to Sir Mark, when he first took possession of the tower; and there had seemed no reason why he should go away; the two suited each other; Sir Mark was sparing of speech, fond of books and of rhymes. Roland was different, loving ease and wine and talk, and finding in Mark a good listener. Mark loved his cousin, and thought it praiseworthy of him to stay and help to cheer so sequestered a house, since there were few neighbours within reach.

And yet Mark was not wholly content with his easy life; there were many days when he asked himself why he should go thus quietly on, day by day, like a stalled ox; still, there appeared no reason why he should do otherwise; there were but few folk on his land, and they were content; yet he sometimes envied them their bondage and their round of daily duties. The only place where he could else have been was with the army, or even with the court; but Sir Mark was no soldier, and even less of a courtier; he hated tedious gaiety, and it was a time of peace. So, because he loved solitude and quiet he lived at home, and sometimes thought himself but half a man; yet was he happy after a sort, but for a kind of little hunger of the heart.

What gave the tower so dark a name was the memory of old Sir James de Nort, Mark's grandfather, an evil and secret man, who had dwelt at Nort under some strange shadow; he had driven his son from his doors, and lived at the end of his life with his books and his own close thoughts, spying upon the stars and tracing strange figures in books; since his death the old room in the turret top, where he came by his end in a dreadful way, had been closed; it was entered by a turret-door, with a flight of steps from the chamber below. It had four windows, one to each of the winds; but the window which looked upon the down was fastened up, and secured with a great shutter of oak.

One day of heavy rain, Roland, being wearied of doing nothing, and vexed because Mark sat so still in a great chair, reading in a book, said to his cousin at last that he must go and visit the old room, in which he had never set foot. Mark closed his book, and smiling indulgently at Roland's restlessness, rose, stretching himself, and got the key; and together they went up the turret stairs. The key groaned loudly in the lock, and, when the door was thrown back, there appeared a high faded room, with a timbered roof, and with a dose, dull smell. Round the walls were presses, with the doors fast; a large oak table, with a chair beside it, stood in the middle. The walls were otherwise bare and rough; the spiders had spun busily over the windows and in the angles.

Roland was full of questions, and Mark told him all he had heard of old Sir James and his silent ways, but said that he knew nothing of the disgrace that had seemed to envelop him, or of the reasons why he had so evil a name. Roland said that he thought it a shame that so fair a room should lie so nastily, and pulled one of the casements open, when a sharp gust broke into the room, with so angry a burst of rain, that he closed it again in haste; little by little, as they talked, a shadow began to fall upon their spirits, till Roland declared that there was still a blight upon the place; and Mark told him of the death of old Sir James, who had been found after a day of silence, when he had not set foot outside his chamber, lying on the floor of the room, strangely bedabbled with wet and mud, as though he had come off a difficult journey, speechless, and with a look of anguish on his face; and that he had died soon after they had found him, muttering words that no one understood.

Then the two young men drew near to the closed window; the shutters were tightly barred, and across the panels was scrawled in red, in an uncertain hand, the words *claudit et nemo aperit*, which Mark explained was the Latin for the text, *he shutteth and none openeth*. And then Mark said that the story went that it was ill for the man that opened the window, and that shut it should remain for him. But Roland girded at him for his want of curiosity, and had laid a hand upon the bar as though to open it, but Mark forbade him urgently.

"Nay," said he, "let it remain so—we must not meddle with the will of the dead!" and as he said the word, there came so furious a gust upon the windows that it seemed as though some stormy thing would beat them open; so, they left the room together, and presently descending, found the sun struggling through the rain.

But both Mark and Roland were sad and silent all that day; for though they spake not of it, there was a desire in their minds to open the closed window, and to see what would befall; in Roland's mind it was like the desire of a child to peep into what is forbidden; but in Mark's mind a sort of shame to be so bound by an old and weak tale of superstition.

Now it seemed to Mark, for many days, that the visit to the turret-room had brought a kind of shadow down between them. Roland was peevish and ill-at-ease; and ever the longing grew upon Mark, so strongly that it seemed to him that something drew him to the room, some beckoning of a hand or calling of a voice.

Now one bright and sunshiny morning it happened that Mark was left alone within the house. Roland had ridden out early, not saying where he was bound. And Mark sat, more listlessly than was his wont, and played with the ears of his great dog, that sat with his head upon his master's knee, looking at him with liquid eyes, and doubtless wondering why Mark went not abroad.

Suddenly Sir Mark's eye fell upon the key of the upper room, which lay on the window-ledge where he had thrown it; and the desire to go up and pluck the heart from the little mystery came upon him with a strength that he could not resist; he rose twice and took up the key, and fingering it doubtfully, laid it down again; then suddenly he took it up, and went swiftly into the turret stair, and up, turning, turning, till his head was dizzy with the bright peeps of the world through the loophole windows. Now all was green, where a window gave on the down; and now it was all clear air and sun, the warm breeze coming pleasantly into the cold stairway; presently Mark heard the pattering of feet on the stair below, and knew that the old hound had determined to follow him; and he waited a moment at the door, half pleased, in his strange mood, to have the company of a living thing. So, when the dog was at his side, he stayed no longer, but opened the door and stepped within the room.

The room, for all its faded look, had a strange air about it, and though he could not say why, Mark felt that he was surely expected. He did not hesitate, but walked to the shutter and considered it for a moment; he heard a sound behind him. It was the old hound who sat with his head aloft, sniffing the air uneasily; Mark called him and held out his hand, but the hound would not move; he wagged his tail as though to acknowledge that he was called, and then he returned to his uneasy quest.

Mark watched him for a moment, and saw that the old dog had made up his mind that all was not well in the room, for he lay down, gathering his legs under him, on the threshold, and watched his master with frightened eyes, quivering visibly. Mark, no lighter of heart, and in a kind of fearful haste, pulled the great staple off the shutter and set it on the ground, and then wrenched the shutters back; the space revealed was largely filled by old and dusty webs of spiders, which Mark lightly tore down, using the staple of the shutters to do this; it was with a strange shock of surprise that he saw that the window was dark, or nearly so; it seemed as though there were some further obstacle outside; yet Mark knew that from below the leaded panes of the window were visible.

He drew back for a moment, but, unable to restrain his curiosity, wrenched the rusted casement open. But still all was dark without; and there came in a gust of icy wind from outside; it was as though something had passed him swiftly, and he heard the old hound utter a strangled howl; then turning, he saw him spring to his feet with his hair bristling and his teeth bare, and next moment the dog turned and leapt out of the room.

Mark, left alone, tried to curb a tide of horror that swept through his veins; he looked round at the room, flooded with the southerly sunlight, and then he turned again to the dark window, and putting a strong constraint upon himself, leaned out, and saw a thing which bewildered him so strangely that he thought for a moment his senses had deserted him. He looked out on a lonely dim hillside, covered with rocks and stones; the hill came up close to the window, so that he could have jumped down upon it, the wall below seeming to be built into the rocks. It was all dark and silent, like a clouded night, with a faint light coming from whence he could not see. The hill sloped away very steeply from the tower, and he seemed to see a plain beyond, where at the same time he knew that the down ought to lie.

In the plain there was a light, like the firelit window of a house; a little below him some shape like a crouching man seemed to run and slip among the stones, as though suddenly surprised, and seeking to escape. Side by side with a deadly fear which began to invade his heart, came an uncontrollable desire to leap down among the rocks; and then it seemed to him that the figure below stood upright, and began to beckon him.

There came over him a sense that he was in deadly peril; and, like a man on the edge of a precipice, who has just enough will left to try to escape, he drew himself by main force away from the window, closed it, put the shutters back, replaced the staple, and, his limbs all trembling, crept out of the room, feeling along the walls like a palsied man. He locked the door, and then, his terror overpowering him, he fled down the turret-stairs. Hardly thinking what he did, he came out on the court, and going to the great well that stood in the centre of the yard, he went to it and flung the key down, hearing it clink on the sides as it fell. Even then he dared not re-enter the house, but glanced up and down, gazing about him, while the cloud of fear and horror by insensible degrees dispersed, leaving him weak and melancholy.

Presently Roland returned, full of talk, but broke off to ask if Mark were ill. Mark, with a kind of surliness, an unusual mood for him, denied it somewhat sharply. Roland raised his eyebrows, and said no more, but prattled on. Presently after a silence he said to Mark, "What did you do all the morning?" and it seemed to Mark as though this were accompanied with a spying look.

An unreasonable anger seized him. "What does it matter to you what I did?" he said. "May not I do what I like in my own house?"

"Doubtless," said Roland, and sate silent with uplifted brows; then he hummed a tune, and presently went out.

They sate at dinner that evening with long silences, contrary to their wont, though Mark bestirred himself to ask questions. When they were left alone, Mark stretched out his hand to Roland, saying, "Roland, forgive me! I spoke to you this morning in a way of which I am ashamed; we have lived so long together—and yet we came nearer to quarrelling today than we have ever done before; and it was my fault."

Roland smiled, and held Mark's hand for a moment. "Oh, I had not given it another thought," he said; "the wonder is that you can bear with an idle fellow as you do."

Then they talked for a while with the pleasant glow of friendliness that two good comrades feel when they have been reconciled. But late in the evening Roland said, "Was there any story, Mark, about your grandfather's leaving any treasure of money behind him?"

The question grated somewhat unpleasantly upon Mark's mood; but he controlled himself and said, "No, none that I know of—except that he found the estate rich and left it poor—and what he did with his revenues no one knows—you had better ask the old men of the village; they know more about the house than I do. But, Roland, forgive me once more if I say that I do not desire Sir James's name to be mentioned between us. I wish we had not entered his room; I do not know how to express it, but it seems to me as though he had sate there, waiting quietly to be summoned, and as though we had troubled him, and—as though he had joined us. I think he was an evil man, close and evil. And there hangs in my mind a verse of Scripture, where Samuel said to the witch, '*Why hast thou disquieted me to bring me up?*' Oh," he went on, "I do not know why I talk wildly thus"; for he saw that Roland was looking at him with astonishment, with parted lips; "but a shadow has fallen upon me, and there seems evil abroad."

From that day forward a heaviness lay on the spirit of Mark that could not be scattered. He felt, he said to himself, as though he had meddled light-heartedly with something far deeper and more danger-ous than he had supposed—like a child that has aroused some evil beast that slept. He had dark dreams too. The figure that he had seen among the rocks seemed to peep and beckon him, with a mock-ing smile, over perilous places, where he followed unwilling. But the heavier he grew the lighter-hearted Roland became; he seemed to walk in some bright vision of his own, intent upon a large and gra-cious design.

One day he came into the hall in the morning, looking so radiant that Mark asked him half enviously what he had to make him so glad.

"Glad," said Roland, "oh, I know it! Merry dreams, perhaps. What do you think of a good grave fellow who beckons me on with a brisk smile, and shows me places, wonderful places, under banks and in woodland pits, where riches lie piled together? I am sure that some good fortune is preparing for me, Mark—but you shall share it."

Then Mark, seeing in his words a certain likeness, with a difference, to his own dark visions, pressed his lips together and sate looking stonily before him.

At last, one still evening of spring, when the air was intolerably languid and heavy for mankind, but full of sweet promises for trees and hidden peeping things, though a lurid redness of secret thunder had lain all day among the heavy clouds in the plain, the two dined together. Mark had walked alone that day, and had lain upon the turf of the down, fighting against a weariness that seemed to be poisoning the very springs of life within him. But Roland had been brisk and alert, coming and going upon some secret and busy errand, with a fragment of a song upon his lips, like a man preparing to set off for a far country, who is glad to be gone. In the evening, after they had dined, Roland had let his fancy rove in talk. "If we were rich," he said, "how we would transform this old place!"

"It is fair enough for me," said Mark heavily; and Roland had chidden him lightly for his sombre ways, and sketched new plans of life.

Mark, wearied and yet excited, with an intolerable heaviness of spirit, went early to bed, leaving Roland in the hall. After a short and broken sleep, he awoke, and lighting a candle, read idly and gloomily to pass the heavy hours. The house seemed full of strange noises that night. Once or twice came a scraping and a faint hammering in the wall; light footsteps seemed to pass in the turret—but the tower was always full of noises, and Mark heeded them not; at last he fell asleep again, to be suddenly awakened by a strange and desolate crying, that came he knew not whence, but seemed to wail upon the air.

The old dog, who slept in Mark's room, heard it too; he was sitting up in a fearful expectancy. Mark rose in haste, and taking the candle, went into the passage that led to Roland's room. It was empty, but a light burned there and showed that the room had not been slept in. Full of a horrible fear, Mark returned, and went in hot haste up the turret steps, fear and anxiety struggling together in his mind. When he readied the top, he found the little door broken forcibly open, and a light within. He cast a haggard look round the room, and then the crying came again, this time very faint and desolate.

Mark cast a shuddering glance at the window; it was wide open and showed a horrible liquid blackness; round the bar in the centre that divided the casements, there was something knotted. He hastened to the window, and saw that it was a rope, which hung heavily. Leaning out he saw that something dangled from the rope below him—and then came the crying again out of the darkness, like the crying of a lost spirit.

He could see as in a bitter dream the outline of the hateful hillside; but there seemed to his disordered fancy to be a tumult of some kind below; pale lights moved about, and he saw a group of forms which scattered like a shoal of fish when he leaned out. He knew that he was looking upon a scene that no mortal eye ought to behold, and it seemed to him at the moment as though he was staring straight into hell.

The rope went down among the rocks and disappeared; but Mark clenched it firmly and using all his strength, which was great, drew it up hand over hand; as he drew it up he secured it in loops round the great oak table; he began to be afraid that his strength would not hold out, and once when he returned to the window after securing a loop, a great hooded thing like a bird flew noiselessly at the window and beat its wings.

Presently he saw that the form which dangled on the rope was clear of the rocks below; it had come up through them, as though they were but smoke; and then his task seemed to him more sure than ever. Inch by painful inch he drew it up, working fiercely and silently; his muscles were tense, and drops stood on his brow, and the veins hammered in his ears; his breath came and went in sharp sobs. At last the form was near enough for him to seize it; he grasped it by the middle and drew Roland, for it was Roland, over the windowsill. His head dangled and drooped from side to side; his face was dark with strangled blood and his limbs hung helpless.

Mark drew his knife and cut the rope that was tied under his arms; the helpless limbs sank huddling on the floor; then Mark looked up; at the window a few feet from him was a face, more horrible than he had supposed a human face, if it was human indeed, could be. It was deadly white, and hatred, baffled rage, and a sort of devilish malignity glared from the white set eyes, and the drawn mouth. There was a rush from behind him; the old hound, who had crept up unawares into the room, with a fierce outcry of rage sprang on to the window-sill; Mark heard the scraping of his claws upon the stone.

Then the hound leapt through the window, and in a moment there was the sound of a heavy fall outside. At the same instant the darkness seemed to lift and draw up like a cloud; a bank of blackness rose past the window, and left the dark outline of the down, with a sky sown with tranquil stars.

The cloud of fear and horror that hung over Mark lifted too; he felt in some dim way that his adversary was vanquished; he carried Roland down the stairs and laid him on his bed; he roused the household, who looked fearfully at him, and then his own strength failed; he sank upon the floor of his room, and the dark tide of unconsciousness closed over him.

Mark's return to health was slow. One who has looked into the Unknown finds it hard to believe again in the outward shows of life. His first conscious speech was to ask for his hound; they told him that the body of the dog had been found, horribly mangled as though by the teeth of some fierce animal, at the foot of the tower. The dog was buried in the garden, with a slab above him, on which are the words:—

Euge Serve Bone et Fidelis

A silly priest once said to Mark that it was not meet to write Scripture over the grave of a beast. But Mark said warily that an inscription was for those who read it, to make them humble, and not to increase the pride of what lay below.

When Mark could leave his bed, his first care was to send for builders, and the old tower of Nort was taken down, stone by stone, to the ground, and a fair chapel built on the site; in the wall there was a secret stairway, which led from the top chamber, and came out among the elder-bushes that grew below the tower, and here was found a coffer of gold, which paid for the church; because, until it was found, it was Mark's design to leave the place desolate.

Mark is wedded since, and has his children about his knee; those who come to the house see a strange and wan man, who sits at Mark's board, and whom he uses very tenderly; sometimes this man is merry, and tells a long tale of his being beckoned and led by a tall and handsome person, smiling, down a hillside to fetch gold; though he can never remember the end of the matter; but about the springtime he is silent or mutters to himself: and this is Roland; his spirit seems shut up within him in some close cell, and Mark prays for his release, but till God call him, he treats him like a dear brother, and with the reverence due to one who has looked out on the other side of Death, and who may not say what his eyes beheld.

The Gray Cat

The knight Sir James Leigh lived in a remote valley of the Welsh Hills. The manor house, of rough grey stone, with thick walls and mullioned windows, stood on a rising ground; at its foot ran a little river, through great boulders. There were woods all about; but above the woods, the bare green hills ran smoothly up, so high, that in the winter the sun only peeped above the ridge for an hour or two; beyond the house, the valley wound away into the heart of the hills, and at the end a black peak looked over. The place was very sparsely inhabited; within a close of ancient yew trees stood a little stone church, and a small parsonage smothered in ivy, where an old priest, a cousin of the knight, lived. There were but three farms in the valley, and a rough track led over the hills, little used, except by drovers. At the top of the pass stood a stone cross; and from this point you could see the dark scarred face of the peak to the left, streaked with snow, which did not melt until the summer was far advanced.

Sir James was a silent sad man, in ill-health; he spoke little and bore his troubles bitterly; he was much impoverished, through his own early carelessness, and now so feeble in body that he had small hope of repairing the fortune he had lost. His wife was a wise and loving woman, who, though she found it hard to live happily in so lonely a place with a sickly husband, met her sorrows with a cheerful face, visited her poorer neighbours, and was like a ray of sunlight in the gloomy valley. They had one son, a boy Roderick, now about fifteen; he was a bright and eager child, who was happy enough, taking his life as he found it—and indeed he had known no other. He was taught a little by the priest; but he had no other schooling, for Sir James would spend no money except when he was obliged to do so. Roderick had no playmates, but he never found the time to be heavy; he was fond of long solitary rambles on the hills, being light of foot and strong.

211

One day he had gone out to fish in the stream, but it was bright and still, and he could catch nothing; so, at last he laid his rod aside in a hollow place beneath the bank, and wandered without any certain aim along the stream. Higher and higher he went, till he found, looking about him, that he was as high as the pass; and then it came into his mind to track the stream to its source. The Manor was now out of sight, and there was nothing round him but the high green hills, with here and there a sheep feeding. Once a kite came out and circled slowly in the sun, pouncing like a plummet far down the glen; and still Roderick went onwards till he saw that he was at the top of the lower hills, and that the only thing higher than him was the peak itself.

He saw now that the stream ran out of a still black pool some way in front of him, that lay under the very shadow of the dark precipice, and was fed by the snows that melted from the face. It was surrounded by rocks that lay piled in confusion. But the whole place wore an air that was more than desolate; the peak itself had a cruel look, and there was an intent silence, which was only broken, as he gazed, by the sound of rocks falling loudly from the face of the hill and thundering down. The sun warned him that he had gone far enough; and he determined to go homewards, half pleased at his discovery, and half relieved to quit so lonely and grim a spot.

That evening, when he sate with his father and mother at their simple meal, he began to say where he had been. His father heard him with little attention, but when Roderick described the dark pool and the sharp front of the peak he asked him abruptly how near he had gone to the pool. Roderick said that he had seen it from a distance, and then Sir James said somewhat sharply that he must not wander so far, and that he was not to go near that place again. Roderick was surprised at this, for his father as a rule interfered little with what he did; but he did not ask his father the reason, for there was something peevish, even harsh, in his tone.

But afterwards, when he went out with his mother, leaving the knight to his own gloomy thoughts, as his will and custom was, his mother said with some urgency, "Roderick, promise me not to go to the pool again; it has an evil name, and is better left to itself." Roderick was eager to know the story of the place, but his mother would not tell him—only she would have him promise; so he promised, but complained that he would rather have had a reason given for his promise; but his mother, smiling and holding his hand, said that it should be enough for him to please her by doing her will. So, Roderick gave his promise again, but was not satisfied.

The next day Roderick was walking in the valley and met one of the farmers, a young good-humoured man, who had always been friendly with the boy, and had often been to fish with him; Roderick walked beside him, and told him that he had followed the stream nearly to the pool, when the young farmer, with some seriousness, asked him how near he had been to the water. Roderick was surprised at the same question that his father had asked him being asked again, and told him that he had but seen it from a hill-top near, adding, "But what is amiss with the place, for my father and mother have made me promise not to go there again?"

The young farmer said nothing for a moment, but seemed to reflect; then he said that there were stories about the place, stories that perhaps it was foolish to believe, but he went on to say that it was better to be on the safe side in all things, and that the place had an evil fame. Then Roderick with childish eagerness asked him what the stories were; and little by little the farmer told him. He said that something dwelt near or in the pool, it was not known what, that had an enmity to the life of man; that twice since he was a boy a strange thing had happened there; a young shepherd had come by his death at the pool, and was found lying in the water, strangely battered; that, he said, was long before Roderick was born; then he added, "You remember old Richard the shepherd?"

"What!" said Roderick, "the old strange man that used to go about muttering to himself, that the boys threw stones at?"

"Yes," said the farmer, "the very same. Well, he was not always so—I remember him a strong and cheerful man; but once when the sheep had got lost in the hills, he would go to the pool because he thought he heard them calling there, though we prayed him not to go. He came back, indeed, bringing no sheep, but an altered and broken man, as he was thenceforth and as you knew him; he had seen something by the pool, he could not say what, and had had a sore strife to get away."

"But what sort of a thing is this?" said Roderick. "Is it a beast or a man, or what?"

"Neither," said the farmer very gravely. "You have heard them read in the church of the evil spirits who dwelt with men, and entered their bodies, and it was sore work even for the Lord Christ to cast them forth; I think it is one of these who has wandered thither; they say he goes not far from the pool, for he cannot abide the cross on the pass, and the church bell gives him pains."

And then the farmer looked at Roderick and said, "You know that they ring the bell all night on the feast of All Souls?"

"Yes," said Roderick, "I have heard it ring."

"Well, on that night alone," said the farmer, "they say that spirits have power upon men, and come abroad to do them hurt; and so they ring the bell, which the spirits cannot listen to—but, young master, it is ill to talk of these things, and Christian men should not even think of them; but as I said, though Satan has but little power over the baptised soul, yet even so, says the priest, he can enter in, if the soul be willing to admit him—and so I say, avoid the place! it may be that these are silly stories to affright folk, but it is ill to touch pitch; and no good can be got by going to the pool, and perhaps evil;—and now I think I have told you enough and more than enough." For Roderick was looking at him pale and with wide open eyes.

Is it strange that from that day the thing that Roderick most desired was to see the pool and what dwelt there? I think not; when hearts are young and before trouble has laid its heavy hand upon them, the hard and cruel things of life, wounds, blows, agonies, terrors, seen only in the mirrors of another spirit, are but as a curious and lively spectacle that feeds the mind with wonder. The stories to which Roderick had listened in church of men that were haunted by demons seemed to him but as dim and distant experiences on which he would fain look; and the fainter the thought of his promise grew, the stronger grew his desire to see for himself.

In the month of June, when the heart is light, and the smell of the woods is fresh and sharp, Roderick's father and mother were called to go him very bright and pure, like a jewel of sapphire, the water being of a deep azure blue; he went all round it. There was no sign of life in the water; at the end nearest the cliff he found a little cool runnel of water that bubbled into the pool from the cliffs. No grass grew round about it, and he could see the stones sloping down and becoming more beautiful the deeper they lay, from the pure tint of the water.

He looked all around him; the moorland quivered in the bright hot air, and he could see far away the hills lie like a map, with blue mountains on the horizon, and small green valleys where men dwelt. He sate down by the pool, and he had a thought of bathing in the water; but his courage did not rise to this, because he felt still as though something sate in the depths that would not show itself, but might come forth and drag him down; so he sate at last by the pool, and presently he fell asleep.

When he woke he felt somewhat chilly; the shadow of the peak had come round, and fell on the water; the place was still as calm as ever, but looking upon the pool he had an obscure sense as though he were being watched by an unclosing eye; but he was thirsting with the heat; so he drew up, in his closed hands, some of the water, which was very cool and sweet; and his drowsiness came upon him, and again he slept.

When next he woke it was with a sense of delicious ease, and the thought that someone who loved him was near him stroking his hand. He looked up, and there close to his side sate very quietly what gave him a shock of surprise. It was a great gray cat, with soft abundant fur, which turned its yellow eyes upon him lazily, purred, and licked his hand; he caressed the cat, which arched its back and seemed pleased to be with him, and presently leapt upon his knee. The soft warmth of the fur against his hands, and the welcoming caresses of this fearless wild creature pleased him greatly; and he sate long in quiet thought, taking care not to disturb the cat, which, whenever he took his hand away, rubbed against him as though to show that it was pleased at his touch.

But at last he thought that he must go homewards, for the day began to turn to the west. So, he put the cat off his knee and began to walk to the top of the pass, as it was quicker to follow the road. For a while the cat accompanied him, sometimes rubbing against his leg and sometimes walking in front, but looking round from time to time as though to consult his pleasure.

Roderick began to hope that it would accompany him home, but at a certain place the cat stopped, and would go no farther. Roderick lifted it up, but it leapt from him as if displeased, and at last he left it reluctantly. In a moment he came within sight of the cross in the hilltop, so that he saw the road was near. Often, he looked round and saw the great cat regarding him as though it were sorry to be left; till at last he could see it no more.

He went home well pleased, his head full of happy thoughts; he had gone half expecting to see some dreadful thing, but had found instead a creature who seemed to love him.

The next day he went again; and this time he found the cat sitting by the pool; as soon as it saw him, it ran to him with a glad and yearning cry, as though it had feared he would not return; today it seemed brighter and larger to look upon; and he was pleased that when he returned by the stream it followed him much farther, leaping lightly from stone to stone; but at a certain place, where the valley began to turn eastward, just before the little church came in sight, it sate down as before and took its leave of him.

The third day he began to go up the valley again; but while he rested in a little wood that came down to the stream, to his surprise and delight the cat sprang out of a bush, and seemed more than ever glad of his presence. While he sate fondling it, he heard the sound of footsteps coming up the path; but the cat heard the sound too, and as he rose to see who was coming, the cat sprang lightly into a tree beside him and was hidden from his sight. It was the old priest on his way to an upland farm, who spoke fondly to Roderick, and asked him of his father and mother.

Roderick told him that they were to return that night, and said that it was too bright to remain indoors and yet too bright to fish; the priest agreed, and after a little more talk rose to go, and as his manner was, holding Roderick by the hand, he blessed him, saying that he was growing a tall boy. When he was gone—and Roderick was ashamed to find how eager he was that the priest should go—he called low to the cat to come back; but the cat came not, and though Roderick searched the tree into which it had sprung, he could find no sign of it, and supposed that it had crept into the wood.

That evening the travellers returned, the knight seeming cheerful, because the vexatious journey was over; but Roderick was half ashamed to think that his mind had been so full of his new plaything that he was hardly glad to see his parents return. Presently his mother said, "You look very bright and happy, dear child," and Roderick, knowing that he spoke falsely, said that he was glad to see them again; his mother smiled and asked him what he had been doing, and he said that he had wandered on the hills, for it was too bright to fish; his mother looked at him for a moment, and he knew in his heart that she wondered if he had kept his promise; but he thought of his secret, and looked at her so straight and full that she asked him no further questions.

The next day he woke feeling sad, because he knew that there would be no chance to go to the pool. He went to and fro with his mother, for she had many little duties to attend to. At last she said, "What are you thinking of, Roderick? You seem to have little to say to me." She said it laughingly; and Roderick was ashamed, but said that he was only thinking; and so, bestirred himself to talk. But late in the day he went a little alone through the wood, and reaching the end of it, looked up to the hill, kissing his hand towards the pool as a greeting to his friend; and as he turned, the cat came swiftly and lovingly out of the wood to him; and he caught it up in his arms and clasped it close, where it lay as if contented.

Then he thought that he would carry it to the house, and say nothing as to where he had found it; but hardly had he moved a step when the cat leapt from him and stood as though angry. And it came into Roderick's mind that the cat was his secret friend, and that their friendship must somehow be unknown; but he loved it even the better for that.

In the weeks that followed, the knight was ill and the lady much at home; from time to time Roderick saw the cat; he could never tell when it would visit him; it came and went unexpectedly, and always in some lonely and secret place. But gradually Roderick began to care for nothing else; his fishing and his riding were forgotten, and he began to plan how he might be alone, so that the cat would come to him. He began to lose his spirits and to be dull without it, and to hate the hours when he could not see it; and all the time it grew or seemed to grow stronger and sleeker; his mother soon began to notice that he was not well; he became thin and listless, but his eyes were large and bright; she asked him more than once if he were well, but he only laughed.

Once indeed he had a fright; he had been asleep under a hawthorn in the glen on a hot July day; and waking saw the cat close to him, watching him intently with yellow eyes, as though it were about to spring upon him; but seeing him awake, it came wheedling and fondling him as often before; but he could not forget the look in its eyes, and felt grave and sad.

Then he began to be troubled with dreams; the man whom he had seen in his former dream rising from the pool was often with him—sometimes he led him to pleasant places; but one dream he had, that he was bathing in the pool, and caught his foot between the rocks and could not draw it out. Then he heard a rushing sound, and looking round saw that a great stream of water was plunging heavily into the pool, so that it rose every moment, and was soon up to his chin. Then he saw in his dream that the man sate on the edge of the pool and looked at him with a cold smile, but did not offer to help; till at last when the water touched his lips, the man rose and held up his hand; and the stream ceased to run, and presently his foot came out of the rock easily, and he swam ashore but saw no one.

Then it came to the autumn, and the days grew colder and shorter, and he could not be so much abroad; he felt, too, less and less disposed to stir out, and it now began to be on his mind that he had broken his promise to his mother; and for a week he saw nothing of the cat, though he longed to see it. But one night, as he went to bed, when he had put out his light, he saw that the moon was very bright; and he opened the window and looked out, and saw the gleaming stream and the grey valley; he was turning away, when he heard a light sound of the scratching of claws, and presently the cat sprang upon the window-sill and entered the room.

It was now cold and he got into bed, and the cat sprang upon his pillow; and Roderick was so glad that the cat had returned that while he caressed it he talked to it in low tones. Suddenly came a step at the door, and a light beneath it, and his mother with a candle entered the room. She stood for a moment looking, and Roderick became aware that the cat was gone.

Then his mother came near, thinking that he was asleep, and he sate up. She said to him, "Dear child, I heard you speaking, and wondered whether you were in a dream," and she looked at him with an anxious gaze.

And he said, "Was I speaking, mother? I was asleep and must have spoken in a dream."

Then she said, "Roderick, you are not old enough yet to sleep so uneasily—is all well, dear child?" and Roderick, hating to deceive his mother, said, "How should not all be well?" So, she kissed him and went quietly away, but Roderick heard her sighing.

Then it came at last to All Souls' Day; and Roderick, going to his bed that night, had a strange dizziness and cried out, and found the room swim round him. Then he got up into his bed, for he thought that he must be ill, and soon fell asleep; and in his sleep he dreamed a dreadful dream. He thought that he lay on the hills beside the pool; and yet he was out of the body, for he could see himself lying there. The pool was very dark, and a cold wind ruffled the waves. And again the water was troubled, and the man stepped out; but behind him came another man, like a hunchback, very swarthy of face, with long thin arms, that looked both strong and evil.

Then it seemed as if the first man pointed to Roderick where he lay and said, "You can take him hence, for he is mine now, and I have need of him," adding, "Who could have thought it would be so easy?"

and then he smiled very bitterly. And the hunchback went towards himself; and he tried to cry out in warning, and straining woke; and in the chilly dawn he saw the cat sit in his room, but very different from what it had been. It was gaunt and famished, and the fur was all marred; its yellow eyes gleamed horribly, and Roderick saw that it hated him, he knew not why; and such fear came upon him that he screamed out, and as he screamed the cat rose as if furious, twitching its tail and opening its mouth; but he heard steps without, and screamed again, and his mother came in haste into the room, and the cat was gone in a moment, and Roderick held out his hands to his mother, and she soothed and quieted him, and presently with many sobs he told her all the story.

She did not reproach him, nor say a word of his disobedience, the fear was too urgent upon her; she tried to think for a little that it was the sight of some real creature lingering in a mind that was wrought upon by illness; but those were not the days when men preferred to call the strange afflictions of body and spirit, the sad scars that stain the fair works of God, by reasonable names. She did not doubt that by some dreadful hap her own child had somehow crept within the circle of darkness, and she only thought of how to help and rescue him; that he was sorry and that he did not wholly consent was her hope.

So, she merely kissed and quieted him, and then she told him that she would return *anon* and he must rest quietly; but he would not let her leave him, so she stood in the door and called a servant softly. Sir James was long abed, for he had been in ill-health that day, and she gave word that someone must be found at once and go to call the priest, saying that Roderick was ill and she was uneasy. Then she came back to the bed, and holding Roderick's hand she said, that he must try to sleep. Roderick said to her, "Mother, say that you forgive me."

To which she only replied, "Dear child, do I not love you better than all the world? Do not think of me now, only ask help of God."

So she sate with his hand in both of her own, and presently he fell asleep; but she saw that he was troubled in his dreams, for he groaned and cried out often; and now through the window she heard the soft tolling of the bell of the church, and she knew that a contest must be fought out that night over the child; but after a sore passage of misery, and a bitter questioning as to why one so young and innocent should thus be bound with evil bonds, she found strength to leave the matter in the Father's hands, and to pray with an eager hopefulness.

But the time passed heavily and still the priest did not arrive; and the ghostly terror was so sore on the child that she could bear it no longer and awakened him. And he told her in broken words of the terrible things that had oppressed him; sore fightings and struggles, and a voice in his ear that it was too late, and that he had yielded himself to the evil. And at last there came a quiet footfall on the stair, and the old priest himself entered the room, looking anxious, yet calm, and seeming to bring a holy peace with him.

Then she bade the priest sit down; and so the two sate by the bedside, with the solitary lamp burning in the chamber; and she would have had Roderick tell the tale, but he covered his face with his hands and could not. So she told the tale herself to the priest, saying, "Correct me, Roderick, if I am wrong;" and once or twice the boy corrected her, and added a few words to make the story plain, and then they sate awhile in silence, while the terrified looks of the mother and her son dwelt on the old priest's strongly lined face; yet they found comfort in the smile with which he met them.

At length he said, "Yes, dear lady and dear Roderick, the case is plain enough—the child has yielded himself to some evil power, but not too far, I think; and now must we meet the foe with all our might. I will abide here with the boy; and, dear lady, you were better in your own chamber, for we know not what will pass; if there were need I would call you."

Then the lady said, "I will do as you direct me. Father, but I would fain stay." Then he said, "Nay, but there are things on which a Christian should not look, lest they should daunt his faith—so go, dear lady, and help us with your prayers."

Then she said, "I will be below; and if you beat your foot thrice upon the floor, I will come. Roderick, I shall be close at hand; only be strong, and all shall be well." Then she went softly away.

Then the priest said to Roderick, "And now, dear son, confess your sin and let me shrive you."

So, Roderick made confession, and the priest blessed him: but while he blessed him there came the angry crying of a cat from somewhere in the room, so that Roderick shuddered in his bed. Then the priest drew from his robe a little holy book, and with a reverence laid it under Roderick's hand; and he himself took his book of prayers and said, "Sleep now, dear son, fear not."

So, Roderick closed his eyes, and being very weary slept. And the old priest in a low whisper said the blessed psalms. And it came near to midnight; and the place that the priest read was, *Thou shall not be afraid for any terror by night, nor for the arrow that flieth by day; for the pestilence that walketh in darkness, nor for the sickness that destroyeth in the noonday;* and suddenly there ran as it were a shiver through his bones, and he knew that the time was come. He looked at Roderick, who slept wearily on his bed, and it seemed to him as though suddenly a small and shadowy thing, like a bird, leapt from the boy's mouth and on to the bed; it was like a wren, only white, with dusky spots upon it; and the priest held his breath; for now, he knew that the soul was out of the body, and that unless it could return uninjured into the limbs of the child, nothing could avail the boy; and then he said quietly in his heart to God that if He so willed He should take the boy's life, if only his soul could be saved.

Then the priest was aware of a strange and horrible thing; there sprang softly on to the bed the form of the great gray cat, very lean and angry, which stood there, as though ready to spring upon the bird, which hopped hither and thither, as though careless of what might be. The priest cast a glance upon the boy, who lay rigid and pale, his eyes shut, and hardly seeming to breathe, as though dead and prepared for burial. Then the priest signed the cross and said *"In Nomine"*; and as the holy words fell on the air, the cat looked fiercely at the bird, but seemed to shrink into itself; and then it slipped away.

Then the priest's fear was that the bird might stray further outside of his care; and yet he dared not try and wake the boy, for he knew that this was death, if the soul was thrust apart from the body, and if he broke the unseen chain that bound them; so, he waited and prayed. And the bird hopped upon the floor; and then presently the priest saw the cat draw near again, and in a stealthy way; and now the priest himself was feeling weary of the strain, for he seemed to be wrestling in spirit with something that was strong and strongly armed. But he signed the cross again and said faintly *"In Nomine"*; and the cat again withdrew.

Then a dreadful drowsiness fell upon the priest, and he thought that he must sleep. Something heavy, leaden-handed, and powerful seemed to be busy in his brain. Meanwhile the bird hopped upon the window-sill and stood as if preparing its wings for a flight. Then the priest beat with his foot upon the floor, for he could no longer battle. In a moment the lady glided in, and seemed as though scared to find the scene of so fierce an encounter so still and quiet. She would have spoken, but the priest signed her to be silent, and pointed to the boy and to the bird; and then she partly understood.

So, they stood in silence, but the priest's brain grew more numb; though he was aware of a creeping blackness that seemed to overshadow the bird, in the midst of which glared two bright eyes. So with a sudden effort he signed the cross, and said "*In Nomine*" again; and at the same moment the lady held out her hand; and the priest sank down on the floor; but he saw the bird raise its wings for a flight, and just as the dark thing rose, and, as it were, struck open-mouthed, the bird sailed softly through the air, alighted on the lady's hand, and then with a light flutter of wings on to the bed and to the boy's face, and was seen no more; at the same moment the bells stopped in the church and left a sweet silence.

The black form shrank and slipped aside, and seemed to fall on the ground; and outside there was a shrill and bitter cry which echoed horribly on the air; and the boy opened his eyes, and smiled; and his mother fell on his neck and kissed him.

Then the priest said, "Give God the glory!" and blessed them, and was gone so softly that they knew not when he went; for he had other work to do. Then mother and son had great joy together.

But the priest walked swiftly and sternly through the wood, and to the church; and he dipped a vessel in the stoup of holy water, turning his eyes aside, and wrapped it in a veil of linen. Then he took a lantern in his hand, and with a grave and fixed look on his face he walked sadly up the valley, putting one foot before another, like a man who forced himself to go unwilling. There were strange sounds on the hillside, the crying of sad birds, and the beating of wings, and sometimes a hollow groaning seemed to come down the stream. But the priest took no heed, but went on heavily till he reached the stone cross, where the wind whistled dry in the grass. Then he struck off across the moorland. Presently he came to a rise in the ground; and here, though it was dark, he seemed to see a blacker darkness in the air, where the peak lay.

But beneath the peak he saw a strange sight; for the pool shone with a faint white light, that showed the rocks about it. The priest never turned his head, but walked thither, with his head bent, repeating words to himself, but hardly knowing what he said.

Then he came to the brink; and there he saw a dreadful sight. In the water writhed large and luminous worms, that came sometimes up to the surface, as though to breathe, and sank again. The priest knew well enough that it was a device of Satan's to frighten him; so he delayed not; but setting the lantern down on the ground, he stood. In a moment the lantern was obscured as by the rush of bat-like wings. But the priest took the veil off the vessel; and holding it up in the air, he let the water fall in the pool, saying softly, "Lord, let them be bound!"

But when the holy water touched the lake, there was a strange sight; for the bright worms quivered and fell to the depth of the pool; and a shiver passed over the surface, and the light went out like a flickering lamp. Then there came a foul yelling from the stones; and with a roar like thunder, rocks fell crashing from the face of the peak; and then all was still.

Then the priest sate down and covered his face with his hands, for he was sore spent; but he rose at length, and with grievous pain made his slow way down the valley, and reached the parsonage house at last.

Roderick lay long between life and death; and youth and a quiet mind prevailed.

Long years have passed since that day; all those that I have spoken of are dust. But in the window of the old church hangs a picture in glass which shows Christ standing, with one lying at his feet from whom he had cast out a devil; and on a scroll are the words, *de abyssis terrae iterum reduxisti me*, the which may be written in English, *Yea, and broughtest me from the deep of the earth again.*

The Hill of Trouble

There was once a great scholar, Gilbert by name, who lived at Cambridge, and was Fellow of St. Peter's College there. He was still young, and yet he had made himself a name for learning, and still more for wisdom, which is a different thing, though the two are often confused. Gilbert was a slender, spare man, but well-knit and well-proportioned. He loved to wear old scholarly garments, but he had that sort of grace in wearing them that made him appear better apparelled than most men in new clothes. His hair was thick and curling, and he had small features clearly cut. His lips were somewhat thin, as though from determined thought.

He carried his eyes a little wrinkled up, as though to spare them from the light; but he had a gracious look which he turned on those with whom he spoke; and when he opened his eyes upon you, they were large and dear, as though charged with dreams; and he had a very sweet smile, trustful and gentle, that seemed to take any that spoke with him straight to his heart, and made him many friends. He had the look rather of a courtier than of a priest, and he was merry and cheerful in discourse, so that you might be long with him and not know him to be learned.

It may be said that he had no enemies, though he did not conceal his beliefs and thoughts, but stated them so courteously and with such deference to opposite views, that he drew men insensibly to his side. It was thought by many that he ought to go into the world and make a great name for himself. But he loved the quiet college life, the familiar talk with those he knew. He loved the great plenty of books and the discourse of simple and wise men. He loved the fresh bright hours of solitary work, the shady college garden, with its butts and meadows, bordered by ancient walls. He loved to sit at meat in the cool and spacious hall; and he loved too the dark high-roofed College Church, and his own canopied stall with the service-books in due order, the low music of the organ, and the sweet singing of the choir. He was not rich, but his Fellowship gave him all that he desired, together with a certain seemly dignity of life that he truly valued; so that his heart was very full of a simple happiness from day to day, and he thought that he would be more than content to live out his life in the peaceful college that he loved so well.

But he was ambitious too; he was writing a great book full of holy learning; and he had of late somewhat withdrawn himself from the life of the college; he sate longer at his studies and he was seen less often in other colleges. Ten years he gave himself to finish his task, and he thought that it would bring him renown; but that was only a far-off dream, gilding his studies with a kind of peaceful glory; and indeed, he loved the doing of his work better than any reward he might get for it.

One summer he felt he wanted some change of life; the sultry Cambridge air, so dry and low, seemed to him to be heavy and lifeless. He began to dream of fresh mountain breezes, and the sound of leaping streams; so at last he packed his books into a box, and set off a long journey into the hills of the West, to a village where an old friend of his was the priest, who he knew would welcome him.

On the sixth day he arrived at the place; he had enjoyed the journey; much of the time he had ridden, but he often walked, for he was very strong and active of body; he had delighted in seeing the places he had passed through, the churches and the towns and the castles that lay beside the way; he had been pleased with the simple friendly inns, and as his custom was had talked with all travellers that he met. And most of all he had loved, as he drew nearer the West, to see the great green slopes of hills, the black heads of mountains, the steep wooded valleys, where the road lay along streams, that dashed among mossy boulders into still pools.

At last he came to the village which he sought, which lay with its grey church and low stone houses by a bridge, in a deep valley. The vicarage lay a little apart in a pleasant garden; and his friend the vicar had made him greatly welcome. The vicar was an old man and somewhat infirm, but he loved the quiet life of the country, and knew all the joys and sorrows of his simple flock.

A large chamber was set apart for Gilbert, who ranged his books on a great table, and prepared for much quiet work. The window of the chamber looked down the valley, which was very still. There was no pattering of feet in the road, as there was at Cambridge; the only sounds were the crying of cocks or the bleating of sheep from the hill-pastures, the sound of the wind in the woods, and the falling of water from the hills. So, Gilbert was well content.

For the first few days he was somewhat restless; he explored the valley in all directions. The Vicar could not walk much, and only crept to and fro in the town, or to church; and though he sometimes rode to the hills, to see sick folk on upland farms, yet he told Gilbert that he must go his walks alone; and Gilbert was not loth; for as he thus went by himself in the fresh air, a stream of pleasant fancies and gentle thoughts passed lightly through his head, and his work shaped itself in his brain, like a valley seen from a height, where the fields and farms lie out, as if on a map, with the road winding among them that ties them with the world.

One day Gilbert walked alone to a very solitary place among the hills, a valley where the woods grew thickly; the valley was an estuary, where the sea came up blue and fresh twice in the day, covering the wide sandbanks with still water that reflected the face of the sky; in the midst of the valley, joined with the hillside by a chain of low mounds, there rose a large round hill, covered with bushes which grew thickly over the slopes, and among little crags, haunted by hawks and crows. It looked a very solitary, peaceful hill, and he stopped at a farm beside the road to inquire of the way thither, because he was afraid of finding himself unable to cross the streams.

At his knock there came out an ancient man, with whom Gilbert entered into simple travellers' talk of the weather and the road; Gilbert asked him the name of the place, and the man told him that it was called the Gate of the Old Hollow. Then Gilbert pointing to the hill that lay in the midst, asked him what that was. The old man looked at him for a moment without answering, and then said in a low voice, "That, sir, is the Hill of Trouble."

"That is a strange name!" said Gilbert.

"Yes," said the old man, "and it is a strange place, where no one ever sets foot—there is a cruel tale about it; there is something that is not well about the place."

Gilbert was surprised to hear the other speak so gravely; but the old man, who was pleased with his company, asked him if he would not rest awhile and eat; and Gilbert said that he would do so gladly, and the more gladly if the other would tell him the story of the place. The old man led him within into a large room, with plain oak furniture, and brought him bread and honey and milk; and Gilbert ate, while the old man told him the legend of the hill.

He said that long years ago it was a place of heathen worship, and that there stood a circle of stones upon it, where sacrifice was done; and that men, it was said, were slain there with savage rites; and that when the Christian teachers came, and the valley became obedient to the faith, it was forbidden the villagers to go there, and for long years it was desolate; but there had dwelt in the manor-house hard by a knight, fearless and rough, who regarded neither God nor man, who had lately wedded a wife whom he loved beyond anything in the world. And one day there was with the knight a friend who was a soldier, and after dinner, in foolish talk, the knight said that he would go to the hill, and he made a wager on it. The knight's lady besought him not to go, but he girded on his sword and went laughing.

Now at the time, the old man said, there was much fighting in the valley, for the people were not yet subject to the English king, but paid tribute to their own Lords; and the knight had been one that fought the best. What the knight saw on the hill no one ever knew, but he came back at sundown, pale, and like a man that has been strangely scared, looking behind him as though he expected to be followed by something; and from that day he kept his chamber, and would not go abroad, or if he went out, he went fearfully, looking about him; and the English men-at-arms came to the valley, but the knight that had ever been foremost in the fight would not ride out to meet them, but kept his bed.

The manor lay off the road, and he ordered a boy to lie in the copse beside the way, and to come up to the house to tell him if any soldiers went by. But a troop of horse came secretly over the hill; and seeing the place lie so solitary and deserted, and being in haste, they came not in, but one of them shot a bolt at a venture; but the knight, it seemed, must have stolen from his bed, and have been peeping through the shutters; for the knight's lady who sate below in sore shame and grief for her husband's cowardice, heard a cry, and coming up found him in his bedgown lying by the window, and a bolt sticking in his brain.

Her grief and misery were so sore at this, that she was for a time nearly mad; they buried the .knight in secret in the churchyard; but the lady sate for many days speaking to no one, beating with her hand upon the table and eating little.

One day it seems that she had the thought to go herself to the Hill of Trouble, so she robed herself in haste, and went at early dawn; she went in secret, and came back at noon, smiling to herself, with all her grief gone; and she sate for three days thus with her hands folded, and from her face it was plain that there was joy in her heart; and on the third evening they found her cold and stiff in her chair, dead an hour since, but she was still smiling. And the lands passed to a distant kinsman. And since that day, said the old man, no one had ever set foot on the hill, except a child not long since that strayed thither, and came back in a great fear, saying that he had seen and spoken with an old man, that had seemed to be angry, but that another person, all in white, had come between them, and had led him by the hand to the right road; it could not be known why the child was frightened, but he said that it was the way the old man looked, and the suddenness with which he came and went; but of the other he had no fear, though he knew him not. "And that, sir, is the tale."

Gilbert was very much astonished at the tale, and though he was not credulous, the story dwelt strongly in his mind. It was now too late to visit the hill, even if he had wished; and he could not have so vexed the old man as to visit it from his house. He stood for a while at the gate looking down at it. It was hot and still in the valley. The tide was out and the warm air quivered over the sandbanks. But the hill had a stillness of its own, as though it guarded a secret, and lay looking out towards the sea. He could see the small crags upon it, in the calm air, and the bushes that grew plentifully all over it, with here and there a little green lawn, or a glade sloping down to the green flat in which it stood.

The old man was beside him and said in his shrill piping voice, "You are not thinking of going to the hill, sir?"

"Not now, at all events," said Gilbert, smiling.

But the old man said, "Ah, sir, you will not go—there are other things in this world of ours, beside the hills and woods and farms; it would be strange if that were all. The spirits of the dead walk at noon-day in the places they have loved; and I have thought that the souls of those who have done wickedness are sometimes bound to a place where they might have done good things, and while they are vexed at all the evil their hands have wrought, they are drawn by a kind of evil habit to do what they chose to do on earth. Perhaps those who are faithful can resist them—but it is ill to tempt them."

Gilbert was surprised at this wise talk from so simple a man; and he said, "How is it that these thoughts come into your mind?"

"Oh, sir," said the other, "I am old and live much alone; and these are some of the thoughts that come into my head as I go about my work, but who sends them to me I cannot tell."

Then Gilbert said farewell, and would have paid for his meal, but the old man courteously refused, and said that it was a pleasure to see a stranger in that lonely place; and that it made him think more kindly of the world to talk so simply with one who was, he was sure, so great a gentleman.

Gilbert smiled, and said he was only a simple scholar; and then he went back to the vicarage house. He told the vicar of his adventure, and the vicar said he had heard of the hill, and that there was something strange in the dread which the place inspired. Then Gilbert said, half impatiently, that it was a pity that people were so ridden by needless superstition, and made fears for themselves when there was so much in the world that it was well to fear.

But the old vicar shook his head. "They are children, it is true," he said, "but children, I often think, are nearer to heaven than ourselves, and perhaps have glimpses of things that it is harder for us to see as we get older and more dull."

But Gilbert made up his mind as they talked that he would see the place for himself; and that night he dreamed of wandering over lonely places with a fear upon him of he knew not what. And waking very early, after a restless night, and seeing the day freshly risen, and the dewy brightness of the valley, he put on his clothes in haste, and taking with him a slice of bread from the table, he set out blithely for the hill, with an eagerness of spirit that he had been used to feel as a child.

He avoided the farm, and took a track that seemed to lead into the valley, which led him up and down through little nooks and pastures, till he came to the base of the hill. It was all skirted by a low wall of piled stones covered with grey lichens, where the brambles grew freely; but the grass upon the hill itself had a peculiar richness and luxuriance, as though it was never trodden or crushed underfoot. Gilbert climbed the wall, but the brambles clung to him as though to keep him back; he disentangled them one by one, and in a moment, he found himself in a little green glade, among small crags, that seemed to lead to the top of the hill. He had not gone more than a few paces when the pleasure and excitement died out of his mind, and left him feeling weary and dispirited. But he said to himself that it was his troubled night, and the walk at the unusual hour, and the lack of food; so, he took out his bread and ate it as he walked, and presently he came to the top.

Then he suddenly saw that he was at the place described; in front of him stood a tall circle of stones, very grey with age. Some of them were flung down and were covered with bushes, but several of them stood upright. The place was strangely silent; he walked round the circle, and saw that it occupied the top of the hill; below him were steep crags, and when he looked over he was surprised to see all down the rocks, on ledges, a number of crows that sate silent in the sun. At the motion he made, a number of them, as though surprised to be disturbed, floated off into the air, with loud jangling cries; and a hawk sailed out from the bushes and hung, a brown speck, with trembling wings.

Gilbert saw the rich plain at his feet and the winding creek of the sea, and the great hills on left and right, in a blue haze. Then he stepped back, and though he had a feeling that it would be wiser not to go, he put it aside and went boldly into the circle of stones. He stood there for a moment, and then feeling very weary, sate down on the turf, leaning his back against a stone; then came upon him a great drowsiness. He was haunted by a sense that it was not well to sleep there, and that the dreaming mind was an ill defence against the powers of the air—yet he put the thought aside with a certain shame and fell asleep.

He woke with a sudden start sometime after; there was a chill in his limbs, not from the air which glowed bright in the steady sun, but a chill of the spirit that made his hair prickle in an unusual way. He raised himself up and looked round him, for he knew by a certain sense that he was not alone; and then he saw leaning against one of the stones and watching him intently, a very old and weary-looking man. The man was pale and troubled; he had a rough cloak such as the peasants wore, the hood of which was pulled over his head; his hair was white and hung about his ears; he had a staff in his hand. But there was a dark look about him, and Gilbert divined in some swift passage of the spirit that he did not wish him well.

Gilbert rose to his feet, and at the same moment the old man drew near; and though he looked so old and feeble, Gilbert had the feeling that he was strong and even dangerous. But Gilbert showed no surprise; he doffed his hat to the old man, and said courteously that he hoped he had not wandered to some private place, where he ought not to be.

"The heat was great, and I slept unawares," he said.

The old man at first made no answer, and then said in a very low and yet clear voice, "Nay, sir, you are welcome. The hill is free to all;

but it has an evil name, I know, and I see but few upon it."

Then Gilbert said courteously that he was but a passer-by, and that he must set of! home again, before the sun was high. And at that the old man said, 'Nay, sir, but as you have come, you will surely wait awhile and speak with me. I see," he added, "so few of humankind, that my mind and tongue are alike stiff with disuse; but you can tell me something of your world—and I," he added, "can tell you something of mine."

Then there came suddenly on Gilbert a great fear, and he looked round on the tall stones of the circle that seemed to be like a prison. Then he said, "I am but a simple scholar from Cambridge, and my knowledge of the world is but small; we work," he said, "we write and read, we talk and eat together, and sometimes we pray."

The old man looked at him with a sudden look, under his brows, as he said the words; and then he said, "So, sir, you are a priest; and your faith is a strong one and avails much; but there is a text about the strong man armed who is overcome of the stronger. And though the faith you teach is like a fort in an enemy's country, in which men may dwell safely, yet there is a land outside; and a fort cannot always hold its own."

He said this in so evil and menacing a tone that Gilbert said, "Come, sir, these are wild words; would you speak scorn of the faith that is the light of God and the victory that overcometh?"

Then the old man said, "Nay, I respect the faith—and fear it even," he added in a secret tone—"but I have grown up in a different belief , and the old is better—and this also is a little stronghold, which holds its own in the midst of foes; but I would not be disputing," he added— and then with a smile, "Nay, sir, I know what is in your mind; you like not this place—and you are right; it is not fit for you to set your holy feet in; but it is mine yet; and so you must even accept the hospitality of the place; you shall look thrice in my glass, and see if you like what you shall see." And he held out to Gilbert a small black shining thing. Gilbert would have wished to refuse it, but his courtesy bade him take it—and indeed he did not know if he could have refused the old man, who looked so sternly upon him. So, he took it in his hand. It was a black polished stone like a sphere, and it was very cold to the touch— so cold that he would fain have thrown it down; but he dared not.

So he said with such spirit as he could muster, "And what shall I see beside the stone?—it seems a fair and curious jewel—I cannot give it a name."

232

"Nay," said the old man sharply, "it is not the stone; the stone is naught; but it hides a mystery. You shall see it in the stone."

And Gilbert said, "And what shall I see in the stone?"

And the old man said, "What shall be."

So, Gilbert looked upon the stone; the sun shone upon it in a bright point of light—and for an instant he saw nothing but the gleaming sides of the ball. But in a moment, there came upon him a dizziness like that which comes upon a man who, walking on a hill-top, finds himself on the edge of a precipice. He seemed to look into a great depth, into the dark places of the earth—but in the depth there hung a mist like a curtain. Now while he looked at it he saw a commotion in the mist; and looking closer, he saw that it seemed to be something waving to and fro that drove the mist about; and presently he saw the two arms of a man; and then the mist parted, and he saw the figure of a man standing and waving with his arms, like a man who would fan smoke aside; and the smoke fled from the waving arms and rolled away; and the man stepped aside.

Then Gilbert looked beyond, and he saw a room with a low ceiling and a mullioned window; and he knew it at once for his room in St. Peter's College. There were books on the table; and he saw what seemed like himself, risen to his feet, as though at a sound; and then he saw the door open and a man come in who made an obeisance, and the two seemed to talk together, and presently Gilbert saw the other man pull something from a cloth and put it in his own hands. And the figure of himself seemed to draw near the window to look at the thing; and though it was all very small and distant, yet Gilbert could see that he held in his hands a little figure that seemed a statue. And then the mist rolled in again and all was hid.

He came to himself like a man out of a dream, he had been so intent on what appeared; and he saw the hill-top and the circle of stones, and the old man who stood watching him with a secret smile upon his face. Then Gilbert made as though he would give the stone back, but before he could speak, the old man pointed to the stone again—and Gilbert looked again and saw the deep place, and the cloud, and the man part the cloud.

Then he saw within a garden, and he knew it at once to be the garden of St. Peter's; it seemed to be summer, for the trees were in leaf. He saw himself stand, carrying something in his hand, and looking at a place in the garden wall. There was something on the wall, a patch of white, but he could not see what it was; and beneath it there stood a small group of men in scholars' dress who looked upon the wall, but he could not see their faces; but one whom he recognised as the Master of the College stood with a stick in his hand, and pointed to the white patch on the wall—and then something seemed to run by, a cat or dog, and all at once the cloud flowed in over the picture; and again he came to himself and saw the hill-top, and the stones, and the old man, who had drawn a little nearer, and looked at him with a strange smile. And again, he pointed to the stone; and Gilbert looked again and saw the cloud work very swiftly and part, and the man who swept the clouds oft came forth for an instant, and then was lost to view.

And Gilbert saw a very dark place, with something long and white, that glimmered faintly, lying in the midst; and he bent down to look at it, but could not discern what it was. Then he saw in the darkness which surrounded the glimmering thing some small threads of dusky white, and some small round things; and he looked at them long; and presently discerned that the round things were pebbles, and that the white threads were like the roots of trees; and then he perceived that he was looking into the earth; and then with a sickly chill of fear he saw that the long and glimmering thing was indeed the body of a man, wrapped in grave-clothes from head to foot.

And he could now distinguish—for it grew more distinct—the sides of a coffin about it, and some worms that moved to and fro in their dark burrows; but the corpse seemed to shine with a faint light of its own—and then he could see the wasted feet, and the thin legs and arms of the body within; the hands were folded over the breast; and then he looked at the face; and he saw his own face, only greatly sunk and fallen, with a bandage that tied up the chin, and leaden eyes; and then the clouds swept in upon it; and he came to himself like a drowning man, and saw that he was in the same place; and his first thought was a thrill of joy to know that he was alive; but then he groaned aloud, and he saw the old man stand beside him with a very terrible look upon his face, holding out his hand for the stone in silence so Gilbert gave him back the stone, and then with a fierce anger said, "Why have you shown me this? for this is the trickery of hell."

And the old man looked at him very sternly and said, "Why then did you come to this place? You were not called hither, and they that pry must be punished. A man who pulls open the door which leads from the present into the future must not be vexed if he sees the truth—and now, sir," he added very angrily, "depart hence in haste; you have seen what you have seen."

So, Gilbert went slowly from the circle, and very heavily, and as he stepped outside he looked back. But there was nothing there but the turf and the grey stones.

Gilbert went slowly down the hill with a shadow upon him, like a man who has passed through a sudden danger, or who has had a sudden glimpse into the dark realities of life. But the whole experience was so strange and dreamlike, so apart from the wholesome current of his life, that his fears troubled him less than he had supposed; still, a kind of hatred for the quiet valley began to creep over him, and he found himself sitting long over his books, looking down among the hills, and making no progress. If he was not silent when in company with the old vicar, it was because he made a strong effort, and because his courtesy came to his assistance. Indeed, the old vicar thought that he had never known Gilbert so tender or thoughtful as he had been in the last week of his visit.

The truth was that it was an effort to Gilbert to talk about himself, and he therefore drew the old priest on to talk about the details of his own life and work. Thus, though Gilbert talked less himself, he was courteously attentive, so that the old man had a sense that there had been much pleasant interchange of feeling, whereas he had contributed the most of the talk himself. Gilbert, too, found a great comfort in the offices of the Church in these days, and prayed much that, whatever should befall him, he might learn to rest in the mighty will of God for himself, whatever that will might be.

Soon after this he went back to Cambridge, and there, among his old friends and in his accustomed haunts, the whole impression of the vision on the Hill of Trouble grew faint and indistinct, especially as no incident occurred to revive it. He threw himself into his work, and the book grew under his hands; and he seemed to be more eager to fill his hours than before, and avoided solitary meditation.

Some three years after the date of his vision, there was announced to him by letter the advent of a great scholar to Cambridge, who had read one of Gilbert's books, and was desirous to be introduced to him. Gilbert was sitting one day in his rooms, after a happy quiet morning, when the porter came to the door and announced the scholar. He was a tall eager man, who came forward with great friendliness, and said some courteous words about his pleasure at having met one whom he was so desirous to see. He carried something in his hand, and after the first compliments, said that he had ventured to bring Gilbert a little curiosity that had lately been dug up at Rome, and which he had been fortunate in securing.

He drew off a wrapper, and held out to Gilbert a little figure of a Muse, finely sculptured, with an inscription on the pedestal. Gilbert stepped to the window to look at it, and as he did so it flashed across his mind that this was surely the scene that he had observed in the black stone. He stood for a moment with the statue in his hand, with such a strange look in his face, that the newcomer thought for an instant that his gift must have aroused some sad association. But Gilbert recovered himself in a moment and resolutely put the thought out of his mind, praised the statue, and thereupon entered into easy talk.

The great scholar spent some days at Cambridge, and Gilbert was much with him. They talked of learned matters together, but the great scholar said afterwards that though Gilbert was a man of high genius and of great insight into learning, yet he felt in talking with him as though he had some further and deeper preoccupation of thought.

Indeed, when Gilbert, by laying of dates together, became aware that it was three years to a day since he had seen the vision in the stone, he was often haunted by the thought of his visit to the hill. But this lasted only a few days; and he took comfort at the thought that he had seen a further vision in the stone which seemed at least to promise him three more peaceful years of unchanged work, before he need give way to the heaviness that the third vision had caused him. Yet it lay like a dark background in his thoughts.

He kept very much to his work after this event, and became graver and sterner in face, so that his friends thought that his application to study was harmful. But when they spoke of it to Gilbert, he used to say laughingly that nothing but work made life worthy, and that he was making haste; and indeed, the great book grew so fast that he was within sight of the end. He had many wrestles within himself, about this time, as to the goodness and providence of God. He argued to himself that he had been led very tenderly beside the waters of comfort, that he had served God as faithfully as he could—and indeed he had little to reproach himself with, though he began to blame himself for living a life that pleased him, and for not going about more in the world helping weak brethren along the way, as the Lord Christ had done.

Yet again he said to himself that the great doctors and fathers of the Church had deemed it praiseworthy that a man should devote all the power of his brain to making the divine oracle clear, and that the apostle Paul had spoken of a great diversity of gifts which could be used faithfully in the service of Christ. Still, he reflected that the truest glimpse into the unknown that he had ever received—for he doubted no longer of the truth of the vision—had come to him from one that was, he thought, outside the mercies of God, an unhallowed soul, shut off by his own will and by his wickedness from the fold; and this was a sore burden to him.

At last the book was done; and he went with it to a friend he had at Oxford, a mighty scholar, to talk over some difficult passages. The opinion of the scholar had been cordial and encouraging; he had said that the book was a very great and sound work, useful for doctrine and exhortation, and that many men had given their whole lives to work without achieving such a result. Gilbert had some of the happiness which comes to one who has completed a lengthy task; and though the time drew nigh at which he might expect a further fulfilment of the vision, he was so filled with gratitude at the thought of the great work he had done, that there was little fear or expectation in his mind.

He returned one summer afternoon to Cambridge, and the porter told him that the Master and several of the Fellows were in the garden, and would fain see him on his arrival. So, Gilbert, carrying a little bundle which contained his precious book, went out there at once. The Master had caused to be made a new sundial, which he had affixed in such a way to the wall that those whose chambers gave on the garden could read the time of day without waiting to hear the bells.

When Gilbert came out he saw the little group of Fellows standing by the wall, while the Master with a staff pointed out the legend on the dial, which said that the only hours it told were the hours of sunshine. It came upon Gilbert in a moment that this was the second vision, and though two or three of the group saw him and turned to him with pleasant greetings, he stood for a moment lost in the strangeness of the thing. One of them said, "He stands amazed at the novelty of the design;" and as he said the words, an old grey cat that belonged to the college, and lodged somewhere in the roofs, sprang from a bush and ran past him.

One of the Fellows said, "Aha, cats do not love change!" and then Gilbert came forward, and greeted his friends; but there lay a cold and terrible thought in the background of his mind, and he could not keep it out of his face; so that one of the Fellows, drawing him aside, asked if he had a good verdict on the book, for he seemed as one that was ill-pleased. And the Master, fearing that Gilbert did not like the dial, came and said to him courteously that he knew it was a new-fangled thing, but that it was useful, and in itself not unpleasant, and that it would soon catch a grace of congruity from the venerable walls around. "But," he added, "if you do not like it, it shall be put in some other place." Then Gilbert bestirred himself and said that he liked the dial very well, so that the Master was content.

But Gilbert, as soon as he was by himself, delivered his mind up to heavy contemplation; the vision had twice fulfilled itself, and it was hardly to be hoped that it would fail the third time. He sent his book to be copied out fair, and when it was gone it was as though he had lost his companion. The hours passed very slowly and drearily; he wrote a paper, to fill the time, of his wishes with regard to what should be done with his books and little property after his death, and was half minded to tear it up again. And then after a few days of purposeless and irresolute waiting, he made up his mind that he must go again to the West, and see his friend the old priest. And though he did not say it to himself in words, yet a purpose slowly shaped itself in his mind that he must at all cost go to the hill, and learn again what should be, and that thus alone could he break the spell.

He spent a morning in making his farewells; he tried to speak to his friends as usual, but they noticed long afterwards that he had used a special tenderness and wistfulness in all he said; he sate long in his own room, with a great love in his heart for the beautiful and holy peace of the place, and for all the happiness he had known there; and then he prayed very long and earnestly in the chapel, kneeling in his stall; and his heart was somewhat lightened.

Then he set off; but before he mounted his horse he looked very lovingly at the old front of the college, and his servant saw that his eyes were full of tears and that his lips moved; and so Gilbert rode along to the West.

His journey was very different from the same journey taken six years before; he spoke with none, and rode busily, like one who is anxious to see some sad errand through. He found the old vicar still more infirm and somewhat blind; but the vicar said that he was very happy to see him, as he himself was near the end of life, and that he could hope for but few years,—adding that it was far different for Gilbert, who, he supposed, would very soon be a dean with a cathedral of his own, and would forget his humble friend the old vicar. But Gilbert put the wit aside, and talked earnestly with the vicar about the end of life and what might be hereafter. But the old vicar said solemnly that he knew not, and indeed cared little. But that he would go into the dark like a child holding a loving hand, and would have no need to fear.

That night Gilbert lay in his bed awake, and very strange thoughts passed through his mind, which he strove to quiet by prayers; and so, fell asleep; till at last in the dim dawn he awoke. Then after a moment's thought he took a paper and wrote on it, saying that he was gone out and knew not when he would return; but he prayed the vicar that when he should find the paper, he should at once fall to prayer for him, for there was a sore conflict before him to fight out, both in soul and body, and what would be the issue he knew not.

"And if," the end of the writing ran, "I must depart hence, then pray that my passage may be easy, and that I may find the valley bright."

And he laid the paper upon the table. Then he dressed himself, and went out alone into the valley, walking swiftly and intently—so intently that when he passed the farm he marked not that the old farmer was sitting in an arbour in the garden, who called shrilly to him; but Gilbert heard not, and the old farmer was too weak to follow; so, Gilbert went down to the Hill of Trouble.

It lay, as it had lain six years before, very still and beautiful in the breathless sunshine. The water was in the creek, a streak of sapphire blue; the birds called in the crags, and the bushes and lawns glistened fresh with dew.

But Gilbert, very pale and with his heart beating fast, came to the wall and surmounted it, and went swiftly up the hill, till he found himself near the stones; then he looked once round upon the hills and the sea, and then with a word of prayer he stepped within the circle.

This time he had not long to wait. As he entered the circle he saw the old man enter from the opposite side and come to meet him, with a strange light of triumph in his eyes. Then Gilbert looked him in the face with a rising horror, and said, "Sir, I have come again; and I doubt the truth of your vision no longer; I have done my work, and I have twice seen the fulfilment—now therefore, tell me of my end—that I may be certified how long I have to live. For the shadow of the doubt I cannot bear."

And the old man looked at him with something of compassion and said, "You are young, and you fear the passage hence, knowing not what may be on the other side of the door; but you need not fear. Even I, who have small ground of hope, am ashamed that I feared it so much. But what will you give me if I grant your boon?"

Then Gilbert said, "I have nothing to give."

Then the old man said, "Think once more."

Then was there a silence; and Gilbert said;

"Man, I know not what or who thou art; but I think that thou art a lost soul; one thing I can give thee. . . . I will myself intercede for thee before the Throne."

Then the old man looked at him for a moment, and said, "I have waited long . . . and have received no comfort till now;" and then he said, "Wilt thou promise?"

And Gilbert said, "In the name of God, Amen."

Then the old man stretched out his hand and said, "Art thou ready? for the time is come; and thou art called now;" and he touched Gilbert on the breast.

Gilbert looked into the old man's eyes, and seemed to see there an unfathomable sadness, such as he had never seen; but at the touch a pain so fierce and agonising passed through him, that he sank upon the ground and covered his face with his hands.

Just at this time the old priest found the paper; and he divined the truth. So, he called his servant and bade him saddle his horse in haste; and then he fell to prayer.

Then he rode down the valley: and though he feared the place, yet he rode to the Hill of Trouble; and though his sight was dim and his limbs feeble, it seemed to him that someone walked beside the horse and guided him; and as he prayed he knew that all was over, and that Gilbert had peace.

He came soon to the place; and there he found Gilbert lying on the turf; and his sight was so dim that it seemed to him as though someone slipped away from Gilbert's side He put Gilbert on his horse, and held the poor helpless body thereon, but there was so gentle a smile on the face of the dead that he could not fear.

The body of Gilbert lies in the little churchyard; his great book keeps his memory bright; and on the top of the Hill of Trouble stands a little chapel, built out of the stones of the circle; and on the wall, painted at the old priest's charge, is a picture of the Lord Christ, with wounded hands and side, preaching to the disobedient spirits in prison; and they hear him and are glad.

The Red Camp

It was a sultry summer evening in the old days, when Walter Wyatt came to the house of his forefathers. It was in a quiet valley of Sussex, with the woods standing very steeply on the high hillsides. Among the woods were pleasant stretches of pasture, and a little stream ran hidden among hazels beside the road; here and there were pits in the woods, where the men of ancient times had dug for iron, pits with small sandstone cliffs, and full to the brim of saplings and woodland plants. Walter rode slowly along, his heart full of a happy content. Though it was the home of his family he had never even seen Restlands—that was the peaceful name of the house. Walter's father had been a younger son, and for many years the elder brother, a morose and selfish man, had lived at Restlands, often vowing that none of his kin should ever set foot in the place, and all out of a native malice and churlishness, which discharged itself upon those that were nearest to him.

Walter's father was long dead, and Walter had lived a very quiet homely life with his mother. But one day his uncle had died suddenly and silently, sitting in his chair; and it was found that he had left no will. So that Restlands, with its orchards and woods and its pleasant pasture-lands, fell to Walter; and he had ridden down to take possession. He was to set the house in order, for it was much decayed in his uncle's time; and in a few weeks his mother was to follow him there.

He turned a corner of the road, and saw in a glance a house that he knew must be his; and a sudden pride and tenderness leapt up within his heart, to think how fair a place he could call his own.

An avenue of limes led from the road to the house, which was built of ancient stone, the roof tiled with the same. The front was low and many-windowed. And Walter, for he was a God-fearing youth, made a prayer in his heart, half of gratitude and half of hope.

He rode up to the front of the house, and saw at once that it was sadly neglected; the grass grew among the paving-stones, and several of the windows were broken. He knocked at the door, and an old serving-man came out, who made an obeisance. Walter sent his horse to the stable; his baggage was already come; and his first task was to visit his new home from room to room. It was a very beautiful solidly built house, finely panelled in old dry wood, and had an abundance of solid oak furniture; there were dark pictures here and there; and that night Walter sate alone at his meat, which was carefully served him by the old serving-man, his head full of pleasant plans for his new life; he slept in the great bedroom, and many times woke wondering where he was; once he crept to the window, and saw the barns, gardens, and orchards lie beneath, and the shadowy woods beyond, all bathed in a cold dear moonlight.

In the morning when he had breakfasted, the lawyer who had charge of his business rode in from the little town hard by to see him; and when Walter's happiness was a little dashed; for though the estate brought in a fair sum, yet it was crippled by a mortgage which lay upon it; and Walter saw that he would have to live sparely for some years before he could have his estate unembarrassed; but this troubled him little, for he was used to a simple life. The lawyer indeed had advised him to sell a little of the land; but Walter was very proud of the old estate, and of the memory that he was the tenth Wyatt that had dwelt there, and he said that before he did that he would wait a while and see if he could not arrange otherwise.

When the lawyer was gone there came in the bailiff, and Walter went with him all over the estate. The garden was greatly overgrown with weeds, and the yew hedges were sprawling all uncut; they went through the byre, where the cattle stood in the straw; they visited the stable and the barn, the granary and the dovecote; and Walter spoke pleasantly with the men that served him; then he went to the plough-land and the pastures, the orchard and the woodland; and it pleased Walter to walk in the wood-paths, among the copse and under great branching oaks, and to feel that it was all his own.

At last they came out on the brow of the hill, and saw Restlands lie beneath them, with the smoke of a chimney going up into the quiet air, and the doves wheeling about the cote. The whole valley was full of westering sunshine, and the country sounds came pleasantly up through the still air.

They stood in a wide-open pasture, but in the centre of it rose a small, dark, and thickly grown square holt of wood, surrounded by a high green bank of turf, and Walter asked what that was.

The old bailiff looked at him a moment without speaking and then said, "That is the Red Camp, sir."

Walter said pleasantly, "And whose camp is it?" but it came suddenly into his head that long ago his father had told him a curious tale about the place, but he could not remember what the tale was.

The old man answering his question said, "Ah, sir, who can say? perhaps it was the old Romans who made it, or perhaps older men still; but there was a sore battle hereabouts." And then he went on in a slow and serious way to tell him an old tale of how a few warriors had held the place against an army, and that they had all been put to the sword there; he said that in former days strange rusted weapons and bones had been ploughed up in the field, and then he added that the Camp had ever since been left desolate and that no one cared to set foot within it; yet for all that it was said that a great treasure lay buried within it, for that was what the men were guarding, though those that took the place and slew them could never find it; "and that was all long ago," he said.

Walter, as the old man spoke, walked softly to the wood and peered at it over the mound; it was all grown up within, close and thick, an evil tangle of plants and briars. It was dark and even cold looking within the wood, though the air lay warm all about it. The mound was about breast high, and there was a grass-grown trench all round out of which the earth had been thrown up. It came into Walter's head that the place had seen strange things. He thought of it as all rough and newly made, with a palisade round the mound, with spears and helmets showing over, and a fierce wild multitude of warriors surging all round; the Romans, if they had been Romans, within, grave and anxious, waiting for help that never came.

All this came into his mind with a pleasant sense of security, as a man who is at ease looks on a picture of old and sad things, and finds it minister to his content. Yet the place kept a secret of its own, Walter felt sure of that. And the treasure, was that there all the time? buried in some corner of the wood, money lying idle that might do good things if it could but get forth? So, he mused, tapping the bank with his stick. And presently they went on together. Walter said as they turned away, "I should like to cut the trees down, and throw the place into the pasture," but the old bailiff said, "Nay, it is better left alone."

The weeks passed very pleasantly at first; the neighbours came to see him, and he found that an old name wins friends easily; he spent much of the day abroad, and he liked to go up to the Red Camp and see it stand so solitary and dark, with the pleasant valley beneath it. His mother soon came, and they found that with her small jointure they could indeed live at the place, but that they would have to live very sparely at first; there must be no horses in the stable, nor coach to drive abroad; there must be no company at Restlands for many a year, and Walter saw too that he must not think awhile of marriage, but that he must give all his savings to feed the estate.

After a while, when the first happy sense of possession had gone off, and then life had settled down into common and familiar ways, this began to be very irksome to Walter; and what made him feel even more keenly his fortune was that he made acquaintance with a squire that lived hard by, who had a daughter Marjory, who seemed to Walter the fairest and sweetest maiden he had ever seen; and he began to carry her image about with him; and his heart beat very sharply in his breast if he set eyes on her unexpectedly; and she too, seemed to have delight in seeing Walter, and to understand even the thoughts that lay beneath his lightest word. But the squire was a poor man, and Walter felt bound to crush the thought of love and marriage down in his heart, until he began to grow silent and moody; and his mother saw all that was in his heart and pitied him, but knew not what to do; and Walter began even to talk of going into the world to seek his fortune; but it was little more than talk, for he already loved Restlands very deeply.

Now one day when Walter had been dining with the Vicar of the parish, he met at his table an old and fond man, full of curious wisdom, who took great delight in all that showed the history of the old races that had inhabited the land; and he told Walter a long tale of the digging open of a great barrow or mound upon the downs, which it seemed had been the grave of a great prince, and in which they had found a great treasure of gold, cups and plates and pitchers all of gold, with bars of the same, and many other curious things. He said that a third of such things by rights belonged to the King; but that the King's Grace had been contented to take a rich cup or two, and had left the rest in the hands of him whose land it was.

Then the old scholar asked Walter if it were not true that he had in his own land an ancient fort or stronghold, and Walter told him of the Red Camp and the story, and the old man heard him with great attention saying, "Ay, ay," and "Ay, so it would be," and at the last he said that the story of the treasure was most likely a true one, for he did not see how it could have grown up otherwise; and that he did not doubt that it was a great Roman treasure, perhaps a tribute, gathered in from the people of the land, who would doubtless have been enraged to lose so much and would have striven to recover it. "Ay, it is there, sure enough," he said. Walter offered to go with him to the place; but the old vicar, seeing Walter's bright eye, and knowing something of the difficulties, said that the legend was that it would be ill to disturb a thing that had cost so many warriors their lives; and that a curse would rest upon one that did disturb it.

The old scholar laughed and said that the curses of the dead, and especially of the heathen dead, would break no bones—and he went on to say that doubtless there was a whole hen-roost of curses hidden away in the mound upon the downs; but that they had hurt not his friend who had opened it; for he lived very delicately and plentifully off the treasure of the old prince, who seemed to bear him no grudge for it.

"Nay, doubtless," he said, "if we but knew the truth, I dare say that the old heathen man, pining in some dark loom in hell, is glad enough that his treasure should be richly spent by a good Christian gentleman."

They walked together to the place; and the old gentleman talked very learnedly and showed him where the gates and towers of the fort had been—adding to Walter, "And if I were you, Mr. Wyatt, I would have the place cleared and trenched, and would dig the gold out; for it is there as sure as I am a Christian man and a lover of the old days."

Then Walter told his mother of all that had been said; and she had heard of the old tales, and shook her head; indeed when Walter spoke to the old bailiff of his wish to open the place, the old man almost wept; and then, seeing that he prevailed nothing, said suddenly that neither he nor any of the men that dwelt in the village would put out a hand to help for all the gold of England. So, Walter rested for a while; and still his impatience and his hunger grew.

Walter did not decide at once; he turned the matter over in his mind for a week. He spoke no more to the bailiff, who thought he had changed his mind; but all the week the desire grew; and at last it completely overmastered him. He sent for the bailiff and told him he had determined to dig out the camp; the bailiff looked at him without speaking. Then Walter said laughing that he meant to deal very fairly; that no one should bear a hand in the work who did not do so willingly; but that he should add a little to the wages of every man who worked for him at the camp while the work was going on.

The bailiff shrugged his shoulders and made no reply. Walter went and spoke to each of his men and told them his offer. "I know," he said, "that there is a story about the place, and that you do not wish to touch it; but I will offer a larger wage to every man who works there for me; and I will force no man to do it; but done it shall be; and if my own men win not do it, then I will get strangers to help me." The end of it was that three of his men offered to do the work, and the next day a start was made.

The copse and undergrowth was first cleared, and then the big trees were felled and dragged off the place; then the roots were stubbed up. It was a difficult task, and longer than Walter had thought; and he could not disguise from himself that a strange kind of ill-luck hung about the whole affair. One of his men disabled himself by a cut from an axe; another fell ill; the third, after these two mishaps, came and begged off. Walter replaced them with other workers; and the work proceeded slowly, in spite of Walter's great impatience and haste. He himself was there early and late; the men had it in their minds that they were searching for treasure and were well-nigh as excited as himself; and Walter was for ever afraid that in his absence some rich and valuable thing might be turned up, and perhaps concealed or conveyed away secretly by the finder.

But the weeks passed and nothing was found; and it was now a bare and ugly place with miry pools of dirt, great holes where the trees had been; there were cart tracks all over the field in which it lay, the great trunks lay outside the mound, and the undergrowth was piled in stacks. The mound and ditch had all been unturfed; and the mound was daily dug down to the level, every spadeful being shaken loose; and now they came upon some few traces of human use. In the mound was found a short and dinted sword of bronze, of antique shape. A mass of rusted metal was found in a corner, that looked as if it had been armour.

In another corner were found some large upright and calcined stones, with abundance of wood-ashes below, that seemed to have been a rude fireplace. And in one part, in a place where there seemed to have been a pit, was a quantity of rotting stuff, that seemed like the remains of bones. Walter himself grew worn and weary, partly with the toil and still more with the deferred hope. And the men too became sullen and ill-affected. It surprised Walter too that more than one of his neighbours spoke with disfavour of what he was doing, as of a thing that was foolish or even wrong. But still he worked on savagely, slept little, and cared not what he ate or drank.

At last the work was nearly over; the place had been all trenched across, and they had come in most places to the hard sandstone, which lay very near the surface. In the afternoon had fallen a heavy drenching shower, so that the men had gone home early, wet and dispirited; and Walter stood, all splashed and stained with mud, sick at heart and heavy, on the edge of the place, and looked very gloomily at the trenches, which lay like an ugly scar on the green hilltop. The sky was full of ragged inky clouds, with fierce lights on the horizon.

As he paced about and looked at the trenches, he saw in one place that it seemed as if the earth was of a different colour at the side of the trench; he stepped inside to look at this, and saw that the digging had laid bare the side of a place like a pit, that, seemed to have been dug down through the ground; he bent to examine it, and then saw at the bottom of the trench, washed clear by the rain, something that looked like a stick or a root, that projected a little into the trench; he put his hand down to it, and found it cold and hard and heavy, and in a moment saw that it was a rod of metal that ran into the bank. He took up a spade, and threw the earth away in haste; and presently uncovered the rod.

It was a bar, he saw, and very heavy; but examining it closely he saw that there was a stamp of some sort upon it; and then in a moment looking upon a place where the spade had scratched it, he saw that it was a bright yellow metal. It came over him all at once, with a shock that made him faint, that he had stumbled upon some part of the treasure; he put the bar aside, and then, first looking all round to see that none observed him, he dug into the bank. In a moment his spade struck something hard; and he presently uncovered a row of bars that lay close together. He dragged them up one by one, and underneath he found another row, laid crosswise; and another row, and another, till he had uncovered seven rows, making fifty bars in all. Beneath the lowest row his spade slipped on something round and smooth; he uncovered the earth, and presently drew out a brown and sodden skull, which thus lay beneath the treasure. Below that was a mass of softer earth, but out of it came the two thigh-bones of a man.

The sky was now beginning to grow dark; but he dug out the whole of the pit, working into the bank; and he saw that a round hole had been dug straight down from the top, to the sandstone. The bones lay upon the sandstone; but he found other bones at the sides of where the gold had lain; so that it seemed to him as though the gold must have been placed among dead bodies, and have rested among corruption. This was a dim thought that lurked in an ugly way in his mind. But he had now dug out the whole pit, and found nothing else, except a few large blurred copper coins which lay among the bodies. He stood awhile looking at the treasure; but together with the exultation at his discovery there mingled a dark and gloomy oppression of spirit, which he could not explain, which clouded his mind.

But presently he came to himself again, and gathering the bones together, he threw them down to the bottom of the pit, as he was minded to conceal his digging from the men. While he did so, it seemed to him that, as he was bending to the pit, something came suddenly behind him and stood at his back, close to him, as though looking over his shoulder. For a moment the horror was so great that he felt the hair of his head prickle and his heart thump within his breast; but he overcame it and turned, and saw nothing but the trenches, and above them the ragged sky; yet he had the thought that something had slipped away. But he set himself doggedly to finish his task; he threw earth into the holes, working in a kind of fury; and twice as he did so, the same feeling came again that there was someone at his back; and twice turning he saw nothing; but the third time, from the West came a sharp thunder-peal; and he had hardly finished his work when the rain fell in a sheet, and splashed in the trenches.

Then he turned to the treasure which lay beside him. He found that he could not carry more than a few of the bars at a time; and he dared not leave the rest uncovered. So, he covered them with earth and went stealthily down to the house; and there he got, with much precaution, a barrow from the garden. But the fear of discovery came upon him; and he determined to go into the house and sup as usual, and late at night convey the treasure to the house. For the time, his trove gave him no joy; he could not have believed it would have so weighed on him—he felt more like one who had some guilty secret to conceal, than a man to whom had befallen a great joy.

He went to the house, changed his wet clothes, and came to supper with his mother. To her accustomed questions as to what they had found, he took out the coins and showed them her, saying nothing of the gold, but with a jesting word that these would hardly repay him for his trouble. He could scarcely speak at supper for thinking of what he had found; and every now and then there came upon him a dreadful fear that he had been observed digging, and that even now some thief had stolen back there and was uncovering his hoard. His mother looked at him often, and at last said that he looked very weary; to which he replied with some sharpness, so that she said no more.

Then all at once, near the end of the meal, he had the same dreadful fear that he had felt by the pit. It seemed to him as though some one came near him and stood close behind him, bending over his shoulder; and a kind of icy coldness fell on him. He started and looked quickly round. His mother looked anxiously at him, and said, "What is it, dear Walter?" He made some excuse; but presently feeling that he must be alone, he excused himself and went to his room, where he sate, making pretence to read, till the house should be silent.

Then when all were abed, at an hour after midnight, he forced himself to rise and put on his rough clothes, though a terror lay very sore upon him, and go out to the garden, creeping like a thief. He had with him a lantern; and he carried the barrow on his shoulders for fear that the creaking of the wheel should awake someone; and then stumbling and sweating, and in a great weariness, he went by wood-paths to the hilltop. He came to the place, and having lit his lantern he uncovered the bars, and laid them on the barrow; they were as he had left them.

When he had loaded them, the same fear struck him suddenly cold again, of something near him; and he thought for a moment he would have swooned; but sitting down on the barrow in the cool air he presently came to himself. Then he essayed to wheel the barrow in the dark. But he stumbled often, and once upset the barrow and spilled his load. Thus, though fearing discovery, he was forced to light the lantern and set it upon the barrow, and so at last he came to the house; where he disposed the bars at the bottom of a chest of which he had the key, covering them with papers, and then went to bed in a kind of fever, his teeth chattering, till he fell into a wretched sleep which lasted till dawn.

In his sleep he dreamed a fearful dream; he seemed to be sitting on the ground by the camp, holding the gold in his arms; the camp in his dream was as it was before he had cleared it, all grown up with trees. Suddenly out from among the trees there came a man in rusty tarnished armour, with a pale wild face and a little beard, which seemed all clotted with moisture; he held in his hand a pike or spear, and he came swiftly and furiously upon Walter as though he would smite him. But it seemed as though his purpose changed; for standing aside he watched Walter with evil and piercing eyes, so that it seemed to

Walter that he would sooner have been smitten. And then he woke, but in anguish, for the man still seemed to stand beside him; until he made a light and saw no one.

He arose feeling broken and ill; but he met his mother with a smile, and told her that he had determined to do what would please her, and work no more at the camp. And he told the men that he would dig no more, but that they were to level the place and so leave it. And so, they did, murmuring sore.

The next week was a very miserable one for Walter; he could not have believed that a man's heart should be so heavy. It seemed to him that he lay, like the poor bones that he had found beneath the treasure, crushed and broken and stifled under the weight of it. He was tempted to do wild things with the gold; to bury it again in the camp, to drop it into the mud of the pool that lay near the house. In fevered dreams he seemed to row himself in a boat upon a dark sea, and to throw the bars one by one into the water; the reason of this was not only his fear for the treasure itself, but the dreadful sense that he had of being followed by someone, who dogged his footsteps wherever he went.

If ever he sate alone, the thing would draw near him and bend above him; he often felt that if he could but look round swiftly enough he would catch a glimpse of the thing, and that nothing that he could see would be so fearful as that which was unseen; and so it came to pass that, as he sate with his mother, though he bore the presence long that he might not startle her, yet after a time of patient agony he could bear it no more, but looked swiftly behind him; he grew pale and ill, and even the men of the place noticed how often he turned round as he walked; till at last he would not even walk abroad, except early and late when there would be few to see him.

He had sent away his labourers; but once or twice he noticed, as he went by the camp, that someone had been digging and grubbing in the mire. Sometimes for an hour or two his terrors would leave him, till he thought that he was wholly cured; but it was like a cat with a mouse, for he suffered the worse for his respite, till at last he fell so low that he used to think of stories of men that had destroyed themselves, and though he knew it to be a terrible sin to dally with such thoughts, he could not wholly put them from him, but used to plan in his mind how he could do the deed best, that it might appear to be an accident. Sometimes he bore his trouble heavily, but at others he would rage to think that he had been so happy so short a while ago; and even the love that he bore to Marjory was darkened and destroyed by the evil thing, and he met her timid and friendly glances sullenly; his mother was nearly as miserable as himself, for she knew that something was very grievously amiss, but could not divine what it was. Indeed, she could do nothing but wish it were otherwise, and pray for her son, for she knew not where the trouble lay, but thought that he was ill or even bewitched.

At last, after a day of dreadful gloom, Walter made up his mind that he would ride to London and see to the disposing of the treasure. He had a thought often in his mind that if he replaced it in the camp, he would cease to be troubled; but he could not bring himself to that; he seemed to himself like a man who had won a hard victory, and was asked to surrender what he had won.

His intention was to go to an old and wise friend of his father's, who was a canon of a Collegiate Church in London, and was much about the court. So, he hid the treasure in a strong cellar and padlocked the door; but he took one bar with him to show to his friend.

It was a doleful journey; his horse seemed as dispirited as himself; and his terrors came often upon him, till he was fearful that he might be thought mad; and indeed, what with the load at his heart and the short and troubled nights he spent, he believed himself that he was not very far from it.

It was with a feeling of relief and safety, like a ship coming into port, that he stayed his horse at the door of the college, which stood in a quiet street of the city. He carried a valise of clothes in which the bar was secured. He had a very friendly greeting from the old canon, who received him in a little studious parlour full of books. The court was full of pleasant sunshine, and the city outside seemed to make a pleasant and wholesome stir in the air.

But the canon was very much amazed at Walter's looks; he was used to read the hearts of men in their faces like a wise priest, and he saw in Walter's face a certain desperate look such as he had seen, he said to himself, in the faces of those who had a deadly sin to confess. But it was not his way to make inquisition, and so he talked courteously and easily, and when he found that Walter was inclined to be silent, he filled the silence himself with little talk of the news of the town.

After the meal, which they took in the canon's room—for Walter said that he would prefer that to dining in the hall, when the canon gave him the choice—Walter said that he had a strange story to tell him. The canon felt no surprise, and being used to strange stories, addressed himself to listen carefully; for he thought that in the most difficult and sad tales of sin the words of the sufferer most often supplied the advice and the way out, if one but listened warily.

He did not interrupt Walter except to ask him a few questions to make the story clear, but his face grew very grave; and at the end he sate some time in silence. Then he said very gently that it was a heavy judgment, but that he must ask Walter one question. "I do not ask you to tell me," he said very courteously, "what it may be; but is there no other thing in which you have displeased God? For these grievous thoughts and fears are sometimes sent as a punishment for sin, and to turn men back to the light."

Then Walter said that he knew of no such sin by which he could have vexed God so exceedingly. "Careless," he said, "I am and have been; and, father, I would tell you anything that was in my heart; I would have no secrets from you—but though I am a sinner, and do not serve God as well as I would, yet I desire to serve Him, and have no sin that is set like a wall between Him and me."

He said this so honestly and bravely, looking so full at the priest, that he did not doubt him, and said, "Then, my son, we must look elsewhere for the cause; and though I speak in haste, and without weighing my words, it seems to me that, to speak in parables, you are like a man who has come by chance to a den and carried off for his pleasure the cubs of some forest beast, who returns and finds them gone, and tracks the robber out. The souls of these poor warriors are in some mansion of God, we know not where; if they did faithfully in life they are beaten, as the Scripture says, with few stripes; but they may not enjoy His blessed rest, nor the sweet sleep of the faithful souls who lie beneath the altar and wait for His coming. And now though they cannot slay you, they can do you grievous hurt. The Holy Church hath power indeed over the spirits of evil, the devils that enter into men. But I have not heard that she hath power over the spirits of the dead, and least of all over those that lived and died outside the fold.

"It seems to me, though I but grope in darkness, that these poor spirits grudge the treasure that they fought and died for to the hands of a man who hath not fought for it. We may think that it is a poor and childish thing to grudge that which one cannot use; but no discourse will make a child think so; and I reckon that these poor souls are as children yet. And it seems to me, speaking foolishly, as though they would not be appeased until you either restored it to them, or used it for their undoubted benefit; but of one thing I am certain, that it must

252

not be used to enrich yourself. But I must ponder over the story, for it is a strange one, and not such as has ever yet come before me."

Then Walter found fresh courage at these wary and wise words, and told him of his impoverished estate and the love he had to Marjory; and the priest smiled, and said that love was the best thing to win in the world. And then he said that as it was now late, they must sleep; and that the night often brought counsel; and so he took Walter to his chamber, a little precise place with a window on the court; and there he left him; but he first knelt down and prayed, and then laid his hand on Walter's head, and blessed him, and commended him to the merciful keeping of God; and Walter slept sweetly, and was scared that night by no dismal dreams; and in the morning the priest took him to the church, and Walter knelt in a little chapel while the old man said his mass, commending therein the burden of Walter's suffering into the merciful hands of God; so that Walter's heart was greatly lightened.

Then after the mass the priest asked Walter of his health, and whether he had suffered any visitation of evil that night; he said "no," and the priest then said that he had pondered long over the story, which was strange and very dark. But he had little doubt now as to what Walter should do. He did not think that the treasure should be replaced now that it was got up, because it was only flying before the evil and not meeting it, but leaving the sad inheritance for some other man.

The poor spirit must be laid to rest, and the treasure used for God's glory, "And therefore," he said, "I think that a church must be built, and dedicated to All Souls; and thus, your net will be wide enough to catch the sad spirit. And you must buy a little estate for the support of the chaplain thereof, and so shall all be content."

"All but one," said Walter sadly, "for there goes my dream of setting up my own house that tumbles down."

My son," said the old priest very gravely, you must not murmur; it will be enough for you if God take away the sore chastening of your spirit; and for the rest. He will provide,"

"But there is more behind," he said after a pause. "If you, with an impoverished estate, build a church and endow a priest, there will be questions asked; it will needs be known that you have found a treasure, and it will come, perhaps, to the ears of the King's Grace, and inquisition will be made; so I shall go this morning to a Lord of the Court, an ancient friend of mine, a discreet man; and I will lay the story before him, if you give me leave; and he will advise."

Walter saw that the priest's advice was good; and so he gave him leave; and the priest departed to the court; but while he was away, as Walter sate sadly over a book, his terrors came upon him with fresh force; the thing drew near him and stood at his shoulder, and he could not dislodge it; it seemed to Walter that it was more malign than ever, and was set upon driving him to some desperate deed; so he rose and paced in the court; but it seemed to move behind him, till he thought he would have gone distraught; but finding the church doors open, he went inside and, in a corner, knelt and prayed, and got some kind of peace; yet he felt all the while as though the presence waited for him at the door, but could not hurt him in the holy shrine; and there Walter made a vow and vowed his life into the hands of God; for he had found the world a harder place than he had thought, and it seemed to him as though he walked among unseen foes.

Presently he saw the old priest come into the church, peering about; so, Walter rose and came to him; the priest had a contented air, but seemed big with news, and he told Walter that he must go with him at once to the Court. For he had seen the Lord Poynings, that was his friend, who had taken him at once to the king; and the king had heard the story very curiously, and would see Walter himself that day. So, Walter fetched the bar of gold and they went at once together; and Walter was full of awe and fear, and asked the priest how he should bear himself; to which the priest said smiling, "As a man, in the presence of a man." And as they went Walter told him that he had been visited by the terror again, but had found peace in the church; and the priest said, "Ay, there is peace to be had there."

They came down to the palace, and were at once admitted; the priest and he were led into a little room, full of books, where a man was writing, a venerable man in a furred gown, with a comely face; this was the Lord Poynings, who greeted Walter very gently but with a secret attention; Walter shewed him the bar of gold, and he looked at it long, and presently there came a page who said that the king was at leisure, and would see Mr. Wyatt.

Walter had hoped that the priest, or at least the Lord Poynings, would accompany him; but the message was for himself alone; so he was led along a high corridor with tall stands of arms. The king had been a great warrior in his manhood, and had won many trophies. They came to a great doorway, where the page knocked; a voice cried within, and the page told Walter he must enter alone,

Walter would fain have asked the page how he should make his obeisance; but there was no time now, for the page opened the door, and Walter went in.

He found himself in a small room, hung with green arras. The king was sitting in a great chair, by a table spread out with parchments. Walter first bowed low and then knelt down; the king motioned him to rise, and then said in a quiet and serene voice, "So, sir, you are the gentleman that has found a treasure and would fain be rid of it again." At these gentle words Walter felt his terrors leave him; the king looked at him with a serious attention; he was a man just passing into age; his head was nearly hairless, and he had a thin face with a long nose, and small lips drawn together. On his head was a loose velvet cap, and he wore his gown furred; round his neck was a jewel, and he had great rings on his forefingers and thumbs.

The king, hardly pausing for an answer, said, "You look ill. Master Wyatt, and little wonder; sit here in a chair and tell me the tale in a few words."

Walter told his story as shortly as he could with the king's kind eye upon him; the king once or twice interrupted him; he took the bar from Walter's hands, and looked upon it, weighing it in his fingers, and saying, "Ay, it is a mighty treasure." Once or twice he made him repeat a few sentences, and heard the story of the thing that stood near him with a visible awe.

At last he said with a smile, "You have told your story well, sir, and plainly; are you a soldier?"

When Walter said "no," he said, "It is a noble trade, nevertheless."

Then he said, "Well, sir, the treasure is yours, to use as I understand you will use it for the glory of God and for the peace of the poor spirit, which I doubt not is that of a great knight. But I have no desire to be visited of him," and here he crossed himself. "So, let it be thus bestowed—and I will cause a quittance to be made out for you from the Crown, which will take no part in the trove. How many bars did you say?"

And when Walter said "fifty," the king said, "It is great wealth; and I wish for your sake, sir, that it were not so sad an inheritance." Then he added, "Well, sir, that is the matter; but I would hear the end of this, for I never knew the like; when your church is built and all things are in order, and let it be done speedily, you shall come and visit me again." And then the king said, with a kindly smile, "And as for the maiden of whom I have heard, be not discouraged; for yours is an ancient house, and it must not be extinguished—and so farewell; and remember that your king wishes you happiness;" and he made a sign that Walter should withdraw. So, Walter knelt again and kissed the king's ring, and left the chamber.

When Walter came out he seemed to tread on air; the king's gracious kindness moved him very greatly, and loyalty filled his heart to the brim. He found the priest and the Lord Poynings waiting for him; and presently the two left the palace together, and Walter told the priest what the king had said.

The next day he rode back into Sussex; but he was very sorely beset as he rode, and reached home in great misery. But he wasted no time, but rather went to his new task with great eagerness; the foundations of the church were laid, and soon the walls began to rise. Meanwhile Walter had the gold conveyed to the king's Mint; and a message came to him that it would make near upon twenty thousand pounds of gold, a fortune for an earl. So, the church was built very massive and great, and a rich estate was bought which would support a college of priests. But Walter's heart was very heavy; for his terrors still came over him from day to day; and he was no nearer settling his own affairs.

Then there began to come to him a sore temptation; he could build his church, and endow his college with lands, and yet he could save something of the treasure to set him free from his own poverty; and day by day this wrought more and more in his mind.

At last one day when he was wandering through the wood, he found himself face to face in the path with Marjory herself; and there was so tender a look in her face that he could no longer resist, so he turned and walked with her, and told her all that was in his heart. "It was all for the love of you," he said, "that I have thus been punished, and now I am no nearer the end;" and then, for he saw that she wept, and that she loved him well, he opened to her his heart, and said that he would keep back part of the treasure, and would save his house, and that they would be wed; and so he kissed her on the lips.

But Marjory was a true-hearted and wise maiden, and loved Walter better than he knew; and she said to him, all trembling for pity, "Dear Walter, it cannot be; this must be given faithfully, because you are the king's servant, and because you must give the spirit back his own, and because you are he that I love the best; and we will wait; for God tells me that it must be so; and He is truer even than love."

So, Walter was ashamed; and he threw unworthy thoughts away; and with the last of the money he caused a fair screen to be made, and windows of rich glass; and the money was thus laid out.

Now while the church was in building—and they made all the haste they could—Walter had days when he was very grievously troubled; but it seemed to him a different sort of trouble. In the first place he looked forward confidently to the day when the dark presence would be withdrawn; and a man who can look forward to a certain ending to his pain can stay himself on that; but, besides that, it seemed to him that he was not now beset by a foe, but guarded as it were by a sentinel. There were days when the horror was very great, and when the thing was always near him whether he sate or walked, whether he was alone or in company; and on those days he withdrew himself from men, and there was a dark shadow on his brow. So that there grew up a kind of mystery about him; but, besides that, he learnt things in those bitter hours that are not taught in any school.

He learnt to suffer with all the great company of those who bear heavy and unseen burdens, who move in the grip of fears and stumble under the load of dark necessities. He grew more tender and more strong. He found in his hand the key to many hearts. Before this he had cared little about the thoughts of other men; but now he found himself for ever wondering what the inner thoughts of the hearts of others were, and ready if need were to help to lift their load; he had lived before in careless fellowship with light-hearted persons, but now he was rather drawn to the old and wise and sad; and there fell on him some touch of the holy priesthood that falls on all whose sadness is a fruitful sadness, and who instead of yielding to bitter repining would try to make others happier. If he heard of a sorrow or a distress, his thought was no longer how to put it out of his mind as soon as he might, but of how he might lighten it. So, his heart grew wider day by day.

And at last the day came when the church was done; it stood, a fair white shrine with a seemly tower, on the hill-top, and a little way from it was the college for the priests. The bishop came to consecrate it, and the old canon came from London, and there was a little gathering of neighbours to see the holy work accomplished.

The bishop blessed the church very tenderly; he was an old infirm man, but he bore his weakness lightly and serenely. He made Walter the night before tell him the story of the treasure, and found much to wonder at in it.

There was no part of the church or its furniture that he did not solemnly bless; and Walter from his place felt a grave joy to see all so fair and seemly. The priests moved from end to end with the bishop, in their stiff embroidered robes, and there was a holy smell of incense which strove with the sharp scent of the newly-chiselled wood. The bishop made them a little sermon and spoke much of the gathering into the fold of spirits that had done their work bravely, even if they had not known the Lord Christ on earth.

After all was over, and the guests were departed, the old Canon said that he must return on the morrow to London, and that he had a message for Walter from the king—who had not failed to ask him how the work went on—that Walter was to return with him and tell the king of the fulfilment of the design.

That night Walter had a strange dream; he seemed to stand in a dark place all vaulted over, like a cave that stretched far into the earth; he himself stood in the shadow of a rock, and he was aware of some-one passing by him. He looked at him, and saw that he was the war-rior that he had seen before in his dream, a small pale man, with a short beard, with rusty armour much dinted; he held a spear in his hand, and walked restlessly like a man little content. But while Walter watched him, there seemed to be another person drawing near in the opposite direction.

This was a tall man, all in white, who brought with him as he came a strange freshness in the dark place, as of air and light, and the scent of flowers; this one came along in a different fashion, with an assured and yet tender air, as though he was making search for someone to whom his coming would be welcome; so the two met and words passed between them; the warrior stood with his hands clasped upon his spear seeming to drink in what was said—he could not hear the words at first, for they were spoken softly, but the last words he heard were, "And you too are of the number."

Then the warrior kneeled down and laid his spear aside, and the other seemed to stoop and bless him, and then went on his way; and the warrior knelt and watched him going with a look in his face as though he had heard wonderful and beautiful news, and could hardly yet believe it; and so holy was the look that Walter felt as though he intruded upon some deep mystery, and moved further into the shadow of the rock; but the warrior rose and came to him where he stood, and looked at him with a half-doubting look, as though he asked pardon, stretching out his hands; and Walter smiled at him, and the other smiled; and at the moment Walter woke in the dawn with a strange joy in his heart, and rising in haste, drew the window curtain aside, and saw the fresh dawn beginning to come in over the woods, and he knew that the burden was lifted from him and that he was free.

In the morning as the old canon and Walter rode to London, Walter told him the dream; and when he had done, he saw that the old priest was smiling at him with his eyes full of tears, and that he could not speak; so, they rode together in that sweet silence which is worth more than many words.

The next day Walter came to see the king: he carried with him a paper to show the king how all had been expended; but he went with no fear, but as though to see a true friend.

The king received him very gladly, and bade Walter tell him all that had been done; so, Walter told him, and then speaking very softly told the king the dream; the king mused over the story, and then said, "So he has his heart's desire."

Then there was a silence; and then the king, as though breaking out of a pleasant thought, drew from the table a parchment, and said to Walter that he had done well and wisely, and therefore for the trust that he had in him he made him his sheriff for the County of Sussex, to which was added a large revenue; and there was more to come, for the king bade Walter unhook a sword from the wall, his own sword that he had borne in battle; and therewith he dubbed him knight, and said to him, "Rise up. Sir Walter Wyatt." Then before he dismissed him, he said to him that he would see him every year at the court; and then with a smile he added, "And when you next come, I charge you to bring with you my Lady Wyatt."

And Walter promised this, and kept his word.

The Slype House

In the town of Garchester, close to St. Peter's Church, and near
the river, stood a dark old house called the Slype House, from a narrow passage of that name that ran close to it, down to a bridge over
the stream. The house showed a front of mouldering and discoloured
stone to the street, pierced by small windows, like a monastery; and indeed, it was formerly inhabited by a college of priests who had served
the Church. It abutted at one angle upon the aisle of the church, and
there was a casement window that looked out from a room in the
house, formerly the infirmary, into the aisle; it had been so built that
any priest that was sick might hear the Mass from his bed, without
descending into the church.

Behind the house lay a little garden, closely grown up with trees
and tall weeds, that ran down to the stream. In the wall that gave on
the water, was a small door that admitted to an old timbered bridge
that crossed the stream, and had a barred gate on the further side,
which was rarely seen open; though if a man had watched attentively
he might sometimes have seen a small lean person, much bowed and
with a halting gait, slip out very quietly about dusk, and walk, with his
eyes cast down, among the shadowy byways.

The name of the man who thus dwelt in the Slype House, as it
appeared in the roll of *burgesses*, was Anthony Purvis. He was of an
ancient family, and had inherited wealth. A word must be said of his
childhood and youth. He was a sickly child, an only son, his father a
man of substance, who lived very easily in the country; his mother had
died when he was quite a child, and this sorrow had been borne very
heavily by his father, who had loved her tenderly, and after her death
had become morose and sullen, withdrawing himself from all company and exercise, and brooding angrily over his loss, as though God
had determined to vex him. He had never cared much for the child,

who had been peevish and fretful; and the boy's presence had done little but remind him of the wife he had lost; so that the child had lived alone, nourishing his own fancies, and reading much in a library of curious books that was in the house. The boy's health had been too tender for him to go to school; but when he was eighteen, he seemed stronger, and his father sent him to a university, more for the sake of being relieved of the boy's presence than for his good.

And there, being unused to the society of his equals, he had been much flouted and despised for his feeble frame; till a certain bitter ambition sprang up in his mind, like a poisonous flower, to gain power and make himself a name; and he had determined that as he could not be loved he might still be feared; so he bided his time in bitterness, making great progress in his studies; then, when those days were over, he departed eagerly, and sought and obtained his father's leave to betake himself to a university of Italy, where he fell into somewhat evil hands; for he made a friendship with an old doctor of the college, who feared not God and thought ill of man, and spent all his time in dark researches into the evil secrets of nature, the study of poisons that have enmity to the life of man, and many other hidden works of darkness, such as intercourse with spirits of evil, and the black influences that he in wait for the soul; and he found Anthony an apt pupil.

There he lived for some years till he was nearly thirty, seldom visiting his home, and writing but formal letters to his father, who supplied him gladly with a small revenue, so long as he kept apart and troubled him not.

Then his father had died, and Anthony came home to take up his inheritance, which was a plentiful one; he sold his land, and visiting the town of Garchester, by chance, for it lay near his home, he had lighted upon the Slype House, which lay very desolate and gloomy; and as he needed a large place for his instruments and devices, he had bought the house, and had now lived there for twenty years in great loneliness, but not ill-content.

To serve him he had none but a man and his wife, who were quiet and simple people and asked no questions; the wife cooked his meals, and kept the rooms, where he slept and read, clean and neat; the man moved his machines for him, and arranged his phials and instruments, having a light touch and a serviceable memory.

The door of the house that gave on the street opened into a hall; to the right was a kitchen, and a pair of rooms where the man and his wife lived. On the left was a large room running through the house;

the windows on to the street were walled up, and the windows at the back looked on the garden, the trees of which grew dose to the casements, making the room dark, and in a breeze rustling their leaves or leafless branches against the panes.

In this room Anthony had a furnace with bellows, the smoke of which discharged itself into the chimney; and here he did much of his work, making mechanical toys, as a clock to measure the speed of wind or water, a little chariot that ran a few yards by itself, a puppet that moved its arms and laughed—and other things that had wiled away his idle hours; the room was filled up with dark lumber, in a sort of order that would have looked to a stranger like disorder, but so that Anthony could lay his hand on all that he needed. From the hall, which was paved with stone, went up the stairs, very strong and broad, of massive oak; under which was a postern that gave on the garden; on the floor above was a room where Anthony slept, which again had its windows to the street boarded up, for he was a light sleeper, and the morning sounds of the awakening city disturbed him.

The room was hung with a dark arras, sprinkled with red flowers; he slept in a great bed with black curtains to shut out all light; the windows looked into the garden; but on the left of the bed, which stood with its head to the street, was an alcove, behind the hangings, containing the window that gave on the church. On the same floor were three other rooms; in one of these, looking on the garden, Anthony had his meals. It was a plain panelled room. Next was a room where he read, filled with books, also looking on the garden; and next to that was a little room of which he alone had the key. This room he kept locked, and no one set foot in it but himself.

There was one more room on this floor, set apart for a guest who never came, with a great bed and a press of oak. And that looked on the street. Above, there was a row of plain plastered rooms, in which stood furniture for which Anthony had no use, and many crates in which his machines and phials came to him; this floor was seldom visited, except by the man, who sometimes came to put a box there; and the spiders had it to themselves; except for a little room where stood an optic glass through which on clear nights Anthony sometimes looked at the moon and stars, if there was any odd misadventure among them, such as an eclipse; or when a fiery-tailed comet went his way silently in the heavens, coming from none might say whence and going none knew whither, on some strange errand of God.

Anthony had but two friends who ever came to see him. One was an old physician who had ceased to practise his trade, which indeed was never abundant, and who would sometimes drink a glass of wine with Anthony, and engage in curious talk of men's bodies and diseases, or look at one of Anthony's toys. Anthony had come to know him by having called him in to cure some ailment, which needed a surgical knife; and that had made a kind of friendship between them; but Anthony had little need thereafter to consult him about his health, which indeed was now settled enough, though he had but little vigour; and he knew enough of drugs to cure himself when he was ill.

The other friend was a foolish priest of the college, that made belief to be a student but was none, who thought Anthony a very wise and mighty person, and listened with open mouth and eyes to all that he said or showed him. This priest, who was fond of wonders, had introduced himself to Anthony by making believe to borrow a volume of him; and then had grown proud of the acquaintance, and bragged greatly of it to his friends, mixing up much that was fanciful with a little that was true.

But the result was that gossip spread wide about Anthony, and he was held in the town to be a very fearful person, who could do strange mischief if he had a mind to; Anthony never cared to walk abroad, for he was of a shy habit, and disliked to meet the eyes of his fellows; but if he did go about, men began to look curiously after him as he went by, shook their heads and talked together with a dark pleasure, while children fled before his face and women feared him; all of which pleased Anthony mightily, if the truth were told; for at the bottom of his restless and eager spirit lay a deep vanity unseen, like a lake in woods; he hungered not indeed for fame, but for repute—*monstrari digito*, as the poet has it; and he cared little in what repute he was held, so long as men thought him great and marvellous; and as he could not win renown by brave deeds and words, he was rejoiced to win it by keeping up a certain darkness and mystery about his ways and doings; and this was very dear to him, so that when the silly priest called him Seer and Wizard, he frowned and looked sideways; but he laughed in his heart and was glad.

Now, when Anthony was near his fiftieth year, there fell on him a heaviness of spirit which daily increased upon him. He began to question of his end and what lay beyond. He had always made pretence to mock at religion, and had grown to believe that in death the soul was extinguished like a burnt-out flame. He began, too, to question of his life and what he had done. He had made a few toys, he had filled vacant hours, and he had gained an ugly kind of fame—and this was all. Was he so certain, he began to think, after all, that death was the end? Were there not, perhaps, in the vast house of God, rooms and chambers beyond that in which he was set for a while to pace to and fro? About this time, he began to read in a Bible that had lain dusty and unopened on a shelf.

It was his mother's book, and he found therein many little tokens of her presence. Here was a verse underlined; at some gracious passages the page was much fingered and worn; in one place there were stains that looked like the mark of tears; then again, in one page, there was a small tress of hair, golden hair, tied in a paper with a name across it, that seemed to be the name of a little sister of his mother's that died a child; and again there were a few withered flowers, like little sad ghosts, stuck through a paper on which was written his father's name—the name of the sad, harsh, silent man whom Anthony had feared with all his heart. Had those two, indeed, on some day of summer, walked to and fro, or sate in some woodland corner, whispering sweet words of love together?

Anthony felt a sudden hunger of the heart for a woman's love, for tender words to soothe his sadness, for the laughter and kisses of children—and he began to ransack his mind for memories of his mother; he could remember being pressed to her heart one morning when she lay abed, with her fragrant hair falling about him. The worst was that he must bear his sorrow alone, for there were none to whom he could talk of such things. The doctor was as dry as an old bunch of herbs, and as for the priest, Anthony was ashamed to show anything but contempt and pride in his presence.

For relief he began to turn to a branch of his studies that he had long disused; this was a fearful commerce with the unseen spirits. Anthony could remember having practised some experiments of this kind with the old Italian doctor; but he remembered them with a kind of disgust, for they seemed to him but a sort of deadly juggling; and such dark things as he had seen seemed like a dangerous sport with unclean and coltish beings, more brute-like than human. Yet now he read in his curious books with care, and studied the tales of necromancers, who had indeed seemed to have some power over the souls of men departed.

But the old books gave him but little faith, and a kind of angry disgust at the things attempted. And he began to think that the horror in which such men as made these books abode, was not more than the dark shadow cast on the mirror of the soul by their own desperate imaginings and timorous excursions.

One day, a Sunday, he was strangely sad and heavy; he could settle to nothing, but threw book after book aside, and when he turned to some work of construction, his hand seemed to have lost its cunning. It was a grey and sullen day in October; a warm wet wind came buffeting up from the west, and roared in the chimneys and eaves of the old house. The shrubs in the garden plucked themselves hither and thither as though in pain. Anthony walked to and fro after his midday meal, which he had eaten hastily and without savour; at last, as though with a sudden resolution, he went to a secret cabinet and got out a key; and with it he went to the door of the little room that was ever locked.

He stopped at the threshold for a while, looking hither and thither; and then he suddenly unlocked it and went in, closing and locking it behind him. The room was as dark as night, but Anthony going softly, his hands before him, went to a corner and got a tinder-box which lay there, and made a flame.

A small dark room appeared, hung with a black tapestry; the window was heavily shuttered and curtained; in the centre of the room stood what looked like a small altar, painted black; the floor was all bare, but with white marks upon it, half effaced. Anthony looked about the room, glancing sidelong, as though in some kind of doubt; his breath went and came quickly, and he looked paler than was his wont.

Presently, as though reassured by the silence and calm of the place, he went to a tall press that stood in a corner, which he opened, and took from it certain things—a dish of metal, some small leathern bags, a large lump of chalk, and a book. He laid all but the chalk down on the altar, and then opening the book, read in it a little; and then he went with the chalk and drew certain marks upon the floor, first making a circle, which he went over again and again with anxious care; at times he went back and peeped into the book as though uncertain. Then he opened the bags, which seemed to hold certain kinds of powder, this dusty, that in grains; he ran them through his hands, and then poured a little of each into his dish, and mixed them with his hands.

Then he stopped and looked about him. Then he walked to a place in the wall on the further side of the altar from the door, and drew the arras carefully aside, disclosing a little alcove in the wall; into this he looked fearfully, as though he was afraid of what he might see.

In the alcove, which was all in black, appeared a small shelf, that stood but a little way out from the wall. Upon it, gleaming very white against the black, stood the skull of a man, and on either side of the skull were the bones of a man's hand. It looked to him, as he gazed on it with a sort of curious disgust, as though a dead man had come up to the surface of a black tide, and was preparing presently to leap out. On either side stood two long silver candlesticks, very dark with disuse; but instead of holding candles, they were fitted at the top with flat metal dishes; and in these he poured some of his powders, mixing them as before with his fingers. Between the candlesticks and behind the skull was an old and dark picture, at which he gazed for a time, holding his taper on high.

The picture represented a man fleeing in a kind of furious haste from a wood, his hands spread wide, and his eyes staring out of the picture; behind him everywhere was the wood, above which was a star in the sky—and out of the wood leaned a strange pale horned thing, very dim. The horror in the man's face was skilfully painted, and Anthony felt a shudder pass through his veins. He knew not what the picture meant; it had been given to him by the old Italian, who had smiled a wicked smile when he gave it, and told him that it had a very great virtue. When Anthony had asked him of the subject of the picture, the old Italian had said, "Oh, it is as appears; he hath been where he ought not, and he hath seen somewhat he doth not like." When Anthony would fain have known more, and especially what the thing was that leaned out of the wood, the old Italian had smiled cruelly and said, "Know you not? Well, you will know some day when you have seen him;" and never a word more would he say.

When Anthony had put all things in order, he opened the book at a certain place, and laid it upon the altar; and then it seemed as though his courage failed him, for he drew the curtain again over the alcove, unlocked the door, set the tinderbox and the candle back in their place, and softly left the room.

He was very restless all the evening. He took down books from the shelves, turned them over, and put them back again. He addressed himself to some unfinished work, but soon threw it aside; he paced up and down, and spent a long time, with his hands clasped behind him, looking out into the desolate garden, where a still, red sunset burnt behind the leafless trees. He was like a man who has made up his mind to a grave decision, and shrinks back upon the brink. When his food was served he could hardly touch it, and he drank no wine as his custom was to do, but only water, saying to himself that his head must be clear. But in the evening he went to his bedroom, and searched for something in a press there; he found at last what he was searching for, and unfolded a long black robe, looking gloomily upon it, as though it aroused unwelcome thoughts; while he was pondering, he heard a hum of music behind the arras; he put the robe down, and stepped through the hangings, and stood awhile in the little oriel that looked down into the church.

Vespers were proceeding; he saw the holy lights dimly through the dusty panes, and heard the low preluding of the organ; then, solemn and slow, rose the sound of a chanted psalm on the air; he carefully unfastened the casement which opened inward and unclosed it, standing for a while to listen, while the air, fragrant with incense smoke, drew into the room along the vaulted roof. There were but a few worshippers in the church, who stood below him; two lights burnt stilly upon the altar, and he saw distinctly the thin hands of a priest who held a book close to his face. He had not set foot within a church for many years, and the sight and sound drew his mind back to his childhood's days.

At last with a sigh he put the window to very softly, and went to his study, where he made pretence to read, till the hour came when he was wont to retire to his bed. He sent his servant away, but instead of lying down, he sate, looking upon a parchment, which he held in his hand, while the bells of the city slowly told out the creeping hours.

At last, a few minutes before midnight, he rose from his place; the house was now all silent, and without the night was very still, as though all things slept tranquilly. He opened the press and took from it the black robe, and put it round him, so that it covered him from head to foot, and then gathered up the parchment, and the key of the locked room, and went softly out, and so came to the door.

This he undid with a kind of secret and awestruck haste, locking it behind him. Once inside the room, he wrestled awhile with a strong aversion to what was in his mind to do, and stood for a moment, listening intently, as though he expected to hear some sound. But the room was still, except for the faint biting of some small creature in the wainscot.

Then with a swift motion he took up the tinderbox and made a light; he drew aside the curtain that hid the alcove; he put fire to the powder in the candlesticks, which at first spluttered, and then swiftly kindling sent up a thick smoky aflame, fragrant with drugs, burning hotly and red. Then he came back to the altar; cast a swift glance round him to see that all was ready; put fire to the powder on the altar, and in a low and inward voice began to recite words from the book, and from the parchment which he held in his hand; once or twice he glanced fearfully at the skull, and the hands which gleamed luridly through the smoke; the figures in the picture wavered in the heat; and now the powders began to burn clear, and throw up a steady light; and still he read, sometimes turning a page, until at last he made an end; and drawing something from a silver box which lay beside the book, he dropped it in the flame, and looked straight before him to see what might befall.

The thing that fell in the flame burned up brightly, with a little leaping of sparks, but soon it died down; and there was a long silence, in the room, a breathless silence, which, to Anthony's disordered mind, was not like the silence of emptiness, but such silence as may be heard when unseen things are crowding quietly to a closed door, expecting it to be opened, and as it were holding each other back.

Suddenly, between him and the picture, appeared for a moment a pale light, as of moonlight, and then with a horror which words cannot attain to describe, Anthony saw a face hang in the air a few feet from him, that looked in his own eyes with a sort of intent fury, as though to spring upon him if he turned either to the right hand or to the left. His knees tottered beneath him, and a sweat of icy coldness sprang on his brow; there followed a sound like no sound that Anthony had ever dreamed of hearing; a sound that was near and yet remote, a sound that was low and yet charged with power, like the groaning of a voice in grievous pain and anger, that strives to be free and yet is helpless.

And then Anthony knew that he had indeed opened the door that looks into the other world, and that a deadly thing that held him in enmity had looked out. His reeling brain still told him that he was safe where he was, but that he must not step or fall outside the circle; but how he should resist the power of the wicked face he knew not. He tried to frame a prayer in his heart; but there swept such a fury of hatred across the face that he dared not. So, he closed his eyes and stood dizzily waiting to fall, and knowing that if he fell it was the end.

Suddenly, as he stood with closed eyes, he felt the horror of the spell relax; he opened his eyes again, and saw that the face died out upon the air, becoming first white and then thin, like the husk that

269

stands on a rush when a fly draws itself from its skin, and floats away into the sunshine.

Then there fell a low and sweet music upon the air, like a concert of flutes and harps, very far away. And then suddenly, in a sweet clear radiance, the face of his mother, as she lived in his mind, appeared in the space, and looked at him with a kind of heavenly love; then beside the face appeared two thin hands which seemed to wave a blessing towards him, which flowed like healing into his soul.

The relief from the horror, and the flood of tenderness that came into his heart, made him reckless. The tears came into his eyes, not in a rising film, but a flood hot and large. He took a step forwards round the altar; but as he did so, the vision disappeared, the lights shot up into a flare and went out; the house seemed to be suddenly shaken; in the darkness he heard the rattle of bones, and the clash of metal, and Anthony fell all his length upon the ground and lay as one dead.

But while he thus lay, there came to him in some secret cell of the mind a dreadful vision, which he could only dimly remember afterwards with a fitful horror. He thought that he was walking in the cloister of some great house or college, a cool place, with a pleasant garden in the court. He paced up and down, and each time that he did so, he paused a little before a great door at the end, a huge blind portal, with much carving about it, which he somehow knew he was forbidden to enter. Nevertheless, each time that he came to it, he felt a strong wish, that constantly increased, to set foot therein. Now in the dream there fell on him a certain heaviness, and the shadow of a cloud fell over the court, and struck the sunshine out of it. And at last he made up his mind that he would enter.

He pushed the door open with much difficulty, and found himself in a long blank passage, very damp and chilly, but with a glimmering light; he walked a few paces down it. The flags underfoot were slimy, and the walls streamed with damp. He then thought that he would return; but the great door was closed behind him, and he could not open it. This made him very fearful; and while he considered what he should do, he saw a tall and angry-looking man approaching very swiftly down the passage. As he turned to face him, the other came straight to him, and asked him very sternly what he did there; to which Anthony replied that he had found the door open. To which the other replied that it was fast now, and that he must go forward.

He seized Anthony as he spoke by the arm, and urged him down the passage. Anthony would fain have resisted, but he felt like a child in the grip of a giant, and went forward in great terror and perplexity. Presently they came to a door in the side of the wall, and as they passed it, there stepped out an ugly shadowy thing, the nature of which he could not clearly discern, and marched softly behind them. Soon they came to a turn in the passage, and in a moment the way stopped on the brink of a dark well, that seemed to go down a long way into the earth, and out of which came a cold fetid air, with a hollow sound like a complaining voice. Anthony drew back as far as he could from the pit, and set his back to the wall, his companion letting go of him. But he could not go backward, for the thing behind him was in the passage, and barred the way, creeping slowly nearer. Then Anthony was in a great agony of mind, and waited for the end.

But while he waited, there came someone very softly down the passage and drew near; and the other, who had led him to the place, waited, as though ill-pleased to be interrupted; it was too murky for Anthony to see the new-comer, but he knew in some way that he was a friend. The stranger came up to them, and spoke in a low voice to the man who had drawn Anthony thither, as though pleading for something; and the man answered angrily, but yet with a certain dark respect, and seemed to argue that he was acting in his right, and might not be interfered with. Anthony could not hear what they said, they spoke so low, but he guessed the sense, and knew that it was himself of whom they discoursed, and listened with a fearful wonder to see which would prevail.

The end soon came, for the tall man, who had brought him there, broke out into a great storm of passion; and Anthony heard him say, "He hath yielded himself to his own will; and he is mine here; so, let us make an end." Then the stranger seemed to consider; and then with a quiet courage, and in a soft and silvery voice like that of a child, said, "I would that you would have yielded to my prayer; but as you will not, I have no choice." And he took his hand from under the cloak that wrapped him, and held something out; then there came a great roaring out of the pit, and a zigzag flame flickered in the dark.

Then in a moment the tall man and the shadow were gone; Anthony could not see whither they went, and he would have thanked the stranger; but the other put his finger to his lip as though to order silence, and pointed to the way he had come, saying, "Make haste and go back; for they will return anon with others; you know not how dear it hath cost me." Anthony could see the stranger's face in the gloom, and he was surprised to see it so youthful; but he saw also that

271

tears stood in the eyes of the stranger, and that something dark like blood trickled down his brow; yet he looked very lovingly at him.

So, Anthony made haste to go back, and found the door ajar; but as he reached it, he heard a horrible din behind him, of cries and screams; and it was with a sense of gratitude, that he could not put into words, but which filled all his heart, that he found himself back in the cloister again. And then the vision all fled away, and with a shock coming to himself, he found that he was lying in his own room; and then he knew that a battle had been fought out over his soul, and that the evil had not prevailed.

He was cold and aching in every limb; the room was silent and dark, with the heavy smell of the burnt drugs all about it. Anthony crept to the door, and opened it; locked it again, and made his way in the dark very feebly to his bed-chamber; he had just the strength to get into his bed, and then all his life seemed to ebb from him, and he lay, and thought that he was dying. Presently from without there came the crying of cocks, and a bell beat the hour of four; and after that, in his vigil of weakness, it was strange to see the light glimmer in the crevices, and to hear the awakening birds that in the garden bushes took up, one after another, their slender piping song, till all the choir cried together.

But Anthony felt a strange peace in his heart; and he had a sense, though he could not say why, that it was as once in his childhood, when he was ill, and his mother had sate softly by him while he slept

So, he waited, and in spite of his mortal weakness that was a blessed hour.

When his man came to rouse him in the morning, Anthony said that he believed that he was very ill, that he had had a fall, and that the old doctor must be fetched to him. The man looked so strangely upon him, that Anthony knew that he had some fear upon his mind. Presently the doctor was brought, and Anthony answered such questions as were put to him, in a faint voice, saying, "I was late at my work, and I slipped and fell." The doctor, who looked troubled, gave directions; and when he went away he heard his man behind the door asking the doctor about the strange storm in the night, that had seemed like an earthquake, or as if a thunderbolt had struck the house. But the doctor said very gruffly, "It is no time to talk thus, when your master is sick to death." But Anthony knew in himself that he would not die yet.

It was long ere he was restored to a measure of health; and indeed, he never rightly recovered the use of his limbs; the doctor held that he had suffered some stroke of palsy; at which Anthony smiled a little, and made no answer.

When he was well enough to creep to and fro, he went sadly to the dark room, and with much pain and weakness carried the furniture out of it. The picture he cut in pieces and burnt; and the candles and dishes, with the book, he cast into a deep pool in the stream; the bones he buried in the earth; the hangings he stored away for his own funeral.

Anthony never entered his workroom again; but day after day he sate in his chair, and read a little, but mostly in the Bible; he made a friend of a very wise old priest, to whom he opened all his heart, and to whom he conveyed much money to be bestowed on the poor; there was a great calm in his spirit, which was soon written in his face, in spite of his pain, for he often suffered sorely; but he told the priest that something, he knew not certainly what, seemed to dwell by him, waiting patiently for his coming; and so Anthony awaited his end.

Out of the Sea

It was about ten of the clock on a November morning in the little village of Blea-on-the-Sands. The hamlet was made up of some thirty houses, which clustered together on a low rising ground. The place was very poor, but some old merchant of bygone days had built in a pious mood a large church, which was now too great for the needs of the place; the nave had been unroofed in a heavy gale, and there was no money to repair it, so that it had fallen to decay, and the tower was joined to the choir by roofless walls. This was a sore trial to the old priest, Father Thomas, who had grown grey there; but he had no art in gathering money, which he asked for in a shamefaced way; and the vicarage was a poor one, hardly enough for the old man's needs. So, the church lay desolate.

The village stood on what must once have been an island; the little River Reddy, which runs down to the sea, there forking into two channels on the landward side; towards the sea the ground was bare, full of sand-hills covered with a short grass. Towards the land was a small wood of gnarled trees, the boughs of which were all brushed smooth by the gales; looking landward there was the green flat, in which the river ran, rising into low hills; hardly a house was visible save one or two lonely farms; two or three church towers rose above the hills at a long distance away.

Indeed, Blea was much cut off from the world; there was a bridge over the stream on the west side, but over the other channel was no bridge, so that to fare eastward it was requisite to go in a boat. To seaward there were wide sands, when the tide was out; when it was in, it came up nearly to the end of the village street. The people were mostly fishermen, but there were a few farmers and labourers; the boats of the fishermen lay to the east side of the village, near the river channel which gave some draught of water; and the channel was marked out by big black stakes and posts that straggled out over the sands, like awkward leaning figures, to the sea's brim.

Father Thomas lived in a small and ancient brick house near the church, with a little garden of herbs attached. He was a kindly man, much worn by age and weather, with a wise heart, and he loved the quiet life with his small flock. This morning he had come out of his house to look abroad, before he settled down to the making of his sermon. He looked out to sea, and saw with a shadow of sadness the black outline of a wreck that had come ashore a week before, and over which the white waves were now breaking. The wind blew steadily from the north-east, and had a bitter poisonous chill in it, which it doubtless drew from the fields of the upper ice.

The day was dark and overhung, not with cloud, but with a kind of dreary vapour that shut out the sun. Father Thomas shuddered at the wind, and drew his patched cloak round him. As he did so, he saw three figures come up to the vicarage gate. It was not a common thing for him to have visitors in the morning, and he saw with surprise that they were old Master John Grimston, the richest man in the place, half farmer and half fisherman, a dark surly old man; his wife, Bridget, a timid and frightened woman, who found life with her harsh husband a difficult business, in spite of their wealth, which, for a place like Blea, was great; and their son Henry, a silly shambling man of forty, who was his father's butt. The three walked silently and heavily, as though they came on a sad errand.

Father Thomas went briskly down to meet them, and greeted them with his accustomed cheerfulness. "And what may I do for you?" he said.

Old Master Grimston made a sort of gesture with his head as though his wife should speak; and she said in a low and somewhat husky voice, with a rapid utterance, "We have a matter, Father, we would ask you about—are you at leisure?"

Father Thomas said, "Ay, I am ashamed to be not more busy! Let us go within the house."

They did so; and even in the little distance to the door, the Father thought that his visitors behaved themselves very strangely. They peered round from left to right, and once or twice Master Grimston looked sharply behind them, as though they were followed. They said nothing but "Ay" and "No" to the Father's talk, and bore themselves like people with a sore fear on their backs. Father Thomas made up his mind that it was some question of money, for nothing else was wont to move Master Grimston's mind. So, he had them into his parlour and gave them seats, and then there was a silence, while the two men continued to look furtively about them, and the goodwife sate with her eyes upon the priest's face. Father Thomas knew not what to make of this, till Master Grimston said harshly, "Come, wife, tell the tale and make an end; we must not take up the Father's time."

"I hardly know how to say it. Father," said Bridget, "but a strange and evil thing has befallen us; there is something come to our house, and we know not what it is—but it brings a fear with it." A sudden paleness came over her face, and she stopped, and the three exchanged a glance in which terror was visibly written.

Master Grimston looked over his shoulder swiftly, and made as though to speak, yet only swallowed in his throat; but Henry said suddenly, in a loud and woeful voice: "It is an evil beast out of the sea."

And then there followed a dreadful silence, while Father Thomas felt a sudden fear leap up in his heart, at the contagion of the fear that he saw written on the faces round him. But he said with all the cheerfulness he could muster, "Come, friends, let us not begin to talk of sea-beasts; we must have the whole tale. Mistress Grimston, I must hear the story—be content—nothing can touch us here." The three seemed to draw a faint content from his words, and Bridget began:—

"It was the day of the wreck. Father. John was up betimes, before the dawn; he walked out early to the sands, and Henry with him—and they were the first to see the wreck—was not that it?"

At these words the father and son seemed to exchange a very swift and secret look, and both grew pale. "John told me there was a wreck ashore, and they went presently and roused the rest of the village; and all that day they were out, saving what could be saved. Two sailors were found, both dead and pitifully battered by the sea, and they were buried, as you know, Father, in the churchyard next day; John came back about dusk and Henry with him, and we sate down to our supper. John was telling me about the wreck, as we sate beside the fire, when Henry, who was sitting apart, rose up and cried out suddenly, 'What is that?'"

She paused for a moment, and Henry, who sate with face blanched, staring at his mother, said, "Ay, did I—it ran past me suddenly."

"Yes, but what was it?" said Father Thomas trying to smile; "a dog or cat, methinks."

"It was a beast," said Henry slowly, in a trembling voice—"a beast about the bigness of a goat. I never saw the like—yet I did not see it clear; I but felt the air blow, and caught a whiff of it—it was salt like the sea, but with a kind of dead smell behind."

"Was that all you saw?" said Father Thomas; "belike you were tired and faint, and the air swam round you suddenly—I have known the like myself when weary."

"Nay, nay," said Henry, "this was not like that—it was a beast, sure enough."

"Ay, and we have seen it since," said Bridget. "At least I have not seen it clearly yet, but I have smelt its odour, and it turns me sick—but John and Henry have seen it often—sometimes it lies and seems to sleep, but it watches us; and again it is merry, and will leap in a corner—and John saw it skip upon the sands near the wreck—did you not, John?"

At these words the two men again exchanged a glance, and then old Master Grimston, with a dreadful look in his face, in which great anger seemed to strive with fear, said, "Nay, silly woman, it was not near the wreck, it was out to the east."

"It matters little," said Father Thomas, who saw well enough this was no light matter. "I never heard the like of it. I will myself come down to your house with a holy book, and see if the thing will meet me. I know not what this is," he went on, "whether it is a vain terror that hath hold of you; but there be spirits of evil in the world, though much fettered by Christ and His Saints—we read of such in Holy Writ—and the sea, too, doubtless hath its monsters; and it may be that one hath wandered out of the waves, like a dog that hath strayed from his home. I dare not say, till I have met it face to face. But God gives no power to such things to hurt those who have a fair conscience."

And here he made a stop, and looked at the three; Bridget sate regarding him with a hope in her face; but the other two sate peering upon the ground; and the priest divined in some secret way that all was not well with them. "But I will come at once," he said, rising, "and I will see if I can cast out or bind the thing, whatever it be—for I am in this place as a soldier of the Lord, to fight with works of darkness." He took a clasped book from a table, and lifted up his hat, saying, "Let us set forth." Then he said as they left the room, "Hath it appeared today?"

"Yes, indeed," said Henry, "and it was ill content. It followed us as though it were angered."

"Come," said Father Thomas, turning upon him, "you speak thus of a thing, as you might speak of a dog—what is it like?"

278

"Nay," said Henry, "I know not; I can never see it clearly; it is like a speck in the eye—it is never there when you look upon it—it glides away very secretly; it is most like a goat, I think. It seems to be horned, and hairy; but I have seen its eyes, and they were yellow, like a flame."

As he said these words Master Grimston went in haste to the door, and pulled it open as though to breathe the air. The others followed him and went out; but Master Grimston drew the priest aside, and said like a man in a mortal fear, "Look you, Father, all this is true—the thing is a devil—and why it abides with us I know not; but I cannot live so; and unless it be cast out it will slay me—but if money be of avail, I have it in abundance."

"Nay," said Father Thomas, "let there be no talk of money—perchance if I can aid you, you may give of your gratitude to God."

"Ay, ay," said the old man hurriedly, "that was what I meant—there is money in abundance for God, if He will but set me free."

So, they walked very sadly together through the street. There were few folk about; the men and the children were all abroad—a woman or two came to the house doors, and wondered a little to see them pass so solemnly, as though they followed a body to the grave.

Master Grimston's house was the largest in the place. It had a walled garden before it, with a strong door set in the wall. The house stood back from the road, a dark front of brick with gables; behind it the garden sloped nearly to the sands, with wooden barns and warehouses. Master Grimston unlocked the door, and then it seemed that his terrors came over him, for he would have the priest enter first. Father Thomas, with a certain apprehension of which he was ashamed, walked quickly in, and looked about him. The herbage of the garden had mostly died down in the winter, and a tangle of sodden stalks lay over the beds.

A flagged path edged with box led up to the house, which seemed to stare at them out of its dark windows with a sort of steady gaze. Master Grimston fastened the door behind them, and they went all together, keeping close one to another, up to the house, the door of which opened upon a big parlour or kitchen, sparely furnished, but very clean and comfortable. Some vessels of metal glittered on a rack. There were chairs, ranged round the open fireplace. There was no sound except that the wind buffeted in the chimney. It looked a quiet and homely place, and Father Thomas grew ashamed of his fears.

"Now," said he in his firm voice, "though I am your guest here, I will appoint what shall be done. We will sit here together, and talk as cheerfully as we may, till we have dined. Then, if nothing appears to us,"—and he crossed himself—"I will go round the house, into every room, and see if we can track the thing to its lair: then I will abide with you till evensong; and then I will soon return, and lie here to-night. Even if the thing be wary, and dares not to meet the power of the Church in the daytime, perhaps it will venture out at night; and I will even try a fall with it. So, come, good people, and be comforted."

So, they sate together; and Father Thomas talked of many things, and told some old legends of saints; and they dined, though without much cheer; and still nothing appeared. Then, after dinner. Father Thomas would view the house. So, he took his book up, and they went from room to room. On the ground floor there were several chambers not used, which they entered in turn, but saw nothing; on the upper floor was a large room where Master Grimston and his wife slept; and a further room for Henry, and a guest-chamber in which the priest was to sleep if need was; and a room where a servant-maid slept. And now the day began to darken and to turn to evening, and Father Thomas felt a shadow grow in his mind. There came into his head a verse of Scripture about a spirit which found a house "empty, swept and garnished," and called his fellows to enter in.

At the end of the passage was a locked door; and Father Thomas said: "This is the last room—let us enter."

"Nay, there is no need to do that," said Master Grimston in a kind of haste; "it leads nowhither—it is but a room of stores."

"It were a pity to leave it unvisited," said the Father—and as he said the word, there came a kind of stirring from within. "A rat, doubtless," said the Father, striving with a sudden sense of fear; but the pale faces round him told another tale.

"Come, Master Grimston, let us be done with this," said Father Thomas decisively; "the hour of vespers draws nigh."

So Master Grimston slowly drew out a key and unlocked the door, and Father Thomas marched in. It was a simple place enough. There were shelves on which various household matters lay, boxes and jars, with twine and cordage. On the ground stood chests. There were some clothes hanging on pegs, and in a corner was a heap of garments, piled up. On one of the chests stood a box of rough deal, and from the corner of it dripped water, which lay in a little pool on the floor. Master Grimston went hurriedly to the box and pushed it further to the wall. As he did so, a kind of sound came from Henry's lips. Father Thomas turned and looked at him; he stood pale and strengthless, his eyes fixed on the comer—at the same moment something dark and shapeless seemed to slip past the group, and there came to the nostrils of Father Thomas a strange sharp smell, as of the sea, only that there was a taint within it, like the smell of corruption.

They all turned and looked at Father Thomas together, as though seeking a comfort from his presence. He, hardly knowing what he did, and in the grasp of a terrible fear, fumbled with his book; and opening it, read the first words that his eye fell upon, which was the place where the Blessed Lord, beset with enemies, said that if He did but pray to His Father, He should send Him forthwith legions of angels to encompass Him. And the verse seemed to the priest so like a message sent instantly from heaven that he was not a little comforted.

But the thing, whatever the reason was, appeared to them no more at that time. Yet the thought of it lay very heavy on Father Thomas's heart. In truth he had not in the bottom of his mind believed that he would see it, but had trusted in his honest life and his sacred calling to protect him. He could hardly speak for some minutes—moreover the horror of the thing was very great—and seeing him so grave, their terrors were increased, though there was a kind of miserable joy in their minds that someone, and he a man of high repute, should suffer with them.

Then Father Thomas, after a pause—they were now in the parlour—said, speaking very slowly, that they were in a sore affliction of Satan, and that they must withstand him with a good courage—"and look you," he added, turning with a great sternness to the three, "if there be any mortal sin upon your hearts, see that you confess it and be shriven speedily—for while such a thing lies upon the heart, so long hath Satan power to hurt—otherwise have no fear at all."

Then Father Thomas slipped out to the garden, and hearing the bell pulled for vespers, he went to the church, and the three would go with him, because they would not be left alone. So, they went together; by this time the street was fuller, and the servant-maid had told tales, so that there was much talk in the place about what was going forward. None spoke with them as they went, but at every comer you might see one check another in talk, and a silence fall upon a group, so that they knew that their terrors were on every tongue. There was but a handful of worshippers in the church, which was dark, save for the light on Father Thomas' book. He read the holy service swiftly and courageously, but his face was very pale and grave in the light of the candle.

When the vespers were over, and he had put off his robe, he said that he would go back to his house, and gather what he needed for the night, and that they should wait for him at the churchyard gate. So, he strode off to his vicarage. But as he shut to the door, he saw a dark figure come running up the garden; he waited with a fear in his mind, but in a moment, he saw that it was Henry, who came up breathless, and said that he must speak with the Father alone. Father Thomas knew that somewhat dark was to be told him. So, he led Henry into the parlour and seated himself, and said, "Now, my son, speak boldly." So, there was an instant's silence, and Henry slipped on to his knees.

Then in a moment Henry with a sob began to tell his tale. He said that on the day of the wreck his father had roused him very early in the dawn, and had told him to put on his clothes and come silently, for he thought there was a wreck ashore. His father carried a spade in his hand, he knew not then why. They went down to the tide, which was moving out very fast, and left but an inch or two of water on the sands. There was but a little light, but, when they had walked a little, they saw the black hull of a ship before them, on the edge of the deeper water, the waves driving over it; and then all at once they came upon the body of a man lying on his face on the sand.

There was no sign of life in him, but he clasped a bag in his hand that was heavy, and the pocket of his coat was full to bulging; and there lay, moreover, some glittering things about him that seemed to be coins. They lifted the body up, and his father stripped the coat off from the man, and then bade Henry dig a hole in the sand, which he presently did, though the sand and water oozed fast into it. Then his father, who had been stooping down, gathering somewhat up from the sand, raised the body up, and laid it in the hole, and bade Henry cover it with the sand. And so, he did till it was nearly hidden.

Then came a horrible thing; the sand in the hole began to move and stir, and presently a hand was put out with clutching fingers; and Henry had dropped the spade, and said, "There is life in him," but his father seized the spade, and shovelled the sand into the hole with a kind of silent fury, and trampled it over and smoothed it down—and then he gathered up the coat and the bag, and handed Henry the spade. By this time the town was astir, and they saw, very faintly, a man run along the shore eastward; so, making a long circuit to the west, they returned; his father had put the spade away and taken the coat upstairs; and then he went out with Henry, and told all he could find that there was a wreck ashore.

The priest heard the story with a fierce shame and anger, and turning to Henry he said, "But why did you not resist your father, and save the poor sailor?"

"I dared not," said Henry shuddering, "though I would have done so if I could; but my father has a power over me, and I am used to obey him."

Then said the priest, "This is a dark matter. But you have told the story bravely, and now will I shrive you, my son." So, he gave him shrift. Then he said to Henry, "And have you seen aught that would connect the beast that visits you with this thing?"

"Ay, that I have," said Henry, "for I watched it with my father skip and leap in the water over the place where the man lies buried."

Then the priest said, "Your father must tell me the tale too, and he must make submission to the law."

"He will not," said Henry.

"Then will I compel him," said the priest.

"Not out of my mouth," said Henry, "or he will slay me too."

And then the priest said that he was in a strait place, for he could not use the words of confession of one man to convict another of his sin. So, he gathered his things in haste, and walked back to the church; but Henry went another way, saying "I made excuse to come away, and said I went elsewhere; but I fear my father much—he sees very deep; and I would not have him suspect me of having made confession."

Then the Father met the other two at the church gate; and they went down to the house in silence, the Father pondering heavily; and at the door Henry joined them, and it seemed to the Father that old Master Grimston regarded him not. So, they entered the house in silence, and ate in silence, listening earnestly for any sound. And the Father looked oft on Master Grimston, who ate and drank and said nothing, never raising his eyes. But once the Father saw him laugh secretly to himself, so that the blood came cold in the Father's veins, and he could hardly contain himself from accusing him. Then the Father had them to prayers, and prayed earnestly against the evil, and that they should open their hearts to God, if He would show them why this misery came upon them.

Then they went to bed; and Henry asked that he might be in the priest's room, which he willingly granted. And so, the house was dark, and they made as though they would sleep; but the Father could not sleep, and he heard Henry weeping silently to himself like a little child.

But at last the Father slept—how long he knew not—and suddenly brake out of his sleep with a horror of darkness all about him, and knew that there was some evil thing abroad. So, he looked upon the room. He heard Henry mutter heavily in his sleep as though there was a dark terror upon him; and then, in the light of the dying embers, the Father saw a thing rise upon the hearth, as though it had slept there, and woke to stretch itself. And then in the half-light it seemed softly to gambol and play; but whereas when an innocent beast does this in the simple joy of its heart, and seems a fond and pretty sight, the Father thought he had never seen so ugly a sight as the beast gambolling all by itself, as if it could not contain its own dreadful joy; it looked viler and more wicked every moment; then, too, there spread in the room the sharp scent of the sea, with the foul smell underneath it, that gave the Father a deadly sickness; he tried to pray, but no words would come, and he felt indeed that the evil was too strong for him.

Presently the beast desisted from its play, and looking wickedly about it, came near to the Father's bed, and seemed to put up its hairy forelegs upon it; he could see its narrow and obscene eyes, which burned with a dull yellow light, and were fixed upon him. And now the Father thought that his end was near, for he could stir neither hand nor foot, and the sweat rained down his brow; but he made a mighty effort, and in a voice, which shocked himself, so dry and husky and withal of so loud and screaming a tone it was, he said three holy words. The beast gave a great quiver of rage, but it dropped down on the floor, and in a moment was gone. Then Henry woke, and raising himself on his arm, said somewhat; but there broke out in the house a great outcry and the stamping of feet, which seemed very fearful in the silence of the night.

The priest leapt out of his bed all dizzy, and made a light, and ran to the door, and went out, crying whatever words came to his head. The door of Master Grimston's room was open, and a strange and strangling sound came forth; the Father made his way in, and found Master Grimston lying upon the floor, his wife bending over him; he lay still, breathing pitifully, and every now and then a shudder ran through him. In the room there seemed a strange and shadowy tumult going forward; but the Father saw that no time could be lost, and kneeling down beside Master Grimston, he prayed with all his might.

Presently Master Grimston ceased to struggle and lay still, like a man who had come out of a sore conflict. Then he opened his eyes, and the Father stopped his prayers, and looking very hard at him he said, "My son, the time is very short—give God the glory."

Then Master Grimston, rolling his haggard eyes upon the group, twice strove to speak and could not; but the third time the Father, bending down his head, heard him say in a thin voice, that seemed to float from a long way off, "I slew him . . . my sin." Then the Father swiftly gave him shrift, and as he said the last word, Master Grimston's head fell over on the side, and the Father said, "He is gone." And Bridget broke out into a terrible cry, and fell upon Henry's neck, who had entered unseen.

Then the Father bade him lead her away, and put the poor body on the bed; as he did so he noticed that the face of the dead man was strangely bruised and battered, as though it had been stamped upon by the hoofs of some beast. Then Father Thomas knelt, and prayed until the light came filtering in through the shutters; and the cocks crowed in the village, and presently it was day. But that night the Father learnt strange secrets, and something of the dark purposes of God was revealed to him.

In the morning there came one to find the priest, and told him that another body had been thrown up on the shore, which was strangely smeared with sand, as though it had been rolled over and over in it; and the Father took order for its burial.

Then the priest had long talk with Bridget and Henry. He found them sitting together, and she held her son's hand and smoothed his hair, as though he had been a little child; and Henry sobbed and wept, but Bridget was very calm. "He hath told me all," she said, "and we have decided that he shall do whatever you bid him; must he be given to justice?" and she looked at the priest very pitifully.

"Nay, nay," said the priest. "I hold not Henry to account for the death of the man; it was his father's sin, who hath made heavy atonement—the secret shall be buried in our hearts."

Then Bridget told him how she had waked suddenly out of her sleep, and heard her husband cry out; and that then followed a dreadful kind of struggling, with the scent of the sea over all; and then he had all at once fallen to the ground and she had gone to him—and that then the priest had come.

Then Father Thomas said with tears that God had shown them deep things and visited them very strangely; and they would henceforth live humbly in His sight, showing mercy.

Then lastly, he went with Henry to the storeroom; and there, in the box that had dripped with water, lay the coat of the dead man, full of money, and the bag of money too; and Henry would have cast it back into the sea, but the priest said that this might not be, but that it should be bestowed plentifully upon shipwrecked mariners unless the heirs should be found. But the ship appeared to be a foreign ship, and no search ever revealed whence the money had come, save that it seemed to have been violently come by.

Master Grimston was found to have left much wealth. But Bridget would sell the house and the land, and it mostly went to rebuild the church to God's glory. Then Bridget and Henry removed to the vicarage and served Father Thomas faithfully, and they guarded their secret. And beside the nave is a little high turret built, where burns a lamp in a lantern at the top, to give light to those at sea.

Now the beast troubled those of whom I write no more; but it is easier to raise up evil than to lay it; and there are those that say that to this day a man or a woman with an evil thought in their hearts may see on a certain evening in November, at the ebb of the tide, a goatlike thing wade in the water, snuffing at the sand, as though it sought but found not. But of this I know nothing.

Basil Netherby

It was five o'clock in the afternoon of an October day that Basil Netherby's letter arrived. I remember that my little clock had just given its warning click, when the footsteps came to my door; and just as the clock began to strike, came a hesitating knock. I called out, "Come in," and after some fumbling with the handle there stepped into the room I think the shyest clergyman I have ever seen. He shook hands like an automaton, looking over his left shoulder; he would not sit down, and yet he looked about the room, as he stood, as if wondering why the ordinary civility of a chair was not offered him; he spoke in a husky voice, out of which he endeavoured at intervals to cast some viscous obstruction by loud hawkings; and when, after one of these interludes, he caught my eye, he went a sudden pink in the face.

However, the letter got handed to me; and I gradually learnt from my visitor's incoherent talk that it was from my friend Basil Netherby; and that he was well, remarkably well, quite a different man from what he had been when he came to Treheale; that he himself (Vyvyan was his name) was curate of St. Sibby. Treheale was the name of the house where Mr. Netherby lived. The letter had been most important, he thought, for Mr. Netherby had asked him as he was going up to town to convey the letter himself and to deliver it without fail into Mr. Ward's own hands. He could not, however, account (here he turned away from me, and hummed, and beat his fingers on the table) for the extraordinary condition in which he was compelled to hand it me, as it had never, so far as he knew, left his own pocket; and presently with a gasp Mr. Vyvyan was gone, refusing all proffers of entertainment, and falling briskly down—to judge from the sounds which came to me—outside my door.

I, Leonard Ward, was then living in rooms in a little street out of Holborn—a poor place enough. I was organist of St. Bartholomew's,

Holborn; and I was trying to do what is described as getting up a connection in the teaching line. But it was slow work, and I must confess that my prospects did not appear to me very cheerful. However, I taught one of the vicar's little daughters, and a whole family, the children of a rich tradesman in a neighbouring street, the piano and singing, so that I contrived to struggle on.

Basil Netherby had been with me at the College of Music. His line was composing. He was a pleasant, retiring fellow, voluble enough and even rhetorical in *tête-à-tête* talk with an intimate; but dumb in company, with an odd streak of something—genius or eccentricity— about him which made him different from other men. We had drifted into an intimacy, and had indeed lodged together for some months. Netherby used to show me his works—mostly short studies—and though I used to think that they always rather oddly broke down in unexpected places, and though he was inaccurate in technique, yet there was always an air of aiming high about them, an attempt to realise the ideal.

He left the college before I did, saying that he had learnt all he could learn and that now he must go quietly into the country some- where and work all alone—he should do no good otherwise. I heard from him fitfully. He was in Wales, in Devonshire, in Cornwall; and then some three months before the day on which I got the letter, the correspondence had ceased altogether; I did not know his address, and was always expecting to hear from him.

I took up the letter from the place where Mr. Vyvyan had laid it down; it was a bulky envelope; and it was certainly true that, as Mr. Vyvyan had said, the packet was in an extraordinary condition. One of the corners was torn off, with a ragged edge that looked like the nibbling of mice, and there were disagreeable stains both on the front and the back, so that I should have inferred that Mr. Vyvyan's pocket had been filled with raspberries—the theory, though improbable, did not appear impossible. But what surprised me most was that near each of the corners in front a rough cross of ink was drawn, and one at the back of the flap.

I had little doubt, however, that Mr. Vyvyan had, in a nervous and absent mood, harried the poor letter into the condition in which I saw it, and that he had been unable to bring himself to confess to the maltreatment.

I tore the letter open—there fell out several pages of MS. music, and a letter in which Basil, dating from "Treheale," and writing in a bold firm hand—bolder and firmer, I thought, than of old—said that he had been making a good deal of progress and working very hard (which must account for his silence), and he ventured to enclose some of his last work which he *hoped* I would like, but he wanted a candid opinion. He added that he had got quarters at a delightful farmhouse, not far from Grampound. That was all.

Stay! That was not all. The letter finished on the third side; but, as I closed it, I saw written on the fourth page, very small, in a weak loose hand, and as if scribbled in a ferocious haste, as a man might write (so it came oddly into my head) who was escaped for a moment from the vigilance of a careful gaoler, a single sentence.

> Vyvyan will take this; and for God's sake, dear Leonard, if you would help a friend who is on the edge (I dare not say of what), come to me tomorrow, *uninvited.* You will think this very strange, but do not mind that—only *come—unannounced,* do you see. . . .

The line broke off in an unintelligible flourish. Then on each corner of the last page had been scrawled a cross, with the same ugly and slovenly haste as the crosses on the envelope.

My first thought was that Basil was mad; my next thought that he had drifted into some awkward situation, fallen under some unfortunate influence—was perhaps being blackmailed—and I knew his sensitive character well enough to feel sure that whatever the trouble was it would be exaggerated ten times over by his lively and apprehensive mind. Slowly a situation shaped itself. Basil was a man, as I knew, of an extraordinary austere standard of morals, singularly guileless, and innocent of worldly matters.

Someone, I augured, some unscrupulous woman, had, in the remote spot where he was living, taken a guileful fancy to my poor friend, and had doubtless, after veiled overtures, resolved on a bolder policy and was playing on his sensitive and timid nature by some threat of nameless disclosures, some vile and harrowing innuendo.

I read the letter again—and still more clear did it seem to me that he was in some strange durance, and suffering under abominable fears. I rose from my chair and went to find a time-table, that I might see when I could get to Grampound, when again a shuffling footstep drew to my door, an uncertain hand knocked at the panel, and Mr. Vyvyan again entered the room. This time his confusion was even greater, if that were possible, than it had previously been. He had forgotten to give me a further message; and he thereupon gave me a filthy scrap of paper, nibbled and stained like the envelope, apologised with unnecessary vehemence, uttered a strangled cough and stumbled from the room. It was difficult enough to decipher the paper, but I saw that. a musical phrase had been written on it; and then in a moment I saw that it was a phrase from an old, extravagant work of Basil's own, a *Credo* which we had often discussed together, the grim and fantastic accompaniment of the sentence "He descended into hell."

This came to me as a message of even greater urgency, and I hesitated no longer. I sat down to write a note to the father of my family of pupils, in which I said that important business called me away for two or three days. I looked out a train, and found that by catching the 10 o'clock limited mail I could be at Grampound by 6 in the morning. I ordered a hasty dinner and I packed a few things into a bag, with an oppressive sense of haste. But, as generally happens on such occasions, I found that I had still two or three hours in hand; so, I took up Netherby's music and read it through carefully.

Certainly, he had improved wonderfully in handling; but what music it was! It was like nothing of which I had ever even dreamed. There was a wild, intemperate voluptuousness about it, a kind of evil relish of beauty which gave me a painful thrill. To make sure that I was not mistaken, owing to the nervous tension which the strange event had produced in *me,* I put the things in my pocket and went out to the house of a friend, Dr. Grierson, an accomplished and critical musician who lived not far away.

I found the great man at home smoking leisurely. He had a bird-like demeanour, like an ancient stork, as he sat blinking through spectacles astride of a long pointed nose. He had a slight acquaintance with Netherby, and when I mentioned that I had received some new music from him, which I wished to submit to him, he showed obvious interest. "A promising fellow," he said, "only of course too transcendental." He took the music in his hand; he settled his spectacles and read. Presently he looked up; and I saw in the kind of shamefaced glance with which he regarded me that he had found something of the same incomprehensible sensuality which had so oddly affected myself in the music. "Come, come," he said rather severely, "this is very strange stuff—this won't do at all, you know. We must just hear this!" He rose and went to his piano; and peering into the music, he played the pieces deliberately and critically.

Heard upon. the piano, the accent of subtle evil that ran through the music became even more obvious. I seemed to struggle between two feelings—an overpowering admiration, and a sense of shame at my own capacity for admiring it. But the great man was still more moved. He broke off in the middle of a bar and tossed the music to me.

"This is filthy stuff," he said. "I should say to you—burn it. It is clever, of course—hideously, devilishly clever. Look at the interlacing of those parts there—look at that progression—F sharp against F natural, you observe" (and he added some technical details with which I need not trouble my readers).

He went on: "But the man has no business to think of such things. I don't like it. Tell him from me that it won't do. There must be some reticence in art, you know—and there is none here. Tell Netherby that he is on the wrong tack altogether. Good heavens," he added, "how could the man write it? He used to be a decent sort of fellow."

It may seem extravagant to write thus of music, but I can only say that it affected me as nothing I had ever heard before. I put it away and we tried to talk of other things; but we could not get the stuff out of our heads. Presently I rose to go, and the doctor reiterated his warnings still more emphatically. "The man is a criminal in art," he said, "and there must be an end once and for all of this: tell him it's abominable!"

I went back; caught my train; and was whirled sleepless and excited to the West. Towards morning I fell into a troubled sleep, in which I saw in tangled dreams the figure of a man running restlessly among stony hills. Over and over again the dream came to me; and it was with a grateful heart, though very weary, that I saw a pale light of dawn in the east, and the dark trees and copses along the line becoming more and more defined, by swift gradations, in the chilly autumn air.

It was very still and peaceful when we drew up at Grampound station. I enquired my way to Treheale; and I was told it was three or four miles away. The porter looked rather enquiringly at me; there was no chance of obtaining a vehicle, so I resolved to walk, hoping that I should be freshened by the morning air.

Presently a lane struck off from the main road, which led up a wooded valley, with a swift stream rushing along; in one or two places the chimney of a deserted mine with desolate rubbish—heaps stood beside the road. At one place a square church-tower, with pinnacles, looked solemnly over the wood. The road rose gradually. At last I came to a little hamlet, perched high up on the side of the valley. The scene was incomparably beautiful; the leaves were yellowing fast, and I could see a succession of wooded ridges, with a long line of moorland closing the view.

The little place was just waking into quiet activity. I found a bustling man taking down shutters from a general shop which was also the post-office, and enquired where Mr. Netherby lived. The man told me that he was in lodgings at Treheale—"the big house itself, where Farmer Hall lives now; if you go straight along the road," he added, "you will pass the lodge, and Treheale lies up in the wood."

I was by this time very tired—it was now nearly seven—but I took up my bag again and walked along a road passing between high hedges. Presently the wood closed in again, and I saw a small plastered lodge with a thatched roof standing on the left among some firs. The gate stood wide open, and the road which led into the wood was grass grown, though with deep ruts, along which heavy laden carts seemed to have passed recently.

The lodge seemed deserted, and I accordingly struck off into the wood. Presently the undergrowth grew thicker, and huge sprawling laurels rose in all directions. Then the track took a sudden turn; and I saw straight in front of me the front of a large Georgian house of brown stone, with a gravel sweep up to the door, but all overgrown with grass.

I confess that the house displeased me strangely. It was substantial, homely, and large; but the wood came up close to it on all sides, and it seemed to stare at me with its shuttered windows with a look of dumb resentment, like a great creature at bay.

I walked on, and saw that the smoke went up from a chimney to the left. The house, as I came closer, presented a front with a stone portico, crowned with a pediment. To left and right were two wings which were built out in advance from the main part of the house, throwing the door back into the shadow.

I pulled a large handle which hung beside the door, and a dismal bell rang somewhere in the house—rang on and on as if unable to cease; then footsteps came along the floor within, and the door was slowly and reluctantly unbarred.

There stood before me a little pale woman with a timid, downcast air. "Does Mr. Netherby live here?" I said.

"Yes; he lodges here, sir."

"Can I see him?" I said.

"Well, sir, he is not up yet. Does he expect you?"

"Well, not exactly," I said, faltering; "but he will know my name—and I have come a long way to see him."

The woman raised her eyes and looked at me, and I was aware, by some swift intuition, that I was in the presence of a distressed spirit, labouring under some melancholy prepossession. "Will you be here long?" she asked suddenly.

"No," I said; "but I shall have to stay the night, I think. I travelled all last night, and I am very tired; in fact, I shall ask to sit down and wait till I can see Mr. Netherby."

She seemed to consider a moment, and then led me into the house. We entered a fine hall, with stone flags and pillars on each side. There hung, so far as I could see in the half light, grim and faded portraits on the walls, and there were some indistinct pieces of furniture, like couched beasts, in the corners. We went through a door and down a passage and turned into a large rather bare room, which showed, however, some signs of human habitation. There was a table laid for a meal.

An old piano stood in a corner, and there were a few books lying about; on the walls hung large pictures in tarnished frames. I put down my bag, and sat down by the fire in an old armchair, and almost instantly fell into a drowse. I have an indistinct idea of the woman returning to ask if I would like some breakfast, or wait for Mr. Netherby. I said hastily that I would wait, being in the oppressed condition of drowsiness when one's only idea is to get a respite from the presence of any person, and fell again into a heavy sleep.

I woke suddenly with a start, conscious of a movement in the room. Basil Netherby was standing close beside me, with his back to the fire, looking down at me with a look which I can only say seemed to me to betoken a deep annoyance of spirit. But seeing me awake, there came on to his face a smile of a reluctant and diplomatic kind. I started to my feet, giddy and bewildered, and shook hands.

"My word," he said, "you sleep sound, Ward. So, you've found me out? Well, I'm very glad to see you; but what made you think of coming? and why didn't you let me know? I would have sent something to meet you."

I was a good deal nettled at this ungenial address, after the trouble to which I had put myself. I said, "Well, really, Basil, I think that is rather strong. Mr. Vyvyan called on me yesterday with a letter from you, and some music; and of course, I came away at once."

"Of course," he said, looking on the ground—and then added

rather hastily, "Now, how did the stuff strike you? I have improved, I think. And it is really very good of you to come off at once to criticise the *music*—*very* good of you," he said with some emphasis; "and, man, you look wretchedly tired—let us have breakfast."

I was just about to remonstrate, and to speak about the postscript, when he looked at me suddenly with so peculiar and disagreeable a glance that the words literally stuck in my throat. I thought to myself that perhaps the subject was too painful to enter upon at once, and that he probably wished to tell me at his own time what was in the background.

We breakfasted; and now that I had leisure to look at Basil, I was surprised beyond measure at the change in him. I had seen him last a pale, rather haggard youth, looselimbed and untidy. I saw before me a strongly-built and firmly-knit man, with a ruddy colour and bronzed cheek. He looked the embodiment of health and well-being. His talk, too, after the first impression of surprise wore off, was extraordinarily cheerful and amusing. Again, and again he broke out into loud laughter—not the laughter of an excited or hectic person, but the firm, brisk laugh of a man full to the brim of good spirits and health.

He talked of his work, of the country people that surrounded him, whose peculiarities he seemed to have observed with much relish; he asked me, but without any appearance of interest, what I thought about his work. I tried to tell him what Dr. Grierson had said and what I had felt; but I was conscious of being at a strange disadvantage before this genial personality. He laughed loudly at our criticisms.

"Old Grierson," he said, "why, he is no better than a clergyman's widow; he would stop his ears if you read Shakespeare to him. My dear man, I have travelled a long way since I saw you last; I have found my tongue—and what is more, I can say what I mean, and as I mean it. Grierson indeed! I can see him looking shocked, like a pelican with a stomach-ache."

This was a felicitous though not a courteous description of our friend, but I could find no words to combat it; indeed, Basil's talk and whole bearing seemed to carry me away like a swift stream; and in my wearied condition I found that I could not stand up to
this radiant personality.

After breakfast he advised me to have a good sleep; and he took me, with some show of solicitude, to a little bedroom which had been got ready for me. He unpacked my things and told me to undress and go to bed, that he had some work to do that he was anxious to finish, and that after luncheon we would have a stroll together.

I was too tired to resist, and fell at once into a deep sleep. I rose a new man; and finding no one in Basil's room, I strolled out for a moment on to the drive, and presently saw the odd and timid figure of Mrs. Hall coming along, in a big white flapping sort of sun-bonnet, with a basket in her hand. She came straight up to me in a curious, resolute sort of way, and it came into my mind that she had come out for the very purpose of meeting me.

I praised the beauty of the place, and said that I supposed she knew it well.

"Yes," she said; adding that she was born in the village and her mother had been as a girl a servant at Treheale. But she went on to tell me that she and her husband had lived till recently at a farm down in the valley, and had only been a year or so in the house itself. Old Mr. Heale, the last owner, had died three or four years before, and it had proved impossible to let the house. It seemed that when the trustees gave up all idea of being able to get a tenant, they had offered it to the Halls at a nominal rent, to act as caretakers. She spoke in a cheerless way, with her eyes cast down and with the same strained look as of one carrying a heavy burden. "You will have heard of Mr. Heale, perhaps?" she said with a sudden look at me.

"No," I said; "I know nothing about the place. Who was Mr. Heale?"

"The old Squire, sir," she said; "but I think people here are unfair to him. He lived a wild life enough, but he was a kind gentleman in his way—and I have often thought it was not his fault altogether. He married soon after he came into the estate—a Miss Tregaskis from down to St. Erne—and they were very happy for a little; but she died after they had been married a couple of years, and they had no child; and then I think Mr. Heale went nearly mad—nothing went right after that. Mr. Heale shut himself up a good deal among his books— he was a very clever gentleman—and then he got into bad ways; but it was the sorrow in his heart that made him bad—and we must not blame people too much, must we?" She looked at me with rather a pitiful look.

"You mean," I said, "that he tried to forget his grief, and did not choose the best way to do it."

"Yes, sir," said Mrs. Hall simply. "I think he blamed God for taking away what he loved, instead of trusting Him; and no good comes of that. The people here got to hate him—he used to spoil the young people, sir—you know what I mean—and they were afraid of seeing him about their houses. I remember, sir, as if it were yesterday, seeing him in the lane to St. Sibby. He was marching along, very upright, with his white hair—it went white early—and he passed old Mr. Miles, the churchwarden, who had been a wild young man too, but he found religion with the Wesleyans, and after that was very hard on everyone.

"It was the first time they had met since Mr. Miles had become serious; and Mr. Heale stopped in his pleasant way, and held out his hand to Mr. Miles; who put his hands behind him and said something—I was close to them—which I could not quite catch, but it was about fellowship with the works of darkness; and then Mr. Miles turned and went on his way; and Mr. Heale stood looking after him with a curious smile on his face—and I have pitied him ever since. Then he turned and saw me; he always took notice of me—I was a girl then; and he said to me:

"'There, Mary, you see that. I am not good enough, it seems, for Mr. Miles. Well, I don't blame him; but remember, child, that the religion which makes a man turn his back on an old friend is not a good religion'; but I could see he was distressed, though he spoke quietly—and as I went on he gave a sigh which somehow stays in my mind. Perhaps, sir, you would like to look at his picture; he was painted at the same time as Mrs. Heale in the first year of their marriage."

I said I should like to see it, and we turned to the house. She led me to a little room that seemed like a study. There was a big book case full of books, mostly of a scientific kind; and there was a large kneehole table much dotted with ink spots.

"It was here," she said," he used to work, hour after hour."

On the wall hung a pair of pictures—one, that of a young woman, hardly more than a girl, with a delightful expression, both beautiful and good. She was dressed in some white material, and there was a glimpse of sunlit fields beyond.

Then I turned to the portrait of Mr. Heale. It represented a young man in a claret-coloured coat, very slim and upright. It showed a face of great power, a big forehead, clear-cut features, and a determined chin, with extraordinarily bright large eyes; evidently the portrait of a man of great physical and mental force, who would do whatever he took in hand with all his might. It was very finely painted, with a dark background of woods against a stormy sky.

I was immensely struck by the picture; and not less by the fact that there was an extraordinary though indefinable likeness to Mrs. Hall herself. I felt somehow that she perceived that I had noticed this, for she made as though to leave the room. I could not help the inference that I was compelled to draw. I lingered for a moment looking at the portrait, which was so lifelike as to give an almost painful sense of the presence of a third person in the room. But Mrs. Hall went out, and I understood that I was meant to follow her.

She led the way into their own sitting-room, and then with some agitation she turned to me. "I understand that you are an old friend of Mr. Netherby's, sir," she said.

"Yes," I said; "he is my greatest friend."

"Could you persuade him, sir, to leave this place?" she went on. "You will think it a strange thing to say—and I am glad enough to have a lodger, and I like Mr. Netherby—but do you think it is a good thing for a young gentleman to live so much alone?"

I saw that nothing was to be gained by reticence, so I said, "Now, Mrs. Hall, I think we had better speak plainly. I am, I confess, anxious about Mr. Netherby. I don't mean that he is not well, for I have never seen him look better; but I think that there is something going on which I don't wholly understand."

She looked at me suddenly with a quick look, and then, as if deciding that I was to be trusted, she said in a low voice, "Yes, sir, that is it; this house is not like other houses. Mr. Heale—how shall I say it?—was a very determined gentleman, and he used to say that he never would leave the house—and—you will think it very strange that I should speak thus to a stranger—I don't think he has left it."

We stood for a moment silent, and I knew that she had spoken the truth. While we thus stood, I can only say what I felt—I became aware that we were not alone; the sun was bright on the woods outside, the clock ticked peacefully in a corner, but there was something unseen all about us which lay very heavily on my mind. Mrs. Hall put out her hands in a deprecating way, and then said in a low and hurried voice, "He would do no harm to me, sir—we are too near for that"—she looked up at me, and I nodded; "but I can't help it, can I, if he is different with other people? Now, Mr. Hall is not like that, sir—he is a plain good man, and would think what I am saying no better than madness; but as sure as there is a God in Heaven, Mr. Heale is *here*—and though he is too fine a gentleman to take advantage of my talk, yet he liked to command other people, and went his own way too much."

While she spoke, the sense of oppression which I had felt a moment before drew off all of a sudden; and it seemed again as though we were alone.

"Mrs. Hall," I said, "you are a good woman; these things are very dark to me, and though I have heard of such things in stories, I never expected to meet them in the world. But I will try what I can do to get my friend away, though he is a wilful fellow, and I think he will go his own way too." While I spoke I heard Basil's voice outside calling me, and I took Mrs. Hall's hand in my own. She pressed it, and gave me a very kind, sad look. And so, I went out.

We lunched together, Basil and I, off simple fare; he pointed with an air of satisfaction to a score which he had brought into the room, written out with wonderful precision.

"Just finished," he said, "and you shall hear it later on; but now we will go and look round the place. Was there ever such luck as to get a harbourage like this? I have been here two months and feel like staying forever. The place is in Chancery. Old Heale of Treheale, the last of his stock—a rare old blackguard—died here. They tried to let the house, and failed, and put Farmer Hall in at last. The whole place belongs to a girl ten years old. It is a fine house—we will look at that tomorrow; but today we will walk round outside. By the way, how long can you stay?"

"I must get back on Friday at latest," I said. "I have a choir practice and a lesson on Saturday."

Basil looked at me with a good-natured smile. "A pretty poor business, isn't it?" he said. "I would rather pick oakum myself. Here I live in a fine house, for next to nothing, and write, write, write—there's a life for a man."

"Don't you find it lonely?" said I.

"Lonely?" said Basil, laughing loud. "Not a bit of it. What do I want with a pack of twaddlers all about me? I tread a path among the stars—and I have the best of company, too." He stopped and broke off suddenly.

"I shouldn't have thought Mrs. Hall very enlivening company," I said. "By the way, what an odd-looking woman! She seems as if she were frightened."

At that innocent remark Basil looked at me suddenly with the same expression of indefinable anger that I had seen in his face at our first meeting; but he said nothing for a moment. Then he resumed:

"No, I want no company but myself and my thoughts. I tell you, Ward, if you had done as I have done, opened a door into the very treasure house of music, and had only just to step in and carry away as much as one can manage at a time, you wouldn't want company."

I could make no reply to this strange talk; and he presently took me out. I was astonished at the beauty of the place. The ground fell sharply at the back, and there was a terrace with a view over a little valley, with pasture—fields at the bottom, crowned with low woods—beyond, a wide prospect over uplands, which lost themselves in the haze. The day was still and clear; and we could hear the running of the stream below, the cooing of doves and the tinkling of a sheep bell. To the left of the house lay large stables and barns, which were in the possession of the farmer.

We wandered up and down by paths and lanes, sometimes through the yellowing woods, sometimes on open ground, the most perfect views bursting upon us on every side, everything lying in a rich still peace, which came upon my tired and bewildered mind like soft music.

In the course of our walk we suddenly came upon a churchyard surrounded by a low wall; at the farther end, beyond the graves, stood a small church consisting of two aisles, with a high perpendicular tower.

"St. Sibby," said Basil, "whether he or she I know not, but no doubt a very estimable person. You would like to look at this? The church is generally open."

We went up a gravel path and entered the porch; the door was open, and there was an odd, close smell in the building. It was a very plain place, with the remains of a roodloft, and some ancient woodwork; but the walls were mildewed and green and the place looked neglected.

"Vyvyan is a good fellow," said Basil, looking round, "but he is single-handed here; the rector is an invalid and lives at Penzance, and Vyvyan has a wretched stipend. Look here, Leonard; here is the old Heale vault."

He led me into a little chapel near the tower, which opened on to the church by a single arch. The place was very dark; but I could see a monument or two of an ancient type and some brasses. There were a couple of helmets on iron supports and the remains of a mouldering banner. But just opposite to us was a tall modern marble monument on the wall.

"That is old Heale's monument," said Basil, "with a long, pious inscription by the old rector. Just look at it—did you ever see such vandalism?"

299

I drew near—then I saw that the monument had been defaced in a hideous and horrible way. There were deep dints in the marble, like the marks of a hammer; and there were red stains over the inscription, which reminded me in a dreadful way of the stains on the letter given me by Vyvyan.

"Good Heavens!" I said, "what inconceivable brutality! Who on earth did this?"

"That's just what no one can find out," said Basil, smiling. "But the inscription was rather too much, I confess—look at this: '*who discharged in an exemplary way the duties of a landowner and a Christian.*' Old Heale's idea of the duties of a landowner was to screw as much as he could out of his farmers—and he had, moreover, some old ideas, which we may call feudal, about his relations with the more attractive of his tenants: he was a cheerful old boy—and as to the Christian part of it, well, he had about as much of that, I gather, as you take up on a two-pronged fork. Still, they might have left the old man alone. I daresay he sleeps sound enough in spite of it all." He stamped his foot on the pavement as he did so, which returned a hollow sound. "Are you inside?" said Basil, laughingly; "perhaps not at home?"

"Don't talk like that," I said to Basil, whose levity seemed to me disgusting.

"Certainly not, my boy," he said, "if you don't like it. I daresay the old man can look after himself."

And so, we left the church. We returned home about four o'clock. Basil left me on the terrace and went into the house to interview Mrs. Hall on the subject of dinner. I hung for a time over the balustrade, but, getting chilly and still not feeling inclined to go in, I strolled to the farther end of the terrace, which ran up to the wood. On reaching the end, I found a stone seat; and behind it, between two yews, a little dark sinister path led into the copse.

I do not know exactly what feeling it was which drew me to enter upon the exploration of the place; the path was slippery and overgrown with moss, and the air of the shrubbery into which it led was close and moist, full of the breath of rotting leaves. The path ran with snakelike windings, so that at no point was it possible to see more than a few feet ahead. Above, the close boughs held hands as if to screen the path from the light. Then the path suddenly took a turn to the left and went straight to the house.

Two yews flanked the way and a small flight of granite steps, slimy and mildewed, led up to a little door in the corner of the house—a door which had been painted brown, like the colour of the stone, and which was let into its frame so as to be flush with the wall. The upper part of it was pierced with a couple of apertures like eyes filled with glass to give light to the passage within. The steps had evidently not been trodden for many months, even years; but upon the door, near the keyhole, were odd marks looking as if scratched by the hoofs of some beast—a goat, I thought—as if the door had been impatiently struck by something awaiting entrance there.

I do not know what was the obsession which fell on me at the sight of this place. A cold dismay seemed to spring from the dark and clutch me; there are places which seem so soaked, as it were, in malign memories that they give out a kind of spiritual aroma of evil. I have seen in my life things which might naturally seem to produce in the mind associations of terror and gloom. I have seen men die; I have seen a man writhe in pain on the ground from a mortal injury; but I never experienced anything like the thrill of horror which passed through my shuddering mind at the sight of the little door with its dark eye-holes.

I went in chilly haste down the path and came out upon the terrace, looking out over the peaceful woods. The sun was now setting in the west among cloud-fiords and bays of rosy light. But the thought of the dark path lying like a snake among the thickets dwelt in my mind and poisoned all my senses. Presently I heard the voice of Basil call me cheerfully from the corner of the house. We went in. A simple meal was spread for us, half tea, half dinner, to which we did full justice. But afterwards, though Basil was fuller than ever, so it seemed to me, of talk and laughter, I was seized with so extreme a fatigue that I drowsed off several times in the course of our talk, till at last he laughingly ordered me to bed.

I slept profoundly. When I awoke, it was bright day. My curtains had been drawn, and the materials for my *toilette* arranged while I still slept. I dressed hastily and hurried down, to find Basil awaiting me.

That morning we gave up to exploring the house. It was a fine old place, full from end to end of the evidences of long and ancestral habitation. The place was full of portraits. There was a great old dining-room—Basil had had the whole house unshuttered for my inspection—a couple of large drawing-rooms, long passages, bedrooms, all full of ancient furniture and pictures, as if the family life had been suddenly suspended. I noticed that he did not take me to the study, but led me upstairs.

301

"This is my room," said Basil suddenly; and we turned into a big room in the lefthand corner of the garden-front. There was a big four-post bedroom here, a large table in the window, a sofa, and some fine chairs. But what at once attracted my observation was a low door in the corner of the room, half hidden by a screen. It seemed to me, as if by a sudden gleam of perception, that this door must communicate with the door I had seen below; and presently, while I stood looking out of the great window upon the valley, I said to Basil, "And that door in the corner—does that communicate with the little door in the wood?"

When I said this, Basil was standing by the table, bending over some MSS. He suddenly turned to me and gave me a very long, penetrating look; and then, as if suddenly recollecting himself, said, "My dear Ward, you are a very observant fellow—yes, there is a little staircase there that goes down into the shrubbery and leads to the terrace. You remember that old Mr. Heale of whom I told you—well, he had this room, and he had visitors at times whom I daresay it was not convenient to admit to the house; they came and went this way; and he too, no doubt, used the stairs to leave the house and return unseen."

"How curious!" I said. "I confess I should not care to have this room—I did not like the look of the shrubbery door."

Well," said Basil, "I do not feel with you; to me it is rather agreeable to have the association of the room. He was a loose old fish, no doubt, but he lived his life, and I expect enjoyed it, and that is more than most of us can claim."

As he said the words he crossed the room, and opening the little door, he said, "Come and look down—it is a simple place enough."

I went across the room, and looking in, saw a small flight of stairs going down into the dark; at the end of which the two square panes of the little shrubbery door were out lined in the shadow.

I cannot account for what happened next: there was a sound in the passage, and some thing seemed to rush up the stairs and past me; a strange, dull smell came from the passage; I know that there fell on me a sort of giddiness and horror, and I went back into the room with hands outstretched, like Elymas the sorcerer, seeking someone to guide me. Looking up, I saw Basil regarding me with a baleful look and a strange smile on his face.

"What was that?" I said. "Surely something came up there . . . I don't know what it was."

There was a silence; then, "My dear Ward," said Basil, "you are

302

behaving very oddly—one would think you had seen a ghost." He looked at me with a sort of gleeful triumph, like a man showing the advantages of a house or the beauties of a view to an astonished friend. But again, I could find no words to express my sense of what I had experienced. Basil went swiftly to the door and shut it, and then said to me with a certain sternness, "Come, we have been here long enough—let us go on. I am afraid I am boring you."

We went downstairs; and the rest of the morning passed, so far as I can remember, in a species of fitful talk. I was endeavouring to recover from the events of the morning; and Basil—well, he seemed to me like a man who was fencing with some difficult question. Though his talk seemed spontaneous, I felt somehow that it was that of a weak antagonist endeavouring to parry the strokes of a persistent assailant.

After luncheon Basil proposed a walk again. We went out on a long ramble, as we had done the previous day; but I remember little of what passed. He directed upon me a stream of indifferent talk; but I laboured, I think, under a heavy depression of spirit, and my conversation was held up merely as it might have been as a shield against the insistent demands of my companion. Anyone who has been through a similar experience in which he wrestles with some tragic fact, and endeavours merely to meet and answer the sprightly suggestions of some cheerful companion, can imagine what I felt. At last the evening began to close in; we retraced our steps: Basil told me that we should dine at an early hour, and I was left alone in my own room.

I became the prey of the most distressing and poignant reflections. What I had experienced convinced me that there was something about the whole place that was uncanny and abnormal. The attitude of my companion, his very geniality, seemed to me to be forced and unnatural; and my only idea was to gain, if I could, some notion of how I should proceed. I felt that questions were useless, and I committed myself to the hands of Providence. I felt that here was a situation that I could not deal with and that I must leave it in stronger hands than my own. This reflection brought me some transitory comfort, and when I heard Basil's voice calling me to dinner, I felt that sooner or later the conflict would have to be fought out, and that I could not myself precipitate matters.

After dinner Basil for the first time showed some signs of fatigue, and after a little conversation he sank back in a chair, lit a cigar, and presently asked me to play something.

I went to the piano, still, I must confess, seeking for some possible opportunity of speech, and let my fingers stray as they moved along the keys. For a time, I extemporised and then fell into some familiar music. I do not know whether the instinctive thought of what he had scrawled upon his note to me influenced me, but I began to play Mendelssohn's anthem *Hear my prayer.* While I played the initial phrase, I became aware that some change was making itself felt in my companion; and I had hardly come to the end of the second phrase when a sound from Basil made me turn round.

I do not think that I ever received so painful a shock in my life as that which I experienced at the sight that met my eyes. Basil was still in the chair where he had seated himself, but instead of the robust personality which he had presented to me during our early interviews, I saw in a sudden flash the Basil that I knew, only infinitely more tired and haggard than I had known him in life. He was like a man who had cast aside a mask, and had suddenly appeared in his own part. He sat before me as I had often seen him sit, leaning forward in an intensity of emotion. I stopped suddenly, wheeled round in my chair, and said, "Basil, tell me what has happened."

He looked at me, cast an agitated glance round the room—and then all on a sudden began to speak in a voice that was familiar to me of old.

What he said is hardly for me to recount. But he led me step by step through a story so dark in horrors that I can hardly bring myself to reproduce it here. Imagine an untainted spirit, entering cheerfully upon some simple entourage, finding himself little by little within the net of some overpowering influence of evil.

He told me that he had settled at Treheale in his normal frame of mind. That he had intended to tell me of his whereabouts, but that there had gradually stolen into his mind a sort of unholy influence. "At first," he said, "I resisted it," but it was accompanied by so extraordinary an access of mental power and vigour that he had accepted the conditions under which he found himself. I had better perhaps try to recount his own experience.

He had come to Grampound in the course of his wanderings and had enquired about lodgings. He had been referred to the farmer at Treheale. He had settled himself there, only congratulating himself upon the mixture of quiet and dignity which surrounded him. He had arranged his life for tranquil study, had chosen his rooms, and had made the best disposition he could of his affairs.

"The second night," he said, "that I was here, I had gone to bed thinking of nothing but my music. I had extinguished my light and was lying quietly in bed watching the expiring glimmer of the embers on my hearth. I was wondering, as one does, weaving all kinds of fancies about the house and the room in which I found myself, lying with my head on my hand, when I saw, to my intense astonishment, the little door in the corner of the bedroom half open and close again. I thought to myself that it was probably Mrs. Hall coming to see whether I was comfortable, and I thereupon said, 'Who is there?' There was no sound in answer, but presently, a moment or two after, there followed a disagreeable laughter, I thought from the lower regions of the house in the direction of the corner. 'Come in, whoever you are,' I said; and in a moment the door opened and closed, and I became aware that there was someone in the room.

"Further than that," said Basil to me in that dreadful hour, "it is impossible to go. I can only say that I became aware in a moment of the existence of a world outside of and intertwined with our own; a world of far stronger influences and powers—how far-reaching I know not—but I know this, that all the mortal difficulties and dilemmas that I had hitherto been obliged to meet melted away in the face of a force to which I had hitherto been a stranger."

The dreadful recital ended about midnight; and the strange part was to me that our positions seemed in some fearful manner to have been now reversed. Basil was now the shrinking, timorous creature, who only could implore me not to leave him. It was in such a mood as this that he had written the letter. I asked him what there was to fear. "Everything," he said with a shocking look. He would not go to bed; he would not allow me to leave the room.

Step by step I unravelled the story, which his incoherent statement had only hinted at. His first emotion had been that of intense fright; but he became aware almost at once that the spirit who thus so unmistakably came to him was not inimical to him; the very features of the being—if such a word can be used about so shadowy a thing—appeared to wear a smile. Little by little the presence of the visitant had become habitual to Basil: there was a certain pride in his own fearlessness, which helped him.

Then there was intense and eager curiosity; "and then, too," said the unhappy man, "the influence began to affect me in other ways. I will not tell you how, but the very necessaries of life were provided for me in a manner which I should formerly have contemned with the utmost scorn, but which now I was given confidence to disregard.

The dejection, the languorous reflections which used to hang about me, gradually drew off and left me cheerful, vigorous, and, I must say it, delighting in evil imaginations; but so subtle was the evil influence, that it was not into any gross corruption or flagrant deeds that I flung myself; it was into my music that the poison flowed.

"I do not, of course, mean that evil then appeared to me, as I can humbly say it does now, *as* evil, but rather as a vision of perfect beauty, glorifying every natural function and every corporeal desire. The springs of music rose clear and strong within me, and with the fountain I mingled from my own stores the subtle venom of the corrupted mind. How glorious, I thought, to sway as with a magic wand the souls of men; to interpret for each all the eager and leaping desires which maybe he had dully and dutifully controlled. To make all things fair—for so potent were the whispers of the spirit that talked at my ear that I believed in my heart that all that was natural in man was also permissible and even beautiful, and that it was nothing but a fantastic asceticism that forbids it; though now I see, as I saw before, that the evil that thwarts mankind is but the slime of the pit out of which he is but gradually extricating himself."

"But what *is* the thing," I said, "of which you speak? Is it a spirit of evil, or a human spirit, or what?"

"Good God!" he said, "how can I tell?" and then with lifted hand he sang in a strange voice a bar or two from Stanford's *Revenge*.

"Was he devil or man? he was devil for aught they knew."

This dreadful interlude, the very flippancy of it, that might have moved my laughter at any other time, had upon me an indescribably sickening effect. I stared at Basil. He relapsed into a moody silence with clasped hands and knotted brow. To draw him away from the nether darkness of his thoughts, I asked him how and in what shape the spirit had made itself plain to him.

"Oh, no shape at all," said he; "he is *there*, that is enough. I seem sometimes to see a face, to catch the glance of an eye, to see a hand raised to warn or to encourage; but it is all impossibly remote; I could never explain to you *how* I see him."

"Do you see him now?" I asked.

"Yes," said Basil, "a long way off—and he is running swiftly to me, but he has far to go yet. He is angry; he threatens me; he beats the air with his hands."

"But *where* is this?" I asked, for Basil's eyes were upon the ground.

"Oh, for God's sake, man, be silent," said Basil. "It is in the region of which you and others know little; but it has been revealed to me. It lies all about us—it has its capes and shadowy peaks, and a leaden sea, full of sound; it is there that I ramble with him."

There fell a silence between us.

Then I said, "But, dear Basil, I must ask you this—how was it that you wrote as you did to me?"

"Oh! he made me write," he said, "and I think he overreached himself—or my angel, that beholds the Father's face, smote him down. I was myself again on a sudden, the miserable and abject wretch whom you see before you, and knowing that I had been as a man in a dream. Then I wrote the despairing words, and guarded the letter so that he could not come near me; and then Mr. Vyvyan's visit to me—that was not by chance. I gave him the letter and he promised to bear it faithfully—and what attempts were made to tear it from him I do not know; but that my adversary tried his best I do not doubt. But Vyvyan is a good man and could not be harmed.

"And then I fell back into the old spell; and worked still more abundantly and diligently and produced this—this accursed thing which shall not live to scatter evil abroad." As he said these words he rose, and tore the score that lay on the table into shreds and crammed the pieces in the fire. As he thrust the last pieces down, the poker he was holding fell from his hands.

I saw him white as a sheet, and trembling.

"What is the matter?" I said.

He turned a terrible look on me, and said, "He is here—he has arrived."

Then all at once I was aware that there was a sort of darkness in the room; and then with a growing horror I gradually perceived that in and through the room there ran a thing like the front of a precipice, with some dark strand at its foot on which beat a surge of phantom waves. The two scenes struggled together. At one time I could plainly see the cliff-front, close beside me—and then the lamp and the firelit room was all dimmed even to vanishing; and then suddenly the room would come back and the cliff die into a steep shadow.

But in either of the scenes Basil and I were there—he standing irresolute and despairing, glancing from side to side like a hare when the hounds close in. And once he said—this was when the cliff loomed up suddenly—"There are others with him." Then in a moment it seemed as if the room in which we sat died away altogether and I was in that other place; there was a faint light as from under a stormy sky; and a little farther up the strand there stood a group of dark figures, which seemed to consult together.

All at once the group broke and came suddenly towards us. I do not know what to call them; they were human in a sense—that is, they walked upright and had heads and hands. But the faces were all blurred and fretted, like half—rotted skulls—but there was no sense of comparison in me. I only knew that I had seen ugliness and corruption at the very source, and looked into the darkness of the pit itself.

The forms eluded me and rushed upon Basil, who made a motion as though to seize hold of me, and then turned and fled, his arms outstretched, glancing behind him as he ran—and in a moment he was lost to view, though I could see along the shore of that formless sea something like a pursuit.

I do not know what happened after that. I think I tried to pray; but I presently became aware that I was myself menaced by danger. It seemed—but I speak in parables—as though one had separated himself from the rest and had returned to seek me. But all was over, I knew; and the figure indeed carried something which he swung and shook in his hand, which I thought was a token to be shown to me. And then I found my voice and cried out with all my strength to God to save me; and in a moment there was the firelit room again, and the lamp—the most peaceful-looking room in England.

But Basil had left me; the door was wide open; and in a moment the farmer and his wife came hurrying along with blanched faces to ask who it was that had cried *out,* and what had happened.

I made some pitiful excuse that I had dozed in my chair and had awoke crying out some unintelligible words. For in the quest I was about to engage in I did not wish that any mortal should be with me.

They left me, asking for Mr. Netherby and still not satisfied. Indeed, Mrs. Hall looked at me with so penetrating a look that I felt that she understood something of what had happened. And then at once I went up to Basil's room. I do not know where I found the courage to do it; but the courage came.

The room was dark, and a strong wind was blowing through it from the little door. I stepped across the room, feeling my way; went down the stairs, and finding the door open at the bottom, I went out into the snake like path.

I went some yards along it; the moon had risen now. There came a sudden gap in the trees to the left, through which I could see the pale fields and the corner of the wood casting its black shadow on the ground.

The shrubs were torn, broken, and trampled, as though some heavy thing had crashed through. I made my way cautiously down, endowed with a more than human strength—it was a steep bank covered with trees—and then in a moment I saw Basil.

He lay some distance out in the field on his face. I knew at a glance that all was over; and when I lifted him I became aware that he was in some way strangely mangled, and indeed it was found afterwards that though the skin of his body was hardly contused, yet that almost every bone of the body was broken in fragments.

I managed to carry him to the house. I closed the doors of the staircase; and then I managed to tell Farmer Hall that Basil had had, I thought, a fall and was dead. And then my own strength failed me, and for three days and nights I lay in a kind of stupor.

When I recovered my consciousness, I found myself in bed in my own room. Mrs. Hall nursed me with a motherly care and tenderness which moved me very greatly; but I could not speak of the matter to her, until, just before my departure, she came in, as she did twenty times a day, to see if I wanted anything. I made a great effort and said, "Mrs. Hall, I am very sorry for you. This has been a terrible business, and I am afraid you won't easily forget it. You ought to leave the house, I think."

Mrs. Hall turned her frozen gaze upon me, and said, "Yes, sir, indeed, I can't speak about it or think of it. I feel as if I might have prevented it; and yet I have been over and over it in my mind and I can't see where I was wrong. But my duty is to the house now, and I shall never leave it; but I will ask you, sir, to try and find a thought of pity in your heart for *him*"—I knew she did not mean Basil—"I don't think he clearly knows what he has done; he must have his will, as he always did. He stopped at nothing if it was for his pleasure; and he did not know what harm he did. But he is in God's hands; and though I cannot understand why, yet there are things in this life which He allows to be; and we must not try to be judges—we must try to be merciful. But I have not done what I could have done; and if God gives me strength, there shall be an end of this."

A few hours later Mr. Vyvyan called to see me; he was a very different person to the Vyvyan that had showed himself to me in Holborn.

I could not talk much with him; but I could see that he had some understanding of the case. He asked me no questions, but he told me a few details. He said that they had decided at the inquest that he had fallen from the terrace. But the doctor, who was attending me, seems to have said to Mr. Vyvyan that a fall it must have been, but a fall of an almost inconceivable character. "And what is more," the old doctor had added, "the man was neither in pain nor agitation of mind when he died." The face was absolutely peaceful and tranquil; and the doctor's theory was that he had died from some sudden seizure before the fall.

And so, I held my tongue. One thing I did: it was to have a little slab put over the body of my friend—a simple slab with name and date—and I ventured to add one line, because I have no doubt in my own mind that Basil was suddenly delivered, though not from death. He had, I supposed, gone too far upon the dark path, and he could not, I think, have freed himself from the spell; and so, the cord was loosed, but loosed in mercy—and so I made them add the words:

"And in their hands they shall bear thee up."

I must add one further word. About a year after the events above recorded I received a letter from Mr. Vyvyan, which I give without further comment.

St. Sibby, *Dec.* 18, 189—.

Dear Mr. Ward,

I wish to tell you that our friend Mrs. Hall died a few days ago. She was a very good woman, one of the few that are chosen. I was much with her in her last days, and she told me a strange thing, which I cannot bring myself to repeat to you. But she sent you a message which she repeated several times, which she said you would understand. It is simply this: 'Tell Mr. Ward I have prevailed.' I may add that I have no doubt of the truth of her words, and you will know to what I am alluding.

The day after she died there was a fire at Treheale; Mr. Hall was absolutely distracted with grief at the loss of his wife, and I do not know quite what happened. But it was impossible to save the house; all that is left of it is a mass of charred ruins, with a few walls standing up. Nothing was saved, not even a picture. There is a wholly inadequate insurance, and I believe it is not intended to rebuild the house.

I hope you will bear us in mind; though I know you so little, I shall always feel that we have a common experience which will hold us together. You will try and visit us some day when the memory of what took place is less painful to you. The grass is now green on your poor friend's grave; and I will only add that you will have a warm welcome here. I am just moving into the rectory, as my old rector died a fortnight ago, and I have accepted the living. God bless you, dear Mr. Ward.

Yours very sincerely,

James Vyvyan."

The Snake, the Leper, and the Grey Frost

In the heart of the Forest of Seale lay the little village of Birnewood Fratrum, like a lark's nest in a meadow of tall grass. It was approached by green wood-ways, very miry in winter. The folk that lived there were mostly woodmen. There was a little church, the stones of which seemed to have borrowed the hue of the forest, and close beside it a small timbered house, the parsonage, with a garden of herbs. Those who saw Birnewood in the summer, thought of it as a place where a weary man might rest for ever, in an ancient peace, with the fresh mossy smell of the wood blowing through it, and the dark cool branching covert to muse in on every side. But it was a different place in winter, with ragged clouds rolling overhead and the bare boughs sighing in the desolate gales; though again in a frosty winter evening it would be fair enough, with the red sun sinking over miles of trees.

From the village green a little track led into the forest, and, a furlong or two inside, ended in an open space thickly overgrown with elders, where stood the gaunt skeleton of a ruined tower staring with bare windows at the wayfarer. The story of the tower was sad enough. The last owner, Sir Ralph Birne, was on the wrong side in a rebellion, and died on the scaffold, his lands forfeited to the crown. The tower was left desolate, and piece by piece the villagers carried away all that was useful to them, leaving the shell of a house, though at the time of which I speak the roof still held, and the floors, though rotting fast, still bore the weight of a foot.

In the parsonage lived an old priest, Father John, as he was called, and with him a boy who was held to be his nephew, Ralph by name, now eighteen years of age. The boy was very dear to Father John, who was a wise and loving man. To many it might have seemed a dull life

313

enough, but Ralph had known no other, having come to the parsonage as a child. Of late indeed Ralph had begun to feel a strange desire grow and stir within him, to see what the world was like outside the forest; such a desire would come on him at early morning, in the fresh spring days, and he would watch some lonely traveller riding slowly to the south with an envious look; though as like as not the wayfarer would be envying the bright boy, with his background of quiet woods. But such fancies only came and went, and he said nothing to the old priest about them, who nevertheless had marked the change for himself with the instinct of love, and would sometimes, as he sate with his breviary, follow the boy about with his eyes, in which the wish to keep him strove with the knowledge that the bird must someday leave the nest.

One summer morning, the old priest shut his book, with the air of a man who has made up his mind in sadness, and asked Ralph to walk with him. They went to the tower, and there, sitting in the ruins, Father John told Ralph the story of the house, which he had often heard before. But now there was so tender and urgent a tone in the priest's voice that Ralph heard him wonderingly; and at last the priest very solemnly, after a silence, said that there was something in his mind that must be told; and he went on to say that Ralph was indeed the heir of the tower; he was the grandson of Sir Ralph, who died upon the scaffold; his father had died abroad, dispossessed of his inheritance; and the priest said that in a few days he himself would set out on a journey, too long deferred, to see a friend of his, a canon of a neighbouring church, to learn if it were possible that some part of the lands might be restored to Ralph by the king's grace.

For the young king that had newly come to the throne was said to be very merciful and just, and punished not the sins of the fathers upon the children; but Father John said that he hardly dared to hope it; and then he bound Ralph to silence; and then after a pause he added, taking one of the boy's hands in his own, "And it is time, dear son, that you should leave this quiet place and make a name for yourself; my days draw to an end; perhaps I have been wrong to keep you here to myself, but I have striven to make you pure and simple, and if I was in fault, why, it has been the fault of love." And the boy threw his arms round the priest's neck and kissed him, seeing that tears trembled in his eyes, and said that he was more than content, and that he should never leave his uncle and the peaceful forest that he loved. But the priest saw an unquiet look in his eye, as of a sleeper awakened, and knew the truth.

A few days after, the priest rode away at sunrise; and Ralph was left alone. In his head ran an old tale, which he had heard from the wood-men, of a great treasure of price, which was hidden somewhere in the tower. Then it came into his mind that there dwelt not far away in the wood an ancient wise man who gave counsel to all who asked for it, and knew the virtues of plants, and the courses of buried springs, and many hidden things beside. Ralph had never been to the house of the wise man, but he knew the direction where it lay; so, with the secret in his heart, he made at once for the place. The day was very hot and still, and no birds sang in the wood. Ralph walked swiftly along the soft green road, and came at last upon a little grey house of plaster, with beams of timber, that stood in a clearing near a spring, with a garden of its own; a fragrant smell came from a sprawling bush of box, and the bees hummed busily over the flowers.

There was no smoke from the chimney, and the single window that gave on the road, in a gable, looked at him like a dark eye. He went up the path, and stood before the door waiting, when a high thin voice, like an evening wind, called from within, "Come in and fear not, thou that tarriest on the threshold." Ralph, with a strange stirring of the blood at the silver sound of the voice, unlatched the door and entered. He found himself in a low dark room, with a door opposite him; in the roof hung bundles of herbs; there was a large oak table strewn with many things of daily use, and sitting in a chair, with his back to the light, sate a very old thin man, with a frosty beard, clad in a loose grey gown. Over the fireplace hung a large rusty sword; the room was very clean and cool, and the sunlight danced on the ceiling, with the flicker of moving leaves.

"Your name and errand?" said the old man, fixing his grey eyes, like flint stones, upon the boy, not unkindly.

"Ralph," said the boy.

"Ralph," said the old man, "and why not add Birne to Ralph? that makes a fairer name."

Ralph was so much bewildered at this strange greeting, that he stood confused—at which the old man pointed to a settle, and said, "And now, boy, sit down and speak with me; you are Ralph from Birnewood Parsonage, I know—Father John is doubtless away—he has no love for me, though I know him to be a true man."

Then little by little he unravelled the boy's desire, and the story of the treasure. Then he said, kindly enough, "Yes, it is ever thus—well, lad, I will tell you; and heed my words well. The treasure is there; and you shall indeed find it; but prepare for strange sounds and sights." And as he said this, he took the young hand in his own for a moment and a strange tide of sensation seemed to pass along the boy's veins. "Look in my face," the old man went on, "that I may see that you have faith—for without faith such quests are vain."

Ralph raised his eyes to those of the old man, and then a sensation such as he had never felt before came over him; it was like looking from a window into a wide place, full of darkness and wonder.

Then the old man said solemnly, "Child, the time is come—I have waited long for you, and the door is open."

Then he said, with raised hand, "The journey is not long, but it must be done in a waking hour; sleep not on the journey; that first. And of three things beware—the Snake, and the Leper, and the Grey Frost; for these three things have brought death to wiser men than yourself. There," he added, "that is your note of the way; now make the journey, if you have the courage."

"But, sir," said Ralph in perplexity, "you say to me, make the journey; and you tell me not whither to go. And you tell me to beware of three things. How shall I know them to avoid them?"

"You will know them when you have seen them," said the old man sadly, "and that is the most that men can know; and as for the journey, you can start upon it wherever you are, if your heart is pure and strong."

Then Ralph said, trembling, "Father, my heart is pure, I think; but I know not whether I am strong."

Then the old man reached out his hand, and took up a staff that leant by the chair; and from a pocket in his gown he took a small metal thing shaped like a five-pointed star; and he said, "Ralph, here is a staff and a holy thing; and now set forth." So, Ralph rose, and took the staff and the star, and made a reverence, and murmured thanks; and then he went to the door by which he had entered; but the old man said, "Nay, it is the other door," and then he bent down his head upon his arms like one who wept.

Ralph went to the other door and opened it; he had thought it led into the wood; but when he opened it, it was dark and cold without; and suddenly with a shock of strange terror he saw that outside was a place like a hill-top, with short strong grass, and clouds sweeping over it. He would have drawn back, but he was ashamed; so, he stepped out and closed the door behind him; and then the house was gone in a moment like a dream, and he was alone on the hill, with the wind whistling in his ears.

He waited for a moment in the clutch of a great fear; but he felt he was alive and well, and little by little his fear disappeared and left him eager. He went a few steps forward, and saw that the hill sloped downward, and downward he went, by steep slopes of turf and scattered grey stones. Presently the mist seemed to blow thinner, and through a gap he saw a land spread out below him; and soon he came out of the cloud, and saw a lonely forest country, all unlike his own, for the trees seemed a sort of pine, with red stems, very tall and sombre. He looked round, and presently he saw that a little track below him seemed to lead downward into the pines, so he gained the track; and soon he came down to the wood.

There was no sign as yet of any habitation; he heard the crying of birds, and at one place he saw a number of crows that stood round something white that lay upon the ground, and pecked at it; and he turned not aside, thinking, he knew not why, that there was some evil thing there. But he did not feel alone, and he had a thought which dwelt with him that there were others bound upon the same quest as himself, though he saw nothing of them. Once indeed he thought he saw a man walking swiftly, his face turned away, among the pines; but the trees blotted him from his sight.

Then he passed by a great open marsh with reeds and still pools of water, where he wished to rest; but he pushed on the faster, and suddenly, turning a corner, saw that the track led him straight to a large stone house, that stood solitary in the wood. He knew in a moment that this was the end of his journey, and marvelled within himself at the ease of the quest; he went straight up to the house, which seemed all dark and silent, and smote loudly and confidently on the door; someone stirred within, and it was presently opened to him. He thought now that he would be questioned, but the man who opened to him, a grave serving-man, made a motion with his hand, and he went up a flight of stone steps.

As he went up, there came out from a door, as though to meet him with honour, a tall and noble personage, very cheerful and comely, and with a courteous greeting took him into a large room richly furnished; Ralph began to tell his story, but the man made a quiet gesture with his hand as though no explanation was needed, and went at once to a press, which he opened, and brought out from it a small coffer, which seemed heavy, and opened it before him; Ralph could not see clearly what it contained, but he saw the sparkle of gold and what seemed like jewels.

The man smiled at him, and as though in reply to a question said, "Yes, this is what you came to seek; and you are well worthy of it; and my lord"—he bowed as he spoke—"is glad to bestow his riches upon one who found the road so easy hither, and who came from so honoured a friend." Then he said very courteously that he would willingly have entertained him, and shown him more of the treasures of the house; "but I know," he added, "that your business requires haste and you would be gone;" and so he conducted him very gently down to the door again, and presently Ralph was standing outside with the precious coffer under his arm, wondering if he were not in a dream; because he had found what he sought so soon, and with so little trouble.

The porter stood at the door, and said in a quiet voice, "The way is to the left, and through the wood." Ralph thanked him, and the porter said, "You know, young sir, of what you are to beware, for the forest has an evil name?"

And when Ralph replied that he knew, the porter said that it was well to start betimes, because the way was somewhat long. So, Ralph went out along the road, and saw the porter standing at the door for a long time, watching him, he thought, with a kind of tender gaze.

Ralph took the road that led to the left, very light-hearted; it was pleasant under the pines, which had made a soft brown carpet of needles; and the scent of the pine-gum was sharp and sweet. He went for a mile or two thus, while the day darkened above him, and the wind whispered like a falling sea among the branches. At last he came to another great marsh, but a path led down to it from the road, and in the path were strange marks as though some heavy thing had been dragged along, with footprints on either side. Ralph went a few steps down the path, when suddenly an evil smell passed by him; he had been thinking of a picture in one of Father John's books of a man fighting with a dragon, and the brave horned creature, with its red mouth and white teeth, with ribbed wings and bright blue burnished mail, and a tail armed with a sting, had seemed to him a curious and beautiful sight, that a man might well desire to see; the thought of danger was hardly in his heart.

Suddenly he heard below him in the reeds a great routing and splashing; the rushes parted, and he saw a huge and ugly creature, with black oily sides and a red mane of bristles, raise itself up and regard him. Its sides dropped with mud, and its body was wrapped with clinging weeds. But it moved so heavily and slow, and drew itself out on to the bank with such pain, that Ralph saw that there was little danger to one so fleet as himself, if he drew not near.

The beast opened its great mouth, and Ralph saw a blue tongue and a pale throat; it regarded him hungrily with small evil eyes; but Ralph sprang backwards, and laughed to see how lumberingly the brute trailed itself along. Its hot and fetid breath made a smoke in the still air; presently it desisted, and as though it desired the coolness, it writhed back into the water again. And Ralph saw that it was only a beast that crept upon its prey by stealth, and that though if he had slept, or bathed in the pool, it might have drawn him in to devour him, yet that one who was wary and active need have no fear; so he went on his way; and blew out great breaths to get the foul watery smell of the monster out of his nostrils.

Suddenly he began to feel weary; he did not know what time of day it was in this strange country, where all was fresh like a dewy morning; he had not seen the sun, though the sky was clear, and he fell to wondering where the light came from; as he wondered, he came to a stone bench by the side of the road where he thought he would sit a little; he would be all the fresher for a timely rest; he sate down, and as though to fill the place with a heavenly peace, he heard at once doves hallooing in the thicket close at hand; while he sate drinking in the charm of the sound, there was a flutter of wings, and a dove alighted close to his feet; it walked about crooning softly, with its nodding neck flashing with delicate colours, and its pink feet running swiftly on the grass.

He felt in his pocket and found there a piece of bread which he had taken with him in the morning and had never thought of tasting; he crumbled it for the bird, who fell to picking it eagerly and gratefully, bowing its head as though in courteous acknowledgment. Ralph leant forwards to watch it, and the ground swam before his weary eyes. He sate back for a moment, and then he would have slept, when he saw a small bright thing dart from a crevice of the stone seat on to his knee. He bent forward to look at it, and saw that it was a thing like a lizard, but without legs, of a powdered green, strangely bright. It nestled on his knee in a little coil and watched him with keen eyes. The trustfulness of these wild creatures pleased him wonderfully. Suddenly, very far away and yet near him, he heard the sound of a voice, like a man in prayer; it reminded him, he knew not why, of the Wise Man's voice, and he rose to his feet ashamed of his drowsiness.

319

The little lizard darted from his leg and on to the ground, as though vexed to be disturbed, and he saw it close to his feet. The dove saw it too, and went to it as though inquiringly; the lizard showed no fear, but coiled itself up, and as the dove came close, made a little dart at its breast, and the dove drew back.

Ralph was amused at the fearlessness of the little thing, but in a moment saw that something ailed the dove; it moved as though dizzy, and then spread its wings as if for flight, but dropped them again and nestled down on the ground. In a moment its pretty head fell forwards and it lay motionless. Then with a shock of fear Ralph saw that he had been nearly betrayed; that this was the Snake itself of which he had been warned; he struck with his staff at the little venomous thing, which darted forward with a wicked hiss, and Ralph only avoided it with a spring. Then without an instant's thought he turned and ran along the wood-path, chiding himself bitterly for his folly. He had nearly slept; he had only not been stung to death; and he thought of how he would have lain, a stiffening figure, till the crows gathered round him and pulled the flesh from his bones.

After this the way became more toilsome; the track indeed was plain enough, but it was strewn with stones, and little thorny plants grew everywhere, which tripped his feet and sometimes pierced his skin; it grew darker too, as though night were coming on. Presently he came to a clearing in the forest; on a slope to his right hand, he saw a little hut of boughs, with a few poor garden herbs about it. A man was crouched among them, as though he were digging; he was only some thirty paces away; Ralph stopped for a moment, and the man rose up and looked at him. Ralph saw a strangely distorted face under a hairless brow. There were holes where the eyes should have been, and in these the eyes were so deeply sunk that they looked but like pits of shade.

Presently the other began to move towards him, waving a large misshapen hand which gleamed with a kind of scurfy whiteness; and he cried out unintelligible words, which seemed half angry, half piteous. Ralph knew that the Leper was before him, and though he loathed to fly before so miserable a wretch, he turned and hurried on into the forest; the creature screamed the louder, and it seemed as though he were asking an alms, but he hobbled so slowly on his thick legs, foully bandaged with rags, that Ralph soon distanced him, and he heard the wretch stop and fall to cursing. This sad and fearful encounter made Ralph sick at heart; but he strove to thank God for another danger escaped, and hastened on.

Gradually he became aware by various signs that he was approaching some inhabited place; all at once he came upon a fair house in a piece of open ground, that looked to him at first so like the house of the treasure, that he thought he had come back to it. But when he looked more closely upon it, he saw that it was not the same; it was somewhat more meanly built, and had not the grave and solid air that the other had; presently he heard a sound of music, like a concert of lutes and trumpets, which came from the house, and when it ceased there was clapping of hands.

While he doubted whether to draw near, he saw that the door was opened, and a man, richly dressed and of noble appearance, came out upon the space in front of the house. He looked about him with a grave and serene air, like a prince awaiting guests. And his eyes falling upon Ralph, he beckoned him to draw near. Ralph at first hesitated. But it seemed to him an unkindly thing to turn his back upon this gallant gentleman who stood there smiling; so, he drew near. And then the other asked him whither he was bound. Ralph hardly knew what to reply to this, but the gentleman awaited not his answer, but said that this was a day of festival, and all were welcome, and he would have him come in and abide with them. Ralph excused himself, but the gentleman smiled and said, "I know, sir, that you are bound upon a journey, as many are that pass this way; but you carry no burden with you, as is the wont of others." And then Ralph, with a start of surprise and anguish, remembered that he had left his coffer on the seat where he had seen the Snake.

He explained his loss to the gentleman, who laughed and said that this was easily mended, for he would send himself a servant to fetch it. And then he asked whether he had been in any peril, and when Ralph told him, he nodded his head gravely, and said it was a great danger escaped. And then Ralph told him of the Leper, at which the gentleman grew grave, and said that it was well he had not stopped to speak with him, for the contagion of that leprosy was sore and sudden. And then he added, "But while I send to recover your coffer, you will enter and sit with us; you look weary, and you shall eat of our meat, for it is good meat that strengtheneth; but wine," he said, "I will not offer you, though I have it here in abundance, for it weakeneth the knees of those that walk on a journey; but you shall delight your heart with music, such as the angels love, and set forth upon your way rejoicing; for indeed it is not late."

And so, Ralph was persuaded, and they drew near to the door. Then the gentleman stood aside to let Ralph enter; and Ralph saw within a hall with people feasting, and minstrels in a gallery; but just as he set foot upon the threshold he turned; for it seemed that he was plucked by a hand; and he saw the gentleman, with the smile all faded from his face, and his robe had shifted from his side; and Ralph saw that his side was swollen and bandaged, and then his eye fell upon the gentleman's knee, which was bare, and it was all scurfed and scarred. And he knew that he was in the hands of the Leper himself.

He drew back with a shudder, but the gentleman gathered his robe about him, and said with a sudden sternness, "Nay, it were discourteous to draw back now; and indeed I will compel you to come in." Then Ralph knew that he was betrayed; but he bethought him of the little star that he carried with him, and he took it out and held it before him, and said, "Here is a token that I may not halt." And at that the gentleman's face became evil, and he gnashed with his teeth, and moved towards him, as though to seize him. But Ralph saw that he feared the star. So, he went backwards holding it forth; and as the Leper pressed upon him, he touched him with the star; and at that the Leper cried aloud, and ran within the house; and there came forth a waft of doleful music like a dirge for the dead.

Then Ralph went into the wood and stood there awhile in dreadful thought; but it came into his mind that there could be no turning back, and that he must leave his precious coffer behind, "and perhaps," he thought, "the Wise Man will let me adventure again." So, he went on with a sad and sober heart, but he thanked God as he went for another danger hardly escaped.

And it grew darker now; so dark that he often turned aside among the trees; till at last he came out on the edge of the forest, and knew that he was near the end. In front of him rose a wide hillside, the top of which was among the clouds; and he could see the track faintly glimmering upwards through the grass; the forest lay like a black wall behind him, and he was now deathly weary of his journey, and could but push one foot before the other.

But for all his weariness he felt that it grew colder as he went higher; he gathered his cloak around him, but the cold began to pierce his veins; so that he knew that he was coming to the Grey Frost, and how to escape from it he knew not. The grass grew crisp with frost, and the tall thistles that grew there snapped as he touched them. By the track there rose in several places, tall tussocks of grass, and happening to pass close by one of these, he saw something gleam white amid the grass; so he looked closer upon it, and then his heart grew cold within him, for he saw that the grass grew thick out of the bones of a skeleton, through the white ribs and out of the sightless eyes. And he saw that each of the tussocks marked the grave of a man.

Then he came higher still, and the ground felt like iron below his feet; and over him came a dreadful drowsiness, till his only thought was to lie down and sleep; his breath came out like a white cloud and hung round him, and yet he saw the hill rising in front. Then he marked something lie beside the track; and he saw that it was a man down upon his face, wrapped in a cloak. He tried to lift him up, but the body seemed stiff and cold, and the face was frozen to the ground; and when he raised it the dirt was all hard upon the face.

So, he left it lying and went on. At last he could go no farther; all was grey and still round him, covered with a bleak hoar-frost. To left and right he saw figures lying, grey and frozen, so that the place was like a battlefield; and still the mountain towered up pitilessly in front; he sank upon his knees and tried to think, but his brain was all be-numbed. Then he put his face to the ground, and his breath made a kind of warmth about him, while the cold ate into his limbs; but as he lay he heard a groan, and looking up he saw a figure that lay close to the track rise upon its knees and sink down again.

So, Ralph struggled again to his feet with the thought that if he must die he would like to die near another man; and he came up to the figure; and he saw that it was a boy, younger than himself, wrapped in a cloak. His hat had fallen off, and he could see his curls all frosted over a cheek that was smooth and blue with cold. By his side lay a lit-tle coffer and a staff, like his own. And Ralph, speaking with difficulty through frozen lips, said, "And what do you here? You are too young to be here."

The other turned his face upon him, all drawn with anguish, and said, "Help me, help me; I have lost my way." And Ralph sate down beside him and gathered the boy's body into his arms; and it seemed as though the warmth revived him, for the boy looked gratefully at him and said, "So I am not alone in this dreadful place."

Then Ralph said to him that there was no time to be lost, and that they were near their end. "But it seems to me," he added, "that a lit-tle farther up the grass looks greener, as if the cold were not so bitter there; let us try to help each other a few paces farther, if we may avoid death for a little." So they rose slowly and painfully, and now Ralph would lead the boy a step or two on; and then he would lean upon the boy, who seemed to grow stronger, for a pace or two; till suddenly it came into Ralph's mind that the cold was certainly less; and so like two dying men they struggled on, step by step, until the ground grew softer under their feet and the grass darker, and then, looking round, Ralph could see the circle of the Grey Frost below them, all white and hoary in the uncertain light.

Presently they struggled out on to a ridge of the long hill; and here they rested on their staves, and talked for a moment like old friends; and the boy showed Ralph his coffer, and said, "But you have none?"

And Ralph shook his head and said, "Nay, I left it on the seat of the Snake." And then Ralph asked him of the Leper's house, and the boy told him that he had seen it indeed, but had feared and made a circuit in the wood, and that he had there seen a fearful sight; for at the back of the Leper's house was a cage, like a kennel of hounds, and in it sate a score of wretched men with their eyes upon the ground, who had wandered from the way; and that he had heard a barking of dogs, and men had come out from the house, but that he had fled through the woods.

While they thus talked together, Ralph saw that hard by them was a rock, and in the rock a hole like a cave; so, he said to the boy, "Let us stand awhile out of the wind; and then will we set out again." So, the boy consented; and they came to the cave; but Ralph wondered exceedingly to see a door set in the rock-face; and he put out his hand and pulled the door; and it opened; and a voice from within called him by name.

Then in a moment Ralph saw that he was in the house of the Wise Man, who sate in his chair, regarding him with a smile, like a father welcoming a son. All seemed the same; and it was very grateful to Ralph to see the sun warm on the ceiling, and to smell the honeyed air that came in from the garden.

Then he went forward, and fell on his knees and laid the staff and the star down, and would have told the Wise Man his tale; but the Wise Man said, "Went not my heart with thee, my son?"

Then Ralph told him how he had left his treasure, expecting to be chidden. But the Wise Man said, "Heed it not, for thou hast a better treasure in thy heart."

Then Ralph remembered that he had left his companion outside, and asked if he might bring him in; but the Wise Man said, "Nay, he has entered by another way." And presently he bade Ralph return home in peace, and blessed him in a form of words which Ralph could not afterwards remember, but it sounded very sweet. And Ralph asked whether he might come again, but the Wise Man said, "Nay, my son."

Then Ralph went home in wonder; and though the journey had seemed very long, he found that it was still morning in Birnewood.

Then he returned to the parsonage; and the next day Father John returned, and told him that the lands would be restored to him; and as they talked, Father John said, "My son, what new thing has come to you? for there is a light in your eye that was not lit before." But Ralph could not tell him.

So, Ralph became a great knight, and did worthily; and in his hall there hang three pictures in one frame; to the left is a little green snake on a stone bench; to the right a leprous man richly clad; and in the centre a grey mist, with a figure down on its face. And some folk ask Ralph to explain the picture, and he smiles and says it is a vision; but others look at the picture in a strange wonder, and then look in Ralph's face, and he knows that they understand, and that they too have been to the Country of Dreams.

LEONAUR

ALSO FROM LEONAUR
AVAILABLE IN SOFTCOVER OR HARDCOVER WITH DUST JACKET

MR MUKERJI'S GHOSTS *by S. Mukerji*—Supernatural tales from the British Raj period by India's Ghost story collector.

KIPLINGS GHOSTS *by Rudyard Kipling*—Twelve stories of Ghosts, Hauntings, Curses, Werewolves & Magic.

THE COLLECTED SUPERNATURAL AND WEIRD FICTION OF WASHINGTON IRVING: VOLUME 1 *by Washington Irving*—Including one novel 'A History of New York', and nine short stories of the Strange and Unusual.

THE COLLECTED SUPERNATURAL AND WEIRD FICTION OF WASHINGTON IRVING: VOLUME 2 *by Washington Irving*—Including three novelettes 'The Legend of the Sleepy Hollow', 'Dolph Heyliger', 'The Adventure of the Black Fisherman' and thirty-two short stories of the Strange and Unusual.

THE COLLECTED SUPERNATURAL AND WEIRD FICTION OF JOHN KENDRICK BANGS: VOLUME 1 *by John Kendrick Bangs*—Including one novel 'Toppleton's Client or A Spirit in Exile', and ten short stories of the Strange and Unusual.

THE COLLECTED SUPERNATURAL AND WEIRD FICTION OF JOHN KENDRICK BANGS: VOLUME 2 *by John Kendrick Bangs*—Including four novellas 'A House-Boat on the Styx', 'The Pursuit of the House-Boat', 'The Enchanted Typewriter' and 'Mr. Munchausen' of the Strange and Unusual.

THE COLLECTED SUPERNATURAL AND WEIRD FICTION OF JOHN KENDRICK BANGS: VOLUME 3 *by John Kendrick Bangs*—Including twor novellas 'Olympian Nights', 'Roger Camerden: A Strange Story', and ten short stories of the Strange and Unusual.

THE COLLECTED SUPERNATURAL AND WEIRD FICTION OF MARY SHELLEY: VOLUME 1 *by Mary Shelley*—Including one novel 'Frankenstein or the Modern Prometheus', and fourteen short stories of the Strange and Unusual.

THE COLLECTED SUPERNATURAL AND WEIRD FICTION OF MARY SHELLEY: VOLUME 2 *by Mary Shelley*—Including one novel 'The Last Man', and three short stories of the Strange and Unusual.

THE COLLECTED SUPERNATURAL AND WEIRD FICTION OF AMELIA B. EDWARDS *by Amelia B. Edwards*—Contains two novelettes 'Monsieur Maurice', and 'The Discovery of the Treasure Isles', one ballad 'A Legend of Boisguilbert'and seventeen short stories to cill the blood.

AVAILABLE ONLINE AT **www.leonaur.com**
AND FROM ALL GOOD BOOK STORES
07/09

Printed in April 2019
by Rotomail Italia S.p.A., Vignate (MI) - Italy